I0831905

DREAMS

DREAMS

RICHARD A. LUPOFF

MYTHOS BOOKS LLC

POPLAR BLUFF

MISSOURI

2011

Mythos Books LLC
351 Lake Ridge Road,
Poplar Bluff,
MO 63901
United States of America

www.mythosbooks.com

Published by Mythos Books LLC 2011

FIRST EDITION

ISBN: 0-9728545-7-6

Set in *Cataneo BT* & *Adobe Jenson Pro*.

Cataneo BT by Bitstream.
www.bitstream.com

Adobe Jenson Pro by Adobe Systems Incorporated.
www.adobe.com

Typesetting, layout and design by PAW.

Sources

"The Adventure of the Voorish Sign"

Originally appeared in *Shadows Over Baker Street,* Ballantine Books, edited by John Pelan & Michael Reaves, 2003.

"At the Esquire"

Originally appeared in *Dude* magazine, Dugent Publishing Corporation, edited by Bruce Arthur, November 1968.

"Nothing Personal"

Originally appeared in *Cthulhu Reigns,* DAW Books, edited by Darrell Schweitzer, 2010.

"Tee Shirts"

Original to this collection, Mythos Books, 2011.

"Dingbats"

Originally appeared in *Horrors Beyond,* Elder Signs Press, edited by William Jones, 2005.

"The River of Fog"

Originally appeared in *Ghor Kin-Slayer: The Saga of Genseric's Fifth-Born Son,* Necronomicon Press, edited by Jonathan Bacon, 2007.

"Cairo, Goodbye"

Originally appeared in *Flurb* magazine, edited by Rudy Rucker, issue #9, Spring-Summer, 2010.

"Report of the Admissions Committee"

Originally appeared in *Tales Out of Miskatonic University,* Elder Signs Press, edited by William Jones, 2010.

"Fourth Avenue Interlude"

Originally appeared in *Poe's Lighthouse,* Cemetery Dance Publications, edited by Christopher Conlon, 2006.

"Sergeant Ghost"

Original to this collection, Mythos Books, 2011.

"The Law"

Original to this collection, Mythos Books, 2011.

"Dreemz.biz"

Originally appeared in *Hardboiled Cthulhu,* Dimension Books, edited by James Ambuehl, 2006.

"Wyshes.com"

Originally appeared in *Horrors Beyond II,* Elder Signs Press, edited by William Jones, 2007.

"Heaven.god"

Original to this collection, Mythos Books, 2011.

CONTENTS

Dedication

Dear Friends and Esteemed Colleagues:

Donald Edwin Westlake {1933-2008}

Thomas Michael Disch {1940-2008}

Charles Nikki Brown {1939-2009}

Kage Baker {1952-2010}

James Judson Harmon {1933-2010}

George Harry Scithers {1929-2010}

Alfonso Williamson {1931-2010}

Joseph Nicholas Gores {1931-2011}

The author wishes to thank Peter A. Worthy for his diligent editing and creative design for this book, and publisher David Wynn of Mythos Books for his patient support and encouragement.

Introduction

INTO THE WEIRD BLUE YONDER

Cody Goodfellow

What need is there for science fiction, when the world faces a host of apocalyptic terrors of its own making, and the future is mortgaged to the hilt? What percentage in cosmic horror, when neighbors believe they see aliens living across the street, worshipping unfathomable gods to hasten the apocalypse? And where is the room for fantasy, in a culture devised to blind us to all of these festering, faceless foes with mind-numbing media spin?

In such times, we need to remember our dreams. Not the showers of shiny things we've been nagged to strain and strive for, but the impossible things that only come true in deep sleep, and fade all to quickly out of waking memory.

Amid the endless man-eating mall of the real world and its increasingly prickly, unhealthy ideas about art, Dick Lupoff's body of work is a welcome anachronism. Old-fashioned, certainly—but in the sense that he hungers for wonder, and not dread. In his generosity for humankind and its myriad weird customs, and the wholesome notions of a bygone age (until you get to "Dingbats").

Old-fashioned, indeed, like a fox. Where the cutting edge has stumbled upon monster mash-up lit and cross-genre marketing strategies, Lupoff was always there. Like Beaumont, Bradbury or Leiber, Lupoff nimbly shifts from fantasy to horror to mystery to science fiction in his career, and often in a single story. But unlike most of his eminent contemporaries—or most any of us—Dick absorbs and evolves instead of aging, without succumbing to hardening of the artistries. His hard-won wisdom and wide-eyed curiosity give him the vigor to leap chasms of genre and style: to kick out a fantasy jam like *"Tee Shirts,"* set in a long-lost free-loving San Francisco; then undertake a cosmic shocker like *"Nothing Personal,"* or a loopy, earthbound star-yarn like *"The Law"*; and top it with a rich frosting of nostalgic Americana like *"Cairo, Goodbye,"* or a love letter to the most beloved of all endangered species, the independent bookstore.

What follows are a psychic smorgasbord of Richard Lupoff's wildest, weirdest yarns, but also his most earthy and elemental, human ones. In a jaded genre ghetto scene that has run out of taboos to smash, Lupoff has unwittingly—one assumes—found a new one: simply to ask, what if something *wonderful* happened? And in a world that often dreams most fervently of its own extinction, the stories in *Dreams* often seem to poignantly ask, *what is worth saving?*

Cody Goodfellow
San Pornando, California

"The Adventure of the Voorish Sign" was written at the request of John Pelan for inclusion in the anthology *Shadows Over Baker Street* (Ballantine Books, 2003) co-edited by Pelan and Michael Reeves. Of course Sherlock Holmes and H. P. Lovecraft's Cthulhu Mythos have both fascinated me since I was a small child, the former dating from the matinee showing of *The Hound of the Baskervilles*—the Rathbone and Bruce version!—to which my brother Jerry was forced to bring me, and the latter from the unforgettable Sunday morning when I read "The Dunwich Horror" in a paperback anthology I'd snuck into church and hidden inside my hymnal.

This opportunity to bring together Dr. Doyle's and Mr. Lovecraft's great creations—leavened, perhaps, with a slight element of the Order of the Golden Dawn—was irresistible.

The Adventure of the Voorish Sign

It was by far the most severe winter London had known in human memory, perhaps since the Romans had founded their settlement of Londinium nearly two millennia ago. Storms had swept down from the North Sea, cutting off the Continent and blanketing the great metropolis with thick layers of snow that were quickly blackened by the choking fumes of ten thousand charcoal braziers, turning to a treacherous coating of ice when doused with only slightly warmer peltings of sleet.

Even so, Holmes and I were snug in our quarters at 221B Baker Street. The fire had been laid, we had consumed a splendid dinner of meat pasties and red cabbage served by the ever-reliable Mrs. Hudson, and I found myself dreaming over an aged brandy and a pipe while Holmes devoted himself to his newest passion.

He had raided our slim exchequer for sufficient funds to purchase one of Mr. Emile Berliner's new gramophones, imported by Harrods of Brompton Road. He had placed one of Mr. Berliner's new disk recordings on the machine, advertised as a marked im-provement over the traditional wax cylinders. But the sounds that emerged from the horn were neither pleasant nor tuneful to my ears. Instead they were of a weird and disquieting nature, seem-ingly discordant yet suggestive of strange harmonies which it would be better not to understand.

As I was about to ask Holmes to shut off the contraption, the melody came to an end and Holmes removed the needle from its groove.

Holmes pressed an upraised finger against his thin lips and sharply uttered my name. "Watson!" he repeated as I lowered my pipe. The brandy snifter had very nearly slipped from my grasp, but I was able to catch it in time to prevent a disastrous spill.

"What is it, Holmes?" I inquired.

"Listen!"

He held one hand aloft, an expression of intense concentration upon his saturnine features. He nodded toward the shuttered windows which gave out upon Baker Street.

"I hear nothing except the whistle of the wind against the eaves," I told him.

"Listen more closely."

I tilted my head, straining to hear whatever it was that had caught Holmes's attention. There was a creak from below, followed by the sound of a door opening and closing, and a rapping of knuckles against solid wood, the latter sound muffled as by thin cloth.

I looked at Holmes, who pressed a long finger against his lips, indicating that silence was required. He nodded toward our door, and in a few moments I heard the tread of Mrs. Hudson ascending to our lodging. Her sturdy pace was accompanied by another, light and tentative in nature.

Holmes drew back our front door to reveal our landlady, her hand raised to knock. "Mr. Holmes!" she gasped.

"Mrs. Hudson, I see that you have brought with you Lady Fairclough of Pontefract. Will you be so kind as to permit Lady Fairclough to enter, and would you be so good as to brew a hot cup of tea for my lady. She must be suffering from her trip through this wintry night."

Mrs. Hudson turned away and made her way down the staircase while the slim young woman who had accompanied her entered our sitting room with a series of long, graceful strides. Behind her, Mrs. Hudson had carefully placed a carpetbag valise upon the floor.

"Lady Fairclough." Holmes addressed the newcomer. "May I introduce my associate, Dr. Watson. Of course you know who I am, which is why you have come to seek my assistance. But first, please warm yourself by the fire. Dr. Watson will fetch a bottle of brandy with which we will fortify the hot tea that Mrs. Hudson is preparing."

The newcomer had not said a word, but her face gave proof of her astonishment that Holmes had known her identity and home without being told. She wore a stylish hat trimmed in dark fur and a carefully tailored coat with matching decorations at collar and cuffs. Her feet were covered in boots that disappeared beneath the lower hem of her coat.

I helped her off with her outer garment. By the time I had placed it in our closet, Lady Fairclough was comfortably settled in our best chair, holding slim hands toward the cheerily dancing flames. She had removed her gloves and laid them with seemingly careless precision across the wooden arm of her chair.

"Mr. Holmes," she said in a voice that spoke equally of cultured sensitivity and barely repressed terror, "I apologize for disturbing you and Dr. Watson at this late hour, but—"

"There is no need for apologies, Lady Fairclough. On the contrary, you are to be commended for having the courage to cross the Atlantic in the midst of winter, and the captain of the steamship *Murania* is to be congratulated for having negotiated the crossing successfully. It is unfortunate that our customs agents delayed your disembarkation as they did, but now that you are here, perhaps you will enlighten Dr. Watson and myself as to the problem which has beset your brother, Mr. Philip Llewellyn."

If Lady Fairclough had been startled by Holmes's recognizing her without introduction, she was clearly amazed beyond my meager powers of description by this statement. She raised a hand to her cheek, which showed a smoothness of complexion and grace of curve in the flattering glow of the dancing flames. "Mr. Holmes," she exclaimed, "how did you know all that?"

"It was nothing, Lady Fairclough, one need merely keep one's senses on the alert and one's mind active." A glance that Holmes darted in my direction was not welcome, but I felt constrained from protesting in the presence of a guest and potential client.

"So you say, Mr. Holmes, but I have read of your exploits and in many cases they seem little short of supernatural," Lady Fairclough replied.

"Not in the least. Let us consider the present case. Your valise bears the paper label of the Blue Star Line. The *Murania* and the *Lemuria* are the premiere ocean liners of the Blue Star Line, alternating upon the easterly and westerly transatlantic sea lanes. Even a fleeting glance at the daily shipping news indicates that the *Murania* was due in Liverpool early this morning. If the ship made port at even so late an hour as ten o'clock, in view of the fact that the rail journey from Liverpool to London requires a mere two hours, you should have reached our city by noon. Another hour at most from the rail terminus to Baker Street would have brought you to our door by one o'clock this afternoon. And yet," concluded Holmes, glancing at the ormolu clock that rested upon our mantel, "you arrive at the surprising hour of ten o'clock *post meridian.*"

"But, Holmes," I interjected, "Lady Fairclough may have had other errands to perform before coming to us."

"No, Watson, no. I fear that you have failed to draw the proper inference from that which you have surely observed. You did note, did you not, that Lady Fairclough has brought her carpetbag with her?"

I pled guilty to the charge.

"Surely, had she not been acting in great haste, Lady Fair-clough would have gone to her hotel, refreshed herself, and left her luggage in her quarters there before traveling to Baker Street. The fact that she has but one piece of luggage with her gives further testimony to the urgency with which she departed her home in Canada. Now, Watson, what could have caused Lady Fairclough to commence her trip in such haste?"

I shook my head. "I confess that I am at a loss."

"It was but eight days ago that the *Daily Mail* carried a dispatch marked Merthyr Tydfil, a town situated on the border of England and Wales, concerning the mysterious disappearance of Mr. Philip Llewellyn. There would have been time for word to reach Lady Fairclough in Pontefract by transatlantic cable. Fearing that delay in traveling to the port and boarding the *Murania* would cause intolerable delay, Lady Fairclough had her maid pack the fewest possible necessities in her carpetbag. She then made her way to Halifax, whence the *Murania* departed, and upon reaching Liver-pool this morning would have made her way at once to London. Yet she arrived some nine hours later than she might have been expected to do. Since our rail service remains uninterrupted in even the most severe of climatic conditions, it can only have been the customs service, equally notorious for their punctilio and their dilatory conduct, which could be responsible."

Turning once more to Lady Fairclough, Holmes said, "On behalf of Her Majesty's Customs Service, Lady Fairclough, I tender my apologies."

There was a knock at the door and Mrs. Hudson appeared, bearing a tray with hot tea and cold sandwiches. This she placed upon the table, then took her leave.

Lady Fairclough looked at the repast and said, "Oh, I simply could not."

"Nonsense," Holmes insisted. "You have completed an arduous journey and face a dangerous undertaking. You must keep up your strength." He rose and added brandy to Lady Fairclough's tea, then stood commandingly over her while she consumed the beverage and two sandwiches.

"I suppose I was hungry after all," she admitted at last. I was pleased to see some color returning to her cheeks. I had been seriously concerned about her wellbeing.

"Now, Lady Fairclough," said Holmes, "it might be well for you to go to your hotel and restore your strength with a good night's slumber. You do have a reservation, I trust."

"Oh, of course, at Claridge's. A suite was ordered for me through the courtesy of the Blue Star Line, but I could not rest now, Mr. Holmes. I am far too distraught to sleep until I have explained my need to you, and received your assurance that you and Dr. Watson will take my case. I have plenty of money, if that is a concern."

Holmes indicated that financial details could wait, but I was pleased to be included in our guest's expression of need. So often I find myself taken for granted, while in fact I am Holmes's trusted associate, as he has himself acknowledged on many occasions.

"Very well." Holmes nodded, seating himself opposite Lady Fairclough. "Please tell me your story in your own words, being as precise with details as possible."

Lady Fairclough drained her cup and waited while Holmes filled it once again with brandy and a spot of Darjeeling. She downed another substantial draft, then launched upon her narrative.

"As you know, Mr. Holmes—and Dr. Watson—I was born in England of old stock. Despite our ancient Welsh connections and family name, we have been English for a thousand years. I was the elder of two children, the younger being my brother, Philip. As a daughter, I saw little future for myself in the home islands, and accepted the proposal of marriage tendered by my husband, Lord Fairclough, whose Canadian holdings are substantial and who indicated to me a desire to emigrate to Canada and build a new life there, which we would share."

I had taken out my notebook and fountain pen and begun jotting notes.

"At about this time my parents were both killed in a horrendous accident, the collision of two trains in the Swiss Alps while vacationing abroad. Feeling that an elaborate wedding would be disrespectful of the deceased, Lord Fairclough and I were quietly married and took our leave of England. We lived happily in Pontefract, Canada, until my husband disappeared."

"Indeed," Holmes interjected, "I had read of Lord Fairclough's disappearance. I note that you refer to him as your husband rather than your late husband still, nor do I see any mourning band upon your garment. Is it your belief that your husband lives still?"

Lady Fairclough lowered her eyes for a moment as a flush rose to her cheeks. "Although ours was somewhat a marriage of convenience, I find that I have come to love my husband most dearly. There was no discord between us, if you are concerned over such, Mr. Holmes."

"Not in the least, Lady Fairclough."

"Thank you." She sipped from her teacup. Holmes peered at it, then refreshed its contents once again. "Thank you," Lady Fairclough repeated. "My husband had been corresponding with his brother-in-law, my brother, and later, after my brother's marriage, with my brother's wife, for some time before he disappeared. I saw the envelopes as they came and went, but I was never permitted to so much as lay eyes on their contents. After reading each newly delivered letter, my husband would burn it and crush the ashes beyond recovery. After receiving one very lengthy letter—I could tell it was lengthy by the heft of the envelope in which it arrived—my husband summoned carpenters and prepared a sealed room which I was forbidden to enter. Of course I obeyed my husband's command."

"A wise policy," I put in. "One knows the story of Bluebeard."

"He would lock himself in his private chamber for hours at a time, sometimes days. When he disappeared, in fact, I half expected him to return at any moment." Lady Fairclough put her hand to her throat. "Please," she said softly, "I beg your pardon for the impropriety, but I feel suddenly so warm." I glanced away, and when I looked back at her I observed that the top button of her blouse had been undone.

"My husband has been gone now for two years, and all have given him up for dead save myself, and I will concede that even my hopes are of the faintest. During the period of correspondence between my husband and my brother, my husband began to absent himself from all human society from time to time. Gradually the frequency and duration of his disappearances increased. I feared I knew not what—perhaps that he had become addicted to some drug or unspeakable vice for the indulging of which he preferred isolation. I inferred that he had caused the construction of the sealed room for this purpose, and determined that I should learn its secret."

She bowed her head and drew a series of long, sobbing breaths, which caused her graceful bosom visibly to heave. After a time she raised her face. Her cheeks were wet with tears. She resumed her narrative.

"I summoned a locksmith from the village and persuaded him to aid me in gaining entry. When I stood at last in my husband's secret chamber I found myself confronting a room completely devoid of feature. The ceiling, the walls, the floor were all plain and devoid of ornament. There were neither windows nor fireplace, nor any other means of egress from the room."

Holmes nodded, frowning. "There was nothing noteworthy about the room, then?" he asked at length.

"Yes, Mr. Holmes, there was." Lady Fairclough's response startled me so, I nearly dropped my fountain pen, but I recovered and returned to my note taking.

"At first the room seemed a perfect cube. The ceiling, floor, and four walls each appeared absolutely square and mounted at a precise right angle to one another. But as I stood there, they seemed to—I suppose, *shift* is the closest I can come to it, Mr. Holmes, but they did not actually move in any familiar manner. And yet their shape seemed to be different, and the angles to become peculiar, obtuse, and to open onto other—how to put this?—*dimensions.*"

She seized Holmes's wrist in her graceful fingers and leaned toward him pleadingly. "Do you think I am insane, Mr. Holmes? Has my grief driven me to the brink of madness? There are times when I think I can bear no more strangeness."

"You are assuredly not insane," Holmes told her. "You have stumbled upon one of the strangest and most dangerous of phenomena, a phenomenon barely suspected by even the most advanced of mathematical theoreticians and spoken of even by them in only the most cautious of whispers."

He withdrew his arm from her grasp, shook his head, and said, "If your strength permits, you must continue your story, please."

"I will try," she answered.

I waited, fountain pen poised above notebook.

Our visitor shuddered as with a fearsome recollection. "Once I had left the secret room, sealing it behind myself, I attempted to resume a normal life. It was days later that my husband reappeared, refusing as usual to give any explanation of his recent whereabouts. Shortly after this a dear friend of mine living in Quebec gave birth to a child. I had gone to be with her when word was received of the great Pontefract earthquake. In this disaster a fissure appeared in the earth and our house was completely swallowed. I was, fortunately, left in a state of financial independence, and have never suffered from material deprivation. But I have never again seen my husband. Most believe that he was in the house at the time of its disappearance, and was killed at once, but I retain a hope, however faint, that he may somehow have survived."

She paused to compose herself, then resumed.

"But I fear I am getting ahead of myself. It was shortly before my husband ordered the construction of his sealed room that my brother, Philip, announced his engagement and the date of his impending nuptials. I thought the shortness of his intended period of engagement was unseemly, but in view of my own marriage and departure to Canada so soon after my parents' death, I was in no position to condemn Philip. My husband and I booked passage to England, on the *Lemuria* in fact, and from Liverpool made our way to the family lands in Merthyr Tydfil."

She shook her head as if to free it of an unpleasant memory.

"Upon arriving at Anthracite Palace, I was shocked by my brother's appearance."

At this point I interrupted our guest with a query.

"Anthracite Palace? Is that not an unusual name for a family manse?"

"Our family residence was so named by my ancestor, Sir Llewys Llewellyn, who built the family fortune, and the manor, by operating a network of successful coal mines. As you are probably aware, the region is rich in anthracite. The Llewellyns pioneered modern mining methods which rely upon gelignite explosives to loosen banks of coal for the miners to remove from their native sites. In the region of Merthyr Tydfil, where the Anthracite Palace is located, the booming of gelignite charges is heard to this day, and stores of the explosive are kept at the mine heads."

I thanked her for the clarification and suggested that she continue with her narrative.

"My brother was neatly barbered and clothed, but his hands shook, his cheeks were sunken, and his eyes had a frightened, hunted look to them," she said. "When I toured my childhood home I was shocked to find its interior architecture modified. There was now a sealed room, just as there had been at Pontefract. I was not permitted to enter that room. I expressed my concern at my brothers appearance but he insisted he was well and introduced his fiancée, who was already living at the palace."

I drew my breath with a gasp.

"Yes, Doctor," Lady Fairclough responded, "you heard me correctly. She was a woman of dark, Gypsyish complexion, glossy sable hair, and darting eyes. I disliked her at once. She gave her own name, not waiting for Philip to introduce her properly. Her maiden name, she announced, was Anastasia Romelly. She claimed to be of noble Hungarian blood, allied both to the Habsburgs and the Romanovs."

"Humph," I grunted, "Eastern European nobility is a ha'penny a dozen, and three-quarters of them aren't real even at that."

"Perhaps true," Holmes snapped at me, "but we do not know that the credentials of the lady involved were other than authentic." He frowned and turned away. "Lady Fairclough, please continue."

"She insisted on wearing her native costume. And she had persuaded my brother to replace his chef with one of her own choosing, whom she had imported from her homeland and who replaced our usual menu of good English fare with unfamiliar dishes reeking of odd spices and unknown ingredients. She imported strange wines and ordered them served with meals."

I shook my head in disbelief.

"The final straw came upon the day of her wedding to my brother. She insisted upon being given away by a surly, dark man who appeared for the occasion, performed his duty, and then disappeared. She—"

"A moment, please," Holmes interrupted. "If you will forgive me—you say that this man disappeared. Do you mean that he took his leave prematurely?"

"No, I do not mean that at all." Lady Fairclough was clearly excited. A moment earlier she had seemed on the verge of tears. Now she was angry and eager to unburden herself of her tale.

"In a touching moment, he placed the bride's hand upon that of the groom. Then he raised his own hand. I thought his intent was to place his benediction upon the couple, but such was not the case. He made a gesture with his hand, as if making a mystical sign."

She raised her own hand from her lap, but Holmes snapped, "Do not, I warn you, attempt to replicate the gesture! Please, if you can, simply describe it to Dr. Watson and myself."

"I could not replicate the gesture if I tried," Lady Fairclough said. "It defies imitation. I cannot even describe it accurately, I fear. I was fascinated and tried to follow the movement of the dark man's fingers, but I could not. They seemed to disappear and reappear most shockingly, and then, without further warning, he was simply gone. I tell you, Mr. Holmes, one moment the dark man was there, and then he was gone."

"Did no one else take note of this, my lady?"

"No one did, apparently. Perhaps all eyes were trained upon the bride and groom, although I believe I did notice the presiding official exchanging several glances with the dark man. Of course, that was before his disappearance."

Holmes stroked his jaw, deep in thought. There was a lengthy silence in the room, broken only by the ticking of the ormolu clock and whistling of the wind through the eaves. Finally Holmes spoke.

"It can be nothing other than the Voorish Sign," he said.

"The Voorish Sign?" Lady Fairclough repeated inquiringly.

Holmes said, "Never mind. This becomes more interesting by the moment, and also more dangerous. Another question, if you please. Who was the presiding official at the wedding? He was, I would assume, a priest of the Church of England."

"No." Lady Fairclough shook her head once again. "The official was neither a member of the Anglican clergy nor a *he*. The wedding was performed by a woman."

I gasped in surprise, drawing still another sharp glance from Holmes.

"She wore robes such as I have never seen," our guest resumed. "There were symbols, both astronomical and astrological, embroidered in silver thread and gold, green, blue, and red. There were other symbols totally unfamiliar to me, suggestive of strange geometries and odd shapes. The ceremony itself was conducted in a language I had never before heard, and I am something of a linguist, Mr. Holmes. I believe I detected a few words of Old Temple Egyptian, a phrase in Coptic Greek, and several suggestions of Sanskrit. Other words I did not recognize at all."

Holmes nodded. I could see the excitement growing in his eyes, the excitement that I saw only when a fascinating challenge was presented to him.

He asked, "What was this person's name?"

"Her name," Lady Fairclough voiced through teeth clenched in anger, or perhaps in the effort to prevent their chattering with fear, "was Vladimira Petrovna Ludmilla Romanova. She claimed the title of Archbishop of the Wisdom Temple of the Dark Heavens."

"Why—why," I exclaimed, "I've never heard of such a thing! This is sheer blasphemy!"

"It is something far worse than blasphemy, Watson." Holmes leaped to his feet and paced rapidly back and forth. At one point he halted near our front window, being careful not to expose himself to the direct sight of anyone lurking below. He peered down into Baker Street, something I have seen him do many times in our years together. Then he did something I had not seen before. Drawing himself back still farther, he gazed upward. What he hoped to perceive in the darkened winter sky other than falling snowflakes, I could hardly imagine.

"Lady Fairclough," he intoned at length, "you have been remarkably strong and courageous in your performance here this night. I will now ask Dr. Watson to see you to your hotel. You mentioned Claridge's, I believe. I will ask Dr. Watson to remain in your suite throughout the remainder of the night. I assure you, Lady Fairclough, that he is a person of impeccable character, and your virtue will in no way be compromised by his presence."

"Even so, Holmes," I objected, "the lady's virtue is one thing, her reputation is another."

The matter was resolved by Lady Fairclough herself. "Doctor, while I appreciate your concern, we are dealing with a most serious matter. I will accept the suspicious glances of prudes and the smirks of servants if I must. The lives of my husband and my brother are at stake."

Unable to resist the lady's argument, I followed Holmes's directions and accompanied her to Claridge's. At his insistence I even went so far as to arm myself with my Enfield MK II revolver, which I tucked into the top of my woolen trousers. Holmes warned me, also, to permit no one save himself entry to Lady Fairclough's suite.

Once my temporary charge had retired, I sat in a straight chair, prepared to pass the night in a game of solitaire. Lady Fairclough had donned camisole and hair net and climbed into her bed. I will admit that my cheeks burned, but I reminded myself that in my medical capacity I was accustomed to viewing patients in a disrobed condition, and could surely assume an avuncular role while keeping watch over this courageous lady.

There was a loud rapping at the door. I jerked awake, realizing to my chagrin that I had fallen asleep over my solitary card game. I rose to my feet, went to Lady Fairclough's bedside and assured myself that she was unharmed, and then placed myself at the door to her suite. In response to my demand that our visitor identify him-self, a male voice announced simply, "Room service, guv'ner."

My hand was on the doorknob, my other hand on the latch, when I remembered Holmes's warning at Baker Street to permit no one entry. Surely a hearty breakfast would be welcome; I could almost taste the kippers and the toast and jam that Mrs. Hudson would have served us, had we been still in our home. But Holmes had been emphatic. What to do? What to do?

"We did not order breakfast." I spoke through the heavy oaken door.

"Courtesy of the management, guv."

Perhaps, I thought, I might admit a waiter bearing food. What harm could there be in that? I reached for the latch only to find my hand tugged away by another, that of Lady Fairclough. She had climbed from her bed and crossed the room, barefoot and clad only in her sleeping garment. She shook her head vigorously, drawing me away from the door, which remained latched against any entry. She pointed to me, pantomiming speech. Her message was clear.

"Leave our breakfast in the hall," I instructed the waiter. "We shall fetch it in ourselves shortly. We are not ready as yet."

"Can't do it, sir," the waiter insisted. "Please, sir, don't get me in trouble wif the management, guv'ner. I needs to roll my cart into your room and leave the tray. I'll get in trouble if I don't, guv'ner."

I was nearly persuaded by his plea, but Lady Fairclough had placed herself between me and the door, her arms crossed and a determined expression on her face. Once again she indicated that I should send the waiter away.

"I'm sorry, my man, but I must insist. Simply leave the tray outside our door. That is my final word."

The waiter said nothing more, but I thought I could hear his reluctantly retreating footsteps.

I retired to make my morning ablutions while Lady Fairclough dressed.

Shortly thereafter, there was another rapping at the door. Fearing the worst, I drew my revolver. Perhaps this was more than a misdirected order for room service. "I told you to go away," I commanded.

"Watson, old man, open up. It is I, Holmes."

The voice was unmistakable; I felt as though a weight of a hundred stone had been lifted from my shoulders. I undid the door latch and stood aside as the best and wisest man I have ever known entered the apartment. I peered out into the hall after he had passed through the doorway. There was no sign of a service cart or breakfast tray.

Holmes asked, "What are you looking for, Watson?"

I explained the incident of the room service call.

"You did well, Watson," he congratulated me. "You may be certain that was no waiter, nor was his mission one of service to Lady Fairclough and yourself. I have spent the night consulting my files and certain other sources with regard to the odd institution known as the Wisdom Temple of the Dark Heavens, and I can tell you that we are sailing dangerous waters indeed."

He turned to Lady Fairclough. "You will please accompany Dr. Watson and myself to Merthyr Tydfil. We shall leave at once. There is a chance that we may yet save the life of your brother, but we have no time to waste."

Without hesitation, Lady Fairclough strode to the wardrobe, pinned her hat to her hair, and donned the same warm coat she had worn when first I laid eyes on her, mere hours before.

"But, Holmes," I protested, "Lady Fairclough and I have not broken our fast."

"Never mind your stomach, Watson. There is no time to lose. We can purchase sandwiches from a vendor at the station."

Almost sooner than I can tell, we were seated in a first class compartment heading westward toward Wales. As good as his word, Holmes had seen to it that we were nourished, and I for one felt the better for having downed even a light and informal meal.

The storm had at last abated and a bright sun shone down from a sky of the most brilliant blue upon fields and hillsides covered with a spotless layer of purest white. Hardly could one doubt the benevolence of the universe; I felt almost like a schoolboy setting off on holiday, but Lady Fairclough s fears and Holmes's serious demeanor brought my soaring spirits back to earth.

"It is as I feared, Lady Fairclough," Holmes explained. "Both your brother and your husband have been ensnared in a wicked cult that threatens civilization itself if it is not stopped."

"A cult?" Lady Fairclough echoed.

"Indeed. You told me that Bishop Romanova was a representative of the Wisdom Temple of the Dark Heavens, did you not?"

"She so identified herself, Mr. Holmes."

"Yes. Nor would she have reason to lie, not that any denizen of this foul nest would hesitate to do so, should it aid their schemes. The Wisdom Temple is a little known organization—I would hesitate to dignify them with the title religion—of ancient origins. They have maintained a secretive stance while awaiting some cosmic cataclysm which I fear is nearly upon us."

"Cosmic—cosmic cataclysm? I say, Holmes, isn't that a trifle melodramatic?" I asked.

"Indeed it is, Watson. But it is nonetheless so. They refer to a coming time 'when the stars are right.' Once that moment arrives, they intend to perform an unholy rite that will 'open the portal,' whatever that means, to admit their masters to the earth. The members of the Wisdom Temple will then become overseers and oppressors of all humankind, in the service of the dread masters whom they will have admitted to our world."

I shook my head in disbelief. Outside the windows of our compartment I could see that our train was approaching the trestle that would carry us across the River Severn. It would not be much longer before we should detrain at Merthyr Tydfil.

"Holmes," I said, "I would never doubt your word."

"I know that, old man," he replied. "But something is bothering you. Out with it!"

"Holmes, this is madness. Dread masters, opening portals, unholy rites—this is something out of the pages of a penny dreadful. Surely you don't expect Lady Fairclough and myself to believe all this."

"But I do, Watson. You must believe it, for it is all true, and deadly serious. Lady Fairclough—you have set out to save your brother and if possible your husband, but in fact you have set us in play in a game whose stakes are not one or two mere individuals, but the fate of our planet."

Lady Fairclough pulled a handkerchief from her wrist and dabbed at her eyes. "Mr. Holmes, I have seen that strange room at Llewellyn Hall at Pontefract, and I can believe your every word, for all that I agree with Dr. Watson as to the fantastic nature of what you say. Might I ask how you know of this?"

"Very well," Holmes assented, "You are entitled to that information. I told you before we left Claridge's that I had spent the night in research. There are many books in my library, most of which are open to my associate, Dr. Watson, and to other men of goodwill, as surely he is. But there are others which I keep under lock and key."

"I am aware of that, Holmes," I interjected, "and I will admit that I have been hurt by your unwillingness to share those volumes with me. Often have I wondered what they contain."

"Good Watson, it was for your own protection, I assure you. Watson, Lady Fairclough, those books include *De los Mundos Amenazantes y Sombriosos* of Carlos Alfredo de Torrijos, *Emmorragia Sante* of Luigi Humberto Rosso, and *Das Bestrafen von der Tugendhaft* of Heinrich Ludvig Georg von Feldenstein, as well as the works of the brilliant Mr. Arthur Machen, of whom you may have heard. These tomes, some of them well over a thousand years old and citing still more remote sources whose origins are lost in the mists of antiquity, are frighteningly consistent in their predic-tions. Further, several of them, Lady Fairclough, refer to a certain powerful and fearsome mystical gesture."

Although Holmes was addressing our feminine companion, I said, "Gesture, Holmes? Mystical gesture? What nonsense is this?"

"Not nonsense at all, Watson. You are doubtless aware of the movement that our Romish brethren refer to as 'crossing themselves.' The Hebrews have a gesture of cabalistic origin that is alleged to bring good luck, and the Gypsies make a sign to turn away the evil eye. Several Asian races perform 'hand dances,' ceremonials of religious or magical significance, including the famous *hoola* known on the islands of Oahu and Maui in the Havai'ian archipelago."

"But these are all foolish superstitions, remnants of an earlier and more credulous age. Surely there is nothing to them, Holmes!"

"I wish 1 could have your assuredness, Watson. You are a man of science, for which I commend you, but 'There are more things in heaven and earth, Horatio, than are dreamed of in your philosophy' Do not be too quick, Watson, to dismiss old beliefs.

More often than not they have a basis in fact."

I shook my head and turned my eyes once more to the wintry countryside through which our conveyance was passing. Holmes addressed himself to our companion.

"Lady Fairclough, you mentioned a peculiar gesture that the dark stranger made at the conclusion of your brother's wedding ceremony."

"I did, yes. It was so strange, I felt almost as if I were being drawn into another world when he moved his hand. I tried to follow the movements, but I could not. And then he was gone."

Holmes nodded rapidly.

"The Voorish Sign, Lady Fairclough. The stranger was making the Voorish Sign. It is referred to in the works of Machen and others. It is a very powerful and a very evil gesture. You were fortunate that you were not drawn into that other world, fortunate indeed."

Before much longer we reached the rail terminus nearest to Merthyr Tydfil. We left our compartment and shortly were ensconced in a creaking trap whose driver whipped up his team and headed for the Anthracite Palace. It was obvious from his demeanor that the manor was a familiar landmark in the region.

"We should be greeted by Mrs. Morrissey, our housekeeper, when we reach the manor," Lady Fairclough said. "It was she who notified me of my brother's straits. She is the last of our old family retainers to remain with the Llewellyns of Merthyr Tydfil. One by one the new lady of the manor has arranged their departure and replaced them with a swarthy crew of her own countrymen. Oh, Mr. Holmes, it is all so horrid!"

Holmes did his best to comfort the frightened woman.

Soon the Anthracite Palace hove into view. As its name would suggest, it was built of the local native coal. Architects and masons had carved the jet black deposits into building blocks and created an edifice that stood like a black jewel against the white backing of snow, its battlements glittering in the wintry sunlight.

Our trap was met by a liveried servant who instructed lesser servants to carry our meager luggage into the manor. Lady Fairclough, Holmes, and I were ourselves conducted into the main hall.

The building was lit with oversized candles whose flames were so shielded as to prevent any danger of the coal walls catching fire. It struck me that the Anthracite Palace was one of the strangest architectural conceits I had ever encountered. "Not a place I would like to live in, eh, Holmes?" I was trying for a tone of levity, but must confess that I failed to achieve it.

We were left waiting for an excessive period of time, in my opinion, but at length a tall wooden door swung back and a woman of commanding presence, exotic in appearance with her swarthy complexion, flashing eyes, sable locks and shockingly reddened lips, entered the hall. She nodded to Holmes and myself and exchanged a frigid semblance of a kiss with Lady Fairclough, whom she addressed as "sister."

Lady Fairclough demanded to see her brother, but Mrs. Llewellyn refused conversation until we were shown to our rooms and had time to refresh ourselves. We were summoned, in due course, to the dining hall. I was famished, and both relieved and my appetite further excited by the delicious odors that came to us as we were seated at the long, linen covered table.

Only four persons were present. These were, of course, Holmes and myself, Lady Fairclough, and our hostess, Mrs. Llewellyn.

Lady Fairclough attempted once again to inquire as to the whereabouts of her brother, Philip.

Her sister-in-law replied only, "He is pursuing his devotions. We shall see him when the time comes 'round."

Failing to learn more about her brother, Lady Fairclough asked after the housekeeper, Mrs. Morrissey.

"I have sad news, sister dear," Mrs. Llewellyn said. "Mrs. Morrissey was taken ill very suddenly. Philip personally drove into Merthyr Tydfil to fetch a physician for her, but by the time they arrived, Mrs. Morrissey had expired. She was buried in the town cemetery. This all happened just last week. I knew that you were already en route from Canada, and it seemed best not to further distress you with this information."

"Oh no," Lady Fairclough gasped. "Not Mrs. Morrissey! She was like a mother to me. She was the kindest, dearest of women. She—" Lady Fairclough stopped, pressing her hand to her mouth. She inhaled deeply. "Very well, then." I could see a look of determination rising like a banked flame deep in her eye. "If she has died there is naught to be done for it."

There was a pillar of strength hidden within this seemingly weak female. I would not care to make an enemy of Lady Fairclough. I noted also that Mrs. Llewellyn spoke English fluently but with an accent that I found thoroughly unpleasant. It seemed to me that she, in turn, found the language distasteful. Clearly, these two were fated to clash. But the tension of the moment was bro-ken by the arrival of our viands.

The repast was sumptuous in appearance, but every course, it seemed to me, had some flaw—an excessive use of spice, an overdone vegetable, an undercooked piece of meat or game, a fish that might have been kept a day too long before serving, a cream that had stood in a warm kitchen an hour longer than was wise. By the end of the meal my appetite had departed, but it was replaced by a sensation of queasiness and discomfort rather than satisfaction.

Servants brought cigars for Holmes and myself, an after dinner brandy for the men, and sweet sherry for the women, but I put out my cigar after a single draft and noticed that Holmes did the same with his own. Even the beverage seemed in some subtle way to be faulty.

"Mrs. Llewellyn." Lady Fairclough addressed her sister-in-law when at last the latter seemed unable longer to delay confrontation. "I received a telegram via transatlantic cable concerning the disappearance of my brother. He failed to greet us upon our arrival, nor has there been any sign of his presence since then. I demand to know his whereabouts."

"Sister dear," replied Anastasia Romelly Llewellyn, "that telegram should never have been sent. Mrs. Morrissey transmitted it from Merthyr Tydfil while in town on an errand for the palace. When I learned of her presumption I determined to send her packing, I can assure you. It was only her unfortunate demise that prevented my doing so."

At this point my friend Holmes addressed our hostess.

"Madam, Lady Fairclough has journeyed from Canada to learn of her brother's circumstances. She has engaged me, along with my associate, Dr. Watson, to assist her in this enterprise. It is not my desire to make this affair any more unpleasant than is necessary, but I must insist upon your providing the information that Lady Fairclough is seeking."

I believe at this point that I observed a smirk, or at least the suggestion of one, pass across the face of Mrs. Llewellyn. But she quickly responded to Holmes's demand, her peculiar accent as pronounced and unpleasant as ever.

"We have planned a small religious service for this evening. You are all invited to attend, of course, even though I had expected only my dear sister-in-law to do so. However, the larger group will be accommodated."

"What is the nature of this religious service?" Lady Fairclough demanded.

Mrs. Llewellyn smiled. "It will be that of the Wisdom Temple, of course. The Wisdom Temple of the Dark Heavens. It is my hope that Bishop Romanova herself will preside, but absent her participation we can still conduct the service ourselves."

I reached for my pocket watch. "It's getting late, madam. Might I suggest that we get started, then!"

Mrs. Llewellyn turned her eyes upon me. In the flickering candlelight they seemed larger and darker than ever. "You do not understand, Dr. Watson. It is too early rather than too late to start our ceremony. We will proceed precisely at midnight. Until then, please feel free to enjoy the paintings and tapestries with which the Anthracite Palace is decorated, or pass the time in Mr. Llewellyn's library. Or, if you prefer, you may of course retire to your quarters and seek sleep."

Thus it was that we three separated temporarily, Lady Fairclough to pass some hours with her husband's chosen books, Holmes to an examination of the palace's art treasures, and I to bed.

I was awakened from a troubled slumber haunted by strange beings of nebulous form. Standing over my bed, shaking me by the shoulder, was my friend Sherlock Holmes. I could see a rim of snow adhering to the edges of his boots.

"Come, Watson," said he, "the game is truly afoot, and it is by far the strangest game we are ever likely to pursue."

Swiftly donning my attire, I accompanied Holmes as we made

our way to Lady Fairclough's chamber. She had retired there after spending the hours since dinner in her brother's library, to refresh herself. She must have been awaiting our arrival, for she responded without delay to Holmes's knock and the sound of his voice.

Before we proceeded further Holmes drew me aside. He reached inside his vest and withdrew a small object which he held concealed in his hand. I could not see its shape, for he held it inside a clenched fist, but I could tell that it emitted a dark radiance, a faint suggestion of which I could see between his fingers.

"Watson," quoth he, "I am going to give you this. You must swear to me that you will not look at it, on pain of damage beyond anything you can so much as imagine. You must keep it upon your person, if possible in direct contact with your body, at all times. If all goes well this night, I will ask you to return it to me. If all does not go well, it may save your life."

I held my hand toward him.

Placing the object on my outstretched palm, Holmes closed my own fingers carefully around it. Surely this was the strangest object I had ever encountered. It was unpleasantly warm, its texture like that of an overcooked egg, and it seemed to squirm as if it were alive, or perhaps as if it contained something that lived and strove to escape an imprisoning integument.

"Do not look at it," Holmes repeated. "Keep it with you at all times. Promise me you will do these things, Watson!"

I assured him that I would do as he requested.

Momentarily we beheld Mrs. Llewellyn moving down the hallway toward us. Her stride was so smooth and her progress so steady that she seemed to be gliding rather than walking. She carried a kerosene lamp whose flame reflected from the polished blackness of the walls, casting ghostly shadows of us all.

Speaking not a word, she gestured to us, summoning us to follow her. We proceeded along a series of corridors and up and down staircases until, I warrant, I lost all sense of direction and of elevation. I could not tell whether we had climbed to a room in one of the battlements of the Anthracite Palace or descended to a dungeon beneath the Llewellyns' ancestral home. I had placed the object Holmes had entrusted to me inside my garments. I could feel it struggling to escape, but it was bound in place and could not do so.

"Where is this bishop you promised us?" I asked of Mrs. Llewellyn.

Our hostess turned toward me. She had replaced her colorful Gypsyish attire with a robe of dark purple. Its color reminded me of the emanations of the warm object concealed now within my own clothing. Her robe was marked with embroidery of a pattern that confused the eye so that I was unable to discern its nature.

"You misunderstood me, Doctor," she intoned in her unpleasant accent. "I stated merely that it was my hope that Bishop Romanova would preside at our service. Such is still the case. We shall see in due time."

We stood now before a heavy door bound with rough iron bands. Mrs. Llewellyn lifted a key which hung suspended about her neck on a ribbon of crimson hue. She inserted it into the lock and turned it. She then requested Holmes and myself to apply our combined strength to opening the door. As we did so, pressing our shoulders against it, my impression was that the resistance came from some willful reluctance rather than a mere matter of weight or decay.

No light preceded us into the room, but Mrs. Llewellyn strode through the doorway carrying her kerosene lamp before her. Its rays now reflected off the walls of the chamber. The room was as Lady Fairclough had described the sealed room in her erstwhile home at Pontefract. The configuration and even the number of surfaces that surrounded us seemed unstable. I was unable even to count them. The very angles at which they met defied my every attempt to comprehend.

An altar of polished anthracite was the sole furnishing of this hideous, irrational chamber.

Mrs. Llewellyn placed her kerosene lamp upon the altar. She turned then, and indicated with a peculiar gesture of her hand that we were to kneel as if participants in a more conventional religious ceremony.

I was reluctant to comply with her silent command, but Holmes nodded to me, indicating that he wished me to do so. I lowered myself, noting that Lady Fairclough and Holmes himself emulated my act.

Before us, and facing the black altar, Mrs. Llewellyn also knelt. She raised her face as if seeking supernatural guidance from above, causing me to remember that the full name of her peculiar sect was the Wisdom Temple of the Dark Heavens. She commenced a weird chanting in a language such as I had never heard, not in all my travels. There was a suggestion of the argot of the dervishes of Afghanistan, something of the Buddhist monks of Tibet, and a hint of the remnant of the ancient Incan language still spoken by the remotest tribes of the high Chaco plain of the Chilean Andes, but in fact the language was none of these and the few words that I was able to make out proved both puzzling and suggestive but never specific in their meaning.

As Mrs. Llewellyn continued her chanting, she slowly raised first one hand then the other above her head. Her fingers were moving in an intricate pattern. I tried to follow their progress but found my consciousness fading into a state of confusion. I could have sworn that her fingers twined and knotted like the tentacles of a jellyfish. Their colors, too, shifted: vermilion, scarlet, obsidian. They seemed, even, to disappear into and return from some concealed realm invisible to my fascinated eyes.

The object that Holmes had given me throbbed and squirmed against my body, its unpleasantly hot and squamous presence making me wish desperately to rid myself of it. It was only my pledge to Holmes that prevented me from doing so.

I clenched my teeth and squeezed my eyes shut, summoning up images from my youth and of my travels, holding my hand clasped over the object as I did so. Suddenly the tension was released. The object was still there, but as if it had a consciousness of its own, it seemed to grow calm. My own jaw relaxed and I opened my eyes to behold a surprising sight.

Before me there emerged another figure. As Mrs. Llewellyn was stocky and swarthy, of the model of Gypsy women, this person was tall and graceful. Swathed entirely in jet, with hair a seeming midnight blue and complexion as black as the darkest African, she defied my conventional ideas of beauty with a weird and exotic glamour of her own that defies description. Her features were as finely cut as those of the ancient Ethiopians are said to have been, her movements filled with a grace that would shame the pride of Covent Garden or the Bolshoi.

But whence had this apparition made her way? Still kneeling upon the ebon floor of the sealed room, I shook my head. She seemed to have emerged from the very angle between the walls.

She floated toward the altar, lifted the chimney from the kerosene lamp, and doused its flame with the palm of her bare hand.

Instantly the room was plunged into stygian darkness, but gradually a new light, if so I may describe it, replaced the flickering illumination of the kerosene lamp. It was a light of darkness, if you will, a glow of blackness deeper than the blackness which surrounded us, and yet by its light I could see my companions and my surroundings.

The tall woman smiled in benediction upon the four of us assembled, and gestured toward the angle between the walls. With infinite grace and seemingly glacial slowness she drifted toward the opening, through which I now perceived forms of such maddeningly chaotic configuration that I can only hint at their nature by suggesting the weird paintings that decorate the crypts of the Pharaohs, the carved stele of the mysterious Mayans, the monoliths of Mauna Loa, and the demons of Tibetan sand paintings.

The black priestess—for so I had come to think of her—led our little procession calmly into her realm of chaos and darkness. She was followed by the Gypsy-like Mrs. Llewellyn, then by Lady Fairclough, whose manner appeared as that of a woman entranced.

My own knees, I confess, have begun to stiffen with age, and I was slow to rise to my feet. Holmes followed the procession of women, while I lagged behind. As he was about to enter the opening, Holmes turned suddenly, his eyes blazing. They transmitted to me a message as clear as any words.

This message was reinforced by a single gesture. I had used my hands, pressing against the black floor as I struggled to my feet. They were now at my sides. Fingers as stiff and powerful as a bobby's club jabbed at my waist. The object which Holmes had given me to hold for him was jolted against my flesh, where it created a weird mark which remains visible to this day.

In the moment I knew what I must do.

I wrapped my arms frantically around the black altar, watching with horrified eyes as Holmes and the others slipped from the sealed room into the realm of madness that lay beyond. I stood transfixed, gazing into the Seventh Circle of Dante's hell, into the very heart of Gehenna.

Flames crackled, tentacles writhed, claws rasped, and fangs ripped at suffering flesh. I saw the faces of men and women I had known, monsters and criminals whose deeds surpass my poor talent to record but who are known in the lowest realms of the planet's underworlds, screaming with glee and with agony.

There was a man whose features so resembled those of Lady Fairclough that I knew he must be her brother. Of her missing husband I know not.

Then, looming above them all, I saw a being that must be the supreme monarch of all monsters, a creature so alien as to resemble no organic thing that ever bestrode the earth, yet so familiar that I realized it was the very embodiment of the evil that lurks in the hearts of every living man.

Sherlock Holmes, the noblest human being I have ever encountered, Holmes alone dared to confront this monstrosity. He glowed in a hideous, hellish green flame, as if even great Holmes were possessed of the stains of sin, and they were being seared from within him in the face of this being.

As the monster reached for Holmes with its hideous mockery of limbs, Holmes turned and signaled to me.

I reached within my garment, removed the object that lay against my skin, pulsating with horrid life, drew back my arm, and with a murmured prayer made the strongest and most accurate throw I had made since my days on the cricket pitch of Jammu.

More quickly than it takes to describe, the object flew through the angle. It struck the monster squarely and clung to its body, extending a hideous network of webbing 'round and 'round and 'round.

The monster gave a single convulsive heave, striking Holmes and sending him flying through the air. With presence of mind such as only he, of all men I know, could claim. Holmes reached and grasped Lady Fairclough by one arm and her brother by the other. The force of the monstrous impact sent them back through the angle into the sealed room, where they crashed into me, sending us sprawling across the floor.

With a dreadful sound louder and more unexpected than the most powerful thunderclap, the angle between the walls slammed shut. The sealed room was plunged once again into darkness.

I drew a packet of lucifers from my pocket and lit one. To my surprise, Holmes reached into an inner pocket of his own and drew from it a stick of gelignite with a long fuse. He signaled to me and I handed him another lucifer. He used it to ignite the fuse of the gelignite bomb.

Striking another lucifer, I relit the kerosene lamp that Mrs. Llewellyn had left on the altar. Holmes nodded his approval, and with the great detective in the lead, the four of us—Lady Fairclough, Mr. Philip Llewellyn, Holmes himself, and I—made haste to find our way from the Anthracite Palace.

Even as we stumbled across the great hall toward the chief exit of the palace, there was a terrible rumbling that seemed to come simultaneously from the deepest basement of the building if not from the very center of the earth, and from the dark heavens above. We staggered from the palace—Holmes, Lady Fairclough, Philip Llewellyn, and I—through the howling wind and pelting snow of a renewed storm, through frigid drifts that rose higher than our boot tops, and turned about to see the great black edifice of the Anthracite Palace in flames.

"At the Esquire" was the first short story I ever sold. It appeared in *Dude* magazine for November, 1968. It's based on a real incident involving the late artist Jack Gaughan, myself, and our respective spouses, Phoebe and Patricia. I was working in the computer industry at the time, and when the story appeared in *Dude* I proudly passed a copy of the magazine around my office. It was greeted with enthusiasm, which I found highly flattering until I realized that nobody cared about my story—all eyes were focused on the photos of the unclad ladies featured in *Dude*.

At the Esquire

We were sitting there in the Esquire having brandy and cheesecake. Okay, it isn't the most usual combination but what the hell, after dinner at the slightly ersatz kraut joint that's the most exotic eatery that Asbury sports, even with all the ritzy Valerian College girls, we wanted to stop off *somewhere* for a little after dinner drink before we went home for a real nightcap with Frances and Jack.

So brandy, and Pamela ordered a piece of the Esquire's real cheesecake (imported from Brooklyn, no less) and we asked for extra forks and all four of us picked at the cheesecake when it came. So.

The Esquire is a pretty nice gin mill if that's what you go for. Solid brick walls—it's in an old building, not just pre-prefab but pre-union, when they could lay on a work gang and really *build*—and a nice choice of décor . . . old ads and news pages and magazine covers so you have to tell for yourself (by the light of Tiffany-shaded lamps) whether the intention is antique or camp.

It's crowded, of course, and smoky, of course, and the jukebox is set too loud and it's all bass, but *all*. You throw a dime for *Creeque Alley* and all you get is Denny and John. You know, don't make too much of it, nobody's saying that Wally Wishart—he runs the Esquire—tuned out Michelle and Cass as a kind of sexual protest because he hates making a living off a bunch of horsey Valerian girls. Probably, he just has the bass turned way the hell up to give his place a Big Beat sound. That's the big thing now.

First it was jazz, then it was folk, now it's rock. If you don't stay with it the girls will take their bucks back to Pizza City or worse. Still, it's a little disconcerting to play *I'm In Love With A Big Blue Frog* and get only Peter and Paul plus deep down fiddle thumps.

Jack Gordon, by the ways is, yes, *the* Jack Gordon. Former ad agency art director who went straight and is now just about the top freelance illustrator around. Chances are you know his name; if you don't you've surely seen his work. What brought him to the top, I think, isn't technical skill. He's competent and more, absolutely, but what really makes him so good is a real eye, a talent for showing more than physical appearances in his pictures.

I remember the first time I talked to him about his work. I hardly knew the guy and I figured I'd make an ingratiating first impression by saying something nice about his work. So I picked a then-recent paperback cover painting he'd done and said I liked it. "What really got to me," I told him, "was the oddly flat planes of the faces. Really striking, and it really *says* something."

"Gee, Dave," he said, "I didn't *mean* to make the faces flat, I guess I just didn't paint them very well."

That's Jack. It was a helluva putdown, you can't deny that, but he put himself down in the same breath. How can you complain? But he is a fantastically penetrating observer. And a good storyteller, too. If he'd ever tried to write instead of drawing and painting he would have been just as successful at that too. The writers were lucky.

Let me give you an example. Jack used to tell stories about his ad agency days whenever he was trying to illustrate a point in conversation. He had this idea, for instance, about people and the nature of reality. It had bad effects of course, but it was a terrific insight. "Some people," Jack used to say, "aren't real. They're caricatures!"

You could tell from the way that he said it that an agency days story was in the works. Jack's wife, Frances, and Pamela and I just leaned back and listened. And, with full reliability, "When I was with Folwell, Taylor & Bangs, we used to have these staff meetings. All the Mad Ave types would sit around the polished table wearing the latest identical clothes. I think that season it was four button dark suits and mini-plaid button down Oxford cloth shirts and foulard four-in-hands. And they would stand up in their identical four dollar haircuts and take off their forty buck tortoise shell glasses that they all had to have whether they needed them for their eyes or not, and they'd start mouthing these Mad Ave clichés. You know, the ones that everybody kids about all the time."

Jack stopped talking and picked up his brandy glass and took a big sip. Behind us the juke box was louder than ever, or at least it seemed to be, and all in the lowest registers.

I said to Jack's wife, "That's a good record, Fran, a good lyric."

She said, "All I can hear is boom boom."

"It's a song about this little old man who alternately gets run over by a train and stampeded by elephants at half hour intervals."

"Oh, come on!" she said, so rather than try and convince her I let it drop, and her husband started telling his story again.

"Well, this account exec proudly outlined an idea he had," Jack said, and a vice president said; and I swear it, "Let's run it up the flagpole and see if anybody salutes." Jack brought his palms down on the table with a half smack, half-thump that as much as said, "believe it or don't."

I mumbled, "Life imitates art."

He said, "That wasn't all. Once they were started, the next line was 'Let's put it on the train and see if it gets off at Westport."

Cosby had given way to a Brubeck side, audio potsherd in the fast deepening sands of popular taste, but nobody else at the table seemed to notice. Pamela and Fran looked at Jack, waiting for more.

So did I, hoping that it wouldn't come. See, I really *liked* Jack, in fact: I kind of liked the whole screwy setup we had, sad and irrational as it was in so many ways. And in my role of husband-and-friend I really loved Pamela and even had a sort of low-keyed lech on for Frances that I never did anything worthwhile about except when I was too drunk to do much worthwhile about it.

"And then this senior-senior type—you could tell him by the carefully cultivated graying temples and the boyish suntan—says, so help me God, he actually says," Jack rubs his eyes with the heels of his hands and giggles soundlessly the way he does when he's too amused to speak, "he says, 'Let's lay it on the floor and walk around it a few times.'"

"That was the beginning of the end for me," Jack says, tears of repressed laughter squeezing past closed eyelids and falling on the laminated artificial wood table top.

More than you, Jack, I thought sadly.

Pamela wanted me to throw some coins in the juke box and play some good sides so I stood up and left her with Jack studying the fauna indigenous to a gin mill that's right across the street from a posh institution for the daughters of the moneyed classes. That was one of the things that made Jack a top illustrator.

Unfortunately, it had other results.

I grabbed Frances by the hand and led her over to the juke box, a distance of fully a yard, and we started shooting coins and punching buttons. I'll say this for Wishart: he kept his jukebox up to date. Some gin mills, they think "Blue Suede Shoes" is the latest protest song. But Wishart kept up with the new stuff. Donovan and the Byrds and the Stones and Cream and the *good* Beatle sides, the ones that they won't let on AM at all.

Frances and I slotted a Kennedy half and got seven sides for it and by the time we got back to the table I was really worried about Jack and the whole thing. I tried to swing the conversation around to anything but Jack's too penetrating observations. Even tried talking shop about MPT Computers Inc., the place where I worked in my cover, and how I couldn't tolerate the stories you're always reading about intelligent computers having nervous breakdowns when confronted with logical paradoxes.

Computers just don't *work* that way, I used to tell everybody I could get to listen. They don't and they never will. It just isn't a valid projection, a real personality just isn't in the nature of a computer, it would take a qualitatively different thing that would simply not be a computer any more. I used to spiel on. So.

It didn't do any good.

Jack waved a little fuzzily at the waiter for another round of drinks. Was it the third? Fourth? Plus a couple with dinner, earlier, in the kraut joint. But booze didn't dim his insight. Or his eyesight.

He looked around the Esquire, obviously focusing with difficulty, but also with a new look in his eyes that made me feel very, very sad. And yet, in a way, kind of proud that Jack was my friend. I could see that he understood the whole thing. He was the first person who ever did fully, in this world or any like it.

Oh, others had guessed before, and some had even guessed right. Some nut cults had even been founded on the idea, but they were either wild guesses or lies that happened to be true, if you can grasp that.

But Jack really knew. He really *understood*. It was a shame.

He made a circular motion with a pointing finger, vaguely including everybody in the room, the Valerian girls and their various tweedy-looking Ivy League dates and the phonies and would-be pick-ups who always hang around a place like the Esquire, and he said, "This place isn't real either."

Uh-oh, I thought. I knew it was coming then. I hoped he'd take a big swig and pass out or that a waiter would drop something on his head or anything to distract him, but nothing happened. Hell, I should have made a crude pass at the guy's wife even, that would have distracted him and maybe saved the whole thing, but when he was talking I just froze. Damn it!

Then the fit hit the shan as they say, and it was too late to save anything.

Pamela asked him what he meant.

Jack made his all around gesture again. He said, "I mean mostly—just look at the girls in this place. Look at the perfect hairdo's, and the fresh-from-the-beauty-parlor complexions with just the right amount of just the right makeup. And the clothes, they're all too right, nobody's underdressed or overdressed and you can tell that they're all expensive and all new.

"They can't be real. They're straight out of Mary McCarthy or someplace."

It was the *or someplace* that got me. That was Jack. He had those Valerian girls pegged to the last decimal place but he wouldn't admit it, he had to put on that *or someplace*. It was like Einstein saying that E equals MC squared, "I guess." Modest Jack.

We finished our drinks and settled the tab and went and got in the car, our car not theirs, and I drove. Down College Avenue to Randolph and turned on Randolph headed toward where Jack and Fran had left their station wagon. I turned on the radio loud still hoping to keep Jack from dropping the other shoe, even though I really knew it was too late. It was. He said:

"Wait a minute. If all those Mad Ave types aren't real, and the Valerian girls aren't real . . . I guess maybe we aren't either. In our own way. In fact I don't think that anybody is." Pause. You could almost hear the heavy thinking. "Or anything!"

I told the truth then.

Frances and Pamela took it better than I thought they would. Like real troupers.

But Jack was best of all. That man never wanted to stop

learning, understanding new things all the time. I used a simile to MPT computers and studying mathematical models, and of course his agency background prepared him for understanding things like market research and test studies.

He understood it, and he didn't flinch a bit. I thought he was entitled to something for that, I don't care what the rules say about no exceptions.

So I cut over control and took the car up high, and looking out the windshield it seemed even to me that we were suspended there, completely surrounded by bright points of light, the stars above us and the lights of the Valerian campus and the town of Asbury below. I let him watch the first few lights wink out before he did.

"Nothing Personal" was written at the request of one of my favorite editors, Darrell Schweitzer, for inclusion in his anthology *Cthulhu Reigns* (DAW Books, 2010). It's another Lovecraftian piece, of course.

Nothing Personal

The flashes on the surface of Yuggoth were so brilliant that they shorted out every bit of electronic equipment on *Beijing 11-11*. Dr. Chen Jing-quo was the sole occupant of the observation satellite at the time, and her own eyes were spared only through a lucky break. She had been showering when the flashes occurred, sealed off from the outer universe.

Still, she had a devil of time extricating herself from the shower-stall, now that the fractional horsepower motor that rolled the door open and shut as well as the touch-sensitive keypad that controlled the motor were dead.

Dr. Chen found the manual override control by touch, got the door open, slipped into a jumpsuit and made her way to one of *Beijing 11-11's* visual ports. The series of flashes had jolted the ports' photosensitive intracoating to darken dramatically. Dr. Chen stared at Yuggoth, a pulsing, oblate globe that filled the sky above *Beijing 11-11*. Dr. Chen studied the planet's surface and the flashes briefly; she intuited that the observatory's electron telescopes would be useless. Fortunately the station was also fitted with an array of old-style optical telescopes. Dr. Chen made her way to one of these, a 500-millimeter Zeiss-Asahi model, and trained it upon the site of the most recent flashes.

The flashes continued. Dr. Chen, at first alarmed and confused by the unexpected events, was regaining her calm. She focused the Zeiss-Asahi on the apparent epicenter of the flashes and was rewarded by the sight of another flash. This time she observed a bright dot moving away from the surface of the planet. It flashed away into the black trans-Neptunian space, toward the tiny, distant jewel that she knew was the sun. She followed the brilliant dot as long as she could. When it disappeared from sight she set about repairing the assaulted electronics of *Beijing 11-11*.

As soon as she could do so she set up a hyper-lightspeed link with her superiors on Earth's moon. Even as she did so she trained one of *Beijing 11-11's* powerful electron telescopes on Yuggoth's surface. She knew the planet's cities as well as—no, better than—she knew the cities of Earth. She had been born on the mother world but her recollections of the planet were only the vague images of a small child. Colors and sounds and odors. The feeling of her mother's arms, a flavor that she thought was that of her mother's milk. But she could not be sure.

She had been selected as a toddler and transported to the moon for two decades of training. She had emerged at the top of her class, triumphing in the final competitive examinations over a thousand young men and women who competed for positions in the world's ongoing scientific enterprises.

She had worked with joyous dedication on *Beijing 11-11* for the past decade, observing the enigmatic activities on Yuggoth. That huge planet and its four satellites, Nithan, Zaman, Thog and Thok, rolled eternally in a counterplanar orbit, crossing the plane of the solar ecliptic only once in a thousand years. No wonder it had gone undiscovered for so long, for Earthbound planetary astronomers had long concentrated their studies on the multi-billion-mile disk that surrounded Sol, containing the four rocky planets, the four gas giants, the asteroids and plutoids and the countless meteors and comets.

Barely a century ago Yuggoth and its moons had actually crossed the plane of the ecliptic, and thus it had been detected at last. The discovery of a new major planet had sent shockwaves through the scientific community of Earth. Probes had landed on the major solid bodies of the solar system, the four rock planets and the solid moons of the four gas giants. The variety of worlds was incredible. There were ice-covered bodies, the volcanoes, the nitrogen seas, the mountain ranges and deserts and canyon-like beds of ancient rivers, long run dry.

Above all, there was life and the evidence of past life. Exobiologists on Earth had long given hope of such discoveries. Their mantra: *Where life can exist, it does!* The flaw in their argument lay in the fact that they had only a single model from which to draw their conclusion. True, life flourished in the most astonishing of environments, in water close to boiling, in fissures deep within the Earth, on ocean floors where pressure reached tons per square centimeter and where neither sunlight nor oxygen could be detected. But it was possible—it was vigorously debated—that life had originated but once upon Earth, and that all organisms, however varied their natures and locales, were descended from a single ancestor.

It took the exploration of dozens of moons to find jungles and prairies, natural gardens of unimaginable colors and forms, schools of swimming things that were surely not fish, and flocks of flying things that were anything but birds.

But no people. Not merely no humans like those whose robot explorers first landed on Callisto and Mimas, Miranda and Proteus and Galatea and all the others. The people of Earth both longed for and feared the discovery of alien intelligences, whether they looked like giant grasshoppers or self-conscious cabbages or whales with hands, whether they wrote epic treatises on the meaning of life or built machines to carry them across the dimensional barrier to other universes even stranger than the one from which they had come.

No people. No intelligent cabbages or whales with hands, no ancient cities to put the monuments of Thebes to shame and to make the mysteries of Rapa Nui and Stonehenge and the riddle of Linear B look like child's play.

Until Yuggoth.

Until the first robotic probe had circled Yuggoth sending back to Earth images of structures that were undoubtedly artificial, yet that resembled no city ever built upon Earth. They stretched for thousands of miles across the ruddy, pulsing surface of Yuggoth. They rose for hundreds miles into the roiling, cloudy atmosphere of the planet. At the poles of the monstrous globe black, glossy areas that must be ice caps reflected the light of a billion distant stars.

At this distance from the sun the amount of heat and light from that star was infinitesimal. Clearly, Yuggoth's ruddy pulsations emanated from within the planet, whether the product of radioactivity, of tidal or magnetic forces, or of some other source of unfathomable nature.

Controllers on Earth—for this was before the construction and orbiting of Chen Jing-kuo's observation station—tried sending messages to the occupants of those cyclopean cities, relaying them from their own base of operations on Luna to the satellites orbiting the gigantic "new" planet. There was no response.

Were the Yuggothi extinct? Were their cities like dead like the temples of Preah Pithu or the cities of Chichen Itza and Uxmal in the Yucatán?

But the satellites detected movement on the surface of Yuggoth. Great creatures of alien configuration, beings like nothing encountered on Earth or any other world of the solar system, moved between the buildings, between structures that had to be considered buildings, of those cities, which had to be considered cities.

Chen Jing-quo observed the Yuggothi with both electronic and optical instruments. They had heads and bodies and limbs. To that extent they resembled familiar species found both on Earth and elsewhere in the solar system. But where one might have expected to see facial features the Yuggothi showed clusters of waving, polypoidal tentacular growths. Their limbs were tipped with vicious-looking claws, and on their backs were what appeared to be vestigial, bat-like wings.

They were hairless, their skin of a scaly composition that suggested a onetime marine origin, and indeed Yuggoth was covered in part with dark regions that appeared to be composed of a black, viscid liquid. If these were the seas and oceans of Yuggoth, the winged creatures might have evolved in their depths, using their wings to "fly" through the seas as Earthly manta rays "flew" through the warm waters of the Caribbean Sea.

Once *Beijing 11-11* was launched from its construction site on Luna, it was piloted to the Oort Cloud by a two-member crew comprising Chen Jing-quo and Kimana Hasani. When *Beijing 11-11* settled into orbit around the ruddy pulsing oblate form of Yuggoth, Kimana Hasani informed Chen Jing-quo that he was going to take one of the station's EEPs for a closer look at the new planet.

Dr. Chen protested. *Beijing 11-11* carried only a limited number of EEPs—External Excursion Pods. They were meant to be used only in cases of extreme necessity. For servicing and repairs of the station, for transportation between space vehicles—although there were no other space vehicles within the better part of a billion miles of *Beijing 11-11*—or as lifeboats. They were emphatically not intended for exploration.

But Kimana Hasani would not be deterred. He suited up in protective gear and entered the EEP. He promised Chen Jing-quo that he would maintain a continuous video and audio link with *Beijing 11-11*. Once he had climbed into the EEP he waited for the interlock to click green, hit the launch button and dropped away from *Beijing 11-11*.

Dr. Chen watched twin video screens. On one she followed the progress of her partner's EEP as it dropped away from *Beijing 11-11* and drifted down toward the atmosphere of Yuggoth. On the other she watched Kimana Hasani's face. He in turn concentrated on the instruments and controls of the pod.

As the tiny craft entered the atmosphere of the planet Chen Jing-quo heard her partner mutter something but this phase lasted only a few seconds. She thought she heard Kimana Hasani say something like *sizzling*, heard him speak part of her name. Then she observed a flash. The screen that had carried Kimana Hasani's image went blank. The screen that had carried an exterior image of the EEP flared a brilliant golden-orange. A shock wave spread visibly through the atmosphere where the EEP had been, then rippled outward and downward toward the surface of Yuggoth.

And upward, toward *Beijing 11-11*, where Dr. Chen cried out in startlement and grief at what she had seen, and at what she suspected was its meaning.

The only phenomenon that she could think of that would produce so violent a discharge was a nuclear explosion. She knew the design of the EEP as she knew every surface, every weld, every circuit on *Beijing 11-11*. She knew that Kimana Hasani's pod carried no fissile material. She inferred what had happened. The atmosphere of Yuggoth was composed of SeeTee matter.

SeeTee. CT. Contraterrene. Antimatter.

She experienced a flash of recollection, of her school days, of a student joke: *What do you get if a normal matter boy makes it with an antimatter girl?*

Answer: *No matter*.

No matter. No matter, in truth. Just one hell of a release of pure energy.

Yuggoth was composed of SeeTee matter.

The mountains and plains of Yuggoth, its black, viscid seas, its ebony ice caps, its cyclopean cities with their towering, eye-wrenching structures, its monstrous inhabitants, all were composed of contraterrene matter. Of antimatter.

Chen Jing-kuo returned to the electron telescope. She trained it upon the Yuggothian city directly below the point where Kimana Hasani's pod and Kimana Hasani himself had been converted to pure energy. The city lay in ruins. Titanic structures had been toppled, crushed to rubble. The inhabitants of the city had died by the millions, their terrible bodies torn and scattered hither and yon.

Shaking her head, Chen Jing-kuo wiped her tears. She turned from the telescope and opened a hyperlightspeed link to Luna. The communications operator who received her call was a onetime classmate, Matyah Melajitm. For a moment Melajitm's smile filled Dr. Chen's screen. Then the comm-op saw the expression on Chen Jing-quo's face.

"What's the matter? Something's happened. What is it?"

"Get Dr. Jerom. Kimana is dead. We seem—I think we've started a war. The first interplanetary war!"

It seemed to take hours—more likely less than two minutes—for Harleyann Jerom to replace Matyah Melajitm at the Luna comm-link.

"Dr. Chen, tell me."

Chen Jing-quo gave her a quick summary of the event.

Harleyann Jerom groaned. "All right, Chen. Do nothing now. Better yet, batten down *Beijing 11-11*. Not that I imagine you can do much to defend the station if the Yuggothi choose to counterattack. They're likely to interpret the explosion as an attack. They surely will if they're anything like us."

"There was no way. I mean, how could Kimana ever imagine . . ." Dr. Chen's voice trailed away.

"Never mind blame," Jerom responded. "There will be plenty of time for that later on. Or maybe not. But not now, that's for sure. Keep the link open."

Chen Jing-quo saw Harleyann Jerom turn away, heard her give instructions to Matyah Melajitm. Chen knew that Jerom was going to talk with Earth, get a quick decision from the politicians who ran planetary affairs.

A quick decision.

Fat chance.

Jerom reappeared on *Beijing 11-11's* comm screen. "Chen, was there ever—ever—any indication that the Yuggothi were even aware of *Beijing 11-11?*"

Chen Jing-quo shook her head. "No. That's what was so—we tried—we tried to establish communication with them. They ignored us. Or—it wasn't even that. It was as if they were completely unaware of us. As if we were bacteria, viruses, and they were humans. Or mammoths. How many bacteria does such a beast crush with every step? To the Yuggothi we were bacteria or less. They never even noticed us. Until Kimana hit their atmosphere. Then . . ." She spread her hands, helpless to continue.

Harleyann Jerom nodded. "An apt simile. They probably won't be angry with us. A mersa bacterium doesn't hate its host and a human doesn't hate a bacterium. They're just two kinds of organism, and one will kill the other in order to preserve itself and perpetuate its kind. The infection will kill the host or the host will kill the infection."

"Right." Chen Jing-kuo reacted with a manic grin.

Jerom's voice was harsh. "Get a grip!"

"Nothing personal," Dr. Chen went on.

"I said, *Get a grip!* This is a crisis that could make all the wars in human history look like playground squabbles."

"I'm sorry," Chen said. She was calmer now. Her nerves were jumping. She could feel her heart pounding in her chest. It must be beating close to two hundred beats a minute. Her breath was coming in desperate gasps.

She recognized the phenomena. Some ancestor was reaching down to her, reaching through the genetic matter that carried ancient reflexes. Her body sensed her desperation, prepared itself for combat or for flight. Appropriate reactions for a Cro-Magnon, for Pithecanthropus Erectus, for an ancestor even more ancient. But hardly apt for Homo Interplanetarius.

She was in control of herself. "What are my instructions, Dr. Jerom?"

"For now, observe and report. What do you see on Yuggoth?"

Chen returned to the telescopes. She activated a third screen, one for an electron image, one for an optical image, one for a superimposed combination.

"It's daytime down there. You know, it's always daytime on Yuggoth. The planet rotates but its light comes from its core so it doesn't really matter. The city that was destroyed by the shock wave—I see Yuggothi arriving from all directions. I suppose they're rescue crews. The devastation is terrible. The casualties—I can't even guess at the number. Some of them are still alive, though. I see Yuggothi crawling through the ruins. Some with dreadful injuries. Some are just—just—it looks as if their body parts, when they were ripped off by the shock wave, some of them didn't die and now they're flopping around, moving like torn starfish. And—and—I can't go on, Harleyann. I can't."

"That's all right, Jing-kuo. You've done what you can. And we're getting feeds from *Beijing 11-11's* instruments."

There was a pause, then Harleyann Jerom resumed. "You're convinced that Kimana Hasani's EEP set off the explosion on Yuggoth?"

Dr. Chen's eyes were still focused on the screens showing conditions on the surface of Yuggoth. "I'm certain, Harleyann. The only explanation—I'm convinced it's the only explanation, the only way that little EEP could cause the devastation—the only explanation is that Yuggoth is composed of antimatter. Once Kimana's EEP hit the atmosphere, that was all it took. The EEP and Kimana himself were cancelled out. Converted to pure energy, along with an equivalent mass of Yuggothi atmosphere. He—"

Her words were cut off by a gasp from Harleyann Jerom. Then the voice of the woman on Luna said, "They're here!"

"Who? What are you saying, Harleyann?"

"The Yuggothi."

"Impossible. I just saw them leave their planet."

"They're here. They're circling overhead. Their ships are unlike anything else I've ever seen. They look like—like cyborgs. They're monsters, something like bats, something like octopuses, something like humans. And machines. They're machines, too."

"But—they can't have traveled that far in a few minutes."

"They can, Jing-kuo. They must have—I don't know—we

manage to skip message through wormholes or subspace or however our system works. We don't really understand, do we, we just know that it works. And they've found a way to travel, oh, not through space. Between space. Whatever. And they're heading toward Earth, Jing-kuo. I can see. I can see waves of blackness sweeping across the planet. The atmosphere is burning, the oceans, forests, ice caps. Oh, my God, my God, my God. It's worse than—"

The transmission ended.

Chen Jing-kuo studied the surface of Yuggoth, pulsing red, filling the sky above *Beijing 11-11*.

The virus doesn't hate its host, she thought, and the host doesn't really hate the virus. There is nothing personal about it. Nothing personal. If the host doesn't destroy the virus in time, the virus will kill the host. But even if that happens, once the host is dead, the virus also will die.

Chen Jing-kuo turned the telescope toward Earth. The image was magnified until it filled a screen. As she watched, bits of black appeared on the blue-and-white disk. They spread from points to irregular blots. More of them appeared, and more, until they began to run together.

For a moment the planet disappeared against the solid black background of space. Then points appeared again, became blots, multiplied and grew until Earth was a red disk. Like Yuggoth, it began to pulse, to pulse like a malevolent heart. Now Chen Jing-kuo understood what she was seeing. The Yuggothi, she realized, had devised a means to convert the normal matter of Earth, contact with which would have been instantly, disastrously fatal to them, into contraterrene matter. Anti-matter.

Now they could live in Earth, and now there remained no other life to compete with them.

But Yuggoth itself was also contraterrene. The Yuggothi had erected no shield against a potential plunging space station of terrene matter. For all Chen Jing-kuo could tell, the Yuggothi were as unaware of the station as a human would be of a single fatal bacterium.

Earth was dead. Chen Jing-kuo knew that now. The Yuggothi had wiped it clean. The atmosphere was gone. The oceans, the forests. The ice caps were gone. The planet had been wiped clean. It now had new owners. Octopus-bat-man-machine *things* that even now were walking or slithering or flying across the black, dead surface of the once blue-green, beautiful world. The black surface that was now pulsing with a red, evil beat.

The oblate globe of Yuggoth spun beneath *Beijing 11-11*. Chen Jing-kuo set the controls, activated the verniers, sent *Beijing 11-11* plunging toward Yuggoth. This time, the sequence of events was reversed. The host had killed the virus, but the virus retained enough vitality for one final act. The virus would kill the host.

Richard A. Lupoff

"Tee Shirts" is a thinly disguised memoir of my experiences in the early 1970s as a popular media journalist. It has never been published before. Instead, I have used it as a performance piece with great success and active response from audiences. One person questioned my ability to dredge up these memories with such accuracy and in such detail, and I could only respond that, "I don't do strong drugs any more."

Tee Shirts

Cynics will tell you that no good deed goes unpunished but of course the opposite is true, at least sometimes.

I was walking down Van Ness Avenue in San Francisco with my ultra-married friends Laura and Gordon Tomkins, when I saw an old woman in a wheelchair trying to cross the thoroughfare. Van Ness, in case you're unfamiliar with this city, is a wide street with a center divider. There are traffic lights, but a lot of drivers seem to think it fun to use Van Ness as a raceway, and scampering across is dangerous even for able-bodied pedestrians to attempt.

And this old woman didn't even have one of those modern electric-powered chairs. She was pumping away with arms no thicker than sticks, and it looked as if she was likely to die of overexertion if some superannuated hot-rodder in a monster SUV didn't first grind her into flinders.

To add to the old woman's peril, it was early evening, just the time when visibility is worst. And it was starting to rain.

I told Laura and Gordon, "I'll be right back." I ran after the old woman and grabbed the handles of her wheelchair. Got her onto the island in the middle of Van Ness. I asked where she was going and she gave an address nearby. As soon as I could get her across the rest of the avenue and to her home, I did.

She looked up at me and her eyes were not at all what I expected. Not the rheumy, faded eyes of a feeble old woman. They looked young and bright and a color that I would call emerald green except that description is totally inadequate.

I asked if she needed help getting into the house and she said No. Then she added, "You will be rewarded." And that was that.

Five minutes later I was back with Laura and Gordon. "You know, you took a serious risk," Gordon said.

"What?"

Laura said, "This is a dangerous neighborhood. We're on the edge of the Tenderloin. That woman could have been a decoy working with muggers."

I said, "Oh, I didn't think of that." Nobody said anything for a minute so I said, "You see somebody needs help, you help her. It's not complicated."

We stopped at the office of *Rock! Rock! Rock!* to see if there were any messages, then on to the Civic Auditorium. Joe Cocker was performing that night. I run the West Coast office of *R!R!R!*. Laura is a freelance photog who works for us now and then. Gordon is a software wizard who actually makes a living out of his job.

Cocker was drunk. He threw up onstage and had to cancel the performance. The management had to refund the money of a couple thousand angry customers.

Laura and Gordon and I paid a brief call to the backstage scene, snagged a couple of sandwiches and beers off the catering table, and worked the room. The usual groupies were milling around, looking more stoned and confused than ever.

I spotted Vampirella. She was wearing her customary black satin outfit with opaque shades and blood-red costume jewelry. I tried to make the same approach I did every time I saw her, and she ignored me the way she did every time I tried. If you're wondering why I bothered, I can't give you an answer that makes much sense. She just had her hooks in me. Maybe it was her glossy, sable hair. Maybe it was her amazing complexion. Or her slim, supple figure. I've never gone for the buxom type, but Vampirella—or whatever her real name was—could just crook her finger and I'd come running.

Next day I opened the *R!R!R!* office and checked the day's mail, messages on the answering machine, LP's for review, and promotional loot. The rock business is brutally competitive and the artists' promoters and the record companies are constantly vying for air-time and ink for their precious darlings. People like me get invited to parties, offered generous doses of illegal candies, backstage passes of course, trips to out-of-town conferences, and an endless array of coffee mugs, dinner trays, ballpoint pens, cheap wrist watches, tee shirts, giant belt buckles, and miscellaneous *tchatchkes*.

I sat down to write as charitable a report as I could of last night's debacle. Laura would be in with some photos. I had no idea what she could have got that we could use, but she's a solid pro and I knew she'd give me something good. I wrote the article and started through the day's loot, looking for something I could either use or hock for a few shekels.

Mostly it was junk. I mean—*Andy Kim? Up With People?* What were the A&R geniuses smoking this month? There was a nice tee shirt, though. Black cotton with a nifty logo on the chest in white and the words *Lone Star Beer* in bright yellow lettering. I checked the label and it was my size. Winner!

There was no promotional material with it. I couldn't think of anybody who'd put out an album called *Lone Star Beer*. But what the heck, it was a great shirt and it was a freebie.

There was a show over in Berkeley that night that I wanted to catch. Merl Saunders was playing at the New Monk, and based on past history Jerry Garcia was likely to drop in and jam. I decided to inaugurate the Lone Star Beer shirt. Of course it was chilly and wet, par for the course this time of year, so I bundled up.

Merl was great, Nine Finger Jerry showed up and was amazing, and I wound up in the green room with them between sets. There was good wine and whiskey on the table along with guacamole and chips. There were very few groupies, the bruiser at the door had seen to that, but I did spot Vampirella there.

We made eye contact and for the first time in recorded history she smiled at me. I walked over, half expecting her to cut me dead, but instead she offered me a tortilla chip slathered in green slime. Yow!

Why the change? I was too happy to worry about that, I was just bathing in the divine presence. Jesus, she even smelled good! She said, "That's a great shirt. You from Texas? What's your name, cowboy?"

I told her, "Del Marston and I'm from Chicago."

"Why the shirt?"

"Just a nice shirt."

We made small talk, told each other about trying to earn a living in San Francisco, drank some of the management's booze (excellent!) and headed out along with Merl and Jerry for the second set.

When it was over Vampie invited me up to her apartment for a nightcap. Believe that? Like a character in some old movie. Of course I said yes, and when we got there she opened a bottle of Chardonnay and put on an LP. I wondered what her choice in music was going to be, hoping it wouldn't be too hard or loud, and she astonished me.

Haydn!

* *** *

Next time I saw her was at the Sweetwater in Mill Valley. Maria Muldaur was singing. I'd put on a spiffy new shirt and jeans just in case. And, all right, I spotted Vampirella. I didn't think Muldaur was her kind of music, but what the hell boss what the hell, I walked over and said, "Hi, remember me, Del Marston from Chicago?"

She looked through me.

"We met at the New Monk? Merl Saunders and Jerry Garcia?"

She said, "I'm waiting for a friend," and turned away.

What the heck?

Muldaur was sweet but I watched Vampirella all night and her friend never showed up. And once the show ended she disappeared before I could offer her a ride home.

Jeez.

Incidentally, I don't want you to think that my job is all hanging out at music venues, cadging catered meals in green rooms, drinking wine and smoking dope with hippies. I have to do interviews and write concert and record reviews and keep this little office going. And I don't want you to think that I actually run *Rock! Rock! Rock!* I'm just the so-called West Coast Editor. All my copy and all of Laura's photos wind up in New York where the bigwigs put the magazine together. And I have to keep them happy to keep the checks flowing westward.

Next show I wanted to cover was at the Pierce Street Annex back in the city. Really talented folkie named Paul Siebel, straight from Woodstock. It was a warm night for San Francisco, and I'd come home from the Laundromat with some clean duds just in time to get dressed for Siebel's show. I put on my best safari boots, clean jeans, and my Lone Star Beer tee shirt. The shirt was plenty comfortable and I was getting fond of it, although the dye the manufacturer used must have been pretty cheap because the shirt looked a little bit faded after only one washing.

Well, the price was right, anyhow.

Siebel was even better in person than he was on his self-titled LP. A modest, sweet-natured guy. I introduced myself and told him I wanted to do a piece on him for *R!R!R!* and he acted as if I was some kind of celebrity.

Coming out of the club after Siebel's show, who should I run into on Pierce Street but—right!—Vampirella. I had a little tape recorder in one hand and my notebook in the other and I was headed for my faithful bug. After the brush-off I'd got at the Sweetwater I didn't know what to expect of Vampie but she came running at me and jumped into my arms. Wrapped her legs around my waist, almost knocked the tape recorder out of my hands, planted a hot wet one on my ear and demanded, "Where have you been? Are you mad at me?"

Once she climbed down from my midsection and I got back the breath she'd knocked out of me, I said, "I thought *you* were mad at *me*."

She said, "After that night we saw Jerry and Merl at the New Monk? How could I be mad at you? But then when I ran into you at the Muldaur show, I thought you must be totally pissed. Did I come on too strong at my place, or what?"

Now I was totally baffled. I figured all I could do was pretend the Sweetwater thing never happened. I said, "It's pretty late, do you need a ride or what?"

She said, "I'll tell you what, I'm really famished. You think we could rustle up some food?"

"Mel's should be open."

"That would be okay, but—do you know how to cook? Or I could make something if you have the ingredients."

Well, long story short, for once the bug started without a fuss, I found a parking spot half a block from my modest digs, and we wound up having a bedtime snack of bacon and eggs and English muffins. A bachelor like me learns to cook, at least the simple stuff.

In the morning she woke up first and returned the favor. And before she left she invited me to go to a movie that night. And would you believe, I had a plus-one press invite to exactly that flick. It was *The Last Picture Show,* and I am nuts for anything that Bogdonovich directs.

Amazing. This was starting to look like a match made in heaven.

As planned, I showed up at the theater half an hour before show time. No sign of Vampie, but what the hell, it was early yet and I knew she wanted to see the film. She'd even told me she had a crush on Timothy Bottoms. She wouldn't miss it.

It was one of those chilly nights, a cold mist in the air and glowing nimbuses around street lamps and storefront neon. I wore a sweatshirt under a quilted jacket and still I was freezing ten minutes after I arrived. There was a coffee shop next door to the theater so I headed in to get a hot cup.

She was sitting in a booth with one of the Kerr twins. Oh, jeez.

You don't know the Kerr twins. Frankie and Jimmy. Frank Arthur Kerr and James Otho Kerr. I don't know what their parents were thinking of. Look at the initials. Their names turn into Faker and Joker. They both work for *Scorpion Blues,* my mag's meanest competitor. Every time I try for a plum interview I have to worry about getting to the artist before Faker or Joker. Every time *B!B!B!* loses an important ad, you can guess who got it. *Scorpion Blues.* Right.

And there was Vampie drinking latté and playing footsie with Frankie. Or maybe Jimmy. I stood there, probably looking like a pimply high school nerd who just got dumped in favor of Superjock and knows he's about to become the laughingstock of the junior class.

Vampie displayed a butter-wouldn't-melt-in-her-mouth grin and waved to me and said, "Oh, hi there. Del, isn't it? Del Martin?"

"Marston," I stammered, as if she didn't know.

"You here for *The Last Picture Show?*" Jimmy asked. Or maybe Frankie.

I ignored him. I said, "I thought we were going together, Vampirella. We just talked about it this morning, don't you remember?"

"I'm sorry, Don," the sentence slithered from between her luscious lips like an aerial snake. "I don't know what you're talking about. Maybe you're thinking of somebody else."

Jimmy-Frankie slid his arm around her shoulders and said, "That rag of yours still going, Dan? I don't hear much about it these days."

I couldn't take any more. I went home and turned on Blue Oyster Cult loud and opened a bottle of cheap wine and got stinko. I played "Don't Fear the Reaper" a dozen times and sang along with Roeser and fantasized about Patti Smith.

Next day I enjoyed a hangover that would surely land me in *The Guinness Book of World Records* if I could figure out how to describe it to them. I excavated my favorite shirt out of the hamper and pulled it on. Either the shirt was getting ripe or I was, but I was in no shape to do anything about that. I peered into the mirror and when I saw what was squinting back at me I scrounged up a Commander Cody baseball cap that I'd got as a reward for a nice little article when the Commander was just getting started. Money would have been nicer.

I managed to crawl down to the office and write a couple of record reviews. I ripped into the material and the performances and the production and the cover art, and for all I know I destroyed a dozen promising careers and sent as many sensitive artistic souls back to grad school for MBAs.

Sorry about that.

I drank a pot of coffee wishing I was a private eye who kept a bottle of bourbon in his desk drawer to spike the java with, but I wasn't and I didn't and by mid-afternoon I was feeling at least slightly human.

There was a free show in Golden Gate Park and the sun was shining. I left the bug in the driveway and struggled over to the park on foot. I heard the band tuning up from three blocks away. By the time I got there Hot Tuna was launched into one of their patented all-day versions of "Keep Your Lamps Trimmed and Burning."

A haze of blue-gray stonedness was floating over the crowd. I struggled to a place near the stage and plopped my *tuchuss* onto the grass and tried to get my head into the music. It was then that I heard the unmistakable sound of a female palm colliding with a male physiognomy and caught the wind-up of an angry exclamation that ended with, ". . . and your pitiful little weenie, too, you creep!"

That caught my attention.

I turned in time to see Frankie-Jimmy Kerr slinking away through the mob of stoned Tuna-lovers. And there was Vampirella decked out in black satin with opaque shades and her hair looking as if the sun had no other job than to make it look gorgeous.

"Del!" Vampie squealed. "Del, oh my gosh, I'm so happy to see you. You won't believe what that son of a something wanted me to do. Oh, Del, please, will you stay with me in case he comes back, or sends that louse of a brother of his."

We stayed together and Hot Tuna went on and on, the sky grew dark, the crowd thinned, the stars came out, the gray mist embraced us and we embraced each other and I had an inkling for the first time in my life of what love poetry is all about.

* *** *

And sometimes the world, as they say, is too much with us. I mean, the next day I scrubbed myself down, shampooed a couple of times, scraped the bristles off my face, threw everything except the sweat suit on my back into a couple of pillow cases and headed down to the local Laundromat. I sat there reading a copy of *The Dharma Bums* while my clothes and the soap suds went 'round and 'round and 'round behind the little glass window.

When the machine stopped I transferred everything to a dryer and sat down again with my book only to feel a cool and gentle kiss on my freshly shaven cheek.

And there stood Laura Tomkins, ace girl shutter-bug. "You're looking chipper as hell, boss, how's about buying a lady a cold refreshing brew?"

And off we went to a nearby watering hole. There was a juke box in the corner and somebody had fed it with a bunch of coins and Grace Slick's voice was wailing. There was a TV set over the bar with the picture turned on and the sound turned off. In a totally bizarre way "Somebody to Love" made a perfect soundtrack for Karl Malden and Michael Douglas screeching up and down the streets of San Francisco in their mile-long Ford sedan.

And when Laura and I got back to the Laundromat some skunk had opened the dryer and made off with my personal wardrobe. I collared the dragon who made change and sold overpriced packages of soap powder to customers and demanded to know who had my belongings. She said it wasn't her job to play policeman and couldn't I read, didn't I see all the signs that said, *Keep an eye on your belongings, Management is not responsible for lost or stolen property.*

Jeez.

Laura tried to cheer me up, invited me to join her and Gordon for a pizza and a movie, but I was in no mood. I just went home and sulked for the next several hours. When the walls started to close in on me and the only choice on TV was Lawrence Welk or Art Linkletter, I grabbed my Commander Cody baseball cap—at least I'd left that at home—and headed for North Beach. There's always some kind of distraction in North Beach.

The flashing lights and pathetic barkers and moronic thrill-seekers didn't do it for me. Not tonight. They just depressed me. I walked down to City Lights and looked at the books in the window and decided maybe I'd find something to read. I wandered around picking books up and putting them down. I finally settled on *A Coney Island of the Mind.* I stood in line to pay for the Ferlinghetti until I got to the cashier's counter.

All right, guess who was working the register.

I don't have to tell you. Oh, boy, did she look good to me!

"Vampirella!"

"Yes, sir. You want that book? A great book, great book, excellent choice." She told me the price. It was right there on the cover but she told me anyhow.

"Vampirella, it's me, Del."

She told me the price again and held out her hand.

I slapped the book into her hand and walked out.

All right, all right, why didn't I just write her off as a flake and go look for another lady fair? Right. Try telling that to somebody who's so crazy in love he can't figure out which way is up.

* *** *

For the next couple of weeks I managed to avoid Vampirella. I started getting up early, showering and shaving regularly, working long hours, even freelancing to supplement the meager salary that the East Coast mobsters who owned *Rock! Rock! Rock!* paid me whenever I called up and whined that I was starving.

I got an invitation to a literary conference in Southern California. A library association had decided that the popular music press was worthy of a panel discussion and offered me a cheap ticket on a PSA jet, a rental AMC Gremlin, and a room at the Motel Five-and-a-Half directly under the LAX flight-path.

Strangely enough, by the time my jet touched down I had a hearty appetite so I headed out in my Gremlin, looking for a place to eat. I must have taken a wrong turn on the Hades Freeway because I wound up in an ugly town in the Valley. While I tried to find my way back to LA I spotted an eating establishment with the unlikely name of Uncle Hoggly-Woggly's Tyler Texas Home Style Barbecue. There was a big sign over the door, a painting of a bright pink pig in a chef's hat holding up a plate of barbecue and saying, "Bet You Can't Top This!" surrounded by the name of the establishment in glowing incandescent letters. People were lined up to get into the joint and the ones going in looked happy and the ones coming out looked happier so I figured this was a find.

It was. If I ever get to Texas—God forbid!—I will head straight to Tyler, wherever that may be, and wallow in barbecue until I can't stand it any more.

For now, though, I just feasted on ribs in sauce so hot it hurt but so delicious I couldn't stop eating, and potato salad, and coffee. That was all that Uncle Hoggly-Woggly sold and it was paradise enow as far as I was concerned.

That was the high point of my trip. As for the low point . . .

The conference was a nightmare. My panel was attended by about three bedraggled-looking spinster librarians. Turned out that everybody else was at a cocktail party in honor of the hundredth birthday a professor of medieval *ballades* from some local community college extension branch. The moderator of the panel must have been that professor's mother. She thought my magazine was a journal devoted to the study of petroglyphs. And my fellow panelists—there were two of them—were none other than my old buddies Frankie and Jimmy Kerr. Who of course proceeded to beat up on me verbally for forty minutes while our moderator sat there, open-mouthed and horror-stricken.

I spent the evening sitting on my bed at the Motel Five-and-a-Half eating a stale chicken salad sandwich, drinking warm, flat beer, and watching *The Brady Bunch* in fuzzy black-and-white. I would have headed back to Uncle Hoggly-Woggly's if I thought I could find it again, but the first time had been strictly a lucky strike and I wasn't going to risk those freeways again.

In the morning I packed my minimal luggage, checked out of the Motel Five-and-a-Half, and started across the parking lot, looking for my avocado green Gremlin.

Other people were checking out. I saw a woman pushing a double-width stroller from the office. As she reached the middle of the parking lot some kind of muscle car came screaming around the corner, headed straight for them. I don't think the driver expected anyone to be there and he mashed on his brakes and the car started to skid but there was no way it was going to stop in time and no way that poor mother was going to get her little ones out of its trajectory.

I want to emphasize, I'm no hero. I didn't decide that I was going to do what I did. I didn't even think about that, *When you see somebody who needs help*, business. I just—well, something clicked in my brain, and without thinking I launched myself into a flying tackle, slammed into the woman with my shoulder, grabbed the handle of the stroller with my other hand and yanked it after me. I hit the pavement hard with the woman in one hand and the stroller, complete with a pair of shrieking toddlers, in the other. I was scraped all to hell and gone and bleeding in a bunch of places but the mom and her tykes were untouched.

The driver of the muscle car had stopped and he and his passenger came trotting back to see what had happened. It was, all right, you got it, Frankie and Jimmy, and give them credit, lousy creeps that they are, they were concerned for the woman and her toddlers and remorseful for their carelessness and the tragedy that had almost caused, and one of them even looked at me and said, "Oh, Del Marston, sorry 'bout that, see you back up north."

And they climbed back into their muscle car and went tearing out of the parking lot.

The woman was hugging her toddlers and crying. After a little while she stood up and held me, her hands on my arms. She actually cried into my jacket. Then she brushed off the cloth and said, "Oh, I got you all wet."

In a minute we both started laughing at the incongruity.

She let go of me and leaned back and looked up at me. Her eyes were a color I'd only seen once before in my life. She said, so softly I could hardly hear, "You will be rewarded."

* *** *

I got back to San Francisco without further incident. I was too pumped from the excitement to go home so I opened the crummy little West Coast office of *Rock! Rock! Rock!* and started through the usual accumulation of mail, LP's for review, press releases, invitations to music venues, and promo gifts.

There was a jiffy bag with no return address on it but there was a Los Angeles postmark. I opened it and extracted a tee shirt. It was gorgeous. It featured a picture of a pig wearing a chef's hat, holding up a plate of barbecue, grinning and saying, "Bet You Can't Top This!" Big, clear lettering around the artwork spelled out the name of the establishment, *Doctor Hoggly-Woggly's Tyler Texas Home Style Barbecue.*

* *** *

Tha-tha-tha that's all, f-folks!

"Dingbats" was written for William Jones for inclusion in his anthology *Horrors Beyond* (Elder Signs Press, 2005). My older son reacted to it with shock. "Dad, are you writing lesbian porn now?" I didn't *think* that was what I was writing.

Dingbats

You couldn't pronounce the name of the ship. Heck, neither could I, nor even spell it, for that matter. So let's call it the *Niña*. That's as good a name as any.

And as for the crew—well, they'll still be recognizably human. Their story takes place in the future, but not so far into the future that our descendents have green extrudable pseudopodia or are disembodied brains riding around in nutrient-filled containers or any of that crazy Wilma Deering-Dale Arden stuff.

So since you couldn't pronounce their names and I couldn't spell them either, I'll call them by ordinary present-day names instead.

Diamond Lil.

Amber Annie.

Asparagus.

Well, the others called her Pair o' Guts, but she preferred Asparagus.

The *Niña* was a small ship. She only took a crew of three, and they weren't expected to be off Earth for long. They'd rented the ship, three total strangers but the computer (if you want to call it that) at the rental agency decided they'd be compatible and they'd save a lot of money (see above) by sharing. One worked with numbers, one with organs, one with physics. Nothing there to make for instant enmity.

A little pleasure jaunt for three new pals, maybe zip up to Luna and sightsee a little. They didn't think they'd go even as far as Nergal, or Mars as it had once been known. There were tourist facilities there and the three pals could certainly afford to vacation on the Red Planet, but they all had jobs and this was only supposed to be a weekend getaway, not a full-fledged vacation.

You understand, I hope, that everything I tell you is only approximately what I say it is. Like, try to explain a nuclear reactor or an HDTV or the way an antibiotic works in your body to somebody who lived a couple of hundred years ago, no less a few thousand or even more.

The *Niña* ran into a tiny singularity, the kind of thing that goes zipping around the galaxies, popping in and out of wormholes and wreaking havoc when you least expect it, and whonked out of ordinary time-space and got deposited someplace far away.

Diamond Lil was the captain, at least to the extent that the *Niña* had a captain, and she said, "Wow, what the hell was *that?*" Neither Amber Annie nor Pair o' Guts had any more idea than Lil did. Gradually it dawned on them, what had happened, or at least a vague inkling of it, and they realized they were totally fucked.

"Zapped by a singularity? I thought that only happened in braineries," Amber Annie said.

"Any way to get out of here?" Pair o' Guts wondered aloud.

Diamond Lil shook her head. (Remember, she only approximately shook her head. For that matter, she was only approximately Diamond Lil. But never mind all that.) "I think we're gonna die, girlfriends, but at least we can try and work our way out of this."

"Oh, yeah?" Amber Annie stood with her hands on her hips. "And how do you propose doing that?"

"First thing, let's see what kind of damage that thingamabob did to the *Niña.*" She studied the instrument panel. "Everything looks okay according to the readouts. Who wants to climb into a spacesuit and check the outside?"

Nobody was really eager but eventually Pair o' Guts was pressured into the job. She climbed into a suit, checked her air and power supplies, temp and pressure controls, and crawled into the *Niña's* airlock.

Couple of minutes later she was creeping around on the outside of the ship, looking for damage. She didn't find any so she made her way back to the airlock, opened the hatch, and shortly stood inside the ship once again. The ship was appointed with richly stained wood and polished brass appurtenances. She peeled off her spacesuit and stood in shorts and tee shirt (approximately), the way Diamond Lil and Amber Annie were already dressed.

"Looks okay," she said.

"But take a goose at the meters now." Amber Annie pointed at the *Niña's* bank of readouts. They were acting pretty crazed.

"Hey, I can *feel* this mother moving." Pair o' Guts grabbed onto the back of a polished mahogany and red plush chair. "Something is either pulling or pushing us—*hard.*"

They all strapped in and watched the sights outside the *Niña* go through some changes. There was a star close enough to show as a disk rather than a point of light. It was a beautiful shade of blue. Nobody knew what kind of radiation it might be giving off. They could only tell that it was tugging them toward it.

Diamond Lil tried using the *Niña's* boosters to get away but they were too close already, or the star's gravitational field was too strong, or maybe those are just two ways of saying the same thing.

"Looks like we're headed for stardom, girlfriends." Lil managed a fairly sincere sounding, if somewhat ironic, laugh.

Everybody was surprised, however, when the *Niña* swung away from its apparent death-plunge into the beautiful blue star. Something else was grabbing the ship.

"Holy shit!" Annie muttered, "I think we're going to be rescued."

And in fact they saw something looming up in front of them, something that might actually have been a sizable black hole except it wasn't. It was a black, globular object. It just might be a planet, or maybe a miniature partner of the blue star that had never quite reached ignition mass. In the former case it would probably have a solid surface. Maybe rock or frozen water. If the latter, it might be just a fuzzy gas ball.

By now the *Niña* was moving fast. The drive on the little ship worked okay, at least the readouts indicated as much, but there was no place to go, really, except to the black, globular thing. Otherwise they might be pulled into the blue sun. A nasty death, that, and none of the three were interested in dying even a nice death just now if she could help it. Or they could head off into the depths of space, if they could somehow escape the gravitational pull of the blue star, but that would probably mean a slow death by starvation or suffocation or by strangulation in their own waste products, none of which was an attractive prospect.

So, what the heck, they let themselves be drawn down to the black, globular whatever-it-was. Captain Diamond Lil brought the *Niña* in for a nice smooth landing. If anything, the surface of the black globe seemed to be just made for the landing of a little three-person spacecraft, and *Niña* settled in just fine and Amber Annie, who had by tacit agreement become the ship's engineer (or something like that), turned on the exterior sensors and analyzers.

Shortly these gadgets reported that there was breathable air outside, which was pretty surprising, that gravity was well below Earth-normal but sufficient to keep them from floating off into the depths of space, and that not a damned thing was moving. Not anywhere on this, well, more-or-less, world.

It was daytime outside, or what could pass for daytime.

Amber Annie and Pair o' Guts donned spacesuits just to be on the safe side and exited the *Niña*.

They were confronted by a bleak and featureless landscape. The unnamed blue sun shone like a lovely amethyst and gave their white spacesuits a kind of ghostly tint. They turned around and looked at *Niña* and saw that the ship had been undamaged by its landing.

For the time being they were better off than they would have been if they had continued on toward the blue sun (for sure) or headed out into black space (for pretty sure), but when they considered their situation and likely future here on this small black world, the prospects weren't really very bright after all.

Asparagus cracked her helmet seal, then removed the helmet entirely and breathed deeply of the little world's air. It smelled nasty, something like the bathroom in an apartment where the owner has gone away for a week and left three cats and as many overflowing dishes of cat food and bowls of water and a litter box for the kitties to use.

Pretty ripe.

But, as the ship's instruments had said, breathable.

Annie waited to make sure that Pair o' Guts was all right, then removed her own helmet. She curled her lip and wrinkled her nose but she agreed that the air would do if it had to. Which it did.

No water, though. No food. No sign of life. There was air and water and food in their spaceship, and by careful recycling they could make it last a long time, but not forever. And who wants to live that way anyhow?

They headed back to the *Niña*.

Amber and Asparagus told Lil what they thought of this, well, call it a planet. They didn't like it but they couldn't think of any alternative. If only it weren't so damned dark and dismal they might have found their situation less depressing.

They didn't seem to be in any imminent danger, but the ship's stores were limited and they didn't want to sit there in the middle of a flat, black plain on a round, black, well, sort of planet, and wait for thirst or starvation or suffocation to claim them. The *Niña* had an emergency beacon which they set to pulsing out a distress call, but they had no idea where in the entire time-space continuum they were and the likelihood of rescue looked pretty darned remote.

What if they were in another galaxy?

What if they were a million years in the past or the future?

The planet they were on seemed to have a fairly short day/night cycle, with no real dusk or twilight to speak of. Once night fell the sky blazed with a billion unfamiliar points of light. It was a beautiful sight but it was also depressing as all get out.

What the heck were they going to do?

They decided to sleep on it.

In the morning they woke up and looked outside. The blue sun glittered gorgeously above the horizon and the flat black plain had turned into a flat white plain. It looked something like an Arctic snowfield. It was as featureless as ever but the grim, dim aspect of the day before was transformed into a bright featurelessness tinted azure by the planet's sun.

Lil and Annie and Pair o' Guts held a council of war.

They knew that the *Niña* wasn't going to run out of fuel. It was propelled by hooking into nature's own universal magneto-gravitic grid and unless something bollixed its propulsion and control circuitry they had nothing to worry about on that score.

But was there anyplace to go?

They settled in and lifted off. Diamond Lil set the *Niña's* autocontrols for a low survey of the planet and they went skimming across the featureless terrain. Once they reached the terminator and passed into the planet's shadow stars appeared overhead and the, well, let's call it landscape, darkened. Still, it was a gleaming, porcelain white and it had the ghostly appearance, by starlight, of an old-time Christmas-card snowscape.

The *Niña* was intended as a vacation excursion ship and at this point its circuitry determined that a little musical accompaniment was desirable. It started playing a vocal piece by the eighteenth century composer Elisabetta de Gambarini. Softly, unobtrusively, soothingly. It was really quite lovely.

"What the hell?"

Lil and Asparagus turned. Annie was pointing at something on the ground. It was the first feature any of them had spotted on the surface of the planet.

It looked like a big more or less human head with an arching brow, oversized ears, a sloping nose, a small, pursed mouth, a puzzled look around the eyes and a generally goofy expression on its face. In fact it reminded them of one of the giant stone heads found on Rapa Nui.

"What the hell?" Lil and Asparagus echoed Amber Annie.

Diamond Lil cut the autos and brought *Niña* around in a graceful maneuver so they could get a closer look at the thing.

Damned if it didn't look exactly like one of those wacky stone statues, except it wasn't the color of ordinary stone.

Lil couldn't gauge the size of the head from *Niña's* current altitude so she dropped back, closer to the planet's surface. She realized that the head was big. Really big. Much taller than the ship.

She circled it, around the level of its ear lobes.

The statue was dark red. The ridge of its forehead shadowed its ruby-tinted eyes, but as *Niña* swooped past the face Lil could see two points of light right where the pupils ought to be, for all the world staring out at them, following *Niña* in its path like the eyes of a three-dee religious icon.

It was spooky.

Responding to Lil's touch, the *Niña* hovered briefly in front of the statue, then settled slowly to the ground.

They were still on the planet's night side, but the starlight was bright. Enough of it reflected off the planet's snow white surface to create a kind of ghostly twilight. Lil and Annie and Asparagus could see the statue clearly.

They left the *Niña*. They weren't wearing spacesuits this time. When they breathed the air outside the nasty odor was gone. Either it had been a local phenomenon at their first landing site or it had cleared up. Or maybe they were just getting used to this strange place.

Amber Annie said, "This planet needs a name. Come to think of it, I guess the sun does, too."

Diamond Lil and Pair o' Guts agreed. "What do you want to call them?" Pair o' Guts asked.

Annie shrugged her shoulders. "What the heck. How about Amaterasu for the sun and Sakti for the planet?"

Lil snorted. "You really like rice, don't you? Well, sure, why the hell not."

Pair o' Guts said, "Okay with me."

They walked around the base of the statue. They didn't measure it but if it had been their favorite girlfriend and they'd set out to buy her a shirt for her birthday they would have estimated her collar size at ninety meters. Diamond Lil stood directly in front of the thing and looked up at its face.

She could have seen the insides of its nostrils if she'd brought a hand-laser with her, but all she could see in the ghostly reflection of starlight off Sakti's white surface was darkness.

The eyes, though. The eyes were a different story. The eyes glittered and gleamed so, made Diamond Lil dream so, she fantasized all sorts of things about the statue. She turned to her companions and said, "I wish we had a ladder. I'd like to climb up there and look inside this thing's eyes. There's something going on there, I'm sure of it."

Amber Annie tilted her head to one side. "Does seem to be looking at us, doesn't it? But what the heck is it doing here? I mean, we're stranded on this weird planet a gazillion whatchamacallits from Earth. Nobody's ever found so much as an empty beer can on any planet they've explored. And now—this?"

Asparagus pursed her lips, unconsciously mimicking the statue's expression. "Wonder what it's made of."

They all three advanced to the base of the statue.

Diamond Lil rapped it with her knuckles and it gave off a

peculiar sound that went on until all three visitors were dizzy. Finally it faded into silence. "Sounds like a gong," Lil commented. "Felt like polished metal to me. Definitely hollow."

Amber Annie was the tallest of the three. By standing on her tippy-toes and reaching as far above her head as she could, she was able to run her hand along the bottom of its chin. The statue quivered. "Feels like flesh to me," Annie said. "I wonder if it goes down into the ground. Maybe there's a whole statue here, neck deep in this—whatever this planet is made out of."

She fell to her knees and tried to scrape away the white stuff from around the base of the statue, but she couldn't budge it.

Asparagus pressed her ear to the statue. She stood unmoving for a long time. Finally she moved away.

Diamond Lil asked, "You hear anything?"

Pair o' Guts nodded affirmatively.

"Well?" Lil demanded.

"I can't tell you."

"Can't tell me? What do you mean, can't tell me? What did you hear? Machinery? Voices? A sinister buzzing? The music of the spheres? What?"

Pair o' Guts said, "I can't tell you. Try it, you'll understand what I mean."

Standing ten meters apart Lil and Annie tried it. They pressed their ears to the statue for a long time. Then they moved away. They both nodded. Nobody said anything.

One place was as good as another on the outside of this featureless globe but one place was a lot more interesting than anyplace else and that was by the big red sculpture, or whatever the heck it was. The three travelers ate a picnic dinner by starlight, raiding their ship's stores for foodstuffs.

The temperature was comfortable so they sat around after eating, swapping lies and singing old songs that they half-remembered and drinking some wine that they'd packed with the intention of consuming it on the surface of Earth's moon, toasting the planet of their birth. In the pale light of Sakti's night the wine looked black. It tasted very good and they all got mildly drunk and fell asleep.

Diamond Lil shuffled the deck of cards and looked around the table as she dealt. The gamblers tonight were the usual crew of cowpokes in town for a wild night, merchants who'd closed up their shops for the day and were looking for some entertainment, and a couple of professional gamblers. Lil didn't like the gamblers. They upset the house's take, and that cut into Lil's income. It was tough running a gambling hell in a town like this.

After a couple of hours of rough poker and faro and maybe a few spins of the roulette wheel, and a goodly intake of rotgut, the cowgirls would head upstairs for a tumble with Lil's whores. The merchants would head for home and the bosoms of their families. The professional gamblers would want to keep playing.

What the hell, it was a living.

But it wasn't time for that, not yet. The house had to make its cut of the card table action first.

One of the cowgirls, an oversized, ill-smelling, dirty-faced lug Lil had had to handle before, reached for a card and knocked her whiskey glass over. The whiskey splashed onto the table as the glass rolled off the wood and tumbled to the floor. The cowgirl cursed and leaned over to pick up the bouncing glass.

Opposite the cowgirl sat a professional gambler. Lil recognized her as the only pro at the table. She wore a string tie and a patch over one eye. She squinted at the cowgirl, shot a glance under the table herself, and slid her chair back, reaching for her Samantha Colt.

The cowgirl came back up with her own iron in her hand.

Lil flung the deck of cards at the cowgirl and at the same time aimed a wad of spittle at the gambler. She caught the gambler square in her one good eye. Temporarily blinded, the gambler dropped her gun and wiped frantically at her eye.

While she did that, Lil launched herself across the table. Cowgirls and merchants scattered. Lil had her hands on the big cowgirl's neck, pressing long red-painted fingernails into her throat, going for the vagus nerve. She got it. The big cowgirl fell over backwards.

Standing above the cowgirl, Lil lifted the hem of her lavender satin skirt and kicked her twice, very hard, with the metal-clad, pointed toe of her boot. Once in the ribs, once in the face. The kick to the face tore a gash in the cowgirl's cheek.

"Huh, hardly matters," Lil muttered. "Little scar won't make that ugly mutt any uglier than she is already, but maybe she'll remember me and learn to behave herself."

The bartender strolled over from her station and picked up the cowgirl by the back of her shirt. She dragged the cowgirl out of Lil's place and threw her in the street. Lil picked up the cowgirl's revolver and when the bartender came back she tossed it to her to add to her collection.

"Come on, girls," Lil announced, "a round of booze on me and then start losing your money again. The whores are getting impatient."

There was a chorus of yells from the wooden balcony. Half a dozen whores were leaning over the railing, flaunting tits and ass and pussy at the customers.

All in all, it was the best night Lil's place had ever experienced.

Diamond Lil woke up along with Amber Annie and Asparagus. She was lying in a big featherbed in a rough wooden room. The bed was huge, big enough to sleep four people easily. In fact there were three people in it right now. Amaterasu cast her rays through the window, a brilliant cobalt-blue mirror. Lil was wearing a skimpy nightgown. Amber Annie lay beside her on one side and Asparagus on the other. They were similarly garbed. Lil climbed over Annie and took a couple of steps to the window. There was a livery stable across the street, a newspaper office next to the stable, and an undertaking establishment next to that. The whole scene could have come straight out of some ancient drama.

Amaterasu hovered overhead and the *Niña* stood at the end of the street, its small bulk and insect-like landing legs stark against the dusty landscape. Blue sunlight glinted off its ports.

"Wake up! Wake up! Eleanor, Mamie and Bess!" she growled, "what the hell is going on!" She gave Asparagus's long, loose hair a tug and landed a loud slap on Amber Annie's smooth, round ass. "What the fuck is going on!"

Annie and Pair o' Guts sat up, yawned, stretched and looked around. Annie yelped. Pair o' Guts leaped out of bed, leaned out the window, pulled her head back in, jumped back into bed and pulled the comforter over her head.

"Won't do any good," Lil hissed. "We have sure as hell pulled ourselves a shitload of trouble, sisters! Where are we, Dodge City? Is this a crazy dream? Don't pinch me anybody, I'll wake myself up if I'm asleep. But our little *Niña* is right out there, that's Sakti's crazy blue sun up there, what the fuck has happened?"

There wasn't much to do about their wacko situation but deal with it. They washed up as best they could, donned whatever clothes they could rummage out of a closet and chest of drawers, and trooped downstairs. They found a little restaurant next door to Lil's place and they trooped in and sat down for breakfast.

A big woman wearing gray hair pulled into a topknot strolled over to them and plunked a coffee pot down in the middle of the table. "You ladies sure slept in this morning," she said. "Good night at Lil's?"

Lil grunted and the big woman said, "Got the usual coming up for you."

The breakfast was delicious, fresh eggs scrambled with cream and butter and fried ham and honey and rough black bread.

Asparagus leaned over and whispered in Diamond Lil's ear, "How are we going to pay for this?"

Lil said, "Don't worry. Eat."

When they got up to leave Lil turned to the big woman and said, "Goes on my account, right?"

The big woman looked mildly annoyed. "Certainly. Why not?"

Lil smiled. "No reason. Just appreciate it, that's all."

A few minutes later they huddled in a corner in Lil's place. The saloon was empty at this hour. There was no sign of the bartender or the whores. Lil said, "Any ideas, sisters?"

Amber Annie said, "What if we stay here?"

Lil shook her head. "I guess I could run a saloon for a living. You two girls make a living upstairs, looks like. You feel good about whoring for a few years?"

Annie said, "Not a chance, Lil. My life on Earth wasn't exactly lilacs and lollipops but I enjoy things like running water and solar power and—what if we get sick? What kind of doctors do you think they have in a shithole like this?"

Lil nodded. "Asparagus?"

"We don't know what happened, how we got here, right? How stable is this world? Yesterday it was just a black blob, then it turned white, then we found that statue, then it turned into some kind of neo-primitive restorationist's wet dream Old West amusement park. It might last or it might turn into something else. Maybe something better, maybe something worse. I say, let's climb back in our little spaceship and blow town."

The others agreed.

They started down the wooden sidewalk, boot heels clattering on the planks, passing closed business establishments and vacant lots. The street was made of hardpacked dirt. Amaterasu blazed. There wasn't a soul in sight. When they got to the end of the street the *Niña* was about thirty meters away from them. Asparagus stepped off the end of the sidewalk and saw a bright shimmering in front of her. She put her hands out and they sank into something that felt like warm jelly.

She leaned into the barrier. It gave but it didn't open. Beyond the barrier the surface of Sakti was still white and blank, as it had been before they found the giant statue. And of course the statue was gone, now.

Asparagus and Annie and Lil put their backs to the barrier, joined hands, and pushed for all they were worth.

Lil grunted. "Fuck! Eleanor, Mamie and Bess! Fuck!"

The shimmering barrier let them through and they tumbled to the ground. They were wearing their own tee shirts and shorts and shoes. Their long dresses and sharp-toed boots stayed behind.

They picked themselves up, dusted themselves off, and started all over again.

The scent of the sea hit Ambergris' nostrils like a double dose of cocaine. She squeezed her eyes shut savoring the sensation of salt-laden moisture, fresh and clean. She couldn't contain the great smile that burst from inside her chest. She could feel her heart beating like a *Taiko* drum and the blood rushing through her veins like a million ecstatic school kids turned loose for the summer.

She dropped her hands to her sides and felt her cutlass on her hip, flintlock pistol on the other.

Tyche's canvas cracked like a whip in the tropic wind. The blue Caribbean leaped and frothed as *Tyche* drove west sou'west. Amaterasu's blue rays danced across the choppy sea.

Dead ahead of *Tyche* a royal galleon wallowed, hull down and heavy with loot. Spices and gold from the new lands, and Amber's for the taking. Amber knew this galleon, the *Princesa Alejandra Olga,* and her captain, Doña María Elizabeta Francesca Esperanza Cortez y Gonsalvo.

"Signal-wench," Amber called, "send the *Princesa* this message. Tell her that Captain Ambergris presents her compliments to Doña Cortez and offers the courtesies of the *Tyche* to herself and the mercies of the sea to her crew. Tell her to haul up the flag of surrender or face my wrath!"

Tyche's signaler called back, "Aye, Cap," and began her wigwag.

What happened next was just what Amber expected. *Princesa Alejandra Olga* dropped her gun covers, exposing a row of black-muzzled iron cannon. *Tyche* rushed head-on toward the *Princesa.* There was no way for *Tyche* to fire her own ordnance against the galleon while the *Princesa* could bring her entire port compliment of cannon to bear on *Tyche.*

It was a dangerous maneuver, but Captain Ambergris was known for her willingness to risk her ship and her life for the grand prizes of the ocean trade. To date she had won at every throw of the dice.

Nor was Amber's courage mere foolhardiness. *Tyche* was fitted with a bowsprit in the form of her namesake, the dispenser of riches and poverty, pleasures and misfortunes, blessings and pain. Painted in bright colors, *Tyche's* own Tyche was fitted with hands as sharp as razors and as strong as rails.

Princesa's cannons boomed and hot flaming balls flew across the narrowing distance between the ships. Most fell short and dropped hissing and steaming into the sea. Some flew overhead, sparking and sizzling as they passed *Tyche.* Several slapped against *Tyche's* canvas, ripping holes as they flew onward. Small fires broke out in several places and well-trained girls scurried up the lines, furling flaming canvas and hurling it overboard into the sea.

With a crash and a crunch *Tyche* made contact with *Princesa,* her bowsprit plowing into the galleon's hull and lodging deep in her side. Ambergris's well-trained pirates hurled grapnels across *Princesa's* railing and with the precision of a London timepiece boarders swarmed onto the deck of the galleon.

Ambergris knew Doña Cortez. Their paths had crossed before. Once, long ago, Amber had been María Elizabeta's prisoner, and she had learned that Doña Cortez had a fondness for the barbed whip and the white-hot prod. Amber bore souvenirs of that encounter, scars that crisscrossed her back and memories of indignities less visible but far more painful.

Amber had survived that encounter, escaped from a dungeon in the dead of night, leaving the corpses of a dozen warders and pike-bearers in her wake, vowing to wreak revenge on her tormentor.

The time for that revenge had arrived.

Amber bared her teeth in a fierce vulpine grin.

Princesa Alejandra's crew put up a better fight than Amber had expected, but *Tyche's* crew were freebooters to the heart while *Alejandra Olga's* company were mere merchant sailors, some of them volunteers looking for a way to support themselves and their families in Iberia, others the scum of the docks and grog-houses of Santiago de Compostela and La Coruña, Cartagena and Alicante.

Some battled with belaying pins, others with curved swords or needle-pointed dirks. The fabled steel of Toledo lived up to its reputation, but a weapon is no better than the woman wielding it, as Amber well knew.

Blood ran across *Princesa Alejandra's* decks and into her scuppers. Cries of pain and the moans of departing souls filled the air. *Princesa Alejandra's* officers were armed with flintlock pistols. The sound of their discharges and the stink of their powder smote Ambergris's senses.

The battle seemed all but over when a second wave of defenders rushed from below deck, *Princesa Alejandra's* cannoneers scrambling up ladders to come to the aid of their comrades. These were tougher characters than the ordinary seawomen *Tyche's* boarding party had faced until now. The battle raged back and forth across *Princesa Alejandra's* decks, decks now slippery with the spilled guts and splashing gore of boarders and defenders alike.

But the final outcome was foreordained.

Within the hour Captain Ambergris has put a prize crew aboard *Princesa Alejandra*. The bodies of the dead and the seriously wounded were flung overboard. Hungry sharks caught the scent of blood, circled and feasted on fresh meat. Most of *Princesa Alejandra's* sailors were happy to sail on under command of prize officers from *Tyche*. Those few who refused to cooperate were given a boat, a supply of hardtack and a cask of water and set adrift.

Only Doña María Elizabeta Francesca Esperanza Cortez y Gonsalvo remained unaccounted for.

It wasn't hard for Captain Ambergris to decide where to look for her arch foe. She found her way to Doña Cortez's cabin. She paused outside. She stood before a mirror that Doña Cortez had caused to be mounted on the bulkhead. Her tricorn hat had been lost in the battle, carried away by the ball from a defender's flintlock. Her blue-black hair curled and swayed around her face. She wore a loose satin blouse and skintight trousers that disappeared into floppy-topped boots. Her face was flushed with excitement and exertion, her tongue flicked out to taste the perspiration that made her face shine.

She tried the door to Doña Cortez's cabin and found it unlocked. She stepped inside and confronted Doña Cortez.

Ambergris laughed at the sight before her.

The noblewoman had donned full court dress, a floor-length gown of crimson silk and kid gloves that reached above her elbows. Her face was powdered a deathly white with spots of rouge on both cheeks and smears of blue above her eyes, a beauty mark fixed to one cheek. Most absurd of all, she wore a tall wig.

"A fair fight, Captain Ambergris," she hissed.

"As you wish, my lady."

"As you see, I am unarmed." The noblewoman held her hands to her sides.

"Very well." Amber carefully laid her cutlass and flintlock in a corner.

When she turned back she was startled to see that Doña Cortez had doffed her gloves and gown. She stood stark naked, defiant, clad only in boots and silvery wig.

"As you wish, my lady," Ambergris said again. She swept herself out of her clothing.

They closed, grappling for advantage. The cabin was cramped and their motion was limited. Amber managed to grasp her opponent by the elbow, spun and twisted.

Doña María moved with her action, slipped from Amber's grasp and delivered a backhand slap to the side of her head.

Amber's ears rang with the blow. She lowered her head and launched a head-butt at her enemy.

Doña María dodged, partially avoiding the attack. Amber's shoulder collided with Doña María's midriff and sent her staggering backward to fetch up against a bulkhead. With one hand she reached upward and grasped a Turkish scimitar that was mounted on the wall. With her other hand she reached beneath her wig, sending it tumbling to the floor.

Amber clutched Doña María's wrist, smashing it against the wall, sending the Turkish scimitar clattering and bouncing across the cabin. At the same moment she felt a red-hot agony lance across her ribcage. Crimson spurted as Doña María screamed in triumph, a blood-dripping dagger in her hand.

"Traitor!" Amber gasped. "The dirk was concealed in your wig."

Doña María stood laughing in triumph.

Amber felt her very consciousness failing as blood flowed from her wound. She gathered her remaining strength and launched herself once more at her opponent. To her surprise, Doña María threw open her arms.

The two women collided, tumbling to the floor. Amber felt Doña María's dagger plunge into her flesh again and again. She found herself beneath her opponent but now marshaled her final reserves. She arched her back, literally throwing Doña María off her body. The noblewoman tumbled, flailing, landing with her throat against the Turkish cutlass.

A hair's breadth higher and the cutlass would have sliced thin flesh and glanced off her jawbone. A hair's breadth lower and it would have bounded from her collarbone. But neither was to be the case.

Doña María uttered a single gurgling gasp of pain and rage and mortality and collapsed, dead, on the floor of her cabin.

Amber, her naked body covered with a mixture of sweat and blood and, yes, tears, knelt beside her dead foe's body, softly stroking her locks. A drop of sweat fell from Ambergris' weary face and ran down Doña María's cheek. A drop of sweat, or perhaps a teardrop.

Diamond Lil and Pair o' Guts dragged Amber Annie through the hatch and laid her on her bunk in *Niña's* cabin. Pair o' Guts bathed her tenderly, then she and Lil dressed Amber in tee shirt and shorts. Amber lay quiet, breathing softly and steadily.

Amber watched over her as Lil lifted *Niña* from the surface of Sakti and cruised slowly toward the horizon.

Astarte lay back against satin cushions, the curved mouthpiece of the water pipe lying lightly upon her breast. She thought she must have dozed, but the gentle sound of wind chimes had wakened her, or perhaps it was the soft suggestion of moisture from a tinkling fountain. She let droplets of moisture settle on her tongue. The water held the merest suggestion of honey and the hint of spices.

She drew once on the water pipe, letting its fumes penetrate her being. She smoothed her thin silken garment over her graceful body, letting it whisper over her generous aureolae and the darkness of her crotch.

It was time, she knew, to receive reports from her ministers, and an ambassador was expected to offer her credentials and ceremonial gifts, always a nuisance but a duty which she performed as her mothers had for generations, ever since they had imposed their benevolent rule on the land.

Servants appeared and removed the water pipe. She could always return to it, when she chose. They bathed her in rose water and dressed her in formal silks. When she was ready she summoned her vizier and ordered the reports of the day to be made. A military triumph over a rebellious tribe in the East, an offer of friendship and an eternal treaty from the growing power of the North. She was concerned with the Northerners; for all their allegedly peaceful intentions they were known to come from warlike stock. Astarte did not trust them.

She conferred with counselors and ministers for hours, but at last the day's business was completed, save for the formal reception of the new ambassador from—where was it? Ah, yes, Hai Hui Hsi.

The ambassador was preceded by child musicians blowing strange, reedy melodies on long, strangely curved horns, and others clashing tiny pairs of cymbals. Gift bearers brought carven chests. Each was no larger than an infant's skull, and for all that Astarte could tell, they were indeed carved from small human skulls.

The ambassador herself was a picture of miniature perfection. If all the people of Hai Hui Hsi were as small and as beautiful as the ambassador, they must be an almost toylike race. The ambassador wore a silken coif but around its edges Astarte could see wisps of flame-red hair. The ambassador's eyes glowed like emeralds by lamplight.

She spoke with a soft accent, offering greetings and affection from her ruler to the grand Astarte, craving to represent her land in eternal peace and amity. When Astarte permitted, she ordered the gift bearers to open the carven skulls, one by one. These were four in number.

The first contained a rose of breathtaking beauty and intoxicating fragrance.

The second contained a purple gem, by far the largest and most vibrant of its sort that Astarte had ever seen.

The third contained a spice; at the ambassador's urging Astarte placed a single grain upon her tongue and was wafted to heights of indescribable pleasure.

The fourth contained a tiny serpent, crimson in color, no longer than Astarte's middle finger. As she held the carven skull in her hand the serpent reared and stared into her face. Its eyes were like brilliant emeralds. It opened its mouth, revealing astonishing fangs that glittered in the lamplight and a forked tongue that darted out and back, out and back. "I will serve you faithfully and forever, Astarte," it hissed.

Astarte nodded to the ambassador. "We are well pleased. Our servants will bring you to your apartments. Or if you wish you may remain with us during the evening's entertainment."

The ambassador chose to remain.

The entertainment consisted of a ritual opera performed exactly as it had been performed for ten thousand years. It told the story of three ancient goddesses who had descended to the Earth to spread the seeds of life.

First the Goddess of the Air had created birds of beauty and of prey, shimmering dragonflies and colorful moths, and everything that flew, even the lovely, velvety bats whose presence was taken as the most joyous of all omens of the air.

Then the Goddess of the Sea had created the fishes and the whales, the sea lions and sea cows, aquatic tortoises and toads, crabs and prawns and the clever, elusive octopuses whose presence was taken as the most joyous of all omens of the water.

And last the Goddess of the Earth created snakes and bears, fearsome tigers and mighty rhinoceroses, thoughtful apes and fleet horses and every creature that walks on the land including the splendid wolves who would bless humans with their friendship if it was returned but who would destroy humans and replace them as the rulers of the Earth if humans provoked them overmuch.

And after their work was completed, the goddesses decided to return to Heaven, but together they created Woman in their own image, and left her the stewardship of the world.

When the opera was over Astarte invited the ambassador to stay the night with her in her private chambers. The ambassador, perhaps for political reasons, perhaps because she found the prospect appealing, agreed.

Together they smoked a water pipe for a while, exchanging small talk, petting each other mildly, at last kissing softly on the lips. Astarte asked the ambassador if she would like to tour Astarte's hareem and select a companion for the coming hours. Receiving the ambassador's consent, Astarte took her by the hand and led her through a series of luxuriously appointed chambers. Fountains lifted scented water into the air and musicians played softly. Beautiful women displayed themselves tastefully. Each was more lovely than the next, but somehow the magical moment of joyous harmony did not arrive.

But at last they entered a chamber where the scent of musk and petals was subtly altered. Astarte clapped her hands. "This is the one!" Turning to the ambassador she asked, "What do you think?"

The ambassador looked at the candidate. She lifted her hand to touch golden hair. "Such springy curls! Oh, yes!" She touched the cheek, the chest. "Such fine skin. And the color, golden. And the eyes, eyes of burnished copper, as large and knowing as those of an owl."

She stepped back. "But more a girl than a woman, Astarte. Sweet nipples, to be sure, like the buds of tea roses. I could nibble and tease them for hours. But the chest is flat, the hips are straight. And—and what is that?" She pointed. "What is that thing?"

"Neither a girl nor a woman," Astarte replied. "This is a being different, rare and precious. And as for that thing, well, it is actually a part."

The ambassador stared. "Does it do anything?"

"Ah." Astarte reached long, skillful fingers and it sprang to life.

The ambassador burst into laughter. Her shoulders shook, her breasts bounced, tears of mirth ran from her eyes. When at last she could speak she asked, "How amusing! How cunning! But is it good for anything?"

Astarte said, "You will see."

They returned to Astarte's chamber, the three of them.

In the morning the third of them returned to the hareem bearing gifts. The ambassador bowed to Astarte. "This night has been most truly amazing. My liege will never believe my report. But I hope I may spend a long time at your court, Astarte."

Astarte said, "It will be my pleasure."

Diamond Lil said, "You are full of surprises, girlfriend."

Asparagus blushed.

The *Niña* stood in the shadow of the red statue. Amaterasu shone a quarter of the way up the sky.

"You made us whores, Lil," Amber Annie said.

"You and your pirates," Lil shot back. "And your little set-to with that Doña Cortez was something, wasn't it, Captain Ambergris!"

"But you topped us all, Pair o' Guts. The Empress Astarte. You really know how to live, but what was that golden thing, really?" There was a big grin on Annie's face.

Asparagus took each of the others by the hand. "The golden thing was just some weird creature I made up. I've always had a crazy imagination. They don't exist. Mother Nature isn't that ridiculous. And I've enjoyed your dreams, Lil, Annie. I hope you weren't too shocked by mine."

The others squeezed Asparagus's hands. "Surprised, yes.

Shocked, no," said Annie.

"But we have to do something about this—this situation. I mean, Amaterasu and Sakti and that weird statue."

They stood in front of the statue. Its eyes glowed like two tiny fragments of sky-mirror.

"I think I've got this figured out," Asparagus said. "At least some."

The others waited. "You know, I just used what I'd learned in my job on Earth."

"Which was what?" Lil inquired. "Until the spaceship rental place put us together with *Niña* we were total strangers. I guess we're anything but that now."

"I was a numerical rememberer," said Annie.

"And I was a crop supervisor in an organ farm," said Lil.

Asparagus hesitated, then said, "I didn't want either of you to think I was arrogant or anything, so I didn't go into detail about my work as a hyperphysics visioner."

"Meaning what?" asked Lil.

"Well, I think that might be why we've had these—experiences."

"They weren't just dreams, were they?"

"No, they were real. Or, well, hyperreal, I should say. A hyperphysics visioner can see into the structure of things. Can see lines of force, energy fluxes, matter-energy relationships. We can see equations not as coding or symbols but as thing really happening. In a way I can see your thoughts. I'm not exactly a mind-reader, Lil, Annie, I don't have telepathic talents. But you must have had moments when you felt that you could tell what somebody was thinking. I can do it, actually and literally. That's just one aspect of hyperphysical visioning."

Lil spat, "Holy Eleanor! You can actually do that?"

"I can."

"Well, what can you do for us, sweetie? As far as I can tell we're still stuck on this little lump of muck and we're going to be here forever."

"No," Asparagus demurred. "The singularity that popped us out of Earth's neighborhood—it's a speck small enough to pass through the eye of a needle, with room to spare on both sides. It's right in the middle of Amaterasu up there. Don't look at it, you'll hurt your eyes. You can't see it anyhow, in the middle of a sun. But it's there. And it's conscious."

"What?" Amber Annie shook her head.

"It is. In its own way. Its consciousness isn't much like anything we've ever known, but it's there nonetheless. It's been trying to contact us ever since we got here. That's why it made Sakti for us. That's why it made the red statue. It must have picked up that image out of one our minds. One of us saw a picture of those ancient stone heads on Rapa Nui and we somehow imagined them as being just the top part of complete statues. Why it's red, I have no idea. But I think the singularity has put its—her—consciousness into the statue. I'll bet it's been learning our minds since we got here. That's why we had the dreams that weren't just dreams. It was getting to know us. And when it's ready, we're going to have the most powerful, the most incredible friend in the universe. We're going to be a goddess's favorite darlings."

The huge statue opened its lips, revealing an amazing, cavernous mouth. One of its two blazing blue eyes closed for a moment, then reopened. It was a monumental wink.

"You bet, girlfriends. You bet. The fun is just beginning."

In 1979 editor Jonathan Bacon asked me to write the concluding chapter of a round-robin serial, *Ghor Kin-Slayer: The Saga of Genseric's Fifth-Born Son.* This was based on an opening chapter found among the papers of the late Robert E. Howard. The other authors made up a truly amazing roster of talented fantasists. Some were contemporaries, others were titans whose works I had devoured and whose success I had envied as a teenaged fan, decades before. Just look at this list:

Karl Edward Wagner, Joseph Payne Brennan, Richard L. Tierney, Michael Moorcock, Charles R. Saunders, Andrew J. Offutt, Manly Wade Wellman, Darrell Schweitzer, A. E. van Vogt, Brian Lumley, Frank Belknap Long, Adrian Cole, Ramsey Campbell, H. Warner Munn, and Marion Zimmer Bradley.

The chapters appeared regularly in a semi-professional magazine of the era called *Fantasy Crossroads.* Unfortunately, *Fantasy Crossroads* ceased publication halfway through the serial. Editor Bacon furnished me with back issues containing all published chapters and manuscript copies of those that remained unpublished.

As I read through the installments it became obvious that every chapter had merit, but the overall plotline—if you could even call it that!—was an incoherent jumble. Not surprising, as no overall plan or outline was found among Two-Gun Bob Howard's papers. Fifteen intervening authors had taken off from Howard's opening chapter in fifteen wildly varied directions.

My job: to find a way to tie up all those loose ends. When I delivered my manuscript Jonathan Bacon was certainly pleased. In fact, he told me, "You did a wonderful job—almost as good a job as I'd hoped to get from the first author I asked to write the conclusion, but couldn't recruit." Ah, sharper than a serpent's tooth. The complete book was published by Necronomicon Press in 1997. Its validity as a novel may be debatable but I think "The River of Fog" works as a stand-alone piece.

The River of Fog

"You bastard, James Allison!"

I turned from the window where I had been staring down from my suite atop San Francisco's Nob Hill, watching the fog like a river of ice flow through the Golden Gate. I faced my three guests. They were all seated in deep Moroccan-leather chairs, surrounding the jade-inlaid table near my fireplace.

A fragrant back-log had burned low, but still cast enough of a glow that no artificial lighting was required in the room.

The speaker had been Yuriko Yamash'ta. She was probably the most beautiful woman alive, and the low flames reflected from deep in her dark eyes, her long glossy black hair and the matching costume that did little to conceal her elegant figure. She was also the only human being to climb the perilous north face of Everest alone. And she was known to have killed no fewer than five armed men—three of them on one occasion—with her bare hands.

"Bastard, my dear?" I smiled at her. "In fact, I am not that. Not as James Allison. Although I'm certain that I was indeed a bastard in most of my prior incarnations. Most of us were."

"You really believe in that reincarnation business?"

The speaker now was Abraham Steinman. His wheelchair lay folded in the outer vestibule of my suite. A cursory glance at Abraham as he sat near the hearth would never have suggested that he had been a paraplegic from early childhood. Nor had the injury to his spine that had turned his body into a passive appendage interfered with the development of the most innovative mind since that of Edison.

Steinman's greatest invention to date—the one that had freed the industrialized world of its bondage to OPEC oil and that had made Steinman the world's first self-created billionaire since the original Rockefeller—was the Steinman Universal Conversion Engine. That engine, in sizes anywhere from the dimensions of a wristwatch to those of the Grand Coulee Dam—could convert energy from any form into any other form, including solar, wind, or ther-mal power into electricity. And it could do that with an efficiency of 99%+.

Abe Steinman maintained a giant technological and administrative apparatus to manage his inventions, but he kept a private laboratory in a wooden shed for himself. And from that wooden shed, he had sworn, he would bring forth a set of neural-controlled miniaturized servo-motors by means of which he would walk within three years and would play third base in the American League within five. If he had to buy his own team to get the job, he said, he would do it. And he would hit for .300 or better!

I answered his question. "I don't just believe in reincarnation, Abe. Any more than you 'believe in' rainstorms or the element oxygen. They *exist.* You know they exist, but that isn't what makes them real. There would be rainstorms whether you believed in them or not. There would be oxygen molecules, pairs of atoms with an atomic weight of eight and a valence of two, whether you believed in them or not. We're all reincarnated, time after time after time. Belief has nothing to do with it."

"Not so." He moved his head slowly from side to side, one of the few actual motions he was capable of. "Belief is all important. If we all believed in reincarnation, there would be no reason to struggle for anything in this world. We might as well lie back and wait for a better life if we weren't happy with this one. No, Jim, it's the belief that this life is our one chance at the brass ring that makes us try for the ring—and some of us actually snag it!"

My third guest made the kind of loud, inarticulate sound that writers render as *hmph!* He reached an elegantly-manicured hand for the small cobalt-blue glass-lined silver dish on the jade-topped table, lifted it and an even tinier silver spoon. He filled the spoon carefully with fine white powder and offered it to Yuriko and Abraham, then carefully took a spoon for himself.

After a few seconds he said, "I agree that belief is all important, but belief in reincarnation isn't necessarily as debilitating as you suggest, Abe."

"Come now," Steinman rejoined. "That belief has been the greatest impediment to the development of India. One of the world's great cultures—gone stagnant and flat. Why work?

"Why bother to advance oneself or society, when there's always another chance and another chance and another chance to come? Someday we'll all be kings if we keep our karma right, so why bother to improve the lot of peasants, even if we're all peasants in this turn around the wheel?"

"Ah, Abe, Abe, Abe," the other said. "You ought to get your nose out of the laboratory once in a while and observe the way the world works. It wasn't reincarnation that set India back, it was the British East India Company! And India's still working to undo the distortions in her character that Britain brought about."

Steinman grimaced. "Very well. I certainly bow to your greater understanding of politics, Senator."

Senator McPherson smiled in mock gratitude.

Gardner Hendricks McPherson had been the most brilliant cadet to graduate from West Point since Douglas MacArthur, and had broken even MacArthur's record for a speedy rise from second lieutenant to brigadier general. His star continued to rise in the military firmament until he startled the nation by resigning his commission to run for a seat in the United States Senate.

He had won, had performed with similar brilliance in the Senate, becoming Minority Leader before the end of his first term—another unprecedented achievement for McPherson. It was now a foregone conclusion that he would be President of the United States one day, whether four years hence, or eight, being the major question that remained.

He placed the cobalt-blue dish back on the table, selected a slim, hand-rolled stick of Thai gold from a filigreed tray, and lit it with a solid gold lighter. He exhaled slowly, nodded and passed the stick to his right.

"Surely you didn't mean to direct the conversation onto abstract philosophy, Yuriko, when you called our gracious host a bastard." McPherson inclined his head toward the mountaineer. "But what *did* you have in mind?"

"I had in mind that James was a bastard for leaving his story hanging there. Whether it's gospel truth or whether it's all a cock-and-bull story, I don't even care. With due respect to your convictions, Abraham and Gardner. But James . . ." She shook her head despairingly. The back-log hissed and flared briefly, throwing golden lights dancing across Yuriko's hair.

I crossed the soft Kermanshahan carpeting and stood before the hearth. Yuriko held the Thai toward me, as if to say, *Never mind my words, everything remains between us as before. I* nodded my understanding, inhaled the fragrant gold, held the Thai for Steinman and passed it along to Senator McPherson.

The strains of a Mozart concerto emerged from speakers whose baffle-cloths were indistinguishable from priceless centuries-old tapestry for very good reasons.

"What further did you wish to hear?" I asked.

Yuriko laughed. "James, you're fortunate to have inherited your fortune. You'd never be much good at earning money—at least not if you tried to do it by writing novels."

"I never claimed to be a businessman *or* a novelist," I responded. "But just what is your complaint? I've simply told you the story of Ghor, fifth-born son of Genseric. As I lived it. Yes, my dear, as I lived it, unmeasured millennia ago. You might quarrel with the structure of a novel, but how can you complain about the truth?"

"Well, James, let's see where you left yourself. That is, Ghor."

Her startlingly slim and graceful hands flowed through an arresting gesture. "You started life as an abandoned cripple, suckled by a conveniently lactating wolf-bitch. Certainly a familiar touch, that!"

I agreed.

"You survived your infancy, overcame your twisted leg, were raised as a wolf, returned to human society and took rather sanguine vengeance upon the family that had abandoned you."

"Yes."

"And then you launched yourself on the most extraordinary series of adventures. Including, as the expression has it, arson, rape and bloody murder."

"But what is it that you find so objectionable in my tale?" I asked her.

She smiled at me.

"I'll accept all of the improbabilities, James, and I'll even write off the seemingly supernatural interventions that seem to occur so often. Let's just say that they were the barbaric mind's interpretation of events that we would find other explanations for, today."

"Such as?"

"Well," she reached and touched my hand lightly. I felt the electric thrill that never failed to come with her touch. "Well," she said, "just for one example. That strange incident on the island. What happened? A volcano opened, bronze robots emerged from its molten bowels, wiped out Ghor's followers, then flew away into the sky. Now really!"

"It happened," I said angrily.

"Of course it did. But was it magical? Might there not have been a more advanced civilization in the world at the time? Maybe they were geologists, sent there to study that volcano. Once it blew, they took their findings and left. They weren't robots. They were wearing protective suits."

"Still, Yuriko, why the 'You bastard' treatment?"

"Because, James, at the end of your whole incredible saga, you just left it hanging. All of the blood, all of the suffering, your wife and child dead, your arch-foe Mentumenen dead. You'd been, literally, to hell and back. And there you were, living with the wolves once again. What happened?"

Before I could answer her, Abraham Steinman raised another objection. "I find it hard to reconcile your pantheon, Allison."

I stood with my back to the guttering fire, waiting for Steinman to elaborate.

"At the start of your tale you made reference to some Scandinavian deities. Ymir, of course, is a familiar figure. Ythillin is less so, but your description of her fits into the Norse concept. But then you bring in Mitra, who was worshipped for some centuries as a sort of alternate Jesus. Ishtar, who was the great Babylonian goddess. Set, the Egyptian devil-god who murdered his brother Osiris. Gaea, the Greek earth-mother. And the Hounds of Tindalos, creations, I believe, of the modern genius Belknapius. Not to mention Cthulhu, Yog-Sothoth, Cthugha of Fomalhaut."

He clucked his tongue like a nursery school teacher who had caught a five-year-old in a fib. Compared to that great intellect, I suppose we were all on the level of five-year-olds.

"If all of this took place those untold thousands of generations ago," Abraham resumed, "how to account for the admixture of deities and beings from so many cultures and such widely separated periods?"

"I do not account for them," said. "What I have told you is the baldest outline of a life I lived long before this one. What happened, happened, and I make no effort to defend or justify it. This is not a courtroom. If you choose not to believe me, then consider it all just a tale. I hope that I have amused you, these past hours. You are surely not obliged to believe me."

"Well," Steinman considered, "I suppose that's fair enough."

Now Senator McPherson spoke. "Suppose, though, to satisfy Miz Yamash'ta, you do tell us what happened after you rejoined the wolves. Surely your memory doesn't just fade out at that point?"

"Surely it does not," I said.

* *** *

And so I found myself a wolf once again, a beast in my heart and largely, even, in my body. It was as if I had reverted to the days of my childhood—or cubhood!—in that terrible time after Gudrun of the Shining Locks had rejected me and Genseric the Sworder exposed me on the ice to die.

Werewolf, wolf-man, man-wolf, what difference did it make? I struggled not to think, not to deal with the terrible events that had overtaken me and the terrible deeds that I myself had performed since my first encounters with the Aesir and the Vanir.

Did I change? Did the weird Lycanthropic alteration come over me, there in the snow-riven waste? Did I mutter those few simple syllables that I had learned from Telordric the White Magician, going now on two legs, now on four, fighting now with fist or the metal arm made for me by Dar'ah Humarl, now with the fangs and claws of my animal form?

I knew not, neither did I care.

At times I think I switched back and forth between my Lycanthropic form as a werewolf and my human form as a wolf-man. What difference did it make?

The anguish of my life was forgotten, and that was all that mattered to me. None of the fighting, none of the killing—nor any of the wounds, the pain, the injury that had been inflicted upon me—mattered. It was all like a grand game in which the winning of a battle, the conquest of a nation, the overthrow of a dynasty meant neither more nor less than the gain or loss of a marker.

I had seen enough of death to know both that it came inevitably to all men and indeed to all living things, and that it was to be fought off and avoided only for the purpose of prolonging this game of warfare that we chose to call life. There with the wolves of the ice-pack I could forget the one memory that it had been impossible for me to accept—the memory of my wife Shanara and my nameless infant child, dead in the northern wastes.

Surely this was a rich irony. I who had slain parent and brother with never a moment's hesitancy, who had gloated in their dying agony, had been brought low by the loss of two loved ones of my own.

The Ice Bitch Ythillin laughed her cold and bitter laugh, I am sure, at the irony of my grief! And it was my life with the wolves of the ice-pack, my deliberate and willful abandonment of human identity, human consciousness, human recollection, that alone made it possible for me to live on.

With the wolves I hunted elk, exulting in the acrid stench of fear that emanated from our prey when some great ruminant realized that it was trapped, doomed. I lusted for the feel of living flesh between my fangs, the taste of hotly spurting blood on my tongue.

As a wolf I became respected as a sharp-nosed scout, a peerless and tireless tracker of our prey. In the moment of attack none was more fearless and none more ferocious than I. At the moment of the kill, no wolf was more savage or more terrible than I.

And I rose, not by design but by the inevitable competition of courage and strength and skill that settles the social order of the wolves, to the moment when I was the second leader of our pack. And then one day I felt myself overcome by strange urgings, irresistible urgings. I felt my hairs stiffening, my tongue lolling, my nostrils twitching to the stimulus of a scent like none other: that of the wolf-bitch in heat.

I rose from my place and trotted across the glittering ice. Soon I found the source of that all-powerful stimulus. It was the mate of the leader of our wolf-pack. He was an old and wise wolf who had seen many winters. He had mated as a young hunter, and as do wolves, he had mated for life. But after years of companionship and litters of whelps, his bitch had died, and after a period of mourning—yes, wolves mourn!—he had mated again, this time with a young female of glittering eyes and long, luxuriant fur.

But now her scent called to me and I could no more resist that call than a fir can resist the call of the springtime sun. I trotted to her side. She lay on a bank of soft snow, looked up at me, licked the fur of my muzzle.

I issued a challenge, a mighty howl that said as clearly to the wolves of our pack as ever human speech said to human ear, that I was claiming the mate of the leader. With her, I claimed the leadership of the pack itself.

By the law of the wolves—and, yes, the wolves have law!—the old leader could choose one of three courses. He could accept my challenge and fight me, fight me to the death. He could yield to my claim, yield to me both his mate and his leadership of the wolf-pack, and become a submissive follower. Or he could leave the pack to wander the ice-floes, a loner, a rogue wolf, hunting such small prey as he could bring down alone, picking at the offal left by others, perhaps attacking the despised Man.

He chose to fight.

There are few preliminaries in the life of the wolf-pack. The challenge had been issued. The old leader had accepted. The rest of the pack assembled, ringing us, the leader's bitch settled to one side of the circle of wolves while the old leader and I stood glaring and snarling at each other in the center.

He was older than I. Larger. Immensely strong. But he was an old wolf, his reflexes not as rapid as once they had been, his stamina less than it had been years gone by.

While I was—ageless.

He must, somehow, have sensed that difference between us. He knew that his sole chance for triumph was to carry a rapid and decisive attack.

He charged across the hard-packed snow until he was a half-dozen strides from me, then launched himself into a flying lunge, his bared yellow fangs directed at my throat.

I timed my response, ducking my belly onto the snow and lunging forward just as he descended to complete his attack.

He missed my throat, skidded across my body, his belly sliding over my hind-quarters as he tumbled onto the snow.

In a flash I reversed myself and caught him from the rear, nipping him on a hind haunch as he scrambled to recover from his failed attack.

With a coughing growl he came back to his feet and stood glaring at me. He was hardly injured by the nip I had taken from his haunch. A tiny dribble of blood trickled down his fur. He edged sideways, hying to circle into a more advantageous position to use against me. He had been humiliated, and he did not wish to be humiliated again.

He growled a challenge to me, urging me to attack, but I refrained, taunting him. I edged myself into position before his bitch and urinated into the snow beside her, marking her as my possession with my spoor. With one paw I cuffed her gently, not to hurt but to show that she was my mate now.

The old leader almost choked on his snarl. He charged across the circle at me, this time making a low approach so as to lunge upward at my throat. This was a far more dangerous attack than his earlier, almost contemptible, flying leap.

I skipped sideways with my hindquarters, backing a half-step so that the trajectory of his new attack lay at right angles—what men would call right angles!—to my own position.

He tried to correct his attack, and partially he succeeded.

We lunged and snapped simultaneously, our very fangs clashing as we collided. We both went sprawling; I rolled onto one side as he skidded to a halt. He was on me before I could regain my feet, and his teeth would have closed in the soft flesh of my neck ending the challenge—and my life—save for the thickness of my heavy coat and the force of our previous clash, which had badly hurt his lower jaw.

So instead of my gushing jugular, his only trophy of the attack was a mouthful of thick fur and a single gobbet of my flesh.

This time I growled my fury and resentment, and backed away, belly down, trying to regain my lost advantage.

My opponent spat and sputtered, clearing his mouth of the fur he had ripped from my throat. I uttered a snarl of fury and circled. My opponent had placed himself before the bitch who was both the symbol and prize of our combat. He stood over her, growling his warning to me.

At that moment I almost uttered the brief syllables that would turn me into a man, armed with the bronze mechanical arm of Dar'ah Humarl, prepared to aim some spring-driven blade or spiked ball at my foe, to destroy him as a man destroys a wild, dangerous animal. But no, I was myself an animal, as wild as my opponent and, if anything, even more dangerous.

I resisted the urge to snarl those syllables, and instead threw my bulk into a murderous charge against my opponent. Not ten paces from the bitch I feinted as if I would leap past my opponent to the left. Instead I shifted my course to the right as if I intended to pass him on that side and seize the prize, the bitch, for myself.

The old wolf spun first one way, then the other, trying to compensate for my feint and my change of direction.

Another calculated movement and I had my opponent trying to maneuver in three directions at once. He reared above me, forepaws flailing for balance, hind feet scrambling on the snow for purchase.

I launched myself with all the power of my iron-hard sinews. I aimed my attack not at my opponent's throat nor at his unprotected belly, but at his mighty chest.

My jaws were opened wide, my head twisted to one side to bring my upper and lower jaw together on the two sides of his ribcage. My razor-like fangs cut through the thick fur and the muscular flesh of the old leader as if they had been the soft wool and tender flesh of a newborn lamb.

As the mighty muscles of my jaw snapped shut I felt and heard brittle bones of his ribcage snap. My teeth met in the middle of his chest. I wrenched my head, tearing away the prize of my successful attack. I had ripped the very heart from my opponent, and rugged it away; his body fell, lifeless, to the snow. He did not even twitch.

I dropped my prize on the snow and pawed at it. I stood over body of my defeated opponent while the rest of the tribe stood at in their positions around us. I made a little summoning whimper to the leader's bitch and she minced temptingly toward me. She licked the little wound on my neck. I made the low, whimpering sound that gave her permission to sample the fresh carrion before her.

She sniffed at the flesh of what had been her mate, pulled away a gobbet of steaming bloody flesh and carried it to her place to be consumed.

One by one the remainder of the wolf-pack advanced to make obeisance to me, their new leader, and to receive their share of the flesh of my defeated predecessor.

Once my dominance of the pack was formalized and accepted by all I strode from the circle, growling to the others a warning that none might follow me.

I walked alone across the snow and ice until darkness fell. The sky was black but clear, the stars and moon bright in the crisp, almost polar air. They cast a bright glow that was reflected from the white surface, giving the world a ghostly semblance of daylight.

Now I muttered the syllables I had learned from Telordric before I killed that white magician. They were brief and simple; they must be, to be made by the vocal apparatus of a wolf, apparatus designed for the making of growls and snarls and whines and eerie howls but not for the making of human syllables.

I felt my body shifting, my hind legs growing longer, my forelegs turning into arms and my forepaws into hands. My muzzle shrank to the nose and jaws of a human. My pelt was absorbed, leaving only the poll and beard and coarse body-hairs of a normal if hirsute man. I threw back my face and glared into the sky, shouting my challenge to my enemy, mentor, patroness and tormentor, Ythillin the first daughter of the Ice Gods.

"Bitch," I shouted. "Bitch! I have won the leadership of the wolves! I have won the beautiful wolf-bitch for my prize! Is she not a token of yourself ? What more must I do? Whom else must I conquer? Why can I not die, Ice-Bitch!"

A terrible wind rose and spun glittering crystals of snow and ice around me. Prism-like, they broke the spectrum of the moon- and starlight into a shimmering rainbow that bathed and burned me until I felt like a living, chromatic flame. I was swept from the ground, raised by that icy whirlwind like a sailor caught up in a waterspout or a dirt-grubbing farmer snatched from the earth by a cyclone's whirling black funnel.

I was carried high into the air, spun topsy-turvy until I could not tell whether the glaring white disk and the twinkling specks that whirled past my eyes were the true moon and stars or their icy reflections glittering at me from the frozen slopes beneath. The wind howled in my ears and in it I heard the voices—I thought I heard the voices—of those gods and mortals with whom I struggled these terrible, toilsome years.

Gudrun and Genseric were there, old Bragi and the four broth-ers I had slain, Raki and Sigismund, Alwin and Obri. Harolf was there, the Aesir chieftain and Hetlund his son, Tjarvakka the Aesir priest and Hialmar my companion in arms. Oderic and Guthric, Nald and Cudric, warriors all, of the Vanir, and Hengist Ironarm my uncle and Tostig Bearslayer my cousin.

Gl'erf was there, leader of the half-human Mi-Go, and Klu'do the she with whom I had tried—and failed—to mate.

Agha Junghaz, king in Turan, and the beauteous Jahree the chiefest of his wives. Ushilon and the Stygian sorcerer Mentumenen, Kaius Valkonnus of Aquilonia and Lamaril the Invincible—who had proved, before my attack, to be anything but what his title claimed.

And Lord Garak, king in Belverus, capital of Nemedia, and his sons Tashako and Yashati and his daughter, my wife the Lady Shanara of Jelah and our child.

The wind howled and howled. Somewhere wolves howled. And somehow the howling turned to a terrible baying, the baying of the Hounds of Tindalos.

They were around me now, their eyes shining redly against the black of the sky and the white of the snow and ice. The Hounds who came, once they were summoned, through the very *angles of space.*

I could see the Ice-Bitch Ythillin, and for once she gazed upon an earthly scene—no, upon an unearthly scene!—not with her expression of detached and supercilious amusement, but with one of concern, of alarm, of—I could not believe my own perceptions—fear!

"Ghor!" she cried. "Ghor!"

"What is it, Bitch?" I replied.

"Come with me! Flee, flee the Hounds, for we are not finished, you and I! We are not finished!"

I laughed and laughed. I tugged at my wondrous arm of bronze that had been made for me by Dar'ah Humarl of Zaporakh, tugged at it and hurled it from me to tumble and tumble onto the ice-fields below.

"Escape with me, Ghor!" Ythillin cried again. "Mortal man, beast, Lycanthrope, killer and king! I will make you one with the immortals, one with the very Ice Gods themselves! Come with me!"

She swept toward me, rushing through some transdimensional realm that neither ancient man nor modern scholar can ever hope to comprehend. In some inexplicable way she seemed to move through planes of existence, to approach me without traversing the finite loci that separated us.

She did not move through the volume of space, but through its angles.

The baying of the Hounds rose in triumph, and before me I saw Ythillin the Ice-Bitch surrounded by their panting, slavering throng.

Too late she turned to retreat.

The Hounds had her, dragging her down by the long shards of her raiment, rending her flesh, spilling her blood, blood that flowed not red like that of any earthly creature I had known but an icy pale blue. A drop of that blood—a single drop!—spattered on my flesh.

Here, right here, where you see the scar.

It burned me and froze me, tormented me with unbearable anguish at the same instant that it transported me to realms of ecstasy indescribable.

I lost consciousness. I lost life. All was over. All.

All.

All.

* *** *

The back-log in my fireplace above San Francisco's streets hissed softly. Through the nearest window I could see the river of fog flowing weirdly back through the Golden Gate, to disperse with the morning's warming sun onto the gray Pacific waters.

"And that was all you remember," Abraham Steinman asked me, "until your present life as James Allison? Ghor?"

I realized to my own surprise that I was panting and disheveled, drenched with perspiration that soaked my formal shirt and dark tuxedo jacket. Like a man bewildered—or, I thought, like a wolf emerging from an icy stream—I shook my head and gathered up my wits.

I looked around the room. Steinman and Senator McPherson and Yuriko Yamash'ta sat in their Morocco chairs, waiting for me to answer Steinman's question.

I drew in my breath and mopped my sweat-laden brow with a silken handkerchief.

"By no means, Abraham," I answered him at length. "Oh no, by no means is that the last I remember. Long after Ghor was dust and dried parchment, I lived the life of a warrior-priest in Atlantis. I was a Pict in ancient Britain. I lived in Khitai—you remember fabled Khitai in the East, surely! Ah, there I witnessed events and myself committed acts that you would never believe, had I the temerity to tell you of them.

"Yes. I dwelt in Shem. I know the true origins of the legend of Eden. I trekked across the Bering Strait when the land-bridge stood between this continent and that which we please to call Asia. I was of the Mixtecs of high Middle America, and of a people who dwelt near the South Pole in a city you would not wish to call a city, and had a form you would never dream to call human.

"All of these. All of these, Abe, and as many more, and as many more again! These lives I have lived.

"And after this one, this little life of James Allison, is over—there will be as many more to follow. I do not *believe* this, Abe. I *know* it!"

He snorted.

"Some time I will tell you of these other lives," I resumed. "That is, I will do so if you wish. Otherwise—let us discuss the politics of nations, or the strategy of the Oakland baseball club, eh? Or amuse ourselves, perhaps, with a quiet game of chess?"

"I think we should be going now," Senator Gardner Hendricks McPherson put in. "Can I give you a hand, Steinman?"

Steinman accepted the offer.

Steinman, I knew, would achieve all that he had set himself to achieve. I *knew* that he would walk again, within three years. That he would play third base in the American League within five. I didn't tell him so. It would spoil the fun.

And so he was helped to his wheelchair and wheeled to my private elevator by Senator, ex-General, Gardner Hendricks McPherson, who confidently expected to be elected President of the United States in four years, or perhaps in eight. He would not be, that I also knew, but I did not tell him either. It would spoil the fun.

The elevator door hissed shut behind the Senator and the brilliant paraplegic engineer.

Behind me, the soft voice of Yuriko Yamash'ta blended perfectly with the strains of a Mozart quintet. "I do not wish to leave, James."

I turned and saw that Yuriko had lighted a stick of Thai gold. She held it toward me. "Thank you," I said. "And again, my dear, I thank you."

"Cairo, Good-bye" is a thinly fictionalized memoir of my days in a second-run movie house as I worked my way through college. I used it as a performance piece until an audience member, Rudy Rucker, asked if he might publish it in his online magazine, *Flurb*. It appeared in the that magazine's ninth issue in 2010.

Cairo, Good-bye

Arlen had his driver in his hand and was all tee'd up when he heard his cell phone tinkling *Happy Days Are Here Again,* the old FDR-era Democratic campaign song. He muttered, "Cell phone," opened the flip, and read the incoming ID. "Clarissa," he told his partner. "Hold a sec."

To his wife he said, "What, Norm and I are on the fifth. What's the matter?"

Arlen listened, nodded, said, "Okay," and closed the phone. He slipped it back into his pocket. To his golfing partner he said, "You'll never guess." There was a smile on his face.

Norm said, "Okay, I'll never guess. What?"

"We won."

"Really?"

"Really."

"We never win. We've been buying raffle tickets ever since we've been neighbors. What, thirty, thirty-five years? I always thought you were a Jonah."

Arlen laughed. "Not this time. Come on, I don't feel like playing golf."

They climbed into the electric cart and headed back to the clubhouse. They had a couple of drinks, over-tipped the bartender, and headed for the parking lot. As they climbed into Norm's blue-and-cream Acura Norm said, "Wait. I'd better call Nettie."

Arlen said, "No need of that. You can be sure Clarissa called her as soon as she found out. Probably before she called me."

Norm's cell phone chimed. "Yes. Arlen told me. We're on our way now." He nodded to Arlen. The grin on Arlen's face threatened to crack it wide open.

The four of them celebrated with dinner at Sorrento, their favorite restaurant. At the end of the meal, Norm raised a glass of Chianti and proposed a toast. "To a super vacation. The ladies can even get new wardrobes for the trip, as far as I'm concerned."

Arlen said, "Hear, hear!"

Clarissa and Nettie exchanged smiles.

* *** *

The big Boeing landed at Miami International and they were met at the luggage carousel by a gray-uniformed chauffeur holding a cardboard sign. In big computer-generated letters it said, *Hirsch – Gennario Party*. A limousine whisked them over the MacArthur Causeway to Miami Beach and up Collins Avenue to the Fontainebleu. They were met by a concierge and checked into a Versailles Suite on the thirty-seventh floor.

Once they'd tipped the bellman they separated into plush bedrooms and agreed to meet in an hour. Arlen lowered himself onto the huge bed and sighed.

Clarissa had opened her makeup carrier and was picking through its contents. She turned to her husband. "Well, what do you think?"

"I'm thinking about the last time I was in this hotel. A fraternity party. That was—"

"Let me guess. Forty years ago."

"Would you believe, closer to fifty? Ahh, we are so old, sweetheart, so old."

She shook her head. "Never mind. We have our health. Our children are grown up and married, our grandchildren . . . And not one of them was ever a drug addict or a gangster. Arlen, we're very lucky. And we're here to have fun. Let's just have fun."

After a conference with the Gennarios they phoned downstairs to the Gotham Steakhouse for reservations. They were tired from the day's travel. Staying in the Fontainebleau for dinner seemed a good idea. Dressed to the nines they rode the elevator to the restaurant. The food was splendid. The wine was delicious. Best of all, they could ignore the prices. They'd won the raffle and their vacation was on the cosmetics chain that sponsored the raffle each year.

Arlen enjoyed the best night's sleep he'd had in years.

In the morning they ordered breakfast from room service. Clarissa asked for a cup of tea and toast. Arlen indulged himself: half a grapefruit, eggs sunny side up, an English muffin with butter and orange marmalade, coffee. Clarissa clucked at him but he said it was their vacation, he was entitled to eat what he wanted.

The Versailles Suite included a terrace where they sat enjoying the morning sun.

Breakfast arrived accompanied by a neatly folded copy of the Miami *Herald.* They sat at a table overlooking the ocean. Arlen leafed through the paper, then stopped and read an item in the local news section. He shook his head.

Clarissa asked what was the matter.

"They're tearing it down."

She waited for him to continue.

He read, *The oldest movie theater in Miami Beach, the venerable Cairo Cinema, will be demolished in a matter of days. Efforts by neighborhood preservation groups were rejected by State Superior Court Judge Marisol Gil-Martinez on grounds that the plaintiffs lacked standing and that they had failed to prove any compelling government interest in the preservation of the building.*

Arlen sliced a triangle of egg and swallowed it with a gulp of fresh coffee. He sighed and shook his head, then continued, *Constructed in the late 1920s, the Cairo featured a mixture of faux Egyptian and Art Deco artistic styles. The building survived the transition to sound and other technological developments over the decades, but declining attendance caused its conversion to other uses in recent years. The building was purchased by Timothy Torrance III, great-grandson of the theater's architect, who attempted to convert the Cairo into a repertory art-film venue, but failed to do so.*

"There simply wasn't the money to do what needed to be done," Torrance told the Herald. "This is a real loss to the community, but I guess people just aren't interested any more. They'd rather sit home and watch slasher films on video."

"That's it?" Clarissa asked.

Arlen laid the paper on the table. "I loved that theater."

"I never knew."

"I grew up in that neighborhood, a block away from the Cairo. My parents used to take me there. They had great kid shows on Saturday afternoons. A western with Johnny Mack Brown or Rod Cameron, a comedy with Abbott and Costello or the Bowery Boys, cartoons . . . Mighty Mouse or Bugs Bunny or a Fleisher

Superman . . . and two chapters of a serial. *The Purple Monster Strikes, Secret of Treasure Island, Buck Rogers.*"

He spread marmalade on half the muffin, chewed and swallowed. "When I got older I worked there."

Clarissa said, "That you've told me."

"I was an usher. You should have seen me, sweetheart. What a uniform they gave me! Royal blue jacket with brass buttons and military epaulets. Black trousers with a gold stripe down the side. I wore a cardboard dickey and a clip-on bow tie. Oh, was I ever something!"

He shook his head.

"No more, eh?" He picked up the *Herald* and stared at the story about the pending demolition of the Cairo. He read it again as if that could make it say something different, but it didn't.

The sliding door moved silently on its track. Norm and Nettie joined Arlen and Clarissa on the terrace. Norm said, "I see you've already got your food. We just ordered ours."

Arlen handed the *Herald* to Norm, who opened it to the sports section. "Greyhounds running at Flagler." He folded the newspaper to an ad. "Want to go?"

Nettie was enthusiastic. "We can spend the morning at the pool, have a bite downstairs and see the action."

Clarissa looked dubious. "Isn't it cruel? Don't they chase a rabbit or something?"

Norm laughed. "It's a mechanical rabbit. It isn't alive."

"Still, I've heard they kill the dogs when they get too old to race."

"People adopt them. You know the McKees over on Chestnut Avenue? They adopted a couple of greyhounds. They say they're wonderful pets. They love to sit on the couch and watch television. *Lassie* and *Scooby-Doo*."

Arlen said, "You go ahead. Clar, sweetheart, you go ahead with Nettie and Norm. I'll meet you back here and we'll go out tonight."

Clarissa frowned. "Don't you want to go, Arlen?"

"I don't think so. I think I'm going to . . ." He let the sentence trail away.

Norm said, "Going to what, Arlen? Come on, spill."

"Nothing important. You'd just be bored."

"Maybe not. What?"

Arlen picked up the *Herald.* "I thought I'd take a ride uptown. I used to live there."

"Understand," Norm nodded. "You want to stroll around the old neighborhood. I got it."

Room service arrived with the Gennarios' breakfast.

Later, Nettie and Norm and Clarissa picked up a rental Toyota and pulled into Collins Avenue and headed for the causeway and the Flagler dog track. Arlen waved them away, then walked to the corner and waited for a northbound bus. He was surprised at how expensive the fare was. He was relieved when the driver pointed to a sign that indicated Arlen was entitled to a senior discount. He always drove his car at home, an '04 Oldsmobile Alero. It was the last Olds model ever built. His father had once owned a '61 DeSoto, the last of its breed, and Arlen had vowed to keep the Alero going for the rest of his life.

He got off the bus, waited for the light to change and crossed Collins Avenue.

There was the Cairo Cinema. The paint, once a vivid ocean blue and Egyptian gold, was faded and peeling. Most of the lights on the vertical sign were broken. Lettering on the marquee spelled out a message, *GOOD-BYE FROM THE CAIRO WELL MISS YOU.* The letters were mismatched, there was no apostrophe, one of the E's was a backwards three and the L's were inverted sevens.

The front doors were covered with heavy plywood and the glass cashier's box was boarded up. To the right of the Cairo he could see Kaplan's Kandy Kastle. He grinned. To the left where a children's shoe store had once operated was a franchise hardware establishment. Pedestrians in light clothing, broad-brimmed straw hats, colorful shirts and shorts passed him.

He stood looking at the Cairo for a few minutes, then entered Kaplan's Kandy Kastle. Once upon a time he'd spent most of his allowance at Kaplan's. Ice cream cones were a nickel for a single scoop, eight cents for a double. He used to ask for strawberry and chocolate, *Strawberry on top, please,* and Mrs. Kaplan used to make it that way to oblige a favorite customer. He bought his comic books at Kaplan's. Fat, exciting issues featuring Airboy and his bat -winged airplane, Green Lantern with his power ring. *In brightest day, in darkest night . . .*

The Kaplans had two daughters, Irma and Akiva. Irma was a year older than Arlen. Akiva was three years older than Irma. Akiva, he knew, had gone to college in Oregon, married, and settled permanently on the West Coast. Irma, even though she was older than Arlen, had taken a liking to him. They played together as children and had been sweethearts of a sort during their teens.

Irma worked at Kaplan's while Arlen ushered at the Cairo. On their days off they would often go to the Cairo or to the Suez, the movie house opposite the Cairo on Collins Avenue. By this time the theaters belonged to the same chain and free admission to either was a perk for employees.

There were two females on the staff of the Cairo, Mildred and Sally. The rest of the staff was male: Tim Torrance was the manager. Jack Corelli, Marty Wollner, and Arlen were ushers. Mr. Hopkinson was the projectionist. He ruled his private domain up a flight of stairs at the rear of the auditorium. Everyone else was on first-name terms but he was always Mr. Hopkinson.

And there was Mr. Isaacs, the doorman. Customers would buy their tickets from Mildred or Sally. The two girls alternated selling tickets and operating the candy counter. Nobody knew how old Mr. Isaacs was. There were legends about him. General belief was that he was a retired widower with a fortune in investments and that he worked only because he was bored.

When the Suez showed *The Black Widow*, a thriller with Ginger Rogers, Gene Tierney, and Van Heflin, Arlen and Irma crossed the avenue and found seats in the rear of the auditorium. They were kissing furiously when Arlen got up the courage to sneak his hand over Irma's shoulder, inside her blouse, inside her bra. The thrill of her breast in his hand, the silky warmth of her skin, the rigid nipple in his palm, had never left him.

A year later she left town to attend an Ivy League college. Arlen stayed behind, attended the local university, was drafted into the service, and found himself on an army post near Indianapolis. He managed to pull a cushy assignment. He had most Friday nights off and attended the local synagogue. He met Clarissa there. They married, and when he got his discharge he went to work in her father's business.

From his own parents in Florida he learned that Irma had moved to Israel. She sent him a picture postcard written in Hebrew and English, a rider on a camel with a pyramid in the background. She wrote, *Remember the Cairo! Love, Irma!* A year later, riding in a jeep, she had been killed by a sniper's bullet.

He pushed open the door of Kaplan's Kandy Kastle. The store was filled with straw hats, souvenir tee-shirts with *Kaplan's Kandy Kastle* silk-screened on them in incandescent ink, baseball caps with cartoon characters embroidered on them, bathing trunks, beach towels, plaster fish mounted on plaques blazoned with comic sayings, playing cards, souvenir pens, key chains.

"I used to live here," he said to no one in particular.

A dark-skinned woman wearing an Indian sari behind the counter walked over to face him.

"Can I help you, sir?"

"I used to come in here all the time."

She smiled encouragingly.

"Is Mr. Kaplan here? Mrs. Kaplan?" he asked.

The woman shook her head. She turned aside and called a name. At least Arlen thought it was a name. *Nadisu,* or something like that. A dark-skinned man wearing a black silk suit, white shirt, and midnight blue tie, appeared from somewhere. He had glossy, wavy, black hair. The woman had worn a head scarf.

"Can I help you, sir?"

"The Kaplans," Arlen managed.

"I do not know them."

"This store is called Kaplan's. I used to buy comic books here. And ice cream cones."

"We don't sell comic books or ice cream cones, sir. There is a big comic book store on Lincoln Road. There is an ice cream store nearby."

"The Kaplans."

The man frowned in concentration. "I bought this store from Mr. D'Onofrio six years ago. It was called Kaplan's then. It may have belonged to a Mr. Kaplan before Mr. D'Onofrio."

Arlen nodded. He backed away from the counter, from the courteous, dark-skinned man and woman. He left the store. The afternoon sun was strong but he stood in the shade beneath the Cairo Cinema marquee and it was comfortable there. There was even a hint of a breeze tinctured with the odor of seaweed and salt water.

He examined the plywood covering the theater doors hoping to find a way in but he could not find one. However there was an alley between the Cairo and Kaplan's Kandy Kastle. At the end of the alley he could get to the rear of the theater. In the days when he'd worked at the Cairo he had learned how to jimmy the ring-and-hasp that held the theater's iron delivery doors shut, and swing the doors wide without opening the padlock.

He made his way down the alley. It was strewn with old newspapers and fast food wrappers and other, less savory trash. He used his trick—it came back to him, even after all these years—and managed to get the iron doors open. They were rusted and heavy and he was barely able to squeeze inside.

He was backstage. The room was musty, the air hot and stale. The light was dim, the afternoon daylight seeping through the delivery doors. He knew the theater well enough to make his way to the edge of the old stage, down half a dozen steps into the auditorium itself. He knew where the light switches were but when he tried them, not surprisingly, he found that the power had been cut off.

There wasn't much he could do in the dark.

He made his way back to the alley, back to Collins Avenue, into the hardware store next door. A Puerto Rican-looking clerk took his money for a powerful flashlight, asked in flawless English if there was anything else he wanted, and thanked him for his business when Arlen told him no.

Back into the sunlight. Back into the alley. Back into the theater. He shone his flashlight around the auditorium. The Egyptian style *bas reliefs* that had both fascinated and frightened him as a child were still there. Crocodile-headed and ibis-headed gods, reed boats, women in snow-white gowns, men wearing pale kilts, leopards on leashes and painted pyramids and sphinxes and temples.

He walked to the back of the auditorium, out into the lobby, downstairs to the men's and women's rest rooms. The lower level of the theater had been decorated with oversized photo-portraits of the great movie stars of the era. Gary Cooper in a foreign legion *kepi,* Garbo in a black jersey gown, Gable as Rhett Butler, Harlow in a dress the color of her hair. The pictures were still there. Somehow they had survived the decades of neglect and abuse.

Back in the auditorium he walked to the foot of the stage, turned and sat in a front row seat. Customers had complained when they had to sit in the front of the room, and he could understand that. They had to lean back to see the picture, it was uncomfortable, and the image on the screen was distorted.

He moved to a more comfortable seat, halfway toward the rear of the auditorium. He settled in and half-closed his eyes. He could almost imagine an image before him. Rod Cameron leading a posse, chasing a gang of rustlers across a cactus-studded butte. The camera cut between pursuers and pursued. Clouds of dust rose from the horses' hooves. Puffs of smoke exploded from six-shooters. All in beautiful chiaroscuro. All accompanied by the pounding of hooves, gunfire, shouts, music.

Arlen leaned back. The projector beam danced overhead as light reflected from decades-old dust.

He turned on his flashlight, pushed himself to his feet, struggled to the end of the row and trotted to the back of the room. He climbed the stairs to the projectionist's booth. The flight was longer and steeper than he remembered, but when he got there he found no sign of Mr. Hopkinson. There was no whir of the projector. In fact, there was no projector. The booth was empty.

He made his way carefully back to the auditorium. The screen was dark. He pushed his way through the iron delivery doors, shoved them closed behind him, trudged back to Collins Avenue.

There was a bench at the bus stop, a tasteful sign with a gold Star of David against a maroon background. *ETERNAL JUDEA,* it read in heavy gilt letters, *Funeral Service Since 1948, With Respect for the Deceased and Concern for the Living.*

A very old man sat on the bench, a straw hat shading his head, a short sleeve shirt and light pants offering protection from the sun.

Arlen peered at him.

"Mr. Isaacs?"

The old man turned his face toward Arlen.

"Mr. Isaacs? Is that you?" Good God, the man must be older than Moses!

"Who's that? I can't see you," the old man said.

"Arlen Hirsch."

"Arlen Hirsch the usher?"

"Yes, sir. You are Mr. Isaacs, aren't you?"

"Arlen, you came back. The theater is closed, you know. You can't get your job back. No more Cairo, Arlen. I come here most days just to sit and look at it. I can't see any more, but I like to come and sit. You must be all grown up now, Arlen."

That brought a smile. "Yes, Mr. Isaacs."

The old man hummed tunelessly. It went on so long, Arlen thought he'd forgotten him, or maybe he had fallen asleep, but then the old man said, "How old are you, Arlen Hirsch?"

Arlen told him.

The old man said, "Really? Really? If you're that old now, then I must be—" He shook his head slowly. "No, no, that's impossible." After a pause he said, "Here's your bus, Arlen."

"It is?"

"Coming, it's coming," the old man nodded toward Surfside, farther uptown. "I can tell. I know by the sound."

Arlen looked. The bus was a block away, approaching slowly, the late afternoon sun glinting off its metal body and shield-like windows.

"How will you get home, Mr. Isaacs?"

"Don't worry about me, Arlen. My daughter comes for me every day. No, that's wrong. I mean my granddaughter." He took off his hat and rubbed his forehead. "No, my great-granddaughter. That's who. She comes for me every day. You go ahead. Remember, I come here every day. Almost every day. Good-bye, Arlen. Say good-bye to the Cairo."

* *** *

For dinner they went to Joe's Stone Crabs in South Beach. Everyone had to clean up first, to rid themselves of the day's perspiration. Arlen had a layer of dust to deal with, but their opulent suite had wonderful showers and he luxuriated under the spray and lay on top of the bed for half an hour before dressing.

He knew he was being quiet during dinner. He hoped that no one would press him about his day, and fortunately no one did. Clarissa and the Gennarios had pooled their bets and come away almost two hundred dollars ahead.

"Love those doggies," Norm said, "I just love those doggies. You should have been along, Arlen, you would have had a great time. We were losing money most of the afternoon, and then came the last race. Nobody knew nothing about these dogs, you know? They had a racing form but nobody knew nothing, we didn't have time to study the charts, so how did we decide?"

Before Arlen could answer, Nettie said, "Wait, Norman, wait. Tell 'em who picked the winner."

"You did. Okay, Nettie, you did. You tell 'em."

"Clar and I. We picked the winner, Arlen. You should have been there. Norman wanted to bet on the favorite, you know? A dog named Far Centaurus. Can you imagine? That's a stupid name for a dog."

Norman growled.

"For cripes sake, Nettie, if you want to tell 'em, tell 'em, and if you don't want to tell 'em, say so and I'll tell 'em."

Clarissa had been working on a crab leg with a pair of pliers. She put down the pliers with a clatter. "Norman had been playing favorites all afternoon and losing, so Nettie and I made him put a bundle on the longest shot in the race. A bundle, Arlen. I mean, a bundle. Can you guess what the dog's name was? You can't? It was Mussolini. Can you imagine sticking a poor doggie with a name like that? Why would anybody name a dog Mussolini? He won going away and we got back everything we'd lost and two hundred dollars profit. Two hundred dollars, Arlen."

He had trouble sleeping that night. They'd shared a cab back to the Fontainebleau, paused in the lobby bar for a nightcap, and gone upstairs.

Clarissa found Arlen standing on the balcony, watching the surf as it ran up on the beach and then retreated, bright moonlight reflecting off the Atlantic. A ship stood silhouetted against the horizon.

"Arlen?"

He nodded in response, not knowing whether she observed the movement or not.

"Arlen, are you mad at me?"

He shook his head abstractedly, focusing on the ship, a black freighter in all probability, headed perhaps for Bilbao. "No," he managed.

"Because I was a little bit loud at dinner, wasn't I? I was a little bit tipsy. I mean, Norman is a lovely man but sometimes he seems to get too full of himself. He was picking greyhounds all afternoon and Nettie and I had ideas and he just brushed us aside and kept making bets and kept losing, and then we both picked Mussolini and made him bet on him, we made him bet on him, and Mussolini won and we won all that money, oh, Arlen, you would have loved it. I know he's your friend but you know what I mean. He couldn't decide whether to be happy because we won or angry because he didn't pick a winner all day and Nettie and I picked a long shot and he won. Arlen, you would have loved it."

Arlen said, "It's all right, Clar sweetheart. It's all right. I'm glad you won the money. You and Nettie." He gripped the railing with both hands.

"Won't you come to bed, Arlen? I miss you in bed."

"In a little while."

"Is something the matter?"

"You know what, Clar? I miss the palms. At home it's all different. In Indiana it's all right. But not in Florida. I grew up with my windows open and the palm fronds clattering in the breeze. Did you know the palm fronds make a real clattering sound when the wind blows?"

"No."

Why did she sound frightened?

"They do. They did. I loved this place. Now it's all different. Now there's just the hiss of the air conditioning. So I can't sleep."

"You slept last night."

"I was tired."

"Arlen."

"Please go to bed. I'll be in in a little while."

The next day he begged off again. The girls were going on a shopping spree and Norm wanted Arlen to play golf with him.

"It's our lucky day, Arlen. I can feel it. We won this vacation. We won at the doggies. Come on."

Arlen begged off. He said he wasn't up to it. He told Norm that he could pick up some partners, make a casual foursome. "Good luck, Norm. I'm sure you'll win. We'll meet the girls back here afterwards and celebrate. After all, this is our last night in town. Some vacation. Long weekend is more like it. Well, who can complain, for the price of a raffle ticket?"

He stood on the corner until the bus came and he paid the senior discount price and rode up Collins Avenue looking at all the familiar sights and at all the changes. When the bus pulled to the curb at his stop he climbed off, waited for the light to change, and crossed the avenue. He had brought his flashlight with him.

Someone had pasted crudely-lettered signs on the plywood pleading, *SAVE THE CAIRO! IT ISN'T TOO LATE!* Someone else had posted a professionally-printed notice advertising *Cairo Condos on Collins,* with an artist's rendering of a modern high-rise residential tower and a plastic dispenser full of promotional brochures.

Arlen looked over his shoulder, feeling vaguely guilty, and made his way down the alley between and theater and the now candy-less Kaplan's Kandy Kastle. He worked his trick on the iron delivery doors, scrambled through the narrow opening, and pulled the doors shut behind him. He clicked on his flashlight and followed its beam to the rear of the auditorium, up the narrow flight of stairs and to the projectionist's booth.

The door to the booth was unlocked, as it had been the day before. He edged it open and stepped inside. The dust was thick everywhere except where he saw his own day-old footprints. The heavy wooden table that the projector had stood on was still there, its surface scratched, cracked and dry, but there was no sign of the projector. It could hardly have been sold. It was far too old and too difficult to maintain. Arlen remembered Mr. Hopkinson showing him how to thread it. Not only did the thirty-five millimeter film have to pass through the complex series of gates in the correct order, but every loop had to be of the exact right size or the sound wouldn't synch with the actors' movements. He knew how audiences reacted when the actors' lips moved a second before or two seconds after the loudspeakers carried their words!

Nowadays it was all automated. Mr. Hopkinson and his colleagues were a dying breed. Nowadays every multiplex had an array of flat-pan projectors that practically ran themselves.

Downstairs again he directed his light at the empty candy counter only to discover that it wasn't quite as empty as he'd thought. Apparently someone—surely not Mildred or Sally!—had left crumbs of popcorn or candy on the shelves, and a family of eight-legged scavengers had established a thriving colony amidst the ruins. As soon as the light hit them there was a scurrying and a mass movement and the counter was again deserted.

Arlen returned to the auditorium and found a comfortable seat. He spread his arms over the backs of the adjacent seats and lay back, his eyes fixed on the screen. He felt that he could retrieve a film from the warrens of recollection, one that he'd seen so many times he practically knew it by heart. He could close his eyes and see it, hear it, live it for an hour or two, before saying good-by forever to the Cairo.

At first it seemed a difficult decision, but once he started discarding candidates he realized that there was only one possible choice, at least for him, for Arlen Hirsch. It had to be *Casablanca.*

The music blared, the Warner Bros. logo filled the screen, the images sparkled like diamonds and onyx. Bogie and Bergman, Ilsa and Rick. Paul Henreid as Victor and Claude Rains, the great, underrated, brilliant Claude Rains, as Louie Renault. Conrad Veidt, Sydney Greenstreet, Peter Lorre, Dooley Wilson, Cuddles Sakall.

"What o'clock?"

"Such o'clock!"

"I'm shocked, shocked!"

"Round up the usual suspects."

"We'll always have Paris."

"This could be the start of a beautiful friendship."

The Blue Parrot, the Nazis, the Free French.

He felt the warmth of Irma's cheek against the side of his neck. He slid an arm around her, over her shoulder. With her hand she guided his hand. He felt—he felt a stirring that he hadn't felt in years.

Dooley was playing, *You must remember this, a kiss is just a kiss* . . . That funny little rolling piano. He heard the tinkling notes but they weren't the notes of a piano. They weren't coming from the speakers hidden behind the screen.

He opened his eyes with a jolt. The tune was *Happy Days Are Here Again*. He found his cell phone in his pants pocket, flipped it open.

"Arlen, are you all right?"

He only grunted. He looked around. The screen was dark. The auditorium was dark. He clicked on his flashlight, shone it in a circle; he was alone with the animal-headed gods of Egypt.

"Arlen?"

"I—I must have fallen asleep. What time is it? Clarissa?"

"Nettie and Norm are waiting downstairs. I'm beside myself. Where have you been? I thought something awful had happened. Are you all right?"

He staggered to his feet, shone the flashlight on his wristwatch, stumbled toward the door. He was still holding his cell phone. "I'm coming home," he managed to say. He was still groggy. "I was working late at the office. I must have dozed off."

"Arlen, you're not at the office. We're in Miami Beach. Don't you remember? Is something the matter? Arlen!"

"No," he said, "nothing is the matter, Clar, nothing is the matter, nothing. I remember everything."

"Report of the Admissions Committee" was another story commissioned by William Jones, this time for his anthology *Tales Out of Miskatonic University* (Elder Signs Press, 2010). I find it fascinating that Miskatonic University has achieved so great a presence in our culture. Several times I have had to explain to acquaintances that my Miskatonic U sweatshirt / baseball cap / lapel pin / license holder are artifacts of an institution that doesn't exist.

Report of the Admissions Committee

The scene outside Hutchinson Hall was a merry one. It was the first week of January and snow covered the rolling hills on which the campus of Miskatonic University was situated. The most recent storm had ended, easterly breezes had sent the last heavy clouds scudding into the highlands to the west and a bright winter sun glittered in a perfect azure sky.

Young men and women sported new finery received from their families during the Christmas break. Couples greeted one another, preparing to settle back into their academic routine. A tall girl, bright sunlight dancing in her blond hair, threw a snowball at a boy in a bright red quilted jacket. Nearby a group of students were building a snowman.

Inside Hutchinson Hall's gray stone battlements, in a spacious office, its walls covered with gold-stamped, leather-bound volumes save where space was reserved for oil portraits of academics of past generations, Tivona Sanders, BA, MA, Ph.D., Dean of Admissions, pored over a stack of carefully labeled manila file folders. Each contained the carefully completed application of a high school senior hoping to enroll at Miskatonic for the following fall semester.

Behind Dean Sanders an ancient fireplace fed fragrant wood-smoke into a tall chimney. A fire had been laid by the building's porter and the room was comfortable despite the midwinter chill. From time to time the fire's pleasant crackling was punctuated by a snapping pine knot.

There was the sound of knuckles on wood.

The Dean raised her eyes, her glance passing over a bookshelf that held a row of Miskatonic's yearbooks dating from the university's Seventeenth Century founding to the present. Dean Sanders pressed a button located at the side of her great mahogany desk, releasing the latch on the door of her office.

A tall, gray-haired, bespectacled man entered. The man was smiling. He wore a dark green alpine hat. In one gnarled hand he carried an elaborately carved stick. That this it was not for mere affectation was evidenced by his pronounced limp and the fact that he leaned on the stick with each step.

"I'll bet you love the buzzers as much as I do," he said. He spoke with the nasal twang of a Maine native. Decades of exposure to Massachusetts surroundings had not changed his speech.

"I don't like them a bit," Dean Sanders smiled. She stood and rounded her desk, taking the newcomer's free hand warmly in both of her own. "But ever since the recent series of break-ins, I suppose they can't be helped."

She gestured to a comfortable chair opposite her desk. It was covered in rich maroon leather and studded in brass. The tall man lowered himself gingerly into it, moving with care. He removed his hat and placed it on a corner of the desk, then he leaned his walking stick against the dark stained wood.

Once the newcomer was settled, Dean Sanders returned to her own chair. "Thank you for coming, Doctor Lazarus."

"Bill."

"Of course."

"I'm glad to offer any assistance I can, Dean."

"Please. Tivona. The least you can do is return that favor."

William Lazarus nodded, waiting for her to continue.

"You know I'd rather be in the classroom, teaching my courses in Middle Eastern and Semitic Archaeology. But the President personally asked me to take over Admissions for a year, and Miskatonic has been so good to me, I couldn't refuse."

As Lazarus's speech marked him as a native of Maine, Tivona Sanders's accent was that of a native Hebrew speaker. She sported a modestly stylish sweater and skirt. She still wore her wedding ring, refusing to give up hope that her husband, Riston Sanders, would be found alive.

"When I was a boy we had an expression for that kind of duty," Lazarus said. "Something vulgar involving a barrel."

"I learned that in the army," Tivona Sanders grinned. "Israel can't afford to coddle its delicate flowers of femininity."

She tapped a fingernail on the topmost manila folder near the edge of her desk.

"Most of these are pretty routine," she said. "Of course Miskatonic has recovered from the scandals that hurt us so much under the former administration. We're getting many more applications than we can accept, and the quality of the applicants has risen. We can stand up to the best of the competition, academically."

"That's good news, but not startling."

Lazarus removed his gold-rimmed spectacles, patted his jacket until he located a gray velvet cloth, and polished the lenses. He set the spectacles carefully in place. "This isn't the Miskatonic it was when I was a young instructor of transdimensional geometry. The student body was exclusively male in those days. And exclusively Caucasian. And Christian. I remember the controversy when the Admissions Committee accepted the first Jewish student in—was it 'thirty-one? Poor fellow took a dreadful hazing. People leaving ham sandwiches in his room when he was out, sending him Gospels in the mail. But he stuck it out, I'll give him that. Poor chap enlisted in the Marine Corps after Pearl Harbor and died on Tarawa."

He shook his head. "I'm sorry, Dean. Ah, Tivona. You'll have to forgive an old man for wandering. I think I might retire after the spring semester."

"Don't do that, Bill. Miskatonic needs your wisdom." She closed her eyes, gathering her thoughts, then lifted the folder and extended it toward him. "What do you make of this?"

Lazarus accepted the folder, opened it and studied its contents. After a few moments he raised his eyes to meet Tivona Sanders's.

"I see."

"Indeed."

Tivona Sanders pushed herself back from her desk, turned and stood facing the fire.

Lazarus waited for her to turn back.

"Another Whateley," he muttered.

"I wasn't here when the great scandal occurred. I wasn't even born then, no less in America." Tivona Sanders raised one hand and rubbed her forehead. "Hardly anyone is left at Miskatonic from those days. But you're the most senior faculty member we have, Bill. You were here, weren't you? You knew what happened? You know about the terrible—*thing*—the thing that died in the library? You know about the events up on Sentinel Hill?"

Lazarus nodded. He removed his spectacles, studied them as if some wisdom might be spelled out on their lenses, then donned them once more. "I was on Sentinel Hill that night," he said at last. "But now—it's been so many years. Decades, Tivona. I thought there were no more Whateleys left in Arkham. Nor even in Aylesbury."

"You didn't notice the applicant's address."

Lazarus said, "Sorry." He studied the document once again. "Once I saw the name I'm afraid I stopped reading. All right, give me a few minutes to study this application."

Soon he looked up. "West Athol." He allowed himself a grin. "I played for the West Athol Marauders, did you know that?"

Tivona Sanders said, "Bill, I never heard of the West Athol Marauders."

Lazarus uttered a sound that was mostly a soft, rueful laugh.

"Semi-professional football team. Long gone, now. Professional football wasn't the big business then that it is nowadays. Even the NFL was small potatoes. Most of the players had day jobs, they just played football on Sundays. But that was my ambition. I was a center. I was pretty good, too. Until I got my kneecap shattered."

He looked down at his rough tweed trousers, kneaded his knee as if to work out its soreness, let out a wistful sigh.

Tivona Sanders said, "Football's loss was Miskatonic's gain, Bill. I hope you don't regret your career."

"I'm sorry." He rose partway from his chair, then sank back into it. "You didn't invite me in here to talk about ancient events on a minor-league gridiron. You want to talk about—" he studied the application once more "—Miss Dorcas Whateley, senior valedictorian of West Athol Rural High School. Also senior class president, chairman of the dramatic society, captain of the girls' basketball team, and editor-in-chief of the West Athol *Rustic News*. Tivona, I don't see how you can do other than accept her."

"But she's a Whateley. Do you know what that name means around here?"

Before Lazarus could reply, Tivona Sanders answered her own question. "Of course you do. Of course. When I first came to Miskatonic, mere mention of that name was enough to silence a room full of chattering academics. Now, it's mostly forgotten. But do we want to stir up those ashes again? There are still people who react to the name. Old-timers who insist that they hear rumblings beneath the hills around Arkham, that there are foul odors on certain nights."

"I know, I know."

"Is it just superstition, Bill? Townies don't like Miskatonic much. And to be honest, the university hasn't done a lot to benefit Arkham."

There was a long silence. Lazarus turned his eyes toward mullioned windows. A wind had risen and drifted snow was being lifted and whirled on the campus. Fresh-faced boys and girls—young men and women—were throwing snowballs, playing like children.

"No, Tivona, it is not just superstition. Would that it were. Would that it were."

"Well, then—" The dean left her sentence incomplete.

William Lazarus said, "This is a new era, Tivona. It's a new world. Tradition or no, I would even say, this is a new Miskatonic University. We cannot penalize this young woman for the evils of her ancestors. I don't see how the university can turn her down. Let's hope that she redeems the name Whateley. Give her a chance to eradicate what bad memories remain. She deserves a chance, Tivona. Look at her record. She deserves a chance."

Tivona Sanders retrieved the file folder from William Lazarus. "You're right," she sighed, "I'm sure you're right, Bill. I was hoping you'd tell me to turn her down. Send her a polite letter, tell her we were over-enrolled for the fall semester, even offer to write a letter of recommendation for her to another institution. But no, of course you're right. She'll be here next autumn."

William Lazarus retrieved his walking stick, leaned on it and got to his feet. He picked up his soft hat and pressed it onto his iron-gray hair. "Besides, West Athol would almost certainly be the undecayed branch of the family. Her transcript indicates as much."

Tivona Sanders let out a sigh. "Let us hope."

William Lazarus smiled. "Now that that's settled, Tivona, how about a couple of drinks and a good meal at the Arkham Inn?"

The dean looked at her wristwatch. "I have a lot of work to do. I really shouldn't. I'll probably be here 'til seven or seven-thirty tonight."

"I can wait."

"All right. I'll meet you at the inn. Would eight-thirty be too late? I want to run home and freshen up after work."

"I'll be at the bar." His smile broadened into a grin. "I'll be the tall fellow in the tweed suit with the fancy walking stick in one hand and a brandy snifter in the other." He stood at the window, watching students running and playing. The glass was thick and he couldn't hear their joyful whoops, but in his mind he could hear a long-ago cheering crowd.

"Fourth Avenue Interlude" was written for editor Christopher Conlon. My fiend Kage Baker, since deceased, deeply mourned and sorely missed, told me that Conlon was assembling an anthology based on "The Lighthouse," a fragmentary tale found among the papers of the great Edgar Allan Poe. This is still another thinly fictionalized memoir. It appeared in *Poe's Lighthouse* (Cemetery Dance Publications, 2006).

Fourth Avenue Interlude

They're all gone now, all dead. Both Jacks, and David, and Alice. David was the first to go, then one Jack, then Alice, and then the other Jack. He was the last. I'm still here, of course, but at my age you never know how much longer you're going to be around either.

And I want to tell you this now, because my memory isn't what it used to be and it isn't going to get any better. My wife tells me that I forget things that happened and remember things that didn't. Sometimes I tell the same story over and over, I know that. I guess it goes with the territory, along with the white hair and the stiff joints.

This happened a long time ago. I think it was 1949. I would have been twelve years old then, and I'm pretty sure that's when it happened because people were still talking about the big surprise of the Dewey-Truman election, how old Give-'em-Hell Harry had outsmarted all the poll-takers and pundits and even the fool who wrote that famous headline about DEWEY BEATS TRUMAN for the Chicago *Tribune*.

It was winter, the Christmas and New Year's holidays were over and it was damned slushy and icy and miserable in New York. I was just a kid of twelve. Did I say that already? I guess it goes with the territory along with the white hair and the stiff joints.

I was just a kid of twelve and I was crazy for books. I'd discovered Book Row in New York, Fourth Avenue below Fourteenth Street. You could find anything you wanted to read down there, and at bargain prices, too, if you weren't too picky about things like first editions in dust jackets. If you'd settle for a reading copy you could get anything you wanted to read, and plenty cheap at that.

Even so, I couldn't afford the books I wanted. Arthur Conan Doyle and Edgar Rice Burroughs and Rafael Sabatini and E. Phillips Oppenheim and Octavus Roy Cohen. You could get a nice copy for a quarter and one that was messed up but still readable for a nickel if you prowled Book Row and knew how to look for books. But my father had come up from poverty and he always felt that the best way to teach me and my brother the value of money was to make sure that we never had any.

After a while, all the booksellers along Book Row knew me, and I got to be friends with most of them. Sometimes they'd pay me to do odd jobs, and of course every dime I made went right back into books. Well, I had to save a nickel for the subway ride home, it was too far to walk.

My favorite store was Biblo and Tannen. I remember the address, 63 Fourth Avenue. There were four people who worked there. The owners were Jack Biblo and Jack Tannen, born Jacob Biblowicz and Jacob Tannenbaum. I always thought of them simply as the two Jacks. They'd been in the book trade since the 1920s. They'd been partners for so long that they'd started to look alike and dress alike. Shrinking hairlines, dark fringes, heavy horn-rimmed glasses, bushy graying moustaches. They wore plaid shirts, solid-color knit ties, corduroy trousers. You could tell them apart because Tannen was a little stockier, a little more outgoing, a little more talkative. Biblo was slimmer, quieter, more on the introspective, intellectual side.

Like any couple who had been together for many years they completed each other's sentences. They fought like Tracy and Hepburn, Ameche and Langford, Lee and Dannay, Chevalier and Gingold, Durocher and any umpire who was handy.

They'd let me sweep out the store, re-shelve books that customers left out, bring in the bargain tables from the sidewalk at the end of the day. They paid me fifty cents an hour, that was a dime more than the legal minimum wage, and if I took it out in trade (I always did) I got an employee discount on any book I bought.

The Adventures of Sherlock Holmes.

Tanar of Pellucidar.

The Double Life of Mr. Alfred Burton.

Jim Hanvey, Detective.

I went to public school, of course, and to synagogue when my parents made me, and sometimes to Ebbets Field to see the Dodgers play, especially when they played the Giants, whom my brother and I both hated, and out-of-town teams like the Boston

Braves and the Cincinnati Reds. But I really lived for my days on Fourth Avenue.

On the subway, going, I would rehearse my want-list in my mind: *The Land of Mist, The Land That Time Forgot, The Man Who Changed His Plea, Scrambled Yeggs*. I'd get off at Astor Place and walk up toward Fourteenth Street, stopping at every store along the way—the Colonial Book Service, Stammer's Bookstore, Books 'n' Things, Louis Schucman, the Raven Bookshop. But I'd always wind up at Biblo and Tannen. They had a basement full of fiction, a huge room with all kinds of novels and short stories, and two smaller rooms, one full of mysteries and detective tales and one that was full of science fiction and fantasy and horror stories.

Oh, I was telling you about Jack and Jack and David and Alice and I only told you about Jack and Jack. I'll back up.

David Garfinkel was a retired high school teacher. He was a huge man, he could crush you in one hand if he wanted to. He used to sit in a chair near the counter at the front of the store. He—oh, you want to know what he looked like?

He was balding with a gray fringe, dark-rimmed glasses, and a bushy gray moustache. He wore plaid shirts and solid-color knitted ties. He was a real old-timer. He loved to reminisce about dime novels. He'd talk about Old Sleuth and Young Sleuth, Nick Carter, Buffalo Bill, and Baseball Joe. He used to talk about a series of dime novels about a baseball team, the author helped you remember the players' names by giving them all the same initials as their positions. Pitcher Palmer, Catcher Carruthers, First Baseman Fillstrup, Second Sacker Simmons, like that. David considered pulp magazines a sign of the decay of modern civilization.

Alice Ryter ruled her own little domain from a battered wooden desk near the back of the store. She was the secretary, office manager, financial manager, and general manager of everything. She wore a stern expression, kept her hair pulled back severely, and used heavy, dark-rimmed glasses.

One Saturday I got to work late.

"Where were you?" asked Jack Tannen.

"*Shul*," I told him.

"*Shul?*" Jack was astonished. "Temple? You? Since when did you get religion?"

"My next birthday, I'll be thirteen. I have to be *bar mitzvah*. I have to go and study. I don't care but my brother was *bar mitzvah* and my parents say I have to be, too. So I'm late, I'm sorry. What work can I do today?"

David Garfinkel reached over and grabbed my right biceps between his fingers. He squeezed, I felt like my arm was a tube of Ipana toothpaste.

"He's a strong boy," David said. "I'll bet he can move those boxes upstairs."

"Think you can do it?" asked Jack Biblo.

"Sure I can, what do you think I am?" I knew the boxes he meant. They were heavy and I wasn't so sure at all that I could move them, but one thing I learned from my big brother is, Never say you can't do a thing, always say you can. That's how you get your chance in this world, and that's how you'll get ahead.

"Come on, then," one of the Jacks said. By now I don't even remember which one. It doesn't matter anyhow. I think it was Biblo, though.

We went upstairs. Biblo and Tannen was in an old building on Fourth Avenue, the store occupied the first floor and the basement, the second floor was office space and shipping and receiving and they kept overstock in boxes on the third floor.

When we got to the third floor, Jack pointed to a huge pile of corrugated boxes full of books. "The whole building is starting to settle and we have to even the load before we have a Leaning Tower of Pisa here. You need to climb up there, get a box off the top row, bring it down, and put it over there. Then go back and do another. Come downstairs when you're done."

I started moving boxes.

They were very heavy, and soon I was sweating up a storm, even in the middle of the winter in New York in, I think it was 1949. Could it have been 1948? Maybe November, December, after the election. DEWEY BEATS TRUMAN. After Christmas, after New Year's, it would be 1949. That's what I think.

The boxes were covered with dust that had accumulated on them for, I don't know, certainly years, maybe decades. What books were in them, anyhow? I didn't know, the boxes were sealed with brown paper tape and I couldn't look inside without cutting the tape and I was supposed to be moving boxes, not looking at books, so I just left them as they were and moved the boxes.

Soon the sweat was rolling down my face and getting into my eyes, and stinging like anything. I tried to wipe my eyes with my elbow but I was wearing my first pair of glasses, with heavy, dark rims. I couldn't do it, so I took off my glasses and wiped my face with my hands. Now I was mixing dust with sweat and making a nice coat of salty mud on my face.

I kept moving boxes.

After a while a manila envelope fell out from between a couple of boxes. It must have been put on top of a box, then overlooked when the next row of boxes was added. It had been lying there for, who knows how long?

The envelope was the size of a sheet of typing paper, flat not folded. It wasn't fat, wasn't skinny. It felt like it had maybe a dozen sheets of paper in it, maybe a few more. On the front it had a couple of cancelled two-cent stamps, and was addressed to somebody way up at the tip of Manhattan. That was where the Polo Grounds were, where the Giants played.

Nobody I knew even cared about the Giants. You either were a Yankees fan (boo!) or a Dodgers fan (yay!), but nobody liked the Giants except for some show business people, for some reason I could never understand. People like Toots Shor went to Giants games. Go figure.

Right, I did say that I hated the Giants, didn't I? Well, I only hated them because I was a Dodgers fan and the Dodgers and the Giants were both in the National League, and Ebbets Field and the Polo Grounds were only a subway ride apart, so if you loved one team it was kind of natural to hate the other one, but that isn't the same thing, really, as *caring* about them.

Does that make sense?

David Garfinkel, God rest his big oversized loving soul, would understand. We used to talk about baseball. He approved of my being a Dodgers fan because they had Jackie Robinson and Roy Campanella. He said, "The *schvartzers* should get a chance just like anybody else, it's only right." But—

Oh, right, the envelope. The address on it was in Manhattan.

The name it was addressed to had been scratched out. A few letters were visible but I really couldn't read it. I clambered down off the boxes and put the envelope over near the door so I wouldn't forget it and went back to work moving boxes.

I was just finishing up when I heard somebody coming up the stairs. The stairs were wooden and they were old. I don't know how old that building was, probably a hundred years or a couple of hundred years.

It's gone now. Book Row is all gone now.

So I heard footsteps coming up the stairs. I knew everybody in the company by then and I could tell them apart by their footsteps. When the door opened and Alice Ryter came into the room I knew who was coming before she even opened the door.

Alice took one look at me and burst into laughter. It was the first time I'd ever seen her even smile, much less laugh. I waited for her to say something.

"What happened to you?"

"What do you mean? Nothing. I've been working. Jack told me to move all these boxes. What time is it?" I didn't have a wristwatch, I was expecting one for my *bar mitzvah*. I knew I'd get a Schaeffer fountain pen or maybe a Parker 51, probably some cash that I hoped my parents would let me spend on things that I wanted and not make me buy new clothes or put the money into a college account. And I figured I'd get a wristwatch. I hoped so, anyhow.

Alice looked at her own watch and told me what time it was. Then she said, "Come with me."

She led me into the bathroom. There was a bathroom on each floor at Biblo and Tannen. She pulled the bead chain to turn on the light and made me look in the mirror. I was a mess, I'll have to admit it. My face looked as if I'd been trying out for a blackface part in a minstrel show. My hands were as filthy as my face. My shirt was sweat-stained and blotchy, too.

"Come on," Alice said. She turned on the water in the sink and made me take off my shirt and she made me wash off my face and my chest and arms and hands. When I was finished she made me start all over again. Then she made me bend over the sink and she picked up the soap and washed my hair and told me to rinse it.

Then she took a towel and dried me off like a little kid. There was an old sweatshirt hanging on a wire hanger and she gave it to me to put on instead of my sweaty shirt.

She marched me downstairs and I didn't know whether I was going to get paid or get fired, even though I hadn't done anything except the job that Jack Tannen told me to do. I think it was Tannen, anyhow.

When we got back downstairs it was dark outside. There was a heavy snowfall coming down. I'd lost all track of time while I was moving those boxes. The bargain carts had already been moved inside, the last customer was gone, and the store was closed.

The Jacks and David and Alice had a little ritual that they performed every Saturday after closing. Other nights, they just locked up and went to their respective homes. Both Jacks were married men, as was David Garfinkel. None of them had any children, though, and the two Jacks seemed to regard me as a surrogate son, David Garfinkel thought of me as a grandson, and Alice, who was unmarried, seemed to treat me as a talented but mischievous nephew. This was all wonderful for me. My mother had died when I was a little kid and my father had remarried. I didn't get along with my stepmother and life at home was not exactly like *Andy Hardy's Double Life*, even if I did feel as if I was one kid in Brooklyn and another in Manhattan.

On Saturdays after closing, the Jacks and David and Alice would break out a bottle of *schnapps* and some sponge cake and have a little office party. They would talk over the events of the week, pass around any particular treasures that people had come in and sold them, damn the Republicans, talk about Lenin and Stalin and where Stalin had first gone wrong, and share the common gossip of Fourth Avenue.

They had never invited me to stay for their little Saturday night party before. This Saturday, they did. I said I was afraid I'd get in trouble if I stayed out too late. They conferred briefly, then Alice asked for my telephone number and called my house. There was a long conversation. When she finally hung up she shook her head, but she said, "It's okay. You can stay over at my place. I had to promise not to take you to Mass with me in the morning, to send you straight home."

David Garfinkel said, "Here, have some of this." He handed me a plate with a piece of sponge cake on it and a little glass of *schnapps*. "You ever try this before? No? Okay, be careful. Maybe you better not drink it from the glass. Break off a corner of sponge cake, good, dip it in the *schnapps* and try it that way."

The glass was a shot glass, that's what they were all drinking their *schnapps* from.

He watched while I followed instructions.

He said, "Did I ever tell you about *Frank Reade and His Steam-Man of the Plains*? No? Great story, I'll never forget it. Byline was 'Noname' but a Jew named Harold Cohen wrote it, isn't that something? He wrote three or four Frank Reades and then he left and a Cuban named Senarens took it over. You can have your E. E. Smiths and your Jack Williamsons, there was never anybody who could write science fiction like Harold Cohen."

I don't suppose that *schnapps* was any stronger than any other liquor, but remember that I was a twelve-year-old boy, I'd never even tasted alcohol before, I'd been working hard moving boxes all afternoon, and all I'd had to eat was a few chunks of sponge cake dipped in *schnapps*.

After a little while I think I got woozy, and maybe a little bit drowsy, too. Next thing I knew one of the Jacks was asking me, "What's this?"

He was holding the manila envelope. I must have brought it downstairs with me after my enforced clean-up exercise, and forgot that I had it with me. I told Jack where I had found it. He handed it to the other Jack and said, "Do you recognize this? He found it upstairs." He nodded in my direction when he said that.

The other Jack took the envelope and looked it over. I could see that the back was sealed. Some of those envelopes come with metal clasps, some have two little disks and a string that you wind back and forth to keep them closed, but this one had a plain gummed flap, like a letter-size envelope, and it was sealed shut.

Jack grinned. "I remember this, sure. Did you find this upstairs?"

I said yes.

"What do you think it is?"

I shook my head, or started to, until I realized that it was making me dizzy. So I said, "I don't know what it is."

"Remember, Jack?" he said to the other Jack.

"We got this from that strange guy from Brooklyn."

"Who?"

"What was his name? Dressed like an undertaker. Said he was a big admirer of Poe's."

"Loveman."

"Who?"

"Loveman. Sam Loveman, poet, came from St. Louis, not from Brooklyn."

"Not him. Guy came from Brooklyn, for Christ's sake, not from St. Louis."

"Cool it on the Christ's sake, please." That was Alice Ryter. Fourth Avenue was mostly a Jewish world, for some reason or other, but Alice was a loyal Catholic and she had to stand up for her rights.

"Lovecraft."

"Huh?"

I think everybody was at least a little bit tipsy.

"Howard Lovecraft," David Garfinkel said. "I remember him, a creepy guy, coming through the door." He pointed to the storefront facing onto Fourth Avenue.

"No," one of the Jacks shook his head. "Impossible. That was nineteen twenty—what's the postmark on the envelope?"

The other Jack said, "Nineteen twenty-three."

"See? We were still in the Nineteenth Street store then, he couldn't have come through that door." He pointed. The snow was coming down hard, making drifting halos around streetlights. Once in a while a car would go past, headlights scorching giant white cones in the falling snow.

"It wasn't Lovecraft or Loveman, it was Cornell Woolrich brought that thing in."

"Alice is right," said a Jack. "It was Woolrich. He was trying to be Scott Fitzgerald then, before he started writing for the gangster pulps."

"Pulps killed the dime novels," said David Garfinkel. I thought he was going to cry into his sponge cake when he said it.

Jack said, "As a matter of fact it was John Dickson Carr. Tweedy little dandy with his phony English manners. You'd think he was born on the Sussex Downs. Phony son of a bitch, came from Uniontown fucking Pennsylvania."

"Jack! There's a child present."

Thanks, Alice, I thought, *I needed you to remind him of that.* But I didn't say anything.

"Whoever it was," one of the Jacks said.

"He wanted to sell it to us," the other Jack said.

"What a *goniff*," the first Jack said.

The room got quiet. Alice refilled everybody's glass with *schnapps* except mine, there was still some in my glass. But I leaned over her desk and took another square of sponge cake. Alice reached over to a shelf next to her desk and turned on a radio. I didn't know there was a radio there, until now. She twirled the dial and the radio made weird squealing noises, then she stopped and dance music came on.

David said, "I hate this modern junk, can't you get something decent on there?"

Alice ignored him.

I got up my nerve to ask, "But what was in the envelope?"

"The complete text of *The Lighthouse*," a Jack said.

"What's that?" I asked.

"A Poe story."

I knew all about Poe. *The Pit and the Pendulum, Facts in the Case of M. Valdemar, Murders in the Rue Morgue, The Purloined Letter, The Narrative of Arthur Gordon Pym*. But I'd never heard of *The Lighthouse*. I said, "I never heard of *The Lighthouse*."

"That's because it's the story he was working on when he died. It's only a fragment."

I thought about that for a minute. Then I said, "But you said that was the complete text." I pointed to the manila envelope. It had found its way to Alice's desk by now, and there were a couple of fresh drops of *schnapps* on it, and some sponge cake crumbs.

"That's right," said Jack, "the complete text."

"But you said—"

"Oh, let's don't pick on the kid," David said. I wished I'd had him for a teacher, but he was retired. He was big and strong but he was old. "Tell him the story," David said.

"Okay," said a Jack. "We were on Nineteenth Street then—"

"I don't think so," the other Jack interrupted, "I think we were in this store."

"Look," Jack tapped a square-tipped finger on the manila envelope, "look at the postmark. Nineteen twenty-three. We were still on Nineteenth Street."

"No, I think it was later than that, that postmark doesn't mean anything. It could have been an old envelope that Woolrich had lying around his apartment for years."

"John Dickson Carr."

"Tweedy little runt."

"He needed the money."

"See, it had to be Carr. Woolrich was a millionaire."

"But he lost his money in the Depression."

"That wasn't 'til twenty-nine."

"That's exactly my point. We were on Fourth Avenue by then."

"Damned Republicans. It was Hoover's fault. If FDR hadn't come along to save this country—" David wiped a tear with a paper napkin.

"See, so it was Loveman after all."

"Lovecraft."

"Where the hell would he have got the Poe? I remember that guy. He loved Poe but he didn't have any money either."

"Nobody did in the Depression."

"He said he had something wonderful to show us." Jack finally got the story rolling. That was Jack Tannen. He'd been a small-time stage actor when he was young, and he still had great stage presence. He said the whole trick was vocal dynamics.

"He said it was something priceless. It was the complete Poe story, *The Lighthouse*."

He paused and looked around, an old acting trick, I guess, to make sure that everybody was paying attention or something.

"I said, 'Of course, *The Lighthouse*, everybody in the world has read that. It's in the 1909 Woodberry book. There are three or four copies in the store. In *Literature*.' But Carr, that little fairy, said—"

"Jack!" It only took one word from Alice to bring him back into line.

"Carr said, 'Yes, everybody knows about the Woodberry fragment but this is *the whole story.*' "

"It wasn't Carr."

"God damn it, Jack, please don't interrupt me. All right, whoever the hell it was, Carr or Woolrich or a person from Porlock—"

"Okay, good, it was a person from Porlock."

Everybody stopped talking, as if by unanimous telepathic agreement, and knocked back their *schnapps,* even me, even though it nearly strangled me and I could feel my face getting hot and red.

Then Jack said, "So I figured I'd humor this pathetic nobody. I said, 'How much do you want for the complete *Lighthouse?*' and he said, 'Fifty dollars,' and I kept a straight face and said, 'All right, let's have a look at it.' "

Alice Ryter said, "Show it to the boy."

Jack reached over and took the envelope off her desk and took a letter opener and slit the manila envelope and showed me the contents. The thing was about ten or twelve or fifteen pages, typed on onionskin. It started, *Jan. 1—1796. This day—*

Jack took the envelope back and slid the pages inside and handed it to Alice. She put it on her desk, reached under the desk for her purse, and put the purse on top of the envelope. As if an errant wind was going to whip through the store and carry it away.

I said, "Poe died in 1849." I knew that much. "Did they even have typewriters then?"

"No," Jack laughed. "I pointed that out to the fellow and he said, 'Oh, this was typed from Poe's manuscript a few years ago. Around 1910, I think. I knew the person who typed it. He was a descendant of Rufus Griswold's. There were two versions of the manuscript in the Griswold family all those years. The one in Woodberry was just a false start. Poe put it aside and began all over again and wrote the complete story. That's the one that my friend had. He typed it up from Poe's holograph.' "

David said, "Well, at least he knew a few things."

"So I asked him where was the Poe manuscript," Jack continued, "and he said, 'My friend threw it away after he finished typing it up.' "

The building must have been resettling from all the weight I'd shifted that afternoon, because it gave a loud creak right then.

Jack said, "The guy must have been desperate to try a crazy stunt like that, so I told him I couldn't give him fifty dollars for the thing, I could go maybe a dollar, dollar and a half at the most. He came down, I went up, he came down, I went up. Finally I said, two bucks, absolute tops. Take it or leave it."

Okay, there was the envelope, there was the typescript, so obviously the guy took it.

"He said, 'Do me a favor,' " Jack said. " 'I can't sell this for two dollars but if you'll lend me two I'll leave the Poe story with you for security, I'll come back as soon as I can and buy it back from you for the two plus interest.' So I said okay, and I gave him two bucks and he left the manuscript with me but he never came back for it."

"He went home to Porlock," David suggested.

Alice looked pointedly at her watch and said, "It's getting awfully late. I think we'd better call it a day. Or a night. Time to head for home. You boys can sleep late on Sunday, I go to early Mass."

David said, "What about the kid?"

Alice said, "He can sleep on my couch. I'll feed him an early breakfast and send him home safe and sound. That okay with you?" she asked me.

I said, "Sure." Then everybody stood up and put on their coats because of the weather. I said, "Can I read that thing?"

A Jack said, "What thing?"

"*The Lighthouse.*"

Jack hesitated a second, then he shrugged. He was shrugging into his topcoat and I think he was shrugging in answer to my question, too. "Sure, why not, it isn't worth anything."

That was a long time ago. A long, long time ago. Look at me now, would you? You think I'm the same person who moved a few tons of boxes in one afternoon and only worried about getting dirty? White hair, stiff joints, did I ever tell you about how I got my job, working for Biblo and Tannen? Oh, I did. Okay.

I always loved books. I thought I'd wind up working on Fourth

Avenue at Schulte's or Stammer's or Eureka Bookshop or the Raven Bookshop. Come to think of it, I wonder why that poor guy didn't sell his Poe item to the Raven. Maybe he tried and they wouldn't take it. Jack only took it because he felt sorry for the guy. He never thought he'd come back for his piece of junk. And he never did. Did I mention that? He took the two dollars and said he'd come back for his typescript but he never showed his face at Biblo and Tannen again.

Yes, I thought I'd wind up a bookman, maybe I'd quit school and work for Biblo and Tannen full time. That would teach that wicked witch of a stepmother a lesson. But I'd miss my brother. But if I could do that, maybe they'd let me sleep in the store, I could sleep upstairs in the overstock room, and maybe someday they'd make me a partner or I could even start my own bookstore.

It didn't happen that way. I guess I just wasn't brave enough to go out on my own. After all, I was only twelve. So I was *bar mitzvah* and I finished high school and I went to Columbia the same as Cornell Woolrich only I didn't drop out, I finished my degree and spent a few years in the Army and then I got out and became a writer.

Oh, it's been a long life. I've written a whole shelf of novels. Plus a few screenplays, a bunch of short stories, some essays and books of what I like to call cultural history, literary biography and criticism. Biblo and Tannen would call it *Literature*.

That night we got to Alice Ryter's apartment and she made up a bed for me on the couch and gave me a cup of cocoa to drink before I went to sleep. I wish she'd been my stepmother instead of the woman my father married. I asked if I could stay up and read the Poe story and she said sure, why not, it can't do you any harm.

I turned on a standing lamp and sat on the couch with my feet up and pulled the blankets around myself. I took the typescript out of the envelope and started to read.

Jan. 1—1796. This day—my first on the light-house—I make this entry in my Diary, as agreed on with De Grät. As regularly as I can keep the journal, I will—but there is no telling what may happen to a man all alone as I am—I may get sick, or worse . . . .So far well!

The story went on from there, a wild adventure about the

narrator, *oy!* I can almost remember his name, it's on the tip of my tongue. It'll come back, don't worry.

There was something lurking in the underground foundation of the lighthouse and people hiding out from a place called Norland. There was a wonderful dog in the story, too, named Neptune. Why can I remember the dog's name and not the man's? Anyhow, Neptune was big and friendly and nothing like the spoiled, pampered creature that my stepmother brought with her when she married my father. And there was something about an "aerial caravel" piloted by De Grät. I'm sure I finished reading it before I fell asleep.

In the morning Alice woke me up and gave me breakfast. I said I had a headache and she laughed at me and said, "Your first hangover, congratulations." She sent me home. I left the Poe story next to the couch.

Nineteen-fifty, the spring was beautiful. David Garfinkel came to work, spent the morning sitting in his chair, went out to lunch, came back, sat down in his chair, put his chin down on his chest, and died. Died in a bookshop. I think I'd like to go that way, not lying in a hospital bed with needles in my arms and tubes up my nose.

Jack Tannen retired to Florida, couldn't stand the boredom, and became curator of a rare-books collection for the rest of his life.

Alice Ryter moved to Los Angeles to care for her aged mother and go to Mass without having to worry about snow and ice. She lived to a ripe old age.

Jack Biblo was the last to go. He was well past ninety, still buying and selling used books, bless his soul. He was more of a father to me than my father ever was.

I know what Heaven is going to look like. When my time comes, if I pass muster with Saint Peter, he'll point the way for me. I'll push open the front door at 63 Fourth Avenue and there will be both Jacks and David and Alice and a building filled with thousands and thousands of old books. I'll walk in and one of the Jacks will say, "Come on, kid, where have you been? There's work to be done." But then David will grab me and ask, "Did I ever tell you about those great dime novel detectives, Old Sleuth and Young Sleuth? They were wonderful."

Then Jack would interrupt. "Never mind all that. Here's here to work, not to talk about all that nonsense."

Alice Ryter will be there, and she'll say, "Leave the boy alone, can't you? For heaven's sake, he's only twelve years old. How can be in two places at once?"

And it will be like that, forever.

Did I tell you that Jack Biblo was the last to go? I repeat myself these days, I know. It goes with the white hair and the stiff joints. Jack was still married, and when he died his wife, Frances, telephoned me to tell me the news. I said I was so sorry, and I was sorry that I hadn't stayed in touch all those years, and she said it was all right, they'd always followed my career and were always proud of me and told their friends that they'd helped me get my start with books when I was twelve years old.

We had a nice talk. I'm afraid I cried more than Frances did. I didn't want to hang up, I felt that there was still a link there and once I hung up it would be gone, all gone, all dead. But finally I told Frances that I loved her and Jack and she said she knew that, she'd always known that, and thank you for saying it at last.

I wiped my eyes. I felt like a fool. My turn is coming soon. I thought about all those good times, and I smiled when I remembered moving those heavy boxes and the famous *schnapps* party and sleeping on Alice Ryter's couch. I remembered the Poe story, as much of it as I could. Was it real? Was it really all Poe, or did one of those others complete Poe's fragment and try to pass it off as a great find?

But what if he had? What if the version of *The Lighthouse* that I read at Alice Ryter's place was a collaboration, was part Poe and part Cornell Woolrich or part Poe and part Samuel Loveman or Lovecraft or John Dickson Carr?

Idle speculation. Idle speculation. I stood up slowly—stiff joints, you know—and found the battered *Complete Poe* set on my shelf and pulled down the volume of short stories. Yes, there was *The Lighthouse*, the fragment, the same fragment that Woodberry first published in 1909.

I started to read. *Jan. 1—1796. This day—*

I read to the end of the fragment and then I tried to remember the rest of the story, the version I had read, wrapped up in a blanket, woozy from my first encounter with alcohol, sitting on Alice Ryter's sofa.

There was something about an underground room and something about a flying machine. I remembered imagining that I was there with De Grät and the narrator, I can almost remember his name, and there were clouds around us. What was that fellow's name? I can almost remember it . . .

You may or may not be familiar with *Publishers Weekly,* a very important trade journal that keeps people in the book business informed as to trends and events in our world. *PW,* as it is familiarly known, also carries many book reviews and/or previews.

Some years ago I got a real thrill when I picked up a new copy of *PW* and discovered that I'd rated two reviews in its columns, one for a collection of short stories called *Before 12:01 and After* and the other for a collection of essays called *Writer at Large.*

While both reviews were favorable—good for the ego and eventually for the royalty reports!—*PW*'s reviewer made a most intriguing remark. The reviewer said that my rather folksy narrative style carried over from my essays to my stories until it became difficult to tell memoir from fable.

I recite this incident as a warning to the reader. The following piece, "Sergeant Ghost," is actually and literally true. Every last word of it. So why is it included in a fiction collection? I suppose, because people who have read it in manuscript insist that it can't possibly be true. "It's a fun read," I keep hearing, "but you must be making this up!"

Dear Reader: You don't have to believe this story if you don't want to. It's perfectly okay with me!

Sergeant Ghost

The trouble with most ghost stories is this: the experiences the narrator describes are purely subjective. Your friend Mabel MacGillicuddy collars you and says, "I had a supernatural experience last night. I woke up in my darkened room and felt a chill in the air. I looked around and saw a glowing figure. It looked like my dead ancestor, Lady Clarissa Chalmondley. The figure raised its shrouded arm and pointed a skeletal finger at me and said, 'Beware, beware, your fate awaits you, you are going to die!' Then Lady Chalmondley floated through the wall and was gone."

Well, of course we're all going to die sooner or later, so forget about that. But what about the chill, the glowing figure, the frightening message? Nobody can deny that Mabel actually felt and saw and heard everything that she claims. But also, Mabel can't prove that it really happened, either. So what do we do with it? I guess we just write it off as an intriguing unexplained event and go on with our business.

But this is *my* ghost story, and I can prove that it's true. Stick around for a while and hear the story, and then I'll show you the proof.

But—where to start? When to start?

How about Fort Benning, Georgia, summer of 1954. I was a very young soldier, just a teenager, going through basic training at the US Army Infantry School.

Up at the crack of dawn—sometimes earlier. Calisthenics, hearty breakfast, cleaning barracks, field exercises, map-reading courses, weapons training. After a while I could take apart an M-1 rifle and put it back together blindfolded, as could all my fellow trainees.

The Cold War was in full swing. Some historical revisionists have denied the reality of the challenge of those days, but we took it seriously. We trained against mock units wearing Soviet army uniforms, carrying Soviet weapons, and speaking Russian.

We had a lot of instructors, but the one I remember most vividly was Sergeant John R. Tessein.

Sergeant Tessein had served in the Second World War. During

the Battle of the Bulge, ten years before I encountered him, he had been severely wounded. A piece of shrapnel had torn a gash in his forehead. More seriously, he had been struck in the chest by a chunk of flying metal and very nearly killed.

Evacuated to a hospital in France, then to a rehabilitation facility in England, he had recovered miraculously from his injuries. The gash in his forehead healed, leaving a scar that turned crimson when he was stressed. The chest wound nearly did him in. He lost one lung. He was thus condemned to a lifetime of limited breath.

He was offered a promotion, a medal, an honorable discharge from the army, and a lifetime pension. But Corporal Johnny Tessein loved the army. He told his superiors that he was happy to accept the promotion and the medal, but he didn't want the honorable discharge or the pension. He wanted to stay in the army.

Over the months that followed he fought the military bureaucracy to a standstill. He finally got what he wanted. He was permitted to stay in the army. But there was one proviso: he would never again be certified as combat-qualified. He could serve at desk jobs, as a recruit trainer, work in a weapons depot or a motor pool, or in any other capacity. But he would never again see combat.

By the summer of 1954 he had a couple of rockers under his sergeant's chevrons. If you don't know what that means, you could look it up. He was assigned to duty as a recruit trainer at Fort Benning.

Most such noncommissioned officers are known for getting pretty tough with recruits who fail to perform as required. Oh, you've seen this kind of thing in a zillion movies. Sergeant stands with hands on hips, glaring into face of recruit. Shouts a question. Recruit quails and stammers a reply. Sergeant gets louder. Recruit shakes in his boots. And so on . . .

Not Sergeant Tessein.

If you screwed up, Sergeant Tessein would get a hurt look. He would grow pale. He would start to hyperventilate. His face would become deathly white. The scar on his forehead would begin to glow. He would struggle to pump enough air through his one lung to remain conscious.

His platoon of trainees would stand at attention, terrified lest their drill sergeant drop dead on the spot and they somehow be held responsible for his demise.

In most ways Sergeant Tessein was very old school. In the blazing Georgia sunlight he wore a set of khakis that had been laundered so many times they were almost white. His trousers showed a knife-edge crease. The brass insignia on his shirt-collar were polished to the brightness of miniature suns.

He believed that there were three ways to do anything: the right way, the wrong way, and the Army way. If you were in his platoon you quickly learned the difference and you quickly learned to do things the Army way.

For instance, for bayonet drill he taught us the Army way to fix and unfix bayonets on our M-1 rifles. To fix (attach) the bayonet you placed the butt of the weapon on the ground between your boots, trigger guard away from you, and held the weapon at a 45 degree angle. You held the bayonet by its grip, point upward, and slid it down onto the bayonet lock on your rifle. To unfix the bayonet you reversed this process.

It was easier, Sergeant Tessein explained, to perform these operations with the rifle placed vertically, but that was not the Army way and he'd better not see any of us doing it.

At the end of any lesson, Sergeant Tessein's parting admonition was always, "Don't make me ashamed."

After a while, nobody wanted to make Sergeant Tessein ashamed.

One afternoon we were conducting a bayonet drill and one of my fellow trainees—I'll call him Jimbo Jenkins, not his real name—decided to attach his bayonet to his rifle the easy way rather than the Army way. That worked fine, so at the end of the exercise Jimbo decided to remove his bayonet the easy way rather than the Army way. He stood the weapon on its butt, muzzle (and bayonet) upright, and gave the bayonet a good tug. Propelled by Jimbo's considerable arm strength the bayonet disengaged from the bayonet lock, sped straight up, and plunged into Jimbo's throat.

After that the surviving members of our platoon *really* paid attention to Sergeant Tessein's instructions. Nobody wanted to make him ashamed.

Well, I got through basic all right, had a not-unpleasant career in the peacetime army, actually earned a commission and emerged as an officer. Thence to my civilian, professional life.

Fast forward thirty years or so. Shift the scene to Minneapolis, Minnesota. The occasion is Bouchercon, aka the World Mystery Convention. Along with a couple thousand other mystery writers, readers, and collectors, I'm in town with my Beloved Spouse to see old friends, have a pleasant time, and maybe transact a little business.

One of my editors, Dennis Weiler, is at the convention and has decided that it would be fun and instructive for some of us to get in a little weapons experience. Dennis called for volunteers and dozen or so conventioneers piled aboard a rented van for a magical mystery tour. I was one of them. Beloved Spouse was another.

As the bus rolled through the lovely Minnesota countryside Dennis lectured us on the history and technology of the Thompson caliber .45 submachine gun, familiarly known as the Tommy Gun.

By the time Dennis's lecture concluded the van rolled up to an unobtrusive, low, gray building. Everyone piled out of the van and followed Dennis into the building.

It was a weapons firing range. I knew about these places from my army experience, and this one was well laid out and activities there were meticulously conducted. Safety was a prime concern.

While most persons who used the range for target practice brought their own weapons, the range could also provide rental weapons on an hourly basis. The range owned a Tommy gun in pristine condition. They even paid the federal license fee—reputedly $5,000 a year!—for the right to maintain the weapon as originally built, not modified to prevent its being fired on full automatic.

Dennis announced that each of us would be permitted to buy a magazine of ammunition and participate in target practice. Of course my macho rose and I quickly joined the party. We were offered a choice of targets including a traditional bull's-eye or an alternate version depicting a murderous fiend threatening the life

of an innocent victim. The idea was to "shoot" the fiend without harming his victim.

A word about the Tommy gun.

With the exception of special arms such as sniper's rifles, most modern military weapons are designed for lightness and rapid rate of fire. They're stamped out of light metal and plastic and they aren't expected to have a long service life. The term for their use is "area fire."

Back in the day this was not the case. The M-1 Garand that I used at Fort Benning was a carefully crafted weapon with a heavy wooden stock and a heavier steel barrel and action. It weighed nine-and-a-half pounds and when you fired it, it kicked. It kicked pretty hard.

Sergeant Tessein taught us how to deal with that kick. "Think of the weapon as your sweetheart," Sergeant Tessein told us. "Hold the butt plate tightly to your shoulder. Press your cheek snugly against the stock. Draw a deep breath, then let half of it out, hold your breath briefly as you gently squeeze the trigger and you won't even know when the weapon is about to fire. You'll feel a hard thump on your shoulder but it won't really hurt and you won't be injured."

Fair enough.

"Don't be afraid of the weapon," Sergeant Tessein went on. "If you hold it away from your face and your shoulder, then the kick will hit you hard. I've seen men with black eyes, cracked cheek bones and broken collar bones because they wouldn't follow my advice about holding the M-1."

Everybody remembered the bayonet incident, so everybody paid attention to Sergeant Tessein's lecture on holding the rifle. No black eyes. No broken bones.

The Tommy gun—still in production, believe it or not! —is very much an old school weapon. It's made of beautifully polished wood, I believe walnut, and carefully machined steel. It's heavy—weighs almost 20 pounds, twice the weight of the Garand rifle. And it fires a .45 caliber round. That's a bullet with a diameter of nearly half an inch. That round packs a hell of a wallop. But, surprisingly, the weapon hardly kicks at all, although it does tend to climb a little bit under sustained fire.

Well, people in our party took their turns firing the Tommy gun. Dennis announced that there would be prizes for best marksmanship, worst marksmanship, and a couple of other categories.

When my turn came I picked up the weapon and looked it over. I'd selected to fiend-and-victim target. I'd never fired a Tommy gun, hadn't fired any weapon in several decades. Further, my eyesight is not the world's greatest. I wear bifocals and my ophthalmologist had warned me that I had the beginnings of a cataract in my right eye. That's the sighting eye, of course.

I picked up the Tommy gun and sighted on the target. I set the control on safety and dry-fired a couple of rounds just to get the feel of the weapon. When I felt comfortable with it I took off the safety and set the control on single-fire. I sighted in for real, now, and hesitated.

Above me and off to the right I saw a glowing, cloud-like nimbus. I felt—*something*. I looked up and saw a figure in the cloud. It was Sergeant Tessein.

His uniform was spotlessly clean and the creases were as sharp as ever. The brass insignia on his collar, "US" on the right tab and crossed rifles denoting infantry on the other, glistened as brightly as two miniature suns.

"Remember what I told you," Sergeant Tessein urged me in his characteristic, whispery voice. "Treat the weapon like your sweetheart. Take a breath, let out half, hold, squeeze."

I felt that chill. I nodded my understanding.

Sergeant Tessein whispered, "Don't make me ashamed."

I fired one round. Then another. After a few I reset the control to full automatic but continued to fire single rounds just to see if I could do it. I could. I couldn't see the target as well as I'd have liked to. Certainly not as well as I'd seen targets at Fort Benning thirty years before. But I remembered Sergeant Tessein's instruction. I fired a couple of bursts. The weapon performed beautifully.

And then my ammunition was exhausted.

The range officer wound the target in and Dennis and I examined it. Twenty rounds fired. Twenty holes in the fiend. In his head, in his torso. Twenty. His would-be victim was untouched.

I returned the Tommy gun to the range officer, who handed it to the next conventioneer. When we piled onto the van to return to the convention hotel I had my prize—a little enamel bull's-eye—pinned to my jacket.

A couple of the other conventioneers complained about my winning the prize. "You were in the army," someone whined, "that isn't fair."

"Thirty years ago?" I responded. "Nineteen fifty-four? Where were you in 1954? Where were your *parents* in 1954?"

The complaints stopped. Beloved Spouse, I knew, was proud of me.

And that's my ghost story.

A while ago I said that most ghost stories are intriguing but they rely on purely subjective reports. Not so my ghost story. I know I saw Sergeant Tessein. I have the target to prove it, initialed by Dennis Weiler to prove that it's authentic. I'll be happy to show it to you if you'd like to see it.

"The Law" was written at the request of Marty Halpern for a proposed anthology. As far as I can recall, it's the only "first contact" story I've ever written. Marty complimented me on the story but I never received a formal acceptance and I don't know what became of the anthology. One of the many mysteries of the publishing world. I have a sneaky feeling that the editors wound up with too many stories and that mine was simply squeezed out. Or maybe not.

The Law

When we finally did it the biggest surprise was Who did it, followed in order by Why, How, and anything else you'd care to ask. Of course, some people were surprised that we did it at all, but that's another matter.

We finally settled the answer to the question that anyone with the sense to wonder about such things had been asking for centuries, if not millennia: *Are we alone?*

And the answer—well, before we get to the answer, let's examine the question first, and kick around a handful of ideas. Come on, you have a few minutes to spare, haven't you? If you hadn't, you wouldn't have picked up this book or magazine or logged onto this website or wherever the heck you're reading these pages. Or screens, or pixels, or whatever.

If we treated the thing like some high school debate we'd have started out with something like, *Resolved, that there are other species than humankind in the universe, who are intelligent, civilized, and technologically advanced.*

The argument proffered by the affirmative side would be essentially mathematical. The scratchy-voiced boy in the ill-fitting hounds-tooth jacket would say, "We know that there are billions of stars in our galaxy. We know that there are billions of galaxies in the known universe. And beyond that we can only speculate upon the possibilities of other universes in other dimensions. There are trillions, quadrillions of stars. And we are learning that most stars have planets circling them. The number of worlds upon which life may exist is therefore not only huge, it's gigantic—titanic—incalculable—mind-boggling. If only one planet out of a thousand—a million—pick your number—has life on it, and only one such planet out of a million that has life, achieves intelligence and technology—it's inevitable that there will be huge numbers of technologically advanced civilizations."

Thus would argue the debater taking the affirmative side.

The debater taking the negative—let's imagine an attractive young lady garbed in a short-sleeved sweater and modish skirt—would say something like this, "All of those numbers of stars and galaxies and dimensions and other ideas out of a science fiction television series are very impressive. But if the universe is really teeming with little green men and purple octopus people and intelligent rose-bushes and all the other weird races that those writers dream up, then *Where is everybody?* Why hasn't the proverbial flying saucer ever landed on the White House lawn? As the great Dr. Carl Sagan once said, building upon the argument of the philosopher David Hume, 'Extraordinary claims require extraordinary evidence,' and the evidence for life anywhere but here on Earth is simply absent."

And the kids would resume their seats and make eye contact with each other while the judges conferred and eventually one team would go home with a genuine simulated gold loving cup and the other team would go home with a bucket of sour grapes.

That is, until we did it.

"We" being, actually, a self-styled psychic who used the professional name of Madame Olga. She lived in a modest home on Marwood Drive in Arcata, California, a onetime logging town in the northern end of that state. Once a thriving logging community, Arcata now sustains itself as the home of Humboldt State University and the center of a large and prosperous agricultural community, the chief crop of which is cannabis sativa.

Now, about Madame Olga.

Olga was her name. Really. Olga Smith, believe it or not. She had started life in Wheaton, Illinois, a conservative community whose customs and values bear a greater resemblance to those of the Bible Belt several hundred miles to the south than to those of Chicago, the sprawling, brawling, brilliant city a few miles to the east.

One of some seven children of assorted genders and temperaments in the Smith family, Olga had taken leave of her relatives and her home town at the earliest available opportunity. She was able to hitch-hike to the West Coast, spent time in Los Angeles, San Francisco, Seattle, and both Vancouvers before a friendly middle-aged marijuana farmer gave her a ride in his ancient Toyota Forerunner, planted an avuncular smooch on her pretty cheek, and let her out on the main street of Arcata.

Olga might not have liked the straight-laced lifestyle of

Wheaton, Illinois or the bustling big-city pace of Chicago or Los Angeles, but she was a sociable young woman who made friends easily. She soon had a job waiting tables in a café that catered mostly to college students, and a room in a pleasant Victorian home that had survived the exigencies of more than a century of fog, rain, occasional snowfall, and earthquakes of varying degrees of severity.

Once she'd established California residency she enrolled at Humboldt State, trying out a variety of courses that appealed to her intelligent mind and her variegated interests. She had always been interested in off-beat theories and unconventional philosophies, and wound up absorbing any number of books on reincarnation, Tarot, palm reading, automatic writing, the *I Ching*, Theosophy, telepathy, human auras and the Akashic Records.

Before long she was conducting informal seminars of her own on these esoteric subjects. Friends would assemble in her rented room in the evening and ask her to deliver lectures. Olga found herself concentrating more intensely on these topics of her personal quest than the subjects she was officially studying at Humboldt State.

One thing that her parents had taught, and that Olga did absorb, was the idea that one finished what one started. The Smiths—the Wheaton Smiths—weren't quitters and they didn't like quitters and they taught their children not to be quitters.

So Olga slogged on through four not-unpleasant years in the classroom while waiting tables in the afternoon and conducting her own unofficial classes in the evening. It was a busy life, but a good one. She managed to earn a bachelor's degree with a major in art. Her grades were good but definitely unspectacular. Her senior advisor, a kind-hearted former editorial cartoonist for the San Francisco *Chronicle* who had been downsized into involuntary retirement and semi-rustication, invited her in for a farewell conference.

"You have some talent," Olga was told. "A nice sense of composition, and your renderings are clear. But commercial art is an overcrowded field and the odds against your achieving success are daunting."

Olga thanked her adviser and took her leave. And then she set up in business for herself. Not as an artist, although she still kept sketch pads handy and drew to amuse herself.

She was not a pretentious person. At first she was plain Olga Smith, and she conducted study groups in various esoteric doctrines. She was an interesting lecturer as well as a pleasant and personable individual, and people were quite willing to pay modest tuition fees to enroll in her informal academy.

She also offered personal sessions in such specialized subjects as interested her students. She could read Tarot cards or palms with equal facility. She yielded to suggestions that she obtain a crystal ball as an aid to concentration. For this purpose she consulted an online catalog and selected an inexpensive battery-powered, self-illuminating snow globe that purported to show a scene of the Primal Atom exploding to give birth to the entire sidereal universe. Olga thought it looked like a miniaturized fireworks display, but she liked it.

How plain Olga Smith became Madame Olga isn't much of a story, either. Students—now they were more like clients—started calling her Madame. They seemed to expect her to dress in exotic robes, too, and being an accommodating soul she found a fabric store in town, bought some prints with an astronomical theme, apparently intended for use as children's bedspreads, and made herself a variety of robes and gowns. She even discovered a website that purported to show how to knot a turban and practiced until she was actually quite good at it.

She never made any special claims and she didn't advertise in the local weekly. A reporter for that publication, the Arcata *Argus*, had been a classmate of hers at Humboldt State. The ex-classmate, one Robyn Marten, familiarly known as Birdie, came by Olga's new home one day—Olga had moved from her single rented room into a small house—and suggested doing a feature story for the *Argus*. Olga yielded to some friendly persuasion and the next week's edition of the *Argus* ran a flattering article on Arcata's most famous (and only) psychic. There were even a couple of photos of Olga in her robe and turban, looking suitably exotic and yet very attractive.

Some quirk caused an internet news service to pick up the story, and one of Olga's siblings still living with Mom and Dad in Wheaton, Illinois, stumbled over it while web-browsing. This was

Olga's younger brother, Milton, an inveterate role-playing gamer. He emailed Olga and asked if she was all right and if he could come and live with her as soon as he was of age. She wrote back that she was doing just fine and Milton could come and use her spare room any time he wanted.

By this time you have inferred that Olga had a strong individualistic streak. This applied to many aspects of her life including her taste in music. Her friends were mostly divided into three or four groups when it came to music. There were the rockers, who were looked down upon by the jazz buffs, who were looked down upon by the classical music lovers. That's three, isn't it? Well, the fourth group was the people who just weren't very interested, and as the Romans used to say, *De gustibus non est disputandum*, loosely translated as "Whatever turns you on," and if life on this planet teaches us anything, it's that there's no arguing with that idea.

If you had to put Olga in one of those three or four groups, she would probably fit in best with the classics-lovers. But of course those were divided as to their favorite era, style, and composer. They were a sizable and eclectic crowd and various among them championed Mozart, Beethoven, Bach—and Dmitri Shostakovitch and Philip Glass and Charles Ives and—well, you get the point.

Olga Smith—Madame Olga—used to play recorded music ever so softly during her psychic sessions. And her chief favorite was the Danish-born organist and composer of music for keyboard and voice, Dietrich Buxtehude. Asked what had first attracted her to Herr Buxtehude she quite candidly admitted that it was his interesting name. She'd never heard of a Buxtehude before, she had no idea what the word meant—if anything—but her curiosity had been piqued. She sought out a sampling of his works and decided that, funny name or no, this was the composer for her.

She even researched Buxtehude and discovered that—at least according to musical folklore—the young Johann Sebastian Bach had walked several hundred miles to study organ technique with the master, Dietrich Buxtehude.

Our Olga may or may not have been a phony. After all, what percentage of self-styled psychics, palm readers, crystal gazers, trance mediums, tea-leaf interpreters, mind readers, or spirit channelers do you think actually have supernatural powers? Maybe, oh, zero?

But Olga used to sit in front of that crystal ball with the explosion of the Primal Atom eternally taking place in its center, darken the room, set a couple of sticks of incense going, turn on some Buxtehude music—her very favorite piece was the *Suite for Harpsichord in G Minor*—and go into a trance. There are such things as trances, and you don't have to believe in supernatural forces to believe in trances, or even to have a trance experience.

When the stars are right, or whatever.

And sometimes Olga would feel herself slowly sinking into a state that was neither conscious nor unconscious, as we usually think of those conditions. George Ivanovich Gurdjieff—genius or scoundrel or both, this is not the place to debate that very colorful oddball—would have loved to hear about this. Sometimes Olga would simply fall asleep, and have strange dreams of drifting in formless realms of color and sound, herself bodiless, her reality utterly bereft of physical objects. Sometimes she would feel that she had entered that crystal ball and become one with the Primal Atom and consequently one with the entire sidereal universe.

She would describe these experiences to her closest friends, to her onetime classmate, Birdie, who wrote for the Arcata *Argus*, or to her brother, Milton, who by now had followed his sister's example and made his way to the West Coast and was happily settled in her spare room, waiting out a residency requirement before enrolling at Humboldt State. Sometimes Olga would describe her dreams to her boyfriend.

Oh, about Olga's boyfriend. His name was Walter Macintosh and he sometimes claimed that the computer of the same name was so-called in recognition of his having given the basic design to the Apple Computer Corporation in the interest of promoting the public good. Nobody believed him.

Now here is where the Law comes into the story. Surely you've been wondering why this story is called "The Law." Your patience is appreciated, and it is about to be rewarded. The Law to which the title refers is the famous Law of Unintended Consequences.

You know, Henry Ford invents the Model T to furnish cheap,

reliable transportation for the American family. And in order to get very, very rich, of course. Well, he succeeded at both. But he also provided a means for young swains and the objects of their affections to get out from under the watchful eyes of Mama and Papa and go off by themselves, thereby sparking the greatest change in courting rituals in several centuries and leading, in due course, to the Sexual Revolution.

Law of Unintended Consequences, you see?

Ready for another one?

Okay. At the height of the Cold War some geniuses in the Pentagon and their colleagues in Cambridge, Massachusetts, and Palo Alto, California, get worried about staying in touch under nasty conditions such as a nuclear attack. They invent something called ARPANet or DARPANet—never mind those crazy acronyms—which evolves into the Internet.

Voila!

Next thing you know—well, actually it took several decades—you've got people buying and selling things from their desktop computers, billions of emails zipping around the globe at every hour of the day and night, tens of thousands of brick-and-mortar stores going out of business, the postal service yanking your corner mailbox out by the roots because nobody uses it any more, and—well, you see?

Law of Unintended Consequences.

Well, back to Miss Olga Smith, aka Madame Olga, the greatest (and only) psychic in Arcata, California.

Olga had got into this esoteric realm because she thought it was colorful and interesting. She didn't believe there was anything to it, at first, and in her seminars she treated the material as she would have taught the religious system of the Incas or the phlogiston theory of combustion. That is, not as something one did or did not adhere to, but purely as a complex and ingenious system of belief.

After a while, though, she found herself becoming increasingly curious and even drawn to some of her subject matter. Most of it was obviously superstition. Finding a four-leaf clover did not mean that you would get the much-coveted promotion you were hoping for or win the lottery or sell your novel—at last—after shopping it around for the past decade or so. But—was there something going on, something, however obscure and hard to figure out, that was hidden behind the mumbo-jumbo and the colorful trappings of these esoteric systems?

On the day in question, Olga Smith shut herself in what she had come to think of as her "trance room." She had no other obligations that day. She dimmed the lights, turned on her favorite Buxtehude composition, and touched a match to a couple of sticks of incense and set them in a brass holder. Now she turned off the lights altogether, set her elbows on the table in front of her, pressed her fingertips to her forehead, and leaned over the crystal ball with the self-illuminating representation of the Primal Atom—some glass artist's concept of the Primal Atom, anyway—and let herself relax, thoroughly and completely.

A couple of hours later Olga's boyfriend, Walter Macintosh, showed up with a six-pack of ice-cold Cerveza Negra Modelo and a bag of sandwiches. Olga's brother, Milton, opened the door for Walter and Walter strolled in.

It was a perfect summer's afternoon in Arcata. The sky was clear and the sun was bright but a pleasant breeze had swept inland from the Pacific, carrying with it a touch of fog and just enough moisture and cool air to make everyone comfortable.

"I thought I'd invite Olga for a little picnic," Walter Macintosh announced. "You could come along, too, Milton."

"Olga's busy," Milton replied.

"Client session?"

"Nope. She's just working on her stuff."

"By stuff, you mean stuff and nonsense, don't you?"

Actually the word Walter used was not "nonsense" but "nonsense" will have to do. Walter was quite a skeptic when it came to psychic phenomena, second sight, UFOs and the like.

"Whatever you want to call it," Milton said.

"How long she been at it?" Walter asked.

Milton looked at his wristwatch. "Wow, didn't realize how late it was getting to be. She's been in there since lunchtime. Four, five hours, easy."

Walter didn't bandy any more words than that. He slammed open the door of Olga's trance room and barged in, turning on the lights as he did so.

Milton followed. He pulled back the draperies—they were made of a fabric with the same astronomical pattern as Olga's gown and turban—and let in the daylight.

Olga sat slumped over her table, the Primal Atom snow globe beside her face. Her eyes were closed. Her breathing was slow and steady. Walter laid his hand across her forehead and nodded in relief. He grasped her wrist and took her pulse—he was no medic but he knew how to do that—and told Milton that his sister's heart rate was normal, steady, and strong.

Apparently there was nothing wrong with Olga.

Walter and Milton helped her to sit up. She blinked, a puzzled expression on her face, then smiled and greeted her boyfriend and her brother.

Leaning on their arms to steady herself, she stood up. She looked at her desk and said, "What's this?"

By *this* she referred to a sketch pad and Ticonderoga Number One pencil that lay near the Primal Atom snow globe. On the top sheet of the pad there was a drawing of a jagged landscape. Tall rocks rose into a black sky studded with uncounted stars. In the distance, so small as to be almost indiscernible, stood what seemed to be a city. If city was the right term. The image was tiny. Either the city was very far from the viewpoint of the artist or it was a very, very, very small city. There was no way of telling.

Olga held the sketch pad and gazed at the picture. "I was there," she said.

"Did you draw that?" her boyfriend, Walter, asked.

Olga shrugged her shoulders. "I don't know. I don't remember drawing it."

"But you said you were there," her brother Milton put in.

"I was."

Walter said, "You must have fallen asleep. You were sleeping a minute ago. Do you think you could have made the drawing from a dream?"

Olga shook her head. "I wasn't dreaming."

Walter and Milton waited for her to continue.

"At least, I don't think I was dreaming. I mean—it was so real. I was there. The heavens, the sky, it was beautiful. I've never seen so many stars at once. It was as if—as if I was standing in a cluster of stars close to the center of the galaxy."

"If you were there you would have been gobbled up by a black hole," Milton said.

"Well—" Olga shrugged "—well, whatever happened. It was fun. Even if it was just a dream. Even if I drew that picture in my sleep."

She dropped the sketch pad on her desk. She turned to her boyfriend and smiled. "Did you say a picnic? Sandwiches and brew? Sounds great to me."

And that would have been the end of the matter if Olga hadn't made another drawing a few days later. Again, the scene was an alien world. Again, the rocks rose jaggedly to tower overhead. Again, there was a city. This time the city was closer and you could make out the buildings a little bit. They were strange. If you'd studied non-Euclidean geometry you might be able to make heads or tails of them. And there appeared to be figures moving among the buildings.

A few days later, wearing her plain Olga Smith outfit of blue jeans and Humboldt State Lumberjacks sweatshirt, Olga dropped in at the café where she had once waited tables. She ordered a latté and a Danish pastry and she was quietly enjoying her snack when Robyn Marten appeared and asked if she felt like company.

Olga said, "Sure, take a load off."

They exchanged small talk for a while and Olga mentioned her odd dream drawings. Robyn asked if Olga ever participated in the scenes she drew. Did she walk around? Did she pick things up and examine them? Did she ever visit the distant city or talk with its inhabitants?

No to everything. She just saw what she drew. Drew what she saw. Whichever.

But that set Olga to thinking. She had a class on her schedule that night, and when her students arrived she set out a bowl of fresh fruit and served clear herb tea and talked about automatic writing. Everybody from William Shakespeare to Helena Blavatsky to Margaret Mitchell to Mickey Spillane, it seemed, had dictated important works from the Other Side of the Great Divide. Alas, none of these had stood up to the scrutiny of scholars and critics, but maybe there was something to it. Who knew?

Madame Olga—turbaned and be-robed now—gave some hints about placing oneself in a receptive state, opening one's mind to the departed author, and attempting to achieve a creative trance. Oh, and keep a supply or pencils and paper handy.

One student asked if anybody had ever achieved automatic writing on a typewriter or computer keyboard or dictating machine. Madame Olga intoned that all things were possible. Why not give it a try?

After the students had finished their tea and fruit and departed for the evening, Olga decided to give it a try herself. She laid out not merely a pad and pencils but a set of pastels on her desk, drew the curtains of her trance room (even though it was night) and sat staring into the Primal Atom.

When she awakened she tried to sort out the dreams she had had during the night. She drew back the curtains. It was broad daylight. Her mind was filled with a jumble of images. Strange scenes, not merely of the dream world she had previously drawn but of one world after another. Worlds of water. Worlds of swirling gases. Worlds of endlessly cascading rocks. Worlds of glaciers and worlds of endless storms.

Every world she had dreamed of was inhabited.

She dreamed of creatures living on asteroids, tumbling endlessly in their progression around single suns and double stars and complex groups of stars that danced endlessly around one another. She dreamed of creatures of immeasurably fine gas, swirling endlessly and consciously, definitely consciously, in the incredibly thin and cold vacuum between the galaxies. Some of them were suggestive of sea creatures. Some might have been intelligent plants that communicated with complex sequences and blends of pheromones. Or maybe not.

She knew their thoughts, and their thoughts were beautiful. And ineffable.

Did she believe that all this was real? Well, it's about time to reveal the fact that the neatly dressed teen-aged girl who took the negative side in the high school debate in Wheaton, Illinois, was none other than Olga Smith.

Sometimes skeptics snap and become fanatical believers. Or vice versa. That didn't happen with Olga. She just went from total disbelief to a kind of mild agnosticism to—well, how could she deny her own experience?

And she had used the pastels. In a single night she had covered page after page of her sketch pad with colorful drawings of alien scenes and alien cities and, most notably of all, alien beings. They weren't little green men or hairless humanoids with shiny oblong eyes or any of the familiar images of aliens.

They were totally unlike one another and they were totally unlike human beings.

Olga phoned her friend Robyn Marten. Robyn came over to Olga's house and looked at the pictures. They were remarkable, Robyn announced. She was something of a science fiction buff, had a shelf of paperbacks in her apartment, followed several TV series and tried to catch every science fiction film that reached either the big or small screen, no matter how bad it might be. She called it her guilty pleasure.

Robyn looked over Olga's drawings. By now there were enough of them to fill a portfolio. The black-and-white images were the earliest ones, and were mostly landscapes. The more recent ones placed greater emphasis on alien life forms. Robyn was fascinated. She asked Olga if she might make copies of them with her digital camera, some with the artist in the picture as well, wearing her full Madame Olga regalia.

With the images she'd snapped, Robyn wrote up a feature and got in touch with a friend of hers, a CNN stringer, who came out to Olga's house and shot a feature story for the World's Most Trusted News Source. The Arcata *Argus* ran Robyn's story on page one, complete with a particularly intriguing pastel of a creature that seemed to be made of varicolored ice cubes.

The day after the story ran on CNN (and in the Arcata *Argus*) Olga had a phone call from a NASA scientist at the Ames Research Center in Mountain View, California. He invited Olga to pack up her drawings and come to visit the NASA installation in Mountain View, a community just south of San Francisco, all expenses paid, of course.

Olga declined the invitation, but told the scientist he was

welcome to visit her in Arcata if he wished. He accepted the invitation.

His name was Jaskaran Singh, D.Sc., Ph.D. He drove an all-electric modified Toyota Prius and wore a turban quite different from Olga's and a miniature sword attached to his belt. His English was flawless.

At Dr. Singh's request Olga brought out her portfolio of drawings and permitted her visitor to examine them. He then asked her to describe the experience in which she made the drawings. He nodded understandingly as Olga answered his questions.

Finally, though, Olga had a question for Dr. Singh. She worded it diplomatically but in effect it was, *Why are you interested in my drawings?*

Dr. Singh sorted through the drawings until he found the one he was looking for and laid it on the table. They were sitting in the dining room of Olga's house. Her trance room would have been too cramped for their meeting.

"You see this odd rock configuration?" Dr. Singh asked. He was pointing to a very peculiar formation, something like the intriguing plateaus found in northern Arizona.

Olga said, "I was there."

"You mean, in your dream?"

"Perhaps."

"I don't understand. I thought these were dream images."

Olga said, "I thought so, too, at first. But the experiences are so realistic, I think they may be something more than dreams."

Dr. Singh smiled. "I'm not qualified in psychology, Miss Smith, but I know that dreams can be extremely convincing. Most remarkably so. People sometimes awaken and find themselves confused as to where they are, because they have been elsewhere, as it were, in a very realistic dream."

Olga said, "That might be. But what's so special about this drawing?"

"What you have drawn is an actual rock formation on Mars. We have images from our ground rovers. And I don't think you could have imagined that formation."

"Well, maybe I saw it on TV or in a magazine."

"No. We have millions of images of Mars now, and we try to release only those of the greatest scientific value or general interest to the public. I know this image. I have a printout of it in my car, if you'd like to see it."

"But why is it so important?" Olga asked.

Dr. Singh exhaled and nodded. "For two reasons, Miss Smith. First, that is such an odd formation, I don't understand how you could have made your drawing without seeing it, and yet I don't have any idea how you could have seen it. And second, you have put water in your drawing, clouds in the sky, plant life along the shoreline, and a boat on the water with—with—I'm afraid I'll have call him—if it is a him—a Martian in the boat."

Olga managed a nervous laugh. "Then I guess it was a dream. Even I know there are no lakes on Mars, and certainly no plants or—or—Martians."

Dr. Singh rubbed his jaw. "We're learning a lot about Mars, Miss Smith. We have strong evidence that there was once plenty of water on Mars. Rivers and seas, yes. Percival Lowell and Giovanni Schiapparelli may have been right, and all the skeptics of the past century, wrong. And if you saw what you drew—"

He stopped.

After a while, Olga Smith said, "If I saw what I drew—what, Dr. Singh?"

"I don't know. Astral projection? Second sight? Remote viewing? Conscious time-travel? Each explanation is more far-fetched than the last." After a pause he said, "I wish I could convince you to come back to Mountain View with me. We can assemble a team to try and figure this out. If you are able to travel—or, at any rate, to 'see'—across vast distances of time and space, this could be one of the most amazing tools for research ever discovered."

Long story short, Olga closed up shop in Arcata. Strictly temporarily. She liked that town, she had friends there. She had found a home in Arcata, which she had never done in Wheaton or Chicago or Los Angeles or San Francisco or Seattle or either Vancouver. Walter Macintosh agreed to accompany her to Mountain View. He drove his own car, a lovingly restored 1966 Volvo 544. Olga's brother Milton agreed to stay in the Arcata house until Olga returned.

And in Mountain View, nothing happened. The astronomers were fascinated by Olga's drawings, the psychologists interviewed her endlessly. But nothing happened.

She did meet some interesting and very nice people. The chief headshrinker was the blackest woman she'd ever encountered. Her name was Pamela Snowden. The top mathematician and computer genius looked like a down-on-his-luck professional wrestler badly in need of a shave and a shower. He introduced himself as Biff McGurk. There just happened to be a book lying on a nearby table. Olga read the stamping on the spine. *Inverse Multidimensional Matrix Inversion and Analysis Techniques for Universal Platform Transforms, by Eldon M. J. McGurk, Ph.D., D.Sc.*

Who said that NASA scientists were a humorless bunch?

Olga had brought her Primal Atom snow globe with her, and all of her Dietrich Buxtehude CDs. The NASA people did their best to re-create Olga's trance room, and truth be told they did a remarkably good job of it. They even rounded up some packages of the kind of incense that Olga had used in Arcata.

Nothing happened.

So it was *Thanks very much, Miss Smith,* and *Please stay in touch, Miss Smith,* and *Of course we'll pay all expenses and even give you a consulting fee out of our discretionary budget, Miss Smith,* and Walter Macintosh and Olga Smith rode back from Mountain View to Arcata, California, a picturesque but demanding drive, and Madame Olga was back in business.

But that isn't the end of the story.

Olga and Walter resumed their pleasant lives in Arcata. Milton decided that he wanted to be a software designer and enrolled at Humboldt State. Two more of Olga's siblings, the twins Anna and Hannah, made their way to the West Coast and took up residence in the growing community of Madame Olga's family. They were only kids, eleven years of age, in fact, but the elder Smiths had by now reconciled themselves to Olga's having become the *de facto mater familias* of the Smith demesne.

And Olga continued to play Buxtehude recordings and gaze into her Primal Atom snow globe and produce amazing drawings of exotic scenes and alien beings. She bought a digital camera and took photos of her drawings and sent them to Jaskaran Singh by email.

Things went along tranquilly until the morning Olga's phone rang and an excited Jaskaran Singh told her that she had produced another drawing of a real place. It was Enceladus. Olga said she'd never heard of Enceladus. Dr. Singh said it was one of the moons of Saturn. It was believed to be warmed by tidal forces and to be geologically active.

Olga wasn't sure why Dr. Singh was telling her this.

He said, "You have drawn a picture of a village—I suppose we should call it a village—on Enceladus, and of the inhabitants of that village, who apparently resemble upright bipeds covered with a leafy exoskeleton. And they are looking upward. And in the sky above them you have placed a crewless scientific probe with NASA insignia."

Olga smiled. "That one, I will confess, has to be a dream. Don't you think so?"

"Miss Smith, the probe that you drew has yet to be activated. It's here in Mountain View right now. There's plenty of work still to be done on it. It should be completed and tested within the next year. It's scheduled to be shipped by rail to Florida and launched from Cape Canaveral. And the trip to Saturn—to Enceladus—will take another six years."

Olga held her breath, waiting for Jaskaran Singh to continue.

"It appears, Miss Smith, that you have not only drawn a scene on a world several hundred million miles from Earth. But the event you have drawn will not take place for seven years. It appears that you can see the future."

Dr. Singh definitely sounded breathless.

"Your Martian image was almost certainly of a moment from the remote past. That's remarkable enough. But your image of Enceladus is a vision of the future. That's more than remarkable. It's astonishing. It is going to shake the scientific world to its very foundations."

Olga said, "I hope you're not going to ask me to leave Arcata again."

Dr. Singh said, "No. That was a hard lesson. Your power—I

suppose we have to call it that—your power operates in Arcata but not in Mountain View. But what I would like to do—several of my colleagues and I, members of the team you met when you were here—what we'd like to do is see if anyone else can do the same things you do. And also see which variables have an effect on your performance."

"Variables? What variables?"

"Well, for instance, is the music vital to your visions? Would you have the same experiences in a silent room?"

"I have no idea."

"Nor I. But suppose the choice of music, the selection, had an effect on your power? Would Haydn do as well as Buxtehude? What about, oh, Scarlatti? Or Ralph Vaughan Williams? Do you see what I mean?"

She did.

A week later a van pulled up to Madame Olga's House of Mystery in Arcata, California. Out poured the scientists and technicians and their support crew. Equipment you wouldn't believe, ranging from electroencephalographs to two- and three-dimensional imaging systems, to an array of computers that would set Bill Gates and Steve Jobs to playing rock-paper-scissors for who gets to tinker with them first.

Olga wasn't exactly happy about all this. She'd fled the world of Wheaton, Illinois, because she felt out of place in those surroundings. She'd sampled half a dozen cities from Chicago to Los Angeles to Vancouver (both Vancouvers, right) and not wanted to live in any of them. But if Olga wouldn't come to the big city, it looked as if the big city was coming to Olga, and she didn't care much for it.

She kept her friends in Arcata and she kept her classes going, more because they relaxed her than because she needed her students' fees. Maybe she should move out of Arcata, find a place in a smaller town nearby. Her friend Robyn Marten actually lived in Fickle Hill, and Walter Macintosh had a place in The Bottoms.

But if Olga moved, she knew that Jaskaran Singh and his NASA colleagues would only follow. So she laid down the law about ground rules in Madame Olga's House of Mystery and vowed to make the best of it. She was in favor of science, after all, and if she truly had an unusual, even unique power, she felt that she ought to cooperate with the researchers from Mountain View.

The first experiment involved setting up conditions identical to the ones that had produced her drawings, but without music.

Nothing.

Bach, Mozart, Scarlatti, Hildegard von Bingen. She loved the music. She even had some pleasant dreams. But no drawings.

Okay, bring back Buxtehude.

First try, a beautiful vision of a triple star. Red, white, and blue, no less. Dozens of planets, weaving in an intricate cosmic dance. And objects moving among them that looked more like living beings than artifacts.

Try it without the Primal Atom snow globe.

Nothing.

Try it with a Santa Claus snow globe.

A dream of her childhood in Wheaton, Illinois. Pleasant enough but nothing special about that.

Try it on an empty stomach, try it on an avocado and tomato salad, try it on a glass of wine. Try it with a different brand of incense. Try it with no incense. When one of the Mountain View bigdomes suggested trying it on LSD, Olga refused flat out.

Try it in teams. Olga and Walter, Olga and Milton, Olga and her friend Robyn.

Nix.

Try it with—now here's a concept!—Olga's twin siblings, Anna and Hannah.

Neither twin had shown any particular talent for graphics or any particular interest in drawing or painting. Still Jaskaran Singh thought it would be worth a try. Olga had come to trust Dr. Singh by this time, a feeling that she did not have for most of his colleagues.

Everything was kept as much like Olga's surroundings, the surroundings that had worked for her, as possible. The snow globe, the incense, the drawn drapes, the Buxtehude music. The only difference was the second chair that had been added.

Anna and Hannah were the youngest of the Smith septet, born three minutes apart in the maternity ward of Wheaton Lutheran Hospital and inseparable, in what sometimes seemed virtual telepathic empathy, all their lives. They were eleven years old—oh, you knew that already—and their greatest passion was roller-blading.

There was a question of supervision and observation. Olga Smith was adamant about barring the Mountain View people from the trance room with Anna and Hannah during the experiment. Pamela Snowden—remember her?—the NASA psychologist on site, vetoed Olga's presence. That would distract the twins, the headshrinker insisted, and Olga had to concede that this would be the case.

Anna and Hannah were of the peculiar variety of twins who were alike in every way imaginable, at least genetically. To the NASA biologists, that meant that they had started as a single fertilized ovum. At a very early stage of development, as the cells multiplied, the almost microscopic cluster of protoplasm had split in half, each half carrying a full set of chromosomes. But in this case, instead of being identical, they were each other's mirror images. Anna was left-handed. Hannah was right-handed. Anna's hair parted naturally on the right. Hannah's hair parted naturally on the left.

Sitting at their older sister's desk, the twins tried to maintain silent concentration on the Primal Atom snow globe. At least, that appeared to be the case in the image that Pamela Snowden and the rest of the NASA gang saw in the video monitor that was the compromise agreed to in lieu of having live witnesses in the trance room with the twins.

After the first thirty seconds the girls had their heads together, whispering. Within the next thirty seconds this led to mutual rib-poking and threats of tickling. Next came the giggles.

Pamela Snowden looked at Olga Smith, who looked at Jaskaran Singh, who looked at Pamela Snowden. In short order they were giggling, too.

But the twins settled down, put their elbows on the desk, gazed into the snow globe, and slowly slid forward until their heads lay on the desk.

The sound of Glen Wilson playing a Buxtehude sarabande on a lovingly restored 1805 Marcus Gabriel Sondermann harpsichord filled the air.

Nothing happened except for two twenty-first-century eleven-year-olds snoozing, emitting occasional gentle snores to the accompaniment of seventeenth century music played on a nineteenth century instrument. After a while the Buxtehude harpsichord compositions gave way to organ performances—those are what brought J. S. Bach to Buxtehude's venue in Lübeck—and choral works.

Anna and Hannah slept on.

The watchers drank coffee, took notes, and made sure that the recording apparatus hooked up to the TV monitor was functioning. Eventually they started taking relief in shifts. Several six-packs of beer were obtained and consumed. A table-stakes poker game broke out in the kitchen.

Dr. Singh remarked that it was getting light outside, although the trance room was kept dark. By eight o'clock Arcata was up and bustling but the twins still slumbered.

Followed a brief consultation among the Mountain View contingent and Olga Smith. The music was faded to silence. The incense sticks had long since burned out and were not renewed.

Still the twins slept on.

Olga insisted on being the one to enter the trance room and draw back the drapes.

Slowly, Anna sat up, stretched, yawned, got to her feet, and looked around as if she wasn't quite sure where she was.

Simultaneously, Hannah yawned, sat up, stretched, got to her feet, and looked around with exactly the same expression as her sister. Well, not quite exactly. Each girl's actions reflected the right-for-left, mirror-like reversal of the other.

Then Anna and Hannah began to dance.

Olga started toward them but she felt a hand on her elbow and turned to see Pamela Snowden, the head headshrinker from Mountain View.

"Please," Snowden said, "don't touch them. They're doing something very important. I can't say that I understand it, but we must not interrupt."

Biff McGurk—you remember him, too—growled, "Well, I do understand it. Can't you see the pattern in what they're doing? We're getting all of this down on microchips, I hope."

They were.

First Anna and then Hannah slouched back into their deserted chairs. They looked up at their elder sister, Olga, and first Hannah and then Anna said, "Wow, am I ever hungry!"

One twin wanted ice cream and pizza and the other wanted pizza and ice cream. You are free to decide which girl wanted which treat first. They both got what they asked for.

While the twins were stoking up their eleven-year old bodies with sugar, fats, and carbohydrates, the main nutritional requirements of their generation, Eldon M. J. McGurk, Doctor of Philosophy, Doctor of Science, was uploading the contents of the microchip recording of Anna and Hannah's dance.

Jaskaran Singh, the *de facto* chief of the NASA team, asked Dr. McGurk what he had in mind.

"It's just a lucky thing that those kids are mirror-image twins, Jasko. I need to add in the music that was playing while they were off on another world."

"Why?"

"There's a mathematical basis for music. You know that. Everybody knows that. And you know what they call me around Mountain View."

"Sure. Biffo."

"No. Mr. Matrix. They call me Mr. Matrix. I think I can reduce those kids' dance moves to a long-stream math statement. And I can matrix it onto that bozo's—what's his name again?"

"Dietrich Buxtehude."

"Right. I prefer Bob Wills and his Texas Playboys, Hank Williams, even Johnny Cash, myself. That's my kind of music. But what the hell. Thanks. The music is the matrix. The dance statement is the observational data. Let me see what I can do with it. I have a feeling it's all going to come out as a series of statements that we'll be able to read."

"You mean like the famous mathematical formulas they've been sending up from SETI for a all these years?"

"Something like that. Only better. Keep everybody away from me for a while, will you, Jasko?"

Jaskaran Singh did as Biff McGurk requested. And McGurk did what he said he would do. The result was a flurry of messages.

Here's a sampling:

Hey, kids, welcome to the party.

Hi there, saps, what the heck took you so long?

Last one into the pool is a rotten grudznik!

Listen, folks, whatever you do, puh-lee-uz *stop wrecking your planet.*

We've noticed you have some pretty nasty diseases there on your marble. Anything we can do to help, just let us know.

And so on. Message after message. Tens of thousands of them. Hundreds of thousands of them. From species scattered throughout the galaxy, the galactic cluster, and mega-clusters and mega-mega-clusters in a whole, glorious, infinitely beautiful and infinitely wonderful universe.

After a while Dr. Jaskaran Singh, the friendly fellow with the turban and dagger, frowned. Dr. Pamela Snowden, the headshrinker from Mountain View, asked what was troubling Dr. Singh.

"It's all one way," he said. "These aliens are all talking to us, but we don't seem to have got any messages through to them."

"I see what you mean," Dr. Snowden said. "It's kind of like taking your pet raccoon to the vet's—"

"You have a pet raccoon?" Singh interrupted.

"No, you're being obstructive. I said, 'kind of like,' I didn't say that I had a pet raccoon. In fact I have a year-old doxie and a ginger cat that I adopted from the animal shelter."

"Then why didn't you say it was like taking your doxie or your cat to the vet?"

Dr. Snowden said, "Jaskaran Singh, you are the most maddening man I know. If you weren't a genius I don't know why I would put up with you." She made a face at him.

Then she said, "All right, it's like taking your doxie to the vet. She's been acting listless lately and her nose is hot. If she were a human patient the doctor would say, 'Describe your symptoms, please,' or the famous, 'Where does it hurt?' But a dog can't describe her symptoms so the vet has to look for clues so she can figure out what's the matter."

Dr. Singh sighed. "How did we get onto the subject of

veterinary medicine? I thought we were talking about communication with aliens."

"Are you following me at all? We're the animals. All you have to do is pick up a morning newspaper to see that we're sick. We're very, very sick. And up to now, those aliens, those millions of aliens, are the veterinarians. But if we could find a way to talk to them, we'd be more like human patients in the doctor's examining room."

Dr. Snowden turned to Olga Smith. "Miss Smith, you're the one who invented or discovered this amazing method of communicating with aliens. Do you have any idea how we could turn this one-way communication into a real dialog?

Olga Smith said, "Yes, I have an idea."

Now, here's another remarkable thing. You might expect these clever people gathered in Madame Olga's *salon* in Arcata, California to run through one idea after another in hopes of getting a message through to the aliens, and finally hitting on an approach that actually worked on the tenth or twentieth or fiftieth attempt.

Didn't happen that way. Olga had an idea, they tried it out, and it worked.

Hey, sometimes you get lucky.

"Try playing the music backwards," Olga suggested.

Biff McGurk said, "Sure, invert the matrix."

By this time the twins, Anna and Hannah, had consumed most of their body weight in pizza, ice cream, pizza, hamburgers, pie a la mode, and a couple of extra slices of pizza for dessert. They'd had a good rest and they were not averse to trying another session of extraplanetary (extrasolar?) (extragalactic?) communication.

There was a small problem as to how to play music backwards—nobody seemed to remember the famous secret messages on the Beatles' album *Abbey Road*—but Butch McGurk devised a new and elegant solution, and soon the works of Dietrich Buxtehude, Georg Philip Telemann, and others of their ilk were streaming backwards from the heart of Arcata, California, to the farthest reaches of all creation.

You'd think there would be a problem with the old speed-of-light limitations. Even the nearby planets of our own solar system were ridiculously far away from Earth at speed-of-light. The distance to other stars had to be measured in light-years, and the distance to remote galaxies—hey, as they say in the gangster movies, *Fuggeddaboudit.*

But if this problem bothered Dr. Singh and Dr. Snowden and Dr. McGurk, and maybe even Madame Olga—well, do you remember the old story of the professor and the bumble bee? Okay, here's a gentle reminder.

A physics professor (maybe even at Humboldt State University) was lecturing to a room full of students on the characteristics of the bumble bee. "The bumble bee cannot fly," the professor asserted. "Merely consider the configuration and weight of its body, the size and shape of its wings, and you will quickly realize that this creature is an aerodynamic impossibility."

At this point a bumble bee flew in through the classroom window and stung the professor smartly on the nose.

The moral of the story, of course, is that nobody had explained to the bee that it could not fly, so it proceeded to fly anyway.

Well, back to Doctors Singh and Snowden and McGurk and their problem with the speed of light.

The twins Anna and Hannah, their tummies happily filled with a glorious assortment of junk food, returned to their older sister's trance room. The lights were dimmed. The Primal Atom glowed hypnotically. The audio system proceeded to play the works of Eduhetxub Hcirteid. Don't worry if you can't pronounce that, hardly anybody can.

The twins rose from their seats and initiated a dance similar to the one they had previously performed.

Dr. Eldon M. J. McGurk did his hands-on magic with his computers.

Dr. Pamela Snowden asked, "Biff, can you understand that?"

Dr. McGurk laughed. "Anna just asked the residents of a distant galaxy if their species is divided into boys and girls, and if so, are the boys as icky and disgusting as the ones we have here on earth. Hannah just asked somebody about a billion light years away if they have a curfew and do they get grounded if they get home late. Oh, wait, now this is important. Anna got an answer to her question and she asked her alien counterpart if there was any way they could exchange picture and the alien told her, yes."

Dr. Singh was dancing himself, for pure joy.

Dr. Snowden was rubbing her temples with her fingertips and muttering unintelligible words.

Dr. McGurk was tapping away at several keyboards in rotation.

Olga Smith's brother Milton wandered in and asked if anybody wanted to head out for a burrito with him and his buddy Walter Macintosh. Walter had just got a gigantic royalty check from the Apple Corporation and he was ready to treat.

That's how we did it. That's how we got an answer to the question, *Is anybody out there?* And the answer, very loosely translated, was, *You bet your bottom dollar there is!* And that, of course, changed *everything*.

And all because Olga Smith felt uncomfortable living in Wheaton, Illinois, and decided to move to the West Coast.

Now that is the Law of Unintended Consequences. In spades!

THE WEBSTER SLOAT STORIES

"Dreemz.biz," was written at the request of William Jones, but appeared in an anthology edited by James Ambuehl, *Hardboiled Cthulhu* (Dimension Books, 2006).

"Wyshes.com" was also written at William Jones' request and appeared in *Horrors Beyond II* (Elder Signs Press, 2007).

"Heaven.god" was introduced as a performance piece at Andrew Migliore and Greg Lowney's wonderful H. P. Lovecraft Film Festival and Cthulhu Con in 2010; this is its first appearance in print.

These three stories chronicle the adventures of Webster Sloat, a onetime tech writer now living in northern California, supplementing his income with occasional consulting jobs in Silicon Valley. Any resemblance between Webster and myself is not exactly coincidental.

Dreemz.biz

If you're getting this e-mail it's because you're very special to me. A close relative, former lover, dear friend, or esteemed co-worker. Believe me, it's not spam and I'm not sending it to any huge mailing list I stole off somebody's database or bought from a marketing house.

I know what that's like, I've been annoyed by spam and spoofs for years and I wouldn't do that to you. Truthfully, I couldn't live with myself if I did that. I really couldn't. I get mad when junk email turns up in my computer, too.

Danged if I can figure out how the heck they get through. I've got a firewall, spam-blocker, anti-spyware, anti-adware, and they still get through. Every day I get offers to buy knock-off jeweled wristwatches indistinguishable from Rolex or Cartier except for the fifteen-cent mechanism inside, certified drugs from Canada or Iceland or Cambodia, or pills guaranteed to enlarge my penis, breasts, or other organs and make my partner ecstatically happy. Oh, stock tips galore, don't forget the stock tips. And my favorite, of course, pleadingly illiterate letters from the impoverished widows of Liberian millionaires offering to share their fortunes with me if I'll just kindly send 'em my bank account information and PIN numbers purely as evidence of good faith of course. Of course.

Here's what I do with these. I hit the "forward" button, type abuse@myinternetserver.net in the address box, and send 'em off to the oblivion they well deserve.

Then there are the chain letters. Two dozen rules for having a happy life or half a dozen photos of cute children, cute dogs, cute cats, or cute children hugging cute dogs or cute dogs hugging cute cats or fuzzy ducklings or whatever, or a soppy poem that somebody dug out of a 1946 issue of *Good Housekeeping*, or a joke that you thought was really hilarious when you heard it in the bathroom at your junior high school thirty years ago. Whatever it is, just send it on to your fifteen dearest friends within thirty minutes and *something good will happen to you today—this is absolutely guaranteed!*

Right.

The free offers can be tempting. You've probably got some of these yourself. You've won a free digital camera, a flat-panel giant TV set, a brand new laptop computer loaded with hi-tech features, a shiny late-model automobile or a lovingly restored classic '55 Chevy Bel-Air or '32 Ford roadster, or a free weekend getaway to the Bahamas for two, transportation included. All you have to do is click here and you're a guaranteed winner.

I asked my guru about these. I mean, just click here and I'm a guaranteed winner, right? I'm not greedy. The great car or the Bahamas vacation for two would be terrific. I can think of one special person I'd love to take for a spin in a Little Deuce Coupé or romance beneath the Caribbean stars. But, hey, I'd settle happily for the camera or the laptop.

My guru says, "If you want the camera or the laptop that much, save your money and then buy one. You'll have less grief, far less grief, than if you start jumping through hoops for some online sharpster."

Still, the offers do manage to get through and when I see a particularly attractive one it takes all my will power not to click where indicated.

But I do resist the temptation.

Always.

Almost always.

We all do slip once in a while or we wouldn't be human, would we?

When an email came through from Dreemz.biz with a subject line of *Dreemz 4 Sale* it caught my attention. I've always been fascinated by dreams. I don't think we know nearly everything there is to know about them, and I think all the so-called "sleep labs" at research universities are going about their work the wrong way. They study brainwaves and eye movements and skin temperatures and respiration rates. Okay, that's fine as far as it goes. But the physiology of sleeping, particularly of dreaming, is only one aspect of the subject.

What about the dreams themselves? What do people dream, and why do they dream what they dream, and for that matter what *is* a dream? That's one of those questions that seems simple enough, the answer should be obvious enough, until you start to think seriously about it. Then it gets very tricky, surprisingly complicated and evasive and ambiguous.

Okay, so I received this e-mail titled *Dreemz 4 Sale* and I thought, yes, the fact that it was about dreams was at least slightly interesting. The "4" was also a nice touch. Very post-modern, very hip, very with-it.

I suppose anybody who still uses phrases like post-modern, hip, or with-it is by definition square, dorky, and obsolete.

Oh, well.

I did like the word "Sale." It's honest, you see? Everybody who advertises on the internet or television these days offers something absolutely free of charge and without obligation and you get a free gift just for trying our product. Nobody ever says, "I want to sell you something," but that's all that any of them want to do.

So one point for *Dreemz*, one point for *4*, one point for *sale*. I figured I had nothing to lose by just opening the letter. I know you can get a virus that way, but I'm paying good dollars for protection from viruses. Let the antivirus software company earn its money for once.

<g>

That sign, BTW, the "g" inside the funny angle marks, is computerese for "grin." And BTW stands for By the Way. BTW.

The email is from a company called Dreemz.biz. I've never heard of them before but obviously they've heard of me. The letter is addressed to me by name, c/o the email address I use for my home office. I don't know how the heck I got onto Dreemz.biz's mailing list, but here I am. Here's what the letter says. I saved it to my hard drive and I'll give you a link to it. Here we go:

> Dear Webster Sloat,
>
> The average person spends one-third of his or her life sleeping. For most of us, the other two-third of our lives are divided roughly in half. Half the time is spent working. That leaves just one-third of your lifetime for everything else, and that includes necessities like washing, dressing and undressing, traveling to and from our jobs, preparing meals, folding laundry, and countless other tasks.

How many hours a day are your own? Really your own, to use however you choose? University studies show that for the average person, the answer is barely more than one hour a day!

By joining *Dreemz.biz* you can get back the one-third of your life that you spend asleep. By ordering *Dreemz* from our huge catalog you can *live* those eight hours every night. You need not rely on random chance to determine the contents of your Dreemz. You can choose anything you want. Be anyone you want. Experience adventure, romance, excitement. Explore outer space. Win an athletic championship. Have a rich, rewarding relationship with the person of your choice. Or use our DreamLearning™ experiences to learn a new language, complete courses in physics, chemistry, sociology. Learn anatomy, mechanics, accounting. Prepare yourself for a new career!

Dreemz.biz offers a choice of over 10,000 *Dreemz* in our ever-expanding catalog. Or tell us *your* dream and for a modest additional fee we'll create a custom *dream* just for you. Our *Dreemz* are fully interactive and participatory. This feature is unique, and I'm sure you'll love it once you try it out.

For a free sample membership in *Dreemz.biz* just go to the URL below and fill out a simple application. We here at *Dreemz.biz* are sure that you'll want to become a full member once you've tried our *Dreemz*. If you have any questions, feel free to write to me personally c/o the *Dreemz.biz* website. Every letter receives my prompt and personal attention.

Yours truly,
Carter Thurston Hull

Maybe I was a fool to follow up on that one, but I figured there was nothing to lose by just writing to Mr. Carter Thurston Hull. I wasn't joining Dreemz.biz, I wasn't even signing up for their free trial offer. All I did was send them a simple question in an email one line long. It was this:

> How did you get my name, business identification, and email address?

I figured they'd bought a mailing list somewhere. Or—ah, this was the answer!—I'd filled out a little questionnaire at the electronics store down at the plaza when I took my daughter there to pick out her birthday present. I'd long since given up trying to choose anything that would please her, not even a brand of breakfast cereal, but giving your own pre-pubescent offspring cash for her birthday seemed pretty cold to me. So we compromised. She could pick the store. She could pick the gift. I would hover at a distance and pretend not to know her until it was time to pony up the moolah, then the gift would go on my plastic not hers.

Mr. Hull actually replied, and he was impressively candid as well as prompt. He acknowledged that Dreemz.biz purchased mailing lists, and that they'd got my information from the electronics outlet where I'd filled out the questionnaire.

Was there anything else I'd like to know? If so, Mr. Carter Thurston Hull would be happy to furnish the information. In any case, he would be delighted if I would accept that free trial membership in his organization, but of course he would not try to pressure me and I was still, he emphasized, under no obligation whatever.

In fact I had a couple more questions for Mr. Hull. I sent him another email:

> What do you mean by "fully interactive and participatory?" Sounds like one of those Role-Playing Games that my daughter buys at the software store. What's so special about your product? And, BTW, why do you spell Dreemz.biz that way? Why not Dreams.biz?

I thought Hull would be annoyed by that, but he played it straight and I kind of liked his answer:

> By "fully interactive and participatory" I mean that our Dreemz are *your* Dreemz. When you enter one of our Dreemz you won't just be an observer—not unless you

want to be, and that's a choice you can make. But if your Dream is, let's say, *Washington Crossing the Delaware,* you won't just see our First President in action, you can be one of the soldiers in his Continental Army. You can be right there in the boat with him, that cold December night. If you choose, you can *be* General Washington. It's up to you!

You can be Babe Ruth or Humphrey Bogart, Marilyn Monroe or Eleanor Roosevelt or Madame Curie or Rosa Parks. You can be anyone you choose, for the duration of your Dream. And when you wake up, you'll be yourself again, but very likely you'll be a happier and maybe a wiser self.

You'll find that our Dreemz are as different from any Role-Playing Game and provide as much better an experience as a full symphony orchestra is from a child playing a tin whistle!

Please—give us a try!

Yours truly,

Carter Thurston Hull

P.S.—We call ourselves Dreemz.biz because somebody else already has the domain name Dreamz.com.

Of course, I might merely have been tapping into an automated FAQ routine that produced those seemingly personalized answers. Or there might have been some low-paid computer science major working at an entry-level job, picking canned answers out of a catalog and assembling replies. But I didn't think so. These answers really seemed, if you'll excuse my saying so, real. And I liked the candor of the "P.S."

Carter Thurston Hull and Dreemz.biz seemed to be on the up-and-up, don't you agree? I even got ahold of my guru and invited her over to the house for a sandwich and a glass of beer, which my daughter watched us consume with undisguised scorn. I showed my guru printouts of our emails, and she reluctantly conceded that the catch, if there was one, was so well concealed that she couldn't find it.

After she left I took a second beer with me into my study. I booted up the computer, clicked on my ISP's icon, and shortly found myself in cyberspace. I went back to Mr. Hull's first email and clicked on the URL at the bottom of the screen.

The application that popped up was pretty simple and definitely nonthreatening. It asked for some personal data but not for my credit card number or driver's license number or Social Security number, so I figured this wasn't an identity theft racket. It asked me to create a user ID for myself. I picked Dudley Batson after a minor comic book character of my childhood. It asked me to create a password of six characters minimum and I keyed in ******.

Next came a screen that said I'd need some software to participate in Dreemz.biz. I muttered, *Ahah! At last! Here comes the pitch. How much are they going to want for this?*

But there was no pitch. I could either download the software or they'd send it to me on a CD. My option. No charge either way. And in either case they recommended that I save it on my hard drive for future reference.

And my selected Dreemz would be sent to me the same way—via download or on CD's, as I preferred. They offered any three chosen from their online catalog. Once I'd used them I could order more. I didn't have to return the used Dreemz, they were mine to keep.

I clicked on CD's—see, that's more of my Luddism coming out, I still like things I can see and touch, not just invisible electrons that come whirring along wires or out of the ether.

Finally Dreemz.biz provided a link to their catalog. It was as big as Carter Thurston Hull had said. My first choice was easy.

I'd always been a rock and roll fan, and when the Beatles played San Francisco in 1966 I was frantic to attend their concert.

Wouldn't you know, I was at school that day and started feeling queasy over my Sloppy Joe and soda at lunchtime. I tried to keep going but my friends said I was literally turning green before their eyes. They dragged me to the nurse's office and an hour later I was in SF General having my appendix yanked.

It was a routine operation. The doc told me later that if I'd tried to go the concert I would never have made it. My appendix would have burst and then I would have been in *real* trouble. But as it was, I was out of the hospital in two days and back to school in a week.

And the Beatles had played at Candlestick Park and I'd missed the show.

I still have my unused ticket. Could probably sell it on eBay for a king's ransom.

I clicked on the little box and a check mark appeared.

What was my second choice?

I was starting to feel slightly more ambitious. I've always loved history and wished I could have witnessed the events that decided the course mankind would take. The Manhattan Project fascinates me, the dramatic events, Albert Einstein's famous letter to President Roosevelt, the development and testing process, Robert Oppenheimer, Leslie Groves, Klaus Fuchs.

Would Dreemz.biz have a file on the original test, the world's first nuclear explosion? I scrolled through the online catalog with my fingers crossed and there it was. Trinity, White Sands, New Mexico, July 16, 1945.

Click.

Check.

And what would my third free sample be?

Right then I was sitting at the computer, filling out the form. I swung around in my chair and scanned the walls of my study. The room was lined with bookcases, the books arranged by category. One bookcase was devoted to computer manuals and user's guides. One was filled with reference books—almanacs, dictionaries, atlases, collections of quotations and records and trivia of every sort. And one was filled with my relaxation reading, my guilty pleasures, what my favorite literary critic calls lurid trash.

I rolled over to the last of those and pulled down a volume of collected stories by H. P. Lovecraft, the eccentric antiquarian pulp author of Providence, Rhode Island. I flipped through the pages reading a striking phrase here, a familiar scene there, in one after another of my favorite stories. There was "The Dunwich Horror," "The Rats in the Walls," "The Shadow Over Innsmouth," "The Color Out of Space," "The Shadow Out of Time." I dropped the book on my desk and let it open where it would, and it fell open to

"The Call of Cthulhu," probably Lovecraft's most famous story.

With the book lying open on my desk I keyed in my specs for a custom Dream. I wouldn't Dream "The Call of Cthulhu." I would be there in the room in Providence as Lovecraft wrote the story. I would *be* Howard Phillips Lovecraft.

Once I'd sent off my order to Dreemz.biz I experienced buyer's remorse. What was I getting into? Was this some new internet scheme? Was Carter Thurston Hull a racketeer who would empty my bank account, ruin my credit rating, and destroy my life? Was Dreemz.biz a cult? Would a couple of men in black come calling at my door while ominously silent helicopters hovered overhead? I considered logging onto the website again and canceling my order, but I didn't do it. My curiosity was fighting my caution, and curiosity was winning.

A couple of days later a FedEx truck pulled up in front of my house and the driver handed me a package. I'd ordered software this way in the past and the driver was a regular. We exchanged some small talk, then he said, "I've been delivering a lot of these lately. Never heard of Dreemz.biz myself."

I told him this was the first time I'd dealt with them and I'd let him know what I thought of their product after I'd tried it out.

You understand, I was still working as a technical editor for a Silicon Valley startup that had barely survived the dotcom bust and was struggling to get back into profit. They let me telecommute part-time and show up at the office the rest of the time. On top of this I was raising a thirteen-year-old girl, which, if you've ever tried it, you know can keep you busy forty-eight hours a day. But eventually I was caught up with my work, or as caught up as I ever managed to get, and my daughter was in bed for the night. I felt I was entitled to relax.

A glass of good Scotch helped, and some fine music cleared my mind and elevated my soul. I'm not a religious man, but Mozart's *Coronation Mass* can almost make me believe there is a God. By eleven o'clock I was ready for sleep. I climbed into my pajamas, performed my ablutions, and was ready to climb into bed when I remembered the disks that had arrived from Dreemz.biz.

All right, I thought, I'll give this thing a try.

I slid the first Dreemz.biz CD into my computer. It booted up just fine. I found myself answering some more questions about what I wanted to dream—or *dream*—and hit *enter*. My monitor screen went nuts for about half a minute, with a variety of colors and images swirling around. Then it seemed as if a bolt of light shot out of it and bathed me for a few seconds. It was like the aura that Sri Babaloo-boom-a-lam-bam-boom claims he can see, send $14.95 for his book, only it was *my* aura. I felt a tingling and I think my hair stood on end although I can't swear to that. Then everything went back to normal, except I felt very tired. I shut the thing down and went to bed.

The jet set down at SFO and Astrid and I put down our drinks and peered out the window. It was nice being back in San Francisco, although I had my doubts about playing in a football stadium. Brian got to the door first and made sure everything was copasetic before any of the boys climbed down the stairway.

It was a quick ride to the football stadium and they put us in a smelly locker room where they told us the local baseball team dressed for games. It was August, baseball season in America, and the baseball team shared facilities with the footballers. A couple of the guys had wives or girlfriends with them. I felt lucky that Astrid Kirchherr stuck with me. She's really a mothering type, and I've been having these dreadful headaches since that yobbo in Liverpool let me have it in the noggin with a steel-tipped boot after a show. I should have killed the thug but I was too stunned and nauseous to move.

There was a nice spread of American grub, fried chicken and potatoes and greens, and after the long flight I was ready to pitch in, and I did. Astrid said, "You haff ein schmear uff schmutz on your chin, *liebchen*," and leaned over the licked my chin with her pink little tongue.

We could hear the other performers from the locker room. They weren't very interesting except the Ronettes, but for some reason Ronnie Spector wasn't with them tonight. The other acts finished, I took a big hit off a joint and a slug of tequila, picked up my bass and headed for the runway.

They had to provide bodyguards for us, believe it or not. Some fool preachers had picked up on John's comment about the Beatles being more popular than Jesus Christ and there were a few demonstrators at the show who thought we were Agents of Satan and wanted to skin us alive for the greater glory of the Prince of Peace and the God of Love.

We made it onto the stage and some disk jockey from a local radio station gave us the big build-up which we really didn't need after all, but that was the way it was. There was a big crowd, mostly young girls. Some of them were screaming, some were crying, some were throwing things at us but the platform was set up in the middle of the field, too far for them to reach.

John gave a signal, Ringo started his countdown, and the three guitars rang out. I stayed in the back, near the drum-kit, laying down a bass line. We were playing "Rock and Roll Music." The sound wasn't what you'd call really perfect or even very good, I'm afraid, but it was good and loud and the kids in the stands went nuts.

Brian had told us to keep the numbers short, loud, and fast, and that's the way we played. We wrapped up with "Long Tall Sally" and got off the stage in half an hour, and that was that.

We didn't head back to the airport after the show. They actually put us in an armored car and took us downtown to a posh hotel. It was still early enough to do something else, so Astrid and I showered and dressed again and asked if anybody wanted to head out with us. George was alone on this trip and he said he'd like to, and we managed to sneak out of the hotel without anybody seeing us.

We wound up at a little club called the Keystone Corner. Muddy Waters was playing there. Can you imagine, a genius like Muddy Waters sitting on a rickety wooden stage all alone, McKinley Morganfield sitting in front of a room with maybe seventy-five seats, maybe a hundred seats, playing his guitar and singing that gorgeous blues and probably getting a couple of hundred dollars and a free meal out of it. And the Beatles just finished a show at a football stadium with, I don't know, thirty thousand, fifty thousand, I don't know how many teenaged girls wetting their pants for us.

After the show I went up to Muddy and introduced myself and my girlfriend and George Harrison and told him I was one of the Beatles and I really loved his music.

He said, "I done hoid of the Beatles. I'm pleased to make your acquaintance, Mr. Sutcliffe and Mr. Harrison, Miss Kirchherr."

That was the whole of our conversation. We had a couple of drinks. I offered to buy one for Muddy but he said he was tired and had to go wash up. We caught a cab back to the hotel and went to bed.

That was the high point of my trip to America.

My radio turned itself on with news of the latest political scandal in Washington and the latest war in the Middle East. I climbed out of bed and resumed my life. My name is Webster Sloat and I am a single dad with a thirteen-year-old daughter whom I love madly and who drives me crazy.

So that was the Dreemz.biz experience.

And today there was an all-day meeting scheduled at the office. Could I ever have done without that! But the bills don't stop coming, month after month. I think if I'd been alone I would have quit my job, sold my modest house in Sunnyvale for an absurd profit over the price I'd paid when I was married, and moved into a skuzzy apartment in the city. But having a teenager changes everything, and I mean everything.

Somewhere in my Beatles collection was a CD of the Candlestick concert. I put it on the speakers in the Saab. The music was wonderful, early Beatles rock and roll before they got all arty and experimental. But it was all John, Paul, George, and Ringo. Stu Sutcliffe wasn't on the record.

Or was he? I hit the *back* button and listened to one track in particular. "I Wanna Be Your Man." Was there an extra guitar on that track? If there were three guitars, then Paul was the third guitarist and that meant that Stu Sutcliffe was playing bass. I hit *back* again and tried to filter out the instruments and just hear the voices. Was there an extra voice? Was it Stu Sutcliffe? Or was that voice *my* voice?

I didn't want to try any more Dreemz.biz experiences after that. Not for a while, anyway. The Candlestick concert might have been only a dream, or a *dream,* but it was so real to me, I couldn't distinguish my recollection of the dream from a memory of a real event. Was I Webster Sloat or was I Stu Sutcliffe?

Sutcliffe had died in 1962 of a brain hemorrhage, probably

caused by that kick in the skull at the Litherland Town Hall. At least, that's what I'd always believed. He wasn't one of the Beatles in 1966, he'd been dead for four years.

But I had a clear memory, a vivid, lifelike memory, of the Candlestick show with Sutcliffe playing bass and McCartney playing guitar.

No more Dreemz.biz for me, I decided.

There was no time limit on the three free Dreemz, and I went back to my life and tried to forget about them and about Mr. Carter Thurston Hull. I can't say my life was very exciting. Technical editing, reading for pleasure, listening to Mozart and Dvorak and Shostakovich and Locatelli. I don't know whether I'd grown away from rock and roll or it had grown away from me, but somehow the old pull wasn't there any more.

And of course, raising a thirteen-year-old. Sometimes I thought I should remarry just to have a woman in the house for my daughter to relate to, but I didn't think that was a good enough reason to marry. It wouldn't be fair to the woman involved and it wouldn't be fair to me.

One day my daughter came home from school and asked me for help with an assignment. She had reached the age where she knew everything and anyone older than high school age was a total ignoramus, distinctly including her father, so when she asked me to help out I was flattered, to say the least.

"What was Trinity, Dad?"

"You mean the religious concept?"

"No." She shook her head. "It has something to do with history. Something about an explosion."

I pondered. Aha, she meant the Trinity test in 1945. The first A-bomb explosion, in the New Mexico desert, before they used the bomb against Japan. I wasn't born for ten years after that, but I suppose to a thirteen-year-old anybody as ancient as her father had to have known Julius Caesar personally.

"How soon do you need this?" I asked.

"Tomorrow."

That wasn't time for anything except a quick peek at the encyclopedia and an internet search. Rather than do the work for her, I talked her through the process. There were plenty of sites devoted to the subject. She didn't need any prompting to pick the best sites and print out the documents. We went over them together, highlighting the key names and dates and events, and when we were finished she sat up for the next few hours writing her report.

I read it through and I was totally impressed. No question, this was *A-plus* work.

Of course, there was no convincing her that I didn't remember all the events she was writing about. Still, she actually gave me a good-night kiss before she went to bed. Now I was the one who couldn't get the events of the summer of 1945 out of my head.

The computer was still running so I sat down in front of the monitor and loaded the Dreemz.biz disk for the Trinity explosion. There was that display on the screen, colors and shapes swirling and blending, the bolt of light, the feeling that I was surrounded by a glowing aura, and then the return to the usual computer wallpaper and start-up menu. I shut the thing down and went to bed.

It was still dark out and it was cold in the wooden barracks but there was the sergeant walking up and down shaking us by the shoulder, his own uniform crisp and fresh-looking in the feeble incandescent lights. He growled out the same vulgar witticism that he had every morning since we got here, and nobody even bothered to pretend to be amused. We all grabbed our socks and the rest of our summer gear and got ready to face the glorious New Mexico sunrise.

This was going to be the big day, and once we got to work there might not be time for any meal breaks, so a good breakfast was important. Uncle Sam, I thought, is one considerate son of a bitch. He doesn't want his soldier boys to have to work on empty tummies.

What the hell time was it, anyway? The gadget was supposed to be tested at 0400 hours and it would take us an hour to get to the test site. Leaving at 0300 meant breakfast at 0200. Jesus, it was hardly worth the trouble of climbing into the sack, just to climb back out and go to work. But I was Webster Sloat, Corporal, Corps of Engineers, and I did what I was told.

It was raining cats and dogs. There was almost continuous

thunder and frequent lightning flashes. I wondered how they could ever hope to get the test off under these conditions, but the big shots running the test must know what they were doing.

We formed up outside the barracks, water pouring off our rain gear, and double-timed it to the mess hall. You'd be amazed how cold the New Mexico desert gets at night, even in July. The mess hall was warm and bright inside. I was hungry and I took everything I could get as I pushed my tray past the serving tables.

Not long into the meal I realized that this was pretty boring. I guess there's nothing that says the *Dreemz* have to be exciting. My experience as Stu Sutcliffe had been a trip, but as myself, as a corporal eating breakfast in 1945, life could be dull. I tried to change to another persona. Sometimes you can do that in Dreemz. What was the big boss of the Manhattan Engineering Project doing? Leslie Groves, Major General Leslie Richard Groves. I concentrated my identity into a theoretical point somewhere inside my head and pushed.

To my delight, I found myself rushing up, right through the top of my skull. I was floating over the table. The mess hall full of GI's shoveled scrambled eggs and grilled sausage patties down their throats. The conversation was desultory, the usual GI mix of complaints, boasts, jokes, discussion of movies and of baseball games. The Cards had beat the Browns in the '44 Series but neither team looked likely to repeat. I knew—I *knew*—that in '45 the Tigers would beat the Cubs.

This was amazing. The more I experimented with my trial *Dreemz* from Dreemz.biz, the more impressed I became. I was able to move around, popping instantaneously out of existence at one place and back into existence at another, like one of those theoretical quantum particles that the high-energy physics geniuses write papers about, and ask me to turn into something resembling comprehensible English.

I could also zip into people by directing my, what should I call it, "point of self" into their heads. I tried it on one of the poor KP's in the serving line, then into the mess sergeant. Piece of cake! All right, then, whom should I become?

There was a clock on the wall. It was 0345 hours. My erstwhile buddies would be heading out of the mess hall, forming up and climbing onto two-and-a-half-ton four-by-fours for the jouncing ride to the test site. I didn't bother to travel with them. I headed for the main test site.

There it was, a hundred-foot steel tower, and there was the gadget, already hoisted into position, wired and ready to go. I looked around for another clock and didn't see one, but without benefit of machinery I knew the time. It was 0415 hours. The rain was still falling, but it was not nearly as intense as it had been for most of the night. The thunder and lightning had rolled away and only faint, distant releases flashed now and then.

The test was fifteen minutes overdue. I knew what had happened. Everything had been held up because of the storm. Some of the scientists had argued for scrubbing the test for twenty-four hours, but General Groves had huddled with Oppy and decided to wait the storm out. Of course, their decision was right. I knew that, even if they were nervous about it.

I became General Groves. Major General Leslie Richard Groves. He was forty-eight, almost forty-nine years old. With a start I realized that he was younger than I was, running this billion-dollar enterprise, commanding thousands of brilliant minds, pushing brains far better than his own to complete the gadget before Stalin's slave-scientists could get one of their own.

The official reason for the Manhattan Engineering Project had been to get the gadget before Hitler did. The Allies were going to use it on Berlin and end the war in Europe, but the Nazis crumbled before the gadget was finished. Some of Oppy's scientists had wanted to quit right then. Mostly Jews, they were, freaked out by Hitler and his policies. Not patriots, not real patriots, they couldn't care less about fighting the Japs, but Dickie Groves had held their feet to the fire and kept them on the job and the gadget was done now, ready for the big test, and if it worked then Dickie would be Harry Truman's fair haired boy and then the sky's the limit!

Groves looked at his watch. It was nearly 0600 hours.

I'd had enough of Groves. I shot through the top of his skull and looked around for somebody more interesting to visit. I spotted a painfully thin, harried looking individual in rumpled civvies. He wore wire-rimmed glasses and paced back and forth, muttering to himself. I couldn't understand what he was saying.

Inside his head I realized that he was thinking and muttering in German and in a flash I was able to understand his thoughts. So this was Emil Julius Klaus Fuchs, one of the great spies of his generation. He was only thirty-four years old. He was a genius. He was a Communist who had fled Hitler and wound up in England as a guest of His Majesty's government.

What a time he'd had! The Brits didn't know what to do with him. Once he had his advanced degrees he wound up in an internment camp as an enemy alien—in Quebec, of all places. But once the Brits got their Tube Alloys program under way, their version of the Manhattan Engineering Project, Fuchs was free again, back in England, working on a gadget for Mister Churchill. And when the Brits combined their program with the Americans, Oppy was delighted to have Fuchs at his side in New Mexico.

Oh, Klaus was like a bear in a honey-tree. The honey he was scooping up was going straight to Harry Gold, and from Gold to Russia, where Comrade Stalin would build a gadget of his own, and face down the capitalist aggressors as he'd faced down the Nazis. It was nervous-making, but it was important work.

Most important work.

Enough. Enough of the mind of Comrade Fuchs. My next stop was obvious. Could I find Oppy himself? Did I have to look for him? Did I have to make myself a point of consciousness and go zooming around Alamogordo like a bee in a meadow?

No, *Dreemz* didn't work that way. I wanted Oppy, I found Oppy. He looked at his watch, no, I looked at my watch. It was 0620 hours. Ten minutes to go. What was Oppy thinking?

He was leaning against a wall. He looked casual but in fact he was trembling inside, so wrought up by what he was doing that he feared to stand unsupported lest he fall down. He was wearing his famous floppy broad-brimmed hat and held a cold pipe between his teeth.

Was that reality or was it my *dream*?

He was thinking—I was thinking—of Berkeley, California, of standing in front of a room full of grad students, a blackboard behind him, a piece of chalk in his hand. He'd been outlining a problem, drawing equations on the board. The minds in the room were fine, he could almost see the keen intellects behind those shining eyes. This was the life he wanted, the life of the mind, the life of the disciple of Newton and of Einstein, a life devoted to fathoming out the deepest secrets and the most glorious creations of the mind of God.

I looked at my watch again. 0629, 0629 and ten seconds, 0629 and twenty seconds. How could a minute last so long, so long when the years of Oppy's life had sped so rapidly?

There was a flash.

What had I done? What had I done? The fireball rose, the shockwave, the blast, the flying debris, the heat, the light, what had I done?

I am become death, the shatterer of worlds.

He staggered. I staggered. Oh, Ella, Julius, Frank. Oh, Kitty, what have you married, what is the monster I have become?

And yet the fireball expanded and from it rose the column of dust and earth, the mushroom cloud that the world would know forever. I had seen the films uncounted times, the films of Alamogordo, Hiroshima, Nagasaki, Bikini, Eniwetok. Nothing could compare to being here. Edward would be pleased but he would not be satisfied, not until we build the super.

I laid my head in my arms. There was dancing and cheering around me, but I wept.

In my *dream* could I rewind events, unhappen them, travel into the past and change history? I left Oppy to his grief, shot forward in space, backward in time, climbed the tower like a phantom creature, plunged into the gadget itself. The countdown ended. There was a click, a flare, I thought I might make the gadget fail. This was my *dream*, wasn't it? Mine! I could make happen what I wanted to happen. But I held back.

The light, the screaming of the universe itself, the tears of God.

The alarm sounded and I sat up in bed, drenched in sweat. What was this hanging from my torso? I staggered to the mirror. My pajamas were in shreds.

Because thy heart was tender, and thou didst humble thyself before God, when thou heardest His words against this place, and against the inhabitants thereof, and hast humbled thyself before Me, and hast rent thy clothes, and wept before Me; I also have heard thee, saith the

Lord.

Breakfast for my daughter, and off to school she went.

In the Saab I turned on the radio and channel-surfed until I found a religious station. What was I looking for? What comfort was I seeking?

Whatever it was, I did not find it. The hymns were vapid, the preaching worse. I surfed to a music station and listened to a Shostakovich string quartet. The music was stormy and troubling, a match for my mood.

I still had my third sample *Dream* but I didn't use it for weeks. If Carter Thurston Hull was worried about me, he didn't show it. My emails contained the usual mix of business correspondence, baby photos from cousins in Minnesota and Connecticut, jokes and political rants and spam. I answered the business communications, deleted the jokes and rants and spam, and let the photos of new cousins and nephews and nieces tug at my heartstrings. I sent baby presents to Minneapolis and Westport. The proud parents sent thank you messages by email.

At the Fremont office I attended meetings and did my work on autopilot. At home there were no meetings, that was the only difference. Nobody seemed to detect any change in me. What does it mean when you don't show up for work and nobody notices?

My daughter asked if she could spend the weekend with her best friends. I knew the girls involved, knew their parents. They were all solid citizens. I wasn't worried. I let her go.

I sat in the living room the first night she was gone with a bottle of Laphroig and a stack of CD's. I started with Grieg and moved on through Dvorak, Vivaldi, Michael Haydn, Joseph Haydn, Carl Phillip Emanuel Bach, Carl Friedrich Bach, Johann Sebastian Bach, Sibelius and my old friend Dmitri Dmitrievich. I ended with the incomparable Ludwig. I felt that I had no choice. Not his big works, his chamber music. I fell asleep to the music.

The next day I was not hung over. I ate an apple for breakfast and drove out into the country. I spent the day walking in woods, listening to birds, watching clouds. I went home and phoned the house where my daughter was visiting. I spoke with the father of the house. The girls were having a grand time being thirteen-year-olds. Did I want to speak to my daughter? I wanted to, desperately, but I told him, No, I don't want to intrude on the girls' party.

For dinner I heated a can of soup and ate half of it. I closed myself in the living room in darkness and silence. Somewhere a dog barked.

The third Dreemz.biz disk was on my desk, I knew, next to my computer. It would take me to Providence, to the cramped and cluttered home of Howard Phillips Lovecraft during the brief period of his greatest creativity. I was convinced he was a genius. I had long been intrigued by his strange, dreamlike narratives, his portrayals of the terrors that lurked in every corner of his Id. I had been drawn to him, fascinated by the thought of entering his mind. But my two previous *Dreemz* now made me wonder.

Was this what I really wanted? In *Dreemz* I could be anyone, anything I wanted. I could be Abraham Lincoln. I could be Adolf Hitler. I could be Jesus. I could be the Shadow. I could be the Green Lantern. I could be James Bond.

I could be a woman.

I could be an animal.

I could be an extraterrestrial.

What did I really want?

I knew that I would have to write to Carter Thurston Hull, pay whatever fee was involved, become a member of Dreemz.biz. But I realized, also, that a danger lurked here. I thought I had as good a grip on reality as most modern men. I had experimented with a few of the more popular drugs when I was in college. I enjoyed them, in a mild way, but they did not excite my enthusiasm and there was certainly no chance that I would become addicted.

Dreemz.biz was a lot like drugs. I had tasted a forbidden fruit and now I wanted more. But I was still able, I knew, to distinguish between the experience of *Dreemz* and that of the real world. In my *dream,* Stu Sutcliffe had performed at Candlestick Park in 1966. I had *been* Stu Sutcliffe in my *dream*. But I had not changed reality. When I played the CD of that 1966 concert, Sutcliffe was not on it. When I looked him up on the internet, Sutcliffe had still died in 1962.

But I wasn't sure. My experience on the freeway, playing that

Candlestick Park concert CD, hearing an extra guitar and voice on "I Wanna Be Your Man" was haunting me. Was it all an illusion? Or was my dream—my *dream*—starting to invade my reality? Or—scariest of all—was my *dream* affecting not just my personal, subjective reality, but the objective reality of the real, physical world?

In my *dream* I had been Corporal Webster Sloat, General Leslie Groves, Klaus Fuchs, Oppy, but when I awakened and consulted the history books, there was no change in the Alamogordo test, the Hirsohima and Nagasaki bombings, the test explosions at Bikini and Eniwetok.

Dreemz did not change reality. But did *Dreemz?*

I loaded the third CD into my computer and watched the swirling lights and shapes, winced at the flash, and turned off the machine. I put my dirty clothing in the hamper and donned my pajamas, brushed my teeth, gargled with mouthwash, and climbed into bed.

The ceiling above my pillow was not the one I had stared at every night for the past fifteen years. It was another ceiling in another room in another city three thousand miles from Sunnyvale. I pushed myself upright, slid my feet off the bed and into my slippers, and walked to the bathroom. I turned on the light.

A long face, lantern-jawed, surmounted by dark hair a good deal shorter than I usually kept my own, stared back at me. I shuffled back to my bedroom and drew a gray robe around myself. It was chilly in Providence, chilly here on Federal Hill. I knew I was not alone. I did not wish to disturb my aunt, Mrs. Gamwell.

I made my way to my desk and took up my pen and manuscript paper. I had correspondence to catch up with but the larder was empty and my purse was flat. I had revision clients to keep me occupied but somehow I could not bring myself to rewrite the poor specimens of prose that they sent to me.

Perhaps if I let my mind wander some flash of inspiration would come to me. A story for one of the pulps would bring a few dollars, enough money, if I were lucky, to keep the landlord at bay and perhaps even to buy a bag of groceries.

A streetlight shone through my window casting weird shadows

on the wall. An errant breeze moved the tree limbs outside. They whispered to me. The shadows on the wall danced and wove, making strange shapes. By studying them I could almost read messages coded into them. I had only to try hard enough, to understand the messages, and I would have my inspiration.

What were the creatures who lurked just beyond the edge of our perception? Could we detect them, should we detect them, what would we learn?

For an instant my room was illuminated to the brilliance of midday, then reverted to its former state. I counted seconds, then heard the distant boom of thunder. Another gust of wind, another whisper of leaves, another flash and another boom of thunder, louder this time and closer, closer, almost as if it were inside my bed chamber.

With a roar the clouds released their contents in a torrent that beat upon my window. I turned in my chair and watched rivulets course down the panes, forming themselves into hieroglyphs that twisted and whirled before my eyes. The messages they spelled out became clear to me.

I reached for the chain that would turn on the lamp on my desk. The paper before me was filled with writing that I recognized as my own. When had I written? What had a I written? What had possessed me to create the document that lay before me?

Here was my opportunity to redeem myself. I made an effort to render my mind blank and passive, to give myself over fully to whatever force it was in my subconscious or in the world around me, in the world unseen and unknown but as real, I knew, as an omelet or an aeroplane, that was guiding my pen.

I wrote through the night, having no idea what I was writing, seeking inspiration in the wind and the rain, the shadows of leaves and the booming of thunder. At last I fell, exhausted, upon my narrow bed. The last thing I saw was a vision of something shocking peering at me through the window, rain dripping horridly from it. Its face was a mass of feelers. Its flesh was rubbery and its skin scaly. Its hands and feet were like the webbed and claw-tipped extremities of a giant batrachian. Long wings ribbed like those of a bat hung from its shoulders.

With a snap and a gust of foetor the creature spread its wings and rose from the tree limb where it had crouched so terribly. It circled overhead, and I was no longer in my room in Providence but in some black void between the stars if not beyond them, and the thing was flapping its wings, the feelers that made up its face writhing, its great eyes leering at me in mad and terrible joy.

With a start I realized that I did not have to remain where I was. I fled from the skull I had inhabited but instead of flying freely I was drawn to the thing that wriggled its feelers and flapped its wings. I entered its mind.

Words crowded through my own being, words whose meaning was so vast and so terrible that I wanted to scream but could not. I beat my own hands against my face, trying to wake myself, and at last I succeeded. I sat up in bed, not in Providence but in Sunnyvale, not eighty years ago but in my own time.

A winter wind was blowing outside and rain was falling. A storm had blown in off the Gulf of Alaska, made its way down the coastline and swept inland here in northern California. I could not bring myself to get out of bed, but I reached for the lamp on my night table and switched it on. I looked at my clock. It was still hours before daylight. I wanted daylight desperately, needed it. Could I survive until the sun rose? I tried to leap forward in time but I was no longer in a *dream*, I no longer controlled the world.

Carter Thurston Hull.

I thought of the being I had seen, the being Howard Lovecraft had seen.

Carter Thurston Hull.

The words ran together in my brain.

Carter Thurston Hull.

I realized, at last, who he was.

Send this message to fifteen people today and something good will happen to you. I guarantee it.

Wyshes.com

The reason most clichés are clichés, I think, is that they express an idea well. Once some clever bozo formulates the idea to perfection there's no reason to concoct another way of putting it, so everybody hops on the first guy's phrase and away we go.

Away we go.

Right.

See, I do it myself. I guess we all do.

For instance, "Be careful what you wish for, you just might get it." That, or minor variations on it, has been around for years, and I'll bet a nickel that no day goes past without some pundit using it for the title of a newspaper column or some screenwriter putting it into a script. You doubt that? Paste it into your search engine and see how many hits you get.

And as for me, I was tired of living in the 'burbs. Sunnyvale strikes me as an up-scale, latter-day Levittown for the technologically hip and the economically ambitious. I bought a house there for my family when my wife and I were still getting along and our very little girl was a daily ray of sunshine for us both.

Well, fifteen years and one divorce later, the dotcom boom and bust have swept through our happy little suburb, my daughter wants to go live with her mother because men just don't understand women (and she's right about that one!), and I manage to sell the house for a decent price. Enough to get me into a new condo on Drumm Street in San Francisco and even put a few bucks in the bank. I can see the Bay Bridge and the Bay itself and the lights of Oakland and environs from my living room window.

For a while I made a decent living, most of it by telecommuting, although I must confess that business has been slow of late and I've been casting worried if not panicked glances at my bank account. I do enjoy the variety and color of the city instead of trying to play Jim Anderson of the old *Father Knows Best* sitcom with my own daughter as innocent young Betty. I tried hitting the singles bars briefly but I quit that when I discovered they were full of twenty-year-olds and forty-year-olds trying to look twenty. I didn't want to fall into that pit!

Online dating was something else, and I was amazed at the women I met there. People my own age who shared my attitudes and interests. It was easy to sort out the ones who just wanted to get laid—not that there's anything wrong with that—-and the ones who never wanted to get laid—and before I knew it I was hooked up with a lovely, mature, intelligent woman. She had her place, I had my place, we enjoyed each other's company, and it looked as if the relationship was actually going to have legs.

The only problem, in fact, came from her name. Martha Washington, would you believe it? She's some kind of remote cousin, many times removed, of Our First President. The surname was tough enough but her parents apparently thought it would be fun to name their child for the First, First Lady. After enough years of ribbing and a couple of marriages and divorces (and who am I to criticize on that score?), she decided to take back her maiden name and make it a point of pride rather than an embarrassment.

Well, good for Martha, says I. Besides, she loves good music, she cooks well (as do I), she makes fascinating conversation, and we please each other in bed. A lot.

So it looks as if I came out of my divorce really well, not even hating my ex or being hated by her, and living the pleasant life of a middle-aged single in the first decade of this the twenty-first century.

Then Ed Guenther phoned.

"Can you come in for a meeting, Webster?"

I asked him what about.

"We've got a project we'd like you to consult on."

Okay, that meant at least a day's pay at a fat hourly fee. It would mean renting a car; I'd dumped my faithful Saab when I sold the Sunnyvale house, but I'd hit Ed for the rental. If my business had been booming I would have played hard to get, but revenues were down and I was, to put it mildly, starting to feel uneasy around the money belt. Even so, I wanted a little more info before I agreed.

"You had that experience with the Dreemz.biz outfit, Web."

I grunted.

"I know you were pretty upset by the end of it. Felt they were doing some dangerous stuff."

That was an understatement. Dreemz.biz pretty well scrambled my brain, and I don't know how many others. The Feds got into the act and the company quietly disappeared and its founding guru and CEO, a sharpy named Carter Thurston Hull, did the same. Where was he now, St. Elizabeth's? Guantanamo? Rumania? Just try asking, but if you do, don't blame me for what happens to you next.

"We know you were pretty upset by the end of the gig, Web."

"Sure, Ed, if you call six months in the bin alternating between ultra-high-dose tranks and intensive therapy sessions being pretty upset."

"Well, but you know what that stuff is like, and we think you can give us some important help with a new product." He paused for effect. I knew Ed Guenther well enough to know that he was sitting with his eyes closed, counting down, ". . . four, three, two, one . . ." And then he would open his eyes, inhale sharply, and get rolling again. I also noticed that he was bouncing back and forth between *I* and *we*, another favorite trick of his. Was he talking for himself or was he talking for Silicon Research Labs, Inc? *I* or *we?*

Good old Ed. I'd worked with him before and he was a pretty good guy. Pretty good. But I wouldn't exactly trust him with the only can opener on the island if we were marooned with a case of canned goods and no other source of nourishment.

"Actually it's more than a product, Webster. It's an important new tool. It's really exciting. I think you're going to love this one."

A quick glance at the calendar, a mental calculation of my bank balance and current cash flow, and I made an appointment to spend a day at SRL, Silicon Research Labs, Incorporated, and find out what Ed Guenther had up his sleeve.

The car I rented was a hybrid. I figure I can't reverse global warming—I wish I could!—or even stop it but at least I can limit the damage that I personally do to this planet. I cruised down 280, pulled into a visitor's slot at SRL, and told the five-year-old receptionist that Mr. Sloat was here to see Mr. Guenther.

Ed bustled into the lobby, curly iron-gray hair in need of a trim, five o'clock shadow on his jaw even at ten in the morning, striped sleeves rolled up, and grabbed my hand in a paw the size of a catcher's mitt. He put his arm around my shoulders and practically carried me off to a conference room. There were half a dozen Silicon Valley types there. A couple looked old enough to have survived the big meltdown. The rest were members of the new generation. I felt a rush or relief that I wasn't making the Union Street singles bars trying to compete with the likes of these kids. They looked as if they belonged on the campus at Stanford or Berkeley but I knew they were already looking over their shoulders at the next generation of grads.

Before we got started, Ed delivered a little lecture on the fact that we were going to be exposed to classified information and under penalty of fine or imprisonment and yada-yada-yada. There was nothing there I hadn't heard a dozen times before, and I signed the confidential disclosure form with my trusty Cross ball-point that I'd got from a onetime employer for completing five years of honorable service.

There were carafes of coffee on the table, fake leather folders with the SRL logo emblazoned on the covers, and freshly sharpened pencils for all. Obviously, they were out to impress good old Webster Sloat. Frankly, it made me apprehensive. I opened my folder, trying to look casually curious, and found nothing inside but a fresh pad of lined paper with a different logo ghosted in the middle of each page. It was an abstract sketch that might have been a spiral nebula crossed with a happy face with just a suggestion of God as we know and love Him from Michelangelo's Sistine Chapel painting. The lettering WYSHES.COM ran across it.

Ed Guenther introduced me to the gang. Most likely they'd been briefed in advance. That's the way Ed worked. But he went over my sterling credentials, credited me with heroic public service in the Dreemz.biz affair, considerately overlooked the fact that I'dwound up in the cuckoo's nest after it was over. Then he turned the meeting over to the genius whose work I was supposed to support.

Her name was Miranda Nguyen. She squinted through Harry Potter glasses. Her face was makeup-free. She was as tall as I was and must have weighed sixty-five pounds. She was wearing a Xena Warrior Princess tee shirt that had clearly seen better days. I'm sure she washed her hair on occasion but I wouldn't want to guess how often that occurred.

When Miranda stood up I was afraid for a moment that she was going to topple over. She righted herself, flicked on a computer-fed image projector, switched off the overhead lights and started to lecture.

She did not lose me with her first word, or even with her first sentence, but by the middle of what must have been her first paragraph I was floundering and before I could finish a cup of hot SLR Custom Roast Mocha Java I realized that I had no idea what she was talking about.

Well, almost no idea. I'd made my living for the past decade turning the jargon of programmers and circuit designers and systems engineers into at least semi-literate and somewhat understandable prose. I bore down and managed to get at least the gist of Ms. Nguyen's pitch. She had reverse-engineered the software that my old buddy Carter Thurston Hull had used to make his *dreemz* seem realer than real. Apparently Miranda knew that he'd also come within a hair's breadth of wrecking my brain, and God knows what he did to how many other customers. But Miranda Nguyen had developed some *mixed-ware*—circuitry plus programming—that she claimed would work better than Hull's and would be perfectly safe for the user.

I believed her, every word.

And there's that nice new Bay Bridge they're working on at this very moment, and if you'd like to buy it from Yours Truly, I'm sure we could strike a really attractive bargain.

Ms. Nguyen sat down to a smattering of applause from her colleagues and Ed Guenther introduced the next genius. Alberto Salazar. Alberto Salazar from NASA Ames, a few miles up the freeway from Silicon Research Labs. Alberto was Mexican from the top of his glossy black hair to the tips of his tan fingers. Mexican, yes, but I had a feeling that he was a full-blooded Mayan or something close to it. He had an accent you could cut *con una cuchilla.* And he was living proof that we need all the smart immigrants we can get, *con documentación o sin.*

And he didn't mince words, accent or no accent.

"There are aliens," he said. "They're not here, they're not little greenies or busty blonde princesses or monsters who want to cook us for dinner, Rod Serling and Damon Knight notwithstanding."

He paused and I guessed it was my turn to contribute something, even if it was only a question. "They don't zip around in flying saucers or abduct fishermen from Mississippi, then?"

"Nope. We're not sure where they are, but they're probably very far from Earth. There's some debate in NASA as to whether they're on the other side of the galactic disk or in another galaxy altogether."

"Are they a threat?" I asked.

"As far as I know they're totally unaware that we even exist."

"Then why trouble trouble?"

"Good question." Alberto smiled. "Again, some of our people say we should just pull our heads in and hope they never notice us. Others think we need to go out and say hello, take a risk if we need to, see what happens."

"What do you think, Alberto?"

"Who, me? I'm just a humble astronomer. My ancestors had the chance to wipe out their first European visitors and they didn't. So it's risky, I can't deny it. Still, Mr. Sloat, it's a basic philosophical question. Do we want to be *tortugas o iguanas?*"

"You lost me," I said. "I know what an iguana is but what's a tortuga?"

"Sorry," he said.

I didn't think for a split second he was sorry.

"Sorry," he repeated. "That means *turtles or iguanas*. Do we want to pull our heads in, hide in our shells, and hope nobody notices us, or do we want to get out there and move, make friends if we can or fight like hell if we have to. That was the mistake my ancestors made. They were ready to make friends but they weren't ready to fight, and they wound up in chains. But enough of that. What do you think about playing *Let's Make a Deal* with alien critters?"

"Not my field," I told him. "You want the SETI people, don't you? Or maybe Spielberg?"

"No, Mr. Sloat. We want you."

I felt my brain racing. All I could do was ask the obvious question. "Why me?"

"Because you've experienced *dreemz* and lived to tell the tale. You emerged from the experience with your sanity intact." He shot a glance at another of the conferees, a black-skinned guy in a suit, the only one I'd seen at SRL.

The only suit, that is, not the only black-skinned individual.

The suit nodded almost imperceptibly, emphasize *almost,* and Salazar kept on going. "You'll hear from Mr. Armstrong shortly. But for now, I'll just beg your indulgence. Okay?"

"Okay." I don't think he caught my Señor Wences impression. "Before you go any farther, suppose you tell me how you know these Martians or whoever the hell they are, are out there."

Salazar said, "Miranda?"

Okay, it was Miss Saigon Olive Oyl's turn again.

The giant stringbean put a picture on the screen. I had no idea what it was, a neutron bomb detonator or a new model can opener. There was even a caption underneath the schematic that told me nothing.

"In attempting to resolve the Einsteinian FTL dilemma and achieve tachyonic acceleration," Miranda Nguyen piped—did I tell you that she had a reedy, almost incomprehensible way of speaking?—we felt that a first modest attempt at ultra-high-speed data transmission would be a suitable preliminary to sending matter through a Hawking-Murray-Disch destabilizing filter."

"Good for you," I muttered under my breath.

"We were unable to achieve our goals," she told her tee shirt—anybody else who wanted to listen in, could—"but the Law of Unintended Consequences kicked in and we picked up signals. At first we thought they were random radiation, just as early researchers thought that cosmic rays were messages and our friends at SETI did when they first turned on their giant arrays and got instant results. So we were very cautious about what we were getting, but after a while we were able to translate them into visuals."

"Don't tell me they were old *I Love Lucy* episodes." I know I was being nasty but by this time I couldn't help it.

"No, Mr. Sloat." She didn't bat an eye. Go figure. "They were not old *I Love Lucy* episodes. Not even early *South Parks*. I'll show you what we got."

She tinkered with her Power Point gadget and the screen lit up with something that looked vaguely like two bright pink pool balls and something that I couldn't really describe except that it looked a little like an ebony marble, all in a row. Whatever the something was, my eyes, to honest, just couldn't deal with it. Or maybe my brain was incapable of processing the signal that came zooming up the optic nerve.

"What do you think of that, Mr. Sloat?"

"Deponent knoweth not what he see-eth," I told her.

"It's a complex star system," Salazar put in. "Three stars locked in a gravitational gavotte."

"I see two pink object that I suppose could be stars," I conceded, "but what's that—that other thing?"

"We're not quite sure. Most likely it's a neutron star. We've consulted with some of the best brains in the world, even got to Coleman at Harvard. Lots of suggestions. No certainties. If it's a neutron star, it must have gone nova at some point in time. And if that's the case, it should have destroyed its two partners. Obviously it didn't."

"And you got this image—how?" I asked.

Miranda Nguyen actually flashed me a grin. "I picked it up and decoded it. And we have plenty of others, Mr. Sloat. Treat yourself to a gander at this one."

Treat myself to a gander. Right.

She flashed through a rapid series of images, finally settled on one that showed the two pink stars much more faintly than I'd seen them before. "This took a lot of tweaking," she said, "but we were finally able to get this far."

The image on the screen showed the two pink stars and the I-had-no-way-to-describe-it thingamabob, and several tiny disks apparently caught in mid-flight between them.

I asked, "Are those planets?"

Alberto Salazar said, "Probably."

Miranda Nguyen played with her tinker toy a little more. The two pink stars and the thingamabob grew still fainter, the things that Salazar said were probably planets grew larger, and some specks no larger than single pixels appeared, dancing like dust motes in a sunbeam.

"Jesus."

"You got it, Web." Ed Guenther switched on the overhead lights. "End of slide show. Our Trip to Yosemite, preserved for the ages." He paused and looked around. I hadn't made so much as a doodle in my nice leatherette SRL folder.

I said, "I'll bet I can guess what Wyshes.com does."

Ed Guenther said, "I'll bet you can."

One thing about SRL, they don't skimp. It was time for a lunch break and our hosts treated us to limp sandwiches on balloon bread and bottled water, followed by coffee or something that I guess was supposed to be coffee. Was it stale or just weak?

As the great Nero Wolfe used to say, *Pfui!*

The afternoon session was at least shorter than the morning had been. The star performer was Robert Armstrong from NIMH. Since everybody else in the room knew each other before I arrived, I wasn't surprised when Armstrong reached across the table to shake my hand and repeat his name.

"Any relation to Carl Denham?" Golly, I thought I was being clever. Either he'd never heard that line before or he was an expert at keeping a poker face. I guessed it was the first and pretended I hadn't heard myself, muttered, "Pleased ta meetcha," and sat back down.

"I've studied Mr. Sloat's file and I want to remind everyone present that Mr. Sloat's privacy rights are very important to the United States government and must be respected by us all."

What the heck?

"Mr. Sloat is unique among the 14,293 known cases of persons victimized by the *Dreemz.biz* disorder, in that he apparently achieved a level of complete psychotic dissociation and has fully recovered from said break. Of the other cases, well over 13,000 went into psychic shock as a result of their experience, and emerged with little or no damage but also with little or no memory of their experiences."

Fourteen thousand? I wasn't so egotistical as to think I was the only sucker to fall for Charles Thurston Hull's nasty game, but I had no idea there were that many fools.

"Approximately 1,000 individuals," Armstrong went on, "to be precise, 857, suffered serious damage. Of these, 294 committed suicide, 18 became violent and were killed in accidents or by law enforcement officers, and the remaining 549 remain hospitalized. Their prognosis is not encouraging."

He looked around the table, smiling brilliantly. You'd have thought he had just won the lottery. "Mr. Sloat here, you see, is uniquely qualified to become the subject, should I say the operator, of our newest investigative tool."

"Which," Ed Guenther put in, "we call Wyshes.com."

Guenther had risen to his feet. I don't know why but suddenly he appeared to be at least six inches taller and eighty pounds heavier than anyone else in the room.

After the session I headed back toward San Francisco. Before I pulled onto the freeway I used my cell phone to check calls on my home answering machine. There was one from Martha Washington so I called her back.

She asked if I was busy tonight.

I told her I was not.

She said, "How about dinner out?"

I said I was feeling jangled and had a lot on my mind and could I have a rain check.

She said she thought as much from the sound of my voice and invited me to her place instead. "I'll whip something up, we can drink a glass of wine and listen to some music. I bet you'll feel better."

How could I refuse?

She lives in a restored Victorian in Noe Valley. Built right after the 1906 quake-and-fire, amazing gingerbread trim, bright yellow paint with white trim, high ceilings, cut glass, carved and polished wood. Amazing. Makes my condo look like a Motel 6. Or maybe the Bates Motel, with Tony Perkins ready to jerk back the shower curtain at any moment.

Did I mention that Martha has amazing powers of empathy? She could read my mood like a book. (There, how's that for a cliché?) I showed up on her doorstep after surviving the freeway back from Silicon Valley without even stopping at my condo for a clean-up and fresh clothes. I knew if I tried that I would have flopped on my bed between shower and dressing and that would have been it for good old Webster Sloat.

Another thing I love about Martha is her amazing talent for irony. She met me in the vestibule of her Queen Anne. Of course, nobody has built a house with a vestibule for seventy-five years at least. She was wearing a satiny copper-colored hostess gown that set off her rich, auburn hair and that showed plenty of cleavage with a tiny diamond-and-pearl pendant just above her sternum. She held a glass of pinot noir from a winery we'd visited together up north in Ukiah. The house was illuminated by candles and there was music playing.

Music.

We'd been exploring some difficult composers for the past couple of months, downloading their works and listening to them—*really* listening to them—at her place or at mine, then trying to find live performances to attend. Not easy when you're into Ives, Schoenberg, Edgar Varese or late John Coltrane from his "sheets of sound" period.

But tonight she had put on a Mozart clarinet concerto. Cool, melodic, just involving enough, not too challenging.

You see what I mean? Hostess gown, candles, wine, Mozart. It was just perfect and it made me feel something in my chest that I didn't think I'd ever feel again, after my divorce. But did Martha have her tongue in her cheek, just a little bit?

I didn't worry about that. I took her in my arms, gave her a warm (not hot) kiss, and accepted the glass of wine. We strolled into her Victorian parlor arm-in-arm and made ourselves comfortable. She must have sensed that I wasn't ready to talk about the day's events so she went first. She works in the Mayor's office and she dotes on City Hall gossip the way a soap fan relishes the latest convolutions of a favorite daytime serial.

The Sewers and Streetlamps Commissioner had her nose out of joint because her most recent boyfriend had left her to take up with her former boyfriend, whom she had lusted after so dearly that she had abandoned her own former girlfriend to be with him. Her former girlfriend had even offered to undergo a sex change if it would just keep her steady squeeze in her bed, but the course of true love was clear, leaving a playing field strewn with angry exes and one couple—was it the Commish herself and her new sweetums? I couldn't quite keep up with the comings and goings—reportedly indulging in a nightly sexual circus that would make the Mitchell Brothers blush.

The whole sequence of events had left the San Francisco political community in a state of sexual confusion.

Martha laid out some *hors d'oeuvres* and we snacked on them, finished the bottle of pinot noir, and kissed and cuddled for a while. The Mozart ended and was replaced by Tchaikovsky's Sixth, a transfer of the old 1959 Carl Maria Giulini version. Somewhere along the way Martha disappeared into the kitchen and returned carrying a cold ahi tuna salad and two forks. How we got from there to her bed I cannot tell you; I think that Tchaikovsky may have wafted us through the air.

We made love, and rested, and made love again, and I was finally ready to talk about my visit to Silicon Research Labs and Wyshes.com.

And Martha was ready to listen. By the time I'd reviewed the events of the day, Ed Guenther's butter-wouldn't-melt-in-his-mouth performance and the pitches of the various bigdomes, Martha was interjecting little hmm's and mm's and mm?'s every time I paused for breath. She seemed particularly intrigued by Robert Armstrong's actions. Why would the National Institutes of Mental Health care about Wyshes.com?

I reminded her that Dreemz.biz had walloped almost 15,000 people's sanity, with a variety of outcomes ranging from apparently complete recovery—me—to those poor souls who just couldn't deal with Carter Thurston Hull's nasty gift and took their own lives. Nearly 300 of them.

Martha was sitting against the headboard of her bed by now. She was still naked after our love-making and the flickering candlelight in the room cast a deep shadow between her breasts. I leaned over the planted a kiss right there and she laughed and wrapped her arms around me. She is not a fragile flower.

"Web, I don't want to sound stupid but after everything you've told me I still don't know exactly what this Miranda Nguyen's—what did she call it?— "

"Mixed-ware."

"—what it's supposed to do. And what was that Salazar genius from NASA all about? What do they want you to do? I guess that's the main question, what the hell do they want you to do, Webster?"

"They want me to be the first of a new breed of astronauts. They want me to go play footsie with the aliens. Or potsy. Or poker. Something."

"Not in a spaceship, though." She shook her head. Her medium-long hair swung around her shoulders and made a screen between me and the rest of the world. I wanted to stay inside that screen for good, but I knew that wasn't in the cards.

That wasn't in the cards. Charge one more to my cliché account.

"That's where the Hull events come in." I pushed myself up and stretched. "I'll be right back, Martha." I climbed out of bed and padded to the kitchen. I brought us each a cold mineral water with a slice of lime.

I climbed back into bed with Martha. Jesus, I had a hard time keeping my mind off sex when I was a randy teenager but now that I'm a middle-aged ex-husband with graying hair and the beginning of a pot belly I'm worse than ever. What the hell is the matter with me?

"Okay." I ordered myself to concentrate. "You know, I'm not supposed to talk about this. We could both wind up in the slammer."

"Bullshit, Webster. Come on, spill." Martha is not a blushing rose, either.

"Armstrong says that NASA has been trying to develop an ultra -high-speed communication system. They're serious about sending people to Mars and they don't want the long delay in radio transmissions. Even talking to moon bases involves a little delay, but they can live with that. But once you get much farther away from Earth, it's a serious problem."

I paused to gather my thoughts.

Martha waited.

"They've been trying all sorts of things to get around the speed-of-light problem. Looking for wormholes, trying to produce fourth-dimensional paper-folds, searching for tachyons."

"Science fiction." Martha grinned.

"No," I said. "They're serious about it, and when they set up an experimental transmitter and receiver they started getting messages. I mean, messages that they hadn't sent. Scared the bejesus out of 'em."

Scared the bejesus out of 'em. Rack up another one.

Martha said, "What kind of signals?"

"Visuals." I told her about the three-sun system. I was starting to think of 'em as Big Pink, Little Pink, and Gingrich the Neutron Star. I told her about the planets that didn't so much circle any of those stars as weave among them in a wildly complex dance. And I told her about the dust-motes, if that's what they were, that appeared to weave among the planets. And of course they weren't dust motes. Oh, no. They were certainly not dust motes.

"I ask again, Webster, although I have a feeling I already know the answer, I'll ask you again anyway, What do they want you to do?"

"They want me to go there."

"By super-high-speed wormhole tachyon express?"

"Nope. By Miranda Nguyen's mixed-ware gadget. By Wyshes.com."

Martha swung her legs off the bed and stood between me and a candle. All I could see of her was her silhouette. She said, "You're going."

I said, "You're way ahead of me."

"I'm not trying to influence you."

"I know it. It scares the piss out of me, but I'm going."

Scares the piss out of me. Ding!

"And this will be something like your Dreemz.biz experiences?"

"Not very much."

* *** *

First, Carl Denham's—I mean, Robert Armstrong's—people at NIMH had to run me through every mental health and stability, does this guy have a firm grip on reality, etc., test in the book, plus a couple that I think they made up just for my personal benefit. I won't say that I came through with flying colors but Armstrong did finally sign off.

Every test in the book. Flying colors. Two for the price of one. Whoops! Two for the price of one. Call that a bonus point.

I saw Rorschach blobs variously as grasshoppers, butterflies,

Satanic faces, and vaginas. Once I got to vaginas I think Armstrong let a small smile escape. I associated *mother* with *love, rain* with *wet, pencil* with *paper* and *alien* with *Roberto Salazar.* I think that last one upset Armstrong until he decided I was pulling his leg. I balanced on one foot, admitted that I'd experimented with weed and acid and coke in my wild youth and denied that I'd used anything illegal in the past couple of decades. I told him that I'd masturbated as a teenager, had sex with approximately thirty women in my life and with one man. Didn't like the latter and never repeated the experiment. I told him that I thought maybe there was a God and maybe not, I really didn't know.

Oh, was it ever fun.

Armstrong decided I was sane, or at least sane enough to put at risk once I signed the release form that Ed Guenther kindly provided.

I had to pass a pretty rigorous physical, but nothing excessively demanding. After all, I didn't have to sit on top of a giant firecracker and get launched into outer space. I was going to travel by—what? Might as well be honest and go all the way back to Madame Blavatsky and her gang of wild and crazy partiers and call it astral projection.

Miranda Nguyen personally showed me her wonderful gadget, the Wyshes.com device.

Have you ever had a CT Scan? Computerized Tomography? I did, a few years ago. One of my internal organs blew up and the docs at the Cal Pacific Med Center decided they needed a good look at my innards. First I had to drink a cocktail with some kind of gunk in it to make my insides show up. It came in banana and chocolate flavors. I asked the refugee from Romper Room who ran the dispensing station which one she recommended and she said, "Doesn't matter, Mister. Whichever one I suggest you'll drink it and get mad at me because no matter how bad the other one is, this one has to be worse."

Actually I had to do the do a couple of times, once before a surgeon went in and fixed my plumbing and once after he was finished. I tried the banana once and the chocolate once and they were both worse.

Anyhow, Miranda Nguyen's Wyshes.com device looked

something like a CT Scanner. There's a big donut-shaped thingamy with enough flashing lights on it to make George Lucas wet his pants. You lie down on a powerized gurney and an operator plays Phantom of the Opera at a futuristic looking control panel. The gurney rolls into the giant donut and if you're strapped to it, as I was, even for a dry run, you feel as if somebody made a mistake and sent you to the Fisher and Sons Mortuary for cremation.

It took a couple of weeks for everybody to brief me on what to expect and how to react. Then everybody from the cafeteria manager to the corporate comptroller had to sign off. Then they had a little party in my honor, complete with SRL baseball caps and Wyshes.com tee shirts.

And then there was no more putting it off. I sent a text message to Martha Washington's Blackberry, handed the keys to my rented hybrid and my condo to Ed Guenther, transmitted an internet greeting card to my daughter in care of her mother saying that I loved her, and told my courtiers, "I'm ready."

One of the guards slit the bottoms of my trousers, the chaplain read a few verses from the Bible, and we went a-strolling to the little green Wyshes.com room.

Just kidding.

But it was a creepy feeling. Maybe more like old Boris lying on Dr. Frankenstein's operating table and getting hoisted into the storm than Bogey getting fried in a Warner Brothers gangster epic. Once I was settled comfortably on the gurney, they had to blindfold me and block my ears. An all-out sensory deprivation tank might have served better, but Miranda Nguyen's super-donut wouldn't have worked under water. And lying on soft padding pretty well damped out tactile sensations.

So there I was locked inside my skull with nobody for company but myself and nothing to play with but my own thoughts. I tried to imagine the lights flashing and the micro motors whirring, electrons flashing and data gates opening and shutting in Miranda's mixed-ware. I tried to see that picture that Alberto Salazar had showed me of those three stars, Big Pink and Little Pink and Newt, and the planets that wove among them and the dust motes that floated from one to another.

Except I knew they weren't dust motes.

And then I was out of my head. I don't mean crazy, although upon further review maybe I was at that. I didn't feel myself leaving my body and there was none of the light show folderol that Carter Thurston Hull's Dreemz.biz provided. It was more like falling asleep, where you're not aware of the transition between waking and dream states. Just that, there you are lying in your bed gazing up at the ceiling or maybe at the inside of your eyelids, and then you're walking on the beach in Maui with a lovely naked maiden, the surf is crashing, the breeze is wafting the odor of jasmine to you and—and how the hell did you get from Smallville, Kansas, to Maui?

No idea, right? No sense of transition, certainly no sensation of travel. Just—you were in one place and then you're in another.

I knew where I was, too. I was out there at Big Pink and Little Pink and Newt. I knew where I was but there's no way I can tell you, exactly. I mean, I wasn't at Betelgeuse or Alpha Centauri or Beta Reticuli or NGC 9999 or any other star that we've cataloged and named.

Oh, no.

If you went all the way to the center of our galaxy, tipped your hat to the black hole that's been sitting there gobbling up matter for the past several billion years, continued to the far side of the galaxy and then jumped off, you would just be starting to go where I was. You'd have to hopscotch over a couple of galactic clusters, hang a couple of sharp curves through the third, fourth, and polka -dot dimensions, reach down your own throat until you came to the inside of your great toe, grab hold and pull with all your might.

You would hear a loud *pop!* and you would have a slight idea of where I was.

Or you could just click your ruby slippers together and say, "I wish, I wish, I wish I was in Kansas!"

Hey, worked for Dorothy Gale, didn't it?

How long did it take me to get there, wherever *there* was? I don't know whether I know and can't tell you, or I don't know myself. You know how time passes in a dream? It was a little bit like that. I could have been floating in that sensory-deprived limbo, wondering what the hell I'd let myself in for, for a few seconds or for ten thousand years. Ten million years. It just doesn't make sense. And it wasn't like a Dreemz.biz dream, oh no, this was one of Miranda Nguyen's wyshes. Very different. Very.

There they were, Big Pink, Little Pink, and Newt.

Alberto Salazar had given me a crash course in star types. As far as I could make it out, Big Pink was a Type M red giant. A huge thing, nearing the end of its stellar lifetime, with a relatively low surface temperature of a few thousand degrees Celsius. Little Pink was a red dwarf. They were both variables, Big Red with a long period and Little Red with a much shorter one.

Newt was indeed a neutron star, its diameter not much more than five miles. If you stood on its surface and if you could move you could walk around the mother in a day. But of course its substance was so dense and its gravity so strong, you'd be squashed into a kind of Flatland creature in a fraction of a second, and even if that didn't happen you'd be held down so you couldn't lift a foot no less walk around the star.

I tried to figure out who or what I was. In Carter Thurston Hull's dreemz I'd been able to flit from mind to mind and from person to person. I'd been Stu Sutcliffe at Candlestick Park, Robert Oppenheimer at Alamogordo, and Howard Lovecraft sitting at his desk in Providence, Rhode Island. Did I have to be somebody to function in Miranda Nguyen's wysh?

I tried looking at myself, you know, the way you hold your hand in front of your face in a dream to make sure you're alive, but there was nothing there. At least, there was nothing there for a moment, and then there was. Yes, there was the good old familiar Webster Sloat *mano* that had lifted a thousand brewski's and fondled a hundred derrieres.

Then I blinked.

My hand was changing. The knuckles became smaller, the fingers more tapered, the skin smoother. I looked down and there was the generous cleavage of my squeeze Martha Washington. I picked up a mirror and . . .

Okay, where the hell did I get a mirror?

If I knew the answer to that one I would be totally willing to tell you.

I picked up a mirror, no, I sat down in front of a mirror, no, I stood in front of a mirror and I was Martha Washington. I was starkers except for that tiny diamond and pearl pendant and I won't deny that I was fuckin' gorgeous, baby.

Nice rounded shoulders, but even as I stood there looking at myself I felt myself changing again. I held out my arms and they got longer and longer until I could hardly see my hands. I was getting taller, too, and my head—Martha's good-looking head—was morphing into something a little bit like a god damned pteranodon.

A pteranodon? Fuck me, what the hell was that about? I barely knew what a pteranodon was, some kind of amazing aerial reptile that lived in the age of dinosaurs and disappeared from the Earth fifty or a hundred million years ago.

What?

I turned my head and looked at my arm, now something like a bat-wing with claw-like fingers and thin, hollow bones holding up an impossibly thin membrane. The membrane was pinkish in color, or maybe it was colorless and picked up the glare of pink light from around me.

Okay, calm down, Sloat. You're here, wherever the hell here is. You are a pink pteranodon.

Yiiiiiiikes!

Did I just say what I thought I said? Talking to myself, okay, that's not as crazy as it might be, "thinking out loud" (ding!) isn't that far from talking to yourself, is it? Okay, Sloat, *You are a pink pteranodon.*

This was a lot crazier than anything that happened to me in one of Carter Thurston Hull's dreemz. God bless Miranda Nguyen!

Calm down, calm down,

All right, maybe this is another kind of dream, or dreem, or wysh. If I'm a—don't say it again, just let it go, Sloat—okay, if I am a whatever-the-heck, if that is *what* I am, then *where* am I? Okay, okay, I came out here courtesy of Guenther, Nguyen, Salazar, and Armstrong. Sounds like a high-price downtown law firm but in fact it was my committee of pals at Silicon Research Labs. I'm someplace near Big Pink, Little Pink, and Newt, somewhere in some galaxy someplace in this great big friggin' universe of ours.

Look around, Sloat. Look down. Look at your feet.

Gaak! Big scaly things with claws like the pigeons in Golden Gate Park. Okay, never mind that, what are you standing on, buddy?

A pink surface, pink or maybe white or a sort of colorless translucence picking up the light from Big Pink or Little Pink, whichever one that star up there is. Hey, I can see both of those old red stars up above, and I can even see Newt the neutron star in the distant sky.

Newt the Neutron Star, a picture book for ages three and up, by Webster Sloat. Might be salable. I'll have to look at that when I get back to California.

When I get back to California. Lots of luck.

I can see down into the earth—well, of course it isn't "Earth, earth" but what the heck, close enough for federal work—I can see down into the earth a ways but then things get jumbled and confused looking. I can reach down with my claws, the ones that used to be hands, I think, and feel the surface I'm standing on.

Is it sand? Feels kind of like sand. I pick up a claw full and let it sift through my, er, claws. There's a wind here and the sand, if that's what it is, drifts away. Except it's awfully cold. I pick up some more and hold it close to my eyes. My eyes seem to work very, very well today. This is one pteranodon who doesn't need specs. The stuff is grainy like sand, all right, but I have a feeling it's something else, maybe ice.

The wind is getting stronger and sure enough the sand or ice is getting swept up off the ground (?) ground (?) ground (?) and swirled through the air (?) and it stings as it collides with my skin (?) or membrane.

Just for the heck of it I try running into the wind, spreading my wings, my membranes, and then I jump and I can glide pretty well. I don't land quite so well. In fact I tumble head over ashcan (ding!) and bounce and roll over the icy terrain. But I am undaunted and I give it another try and do better, and then after a while I try flapping my wings once I'm airborne and I discover that, by golly gee, I can actually fly.

Soon I'm soaring over an eerie pink landscape of swirling ice-sand dunes. I can do an Immelmann. I can do an inside loop. I am one hell of a fine pteranodon, I'll tell you that. But am I really a pteranodon? Is this something that I conjured up out of my fevered imagination (hey, "fevered imagination," ding that!) at the behest of Miranda Nguyen, or is it really a native life form here on Pink, whichever Pink, actually on a planet that wandered between the Pinks and Newt, that I somehow morphed into when I arrived courtesy of Wyshes.com?

Pumping for altitude soon gets me high enough to see a hell of a lot of landscape, if that's the right term for miles and miles and miles of ice. Rocky ice, tumbled ice, ice dunes, ice plains.

Oh, boy!

Here comes something else.

One, two, three, many specks in the sky. They're moving in formation. My first thought is that this is a sign of intelligence. Then I think of the Canada geese who love to nest in Lake Merritt over in Oakland, to the delight of local ornithologists and the dismay of joggers and picnickers whose ideas of sanitation do not quite harmonize with those of the geese.

Intelligent? Well, maybe, but certainly not in any sense that implies you could sit down and discuss cosmic philosophy with them. Or even exchange clichés like *Pleased ta meetcha* and *Have a nice day.*

At the same time that I spot the specks the specks spot me. I'm playing at being a kite in the chilly breezes. The specks are already arranged in a chevron and their leader has obviously decided to take a closer gander at me. He-she-or-it does a sharp nose-over, pumps his-her-or-its wings, and comes zooming down at yours truly at a frightening rate. The rest of the formation follows.

There's no way I can fly away from these critters and I don't want to stay there and parlay with them because they seem to be equipped with nasty beaks and claws. I also know that I'm not experienced at this pteranodon business. This situation looks very damned scary, and I don't know whether Ed Guenther, Miranda Nguyen and Company would be more upset to get me back in bloody chunks or not to get me back at all.

And I think Martha Washington would be dismayed. And despite her teenaged rebelliousness, I do believe that my daughter likes the idea of having a father and would not take kindly to being told that I'd been, ah, *Wyshed* off to an alien world in a galaxy far, far away, only to be torn to shreds by a flock of flying pink dinosaurs.

No, this is not good.

At this point some circuit buried deep in my brain takes over. I'm not being modest. I was, to coin a phrase, scared witless. I did not know what to do. Those scary critters were rocketing at me and there couldn't be more than a few seconds before they sampled their first Sloat-kebob dinner.

And then they disappeared. What the hell? I swiveled my reptilian neck looking for them, and there they were, looking comically confused, a couple of thousand feet *below* me. What had happened? Had I jumped to a higher altitude just as they approached my lower one? Or, more intriguingly, had I *time-jumped* a few seconds into the future? I think that's what happened. I think I disappeared from my spot in the Pink firmament just as the nasties were about to reach me. They continued downward and I popped back into being, right where I'd been before, but they had zipped right through momentarily empty space.

You may get a giggle out of this. I automatically moved my arm—except that it was now a wing!—so I could get a look at my wristwatch. It's a genuine counterfeit $10,000 Rolex Oyster, by the way, that I bought over the internet for less than thirty bucks, and beat that if you can!

The predators tried another couple of passes at me, but pretty soon they gave it up as a bad job and went squawking and quarreling away through the sky. I have a feeling that there was going to be a leadership shakeup in that gang before very long.

If there were predators on this world there had to be prey, and if there was prey there had to be something for the prey to live on, too. I'm no expert on ecosystems, but it's just common sense that everything has to eat something. I dropped to a lower altitude. Keeping a watchful eye for more dive-bombers, I started a survey of the region.

After a while the ice dunes gave way to something truly remarkable. There were fields of something vaguely grassy or grain -like. This had to be damned hardy stuff, to thrive under these conditions. I doubted that its metabolism or biochemistry was much like life on Earth, but I also remembered something that an evolutionary biologist named Stephen Jay Gould had once said at a Silicon Valley tech session. Somebody in the audience had asked him to talk about extraterrestrial life forms, and Gould had modestly pointed out that he was not an exobiologist. But then he'd added, "It seems to be a law of nature that, wherever life *can* exist, it *will* exist."

He also added that the range of environments in which life had been found, even on Earth, was truly astonishing. I wondered what he would think of life on the Pink planets!

The fields of grain—apparently wild grain—gave way to forests, and in the forests I detected an astonishing variety of wildlife. There was a slithering, snakelike creature that must have been a couple of miles long and at least a hundred yards across, but not much more than a quarter of an inch thick. It had a face at one end, or something that I guess was a face. It moved through the forest, apparently scooping up small vegetation and any slow-moving creatures that got in its way.

It left behind perfectly round, flat objects that inflated to globular shapes and then sprouted trunks and limbs and leaves. What the heck kind of thing was that? A snake that gave birth to Frisbees that turned into volleyballs that turned into trees? And I suppose there would be little birdies building their nests in those trees. Yeah, sure.

Except there were, only they weren't birds, they were little flying dinosaurs, miniature versions of the current "me."

Oh, Ed Guenther sent the wrong guy out here. He should have recruited an exobiologist. This expedition alone would have brought home enough data to keep a dozen research institutes busy for the next twenty years.

I came to a river that flowed pinkly through the woods. Ahead there was a highland area, obviously the source of the river. I followed the river until it fed into a body of water that had to be a sea if not an ocean.

Pink, too.

There was plenty of marine life doing its stuff in that body of water. I flew out over the surface looking for ships or islands or any sign of civilization. I didn't find any but I was so focused on my search that I didn't notice a storm coming up. No, I didn't notice until I was buffeted by violent, swirling wind and smashed into a roaring wall of pink. I'd hit a waterspout.

I had a feeling that I could die in this world, in this Wysh, and if I did I would really be dead. Die in a dream and you'll really die, right? That's an old wives' tale (ding!) and I didn't take it seriously, but die in a Wysh? I didn't want to find out.

I tried to beat my wings and fly above the waterspout but I didn't have the strength. Things were looking desperate and then that old smart part of my brain took over again. Before you could say Jack Robinson (ding! ding!) I found myself swimming away from the storm. I couldn't see myself very well but I could feel my body, my organs, my beak.

Hot damn, I was a giant squid. An Architeuthis. Hey, don't ask me how I knew what those big guys are called. Must have learned it before dozing off in front of the National Geographic Channel one night. I was one big son of a gun! (Okay, ding!)

But as much fun and adventure as I was having on this world, I wanted at least a quick peek at a couple of other worlds in this cockamamie system.

Back at Silicon Research Labs I'd seen the pictures that Alberto Salazar had brought to our little clambake. They weren't exactly photographs, not exactly CGI's, certainly not drawings. But they were something, and they'd shown specks moving between the planets of the Pink System.

What were those specks?

Okay, subconscious brain, take over. I'm just a-squiddin' along here, happy as a—thought you'd get me, hey?—so let's see what you can do for good old Webster Sloat.

And—*wham!*—ask and it shall be given to thee! I was way, way above the planet, so high that the sky was black, the world was round, and there was hardly any atmosphere at all. I was back in my pteranodon persona. I guess that's a good shape. But this time I was far bigger than I'd ever been before. I was easily a thousand miles across, and I was so thin that a kid's toy balloon would have looked like a fat blob of pancake batter compared to me.

I was so thin, in fact, that I could maneuver in the solar wind coming from Big Pink and Little Pink. I was able to fly or sail or whatever you want to call it, and as I tacked I surveyed no fewer than sixteen planets that wove and danced among the three stars of the Pink System. I could write a book about the things that I saw, the marvels and the monsters of those worlds and their moons and their inhabitants. Hey, come to think of it, maybe I will. Write a book, that is. Why the heck not, it should sell plenty of copies and it'll be a lot more fun than editing software manuals and getting paid by the hour.

The seventeenth world that I visited was a water world, at least when I was there. I realized that those planets must experience amazing changes in their climates as the three stars of the system engaged in their eternal gavotte, and as the planets pirouetted around their primaries. A planet might be frozen solid at one point in its orbit and turn to a boiling hell at another.

This world was cold but not frozen. A global ocean covered it. It was pink, all right, but I hope I haven't given you the impression that the dominant color of the Pink System was that sweet pink that doting parents swathe their darling baby girls in. No, it was an angry pink, a raging magenta that tore at the eyes. Or at least that was the way it made my eyes feel.

And this world was populated by every manner of marine life, animal and vegetable, from microscopic algae to crustaceans and predators that would scare the daylights (okay, you got me) out of Clive Barker on a bad night. There were even flying creatures, the this-world equivalent of amphibians. They could swim to the surface of the world-ocean, use their version of a blowfish's inflatable membrane until they were, are you ready for this, living blimps, then propel themselves into the air and go merrily seeking their dinners.

There I was, just about ready to start packing it in and head for home if I could just figure out how to get back to dear old Earth, when I spotted the first sign of intelligent life I'd encountered on seventeen worlds.

The first thing I saw was, well, I guess you could call it an aircraft. Nothing like a Boeing 777 or a MiG-29 or a Bell helicopter. It had wings, maybe it resembled one of those B-2 stealth bombers just a little bit. But that would be like saying that

Arnold Schwarzenegger resembled Eddie Gaedel.

Yeah, Eddie Gaedel. You could look it up, but I'll save you the trouble. He was the only officially recognized "little person" ever to play major league baseball. He was a pinch-hitter for the 1951 St. Louis Browns, wore number 7/8 on the back of his jersey, used a toy bat, and drew a walk in his one and only appearance in an American League game.

He was later murdered and the case was never solved.

I am digressing, am I not?

This thing that looked like a cross between a mechanical sting ray and an artificial chiropteran was droning through the sky. I don't know where it came from and I didn't wait around to find out where it was headed. I abandoned my shape as a giant solar sail and tried something vaguely sharkish. I plunged into that global ocean. I tried to sense any kind of artificial activity and almost at once, there it was.

Beneath my fins was the largest city I had ever seen or even imagined. If it had been on Earth you could have dumped Tokyo, Beijing, New York, London, Paris, Rome, and Rio de Janeiro into one corner of it and hardly made a splash.

The ocean must have been two hundred miles deep, surrounding an icy core. The buildings of this city were easily twenty miles tall. Their shapes were jagged, projecting into the waters above them like angry, voracious mouths. The pressure must have been immense, but as Stephen Jay Gould had said, where life *can* exist . . .

I swam above the city. To the creatures who inhabited it, I imagine the heavy, cold water was as air is to the inhabitants of any city on Earth.

The denizens of the metropolis were clearly the product of the same evolution that had inspired their flying craft. They had bat-like wings and they swam with them, or in a sense flew through the water as aquatic rays seem to fly through the shallow seas of Earth.

Now I came to something that I can only compare to an outdoor amphitheater on Earth. It was immense, on a scale with everything else in this strange civilization. It must have held—I tried to calculate—no fewer than twenty million of the bat-winged rays. In the center of the arena thousands, no, tens of thousands of similar beings were—were—I can hardly bring myself to say it. They were staked to the ground.

I tried to get a closer look at them, suddenly realizing my peril. If these hideous monsters discovered me, captured me, there was no telling what my fate would be, but I knew it would be terrible. I used my shape-shifting ability to make myself into a tiny creature, so small and inconspicuous that I could observe the proceedings unnoticed.

The rays that were staked to the ground were clearly close biological relatives of the ones looking on, but there were small, subtle differences. Their cranial development was not identical. One species had a small triangular protuberance in the center of what I can almost bring myself to call a forehead. The other species had slightly longer claws on its bat-wings. The one species were a slightly paler shade of angry magenta, and mottled with irregular blotches; the other, a slightly darker shade, and solid in coloration.

Which were the more hideous? Which were the more terrible?

How could such monstrous conduct take place among such an obviously intelligent, obviously advanced race as these bat-rays? At first I was baffled but then I remembered the legendary sport of Vlad the Impaler, the Transylvanian ruler who gave rise to the legend of Dracula. I thought of the death camps of the Nazis and the killing fields of Pol Pot and a hundred other monstrous, cruel slaughters that my own species had carried out against its own.

No, there was nothing surprising here. These monsters were no worse than humans.

And gradually I realized that they were beautiful. They were lovely creatures, and the staking of their victims to the floor of the arena was an act of artistry. The occupants of the front row of the audience swept from their places and swooped down upon their struggling, staked victims and began to have sport with them. They tore at their bodies with their claws and their teeth, they ripped bits of flesh and tossed them back and forth like playthings before devouring them. They danced, they sang. They mated, mated on the writhing bodies of dying victims.

It was glorious.

I used my power to assume a shape like theirs. I plunged into the melee. I gorged. I cavorted. I—

Miranda Nguyen was standing over me, and Robert Armstrong was standing beside her. Armstrong had his hand on my wrist, clearly feeling for a pulse. Nguyen was fussing with the controls of her mixed-ware gadget.

For a moment I thought I was still a bat-ray, that I was surrounded by the magenta waters of the planet of those horrible beings. No, not horrible. Beautiful. They had found the full joy of life. Murder. And I was one of them.

The gurney was rolling out of Nguyen's machine. There were medical personnel there. I struggled to get free. I wanted to sink my teeth into their flesh, into their throats, to gorge myself on their blood.

Then Martha was there. How had they known of our involvement? How had they located her?

She was standing with Ed Guenther. There were tears on her face. She was trying to get to me but Guenther was holding her back. She called my name and I replied not with words but with a savage roar. That was the way to communicate. With roars and screams and death.

And death.

And death.

Trying to figure out how many times I'd lived with someone. Anyone. My parents, of course, and my brothers and sisters. If you've ever lived in a big, chaotic household you know what I mean, and if you haven't, well, maybe you can imagine and maybe you can't.

Summer camp when I was a kid. A dozen of us to a bunkhouse, iron cots lined up along the walls, the counselor's so-called room separated by a beaverboard partition. College, of course, first in a cramped cell called a dorm room and then in a frat house where the noise and booze and dope never let up.

My parents still had Louisa May Alcott, the family mutt we had adopted from the local animal shelter as a bedraggled pup. She had attached herself to me and we fell madly in love the way only a lonely little kid and a needy little dog can fall in love. Lonely with all those brothers and sisters milling around? I guess there were just so many of us, I needed somebody who was just mine, and that was Louisa.

When I finished college I got my first apartment and Louisa moved in with me. She was already pretty long in the tooth, and when she died of some kind of doggie Alzheimer's a couple of years later I cried for days. The only time I've cried from grief since I became a man. The only time I cried, I cried was tears of joy when my daughter was born.

I married young and Beloved Spouse came to live with me in an apartment about the size of a packing crate. Happy? We'd go off to work in the morning, both of us, taking the train up to San Francisco and separating to our jobs in dueling skyscrapers. We'd meet again at quitting time and head for home. We took turns with household chores.

The first meal that Beloved Spouse made for me—oh, how I remember that meal! Burned liver and green string beans and yellow wax beans. I made a face and Beloved Spouse—I didn't use the term sarcastically, at least not then—burst into tears and I comforted her as best I could and we wound up doing what newlyweds do.

Before very long I became a father, bought a house in the 'burbs in Silicon Valley, and lived the good life until my marriage fell apart and Beloved Spouse moved to for God's sake Glendale and divorced me by mail.

Our darling offspring, Daddy's best girl and chief pride and joy, reached the Atrocious Age, decided she hated my guts, and went to live with Mommy. She took our family pet, a shelter foundling named Anna Sewell, with her. I still love the little hellcat and hope she decides someday that I'm not the world's cruelest parent.

I sold the house in Sunnyvale, bought a postmodern condo on Drumm Street in San Francisco and watched 'em build the new Bay Bridge from my living room window. Oh, listen, I don't know what postmodern means either. Just thought I'd throw that in.

Then I met Martha Washington, her actual name, a big, loving, sensitive, sexy, sometimes vulgar woman of a certain age. Couple of years younger than I am, by the way. Martha owns a Queen Anne Victorian near the Panhandle. If you don't know San Francisco don't worry about that. It's a great house in a neighborhood that bottomed out a couple of decades ago and has been on the rebound ever since.

We kept both places so I suppose we're not officially "living together," although we seldom spend a night or a weekend apart.

Right now, though, things got a little bit off-kilter. Martha had to fly up to Seattle on business. There had been a series of burglaries in her neighborhood and she was worried about leaving her house untenanted for a week. My condo, on the other hand, was pretty secure. The building has a twenty-four-hour doorperson (he said with a slight smirk) and spy gadgets up the wazoo. Hasn't been a crime in the building since it opened, if you don't count the blow parties some of my younger, hipper, more affluent neighbors like to toss.

You see where this is going, don't you? Well, you're right.

Martha and I have keys to each other's digs, so I saw her off to the land of Boeing and Microsoft, drove back to her joint, locked my little Tesla (all right, I've worked hard and made a few bucks and I treated myself) in Martha's garage, deposited a couple of bags of groceries from Cala Foods in the kitchen, and settled in for a week of batching it.

I'd brought a stack of books with me. I have a limited repertoire as a chef but I'm pretty good at homemade *tarte aux champignons* and the meal tasted even better after a couple of fingers worth of Laphroaig that was laid down before I was born.

Martha had surprised me, though. On a low table next to my favorite chair she had left a little package and a note:

> **Webster—**
>
> **I know you're not a big TV fan but the new 3D set your friend Ed Guenther gave us for our "anniversary" is really spectacular. Ed sent over this disk and says it's truly amazing. I hope you'll watch it and give me a briefing when I get home.**
>
> **And thanks, sweetie, for watching my place for me. I can't wait to get back and tell you all about everything.**
>
> **Martha**

She was right about my not being a television addict. I don't knock people who have to have their nightly dose of sitcoms or cop shows or whatever, but I'd rather turn on some worthwhile music—Haydn, Vivaldi, Tchaikovsky, Sibelius—and open a good book, a biography or history, and lose myself in the words in the book and the sounds inside my head.

Still, when in Rome do as the Romans do, and in Martha's house, at her suggestion, I took a postprandial brandy, specifically a lovely Cypriot Zivania, into the TV den and loaded Ed Guenther's gift disk into the tray. I put on the fancy 3D glasses that came with the set. I hate those things, but never mind that. I hit the play button on the remote and leaned back in an easy chair.

At first the screen remained black and I thought that I'd done something wrong, but then a point of light appeared at the bottom edge of the screen. It moved toward me, or seemed to. I'd never tried this gadget before and I was impressed with the technology.

The light halted half a foot from my face. That is, it seemed to. I actually reached out but when I tried to touch it there was nothing there.

As I sat there studying the point of light, waiting for something else to happen, I got the very strange feeling that the point of light was intelligent and aware, and that even as I was studying it, it was studying me.

"You're going to die," said the point of light.

"Everybody dies," I answered.

"Doesn't matter," the point of light said. "*You* are going to die. What do you care if some llama-herder in the Andes dies, or a noodle-vendor in Osaka. That's their problem. Your problem is, *you* are going to die."

I felt pretty silly, arguing with a point of light that wasn't even there. When the point said something, it wasn't as if it had grown vocal cords and was actually talking. I didn't hear the voice of God or of James Earl Jones. I've always thought they were the same, anyhow.

But I didn't really hear anything. It wasn't even the way those science fiction writers describe telepathic communication, somehow hearing a voice inside your head. This was more like, oh, try this out: Did you ever have a feeling about reality? Did you ever just *know* something without having any idea in the world *how* you knew it?

Some people call that intuition, but that isn't an explanation, it's just a label.

I've had the experience a few times in my life. Example: When my Beloved Spouse was pregnant with our sole offspring, I knew the child was going to be a girl. I told Beloved Spouse and she asked how I knew. She hadn't had a sonogram or an amniocentesis. Didn't do the old coin-on-a-string test. Didn't try the old boys-carry-high-girls-carry-low thing.

"I just know," I told her.

Well, the child was born and of course she was a girl and I said to Beloved Spouse, "See, what did I tell you?"

To which Beloved Spouse replied, "Jeez, Webster, so you happened to guess right for once. It was a fifty-fifty shot to start with."

If we'd gone on to produce a large brood and I'd kept predicting their genders and getting them right we would have had a better sample, but we never did get more than that one little bundle of joy. But I really did know. I did. It was not a lucky guess. *Nosiree!*

But I digress.

"You're going to die," the point of light had said, and we'd had our little colloquy about the inevitability of universal extinction and then the point said, "Let's put it this way, Webster Sloat old man, you're a fifty-ish middle class American male in pretty decent health. You don't smoke. You don't mess around with any of those really nasty drugs. You drink a little but not to excess. That Cypriot Zivania brandy, by the way, was a superb choice on your part."

I said, "Thank you."

"Barring a meteor-strike, terrorist attack, botulism in your kohlrabi, or a mugging that goes wrong and turns into a murder case, you should live at least another thirty years. Maybe forty."

I said, "Okay." I figured the point of light was going somewhere with this. I wasn't working these days. Ed Guenther had me on call at Silicon Research Labs but SRL seemed to be having a quiet spell. I had some savings and a couple of cute little investments so I wasn't worried about money. So, I figured, I'd play along with Little Pointy, as I was starting to think of that talkative bit of glitter, and see what he, she, or it had to say.

"This wacky thing you call the universe is something like thirteen-and-a-half billion years old. Give or take a few hundred million. And it's about halfway through its life cycle. What went on before the starting gun went off and what will happen after the universe crosses the finish line, well, that's another matter. But even considering the twenty-seven billion year lifespan of the universe, the life cycle of a critter like you, Web, it less than the blink of an eye. In fact, you so-called living things come and go so fast, you hardly even exist at all."

Little Pointy's reference to everything that ever has or ever will draw a breath on this planet, from the biggest dinosaur to the tiniest bacterium as "so-called living things" was mildly nettlesome. But what the hell, I had bigger fish to fry in this conversation, so I hit him with the ultimate weapon of a onetime member of a high school debate team.

"So what?"

Can a point of light laugh scornfully? I think Pointy did. I realized I'd swung wild and missed by a yard, but at least Pointy didn't rub it in. Instead, he just went on with his spiel. And while he did so, I found myself wondering if this was some kind of gag that Ed Guenther had dreamed up, or maybe that Martha had put him up to. Anyway:

"So what do you think is going to happen to you, Web, when you finally hit the wall? *Splat!* Right? *Splat!* No more single malt scotch for you. No more pomace brandy. No more Beethoven. No more Schopenhauer. No more key lime pie. No more Martha Washington."

A pause. Then:

"No more Webster Sloat."

"No more crazy dialogues with pretentious fugitives from a Fourth of July fireworks show, either," I shot back.

"Now, now," scolded Pointy, "let's not be hostile about this. You can always hit the remote and turn me off and go back to—hey, whatever you'd go back t."

"The autobiography of Howard Fast, if you really want to know, and a Locatelli violin concerto. Not that it's any of your business."

Tsk, the point of light said. *Tsk, tsk.* "You won't do it, though, will you, Web? I know you're annoyed but you're curious. Where the hell is this going, you want to know. Is this some kind of interactive 3D video game, or are you just hallucinating? You're a curious old gink, I know that, so I'm sure you won't hit the off button, whatever you do."

I heaved a sigh. One of the classic stunts of software developers, back in the 1960s, was an interactive program designed to create psychological profiles of volunteers. They used college students for the experiment. The whole exercise was set up in the form of questions and answers. The volunteers never knew whether they were really engaged in a keyboard-based conversation with a psychologist or with a piece of software.

Maybe this disk from Ed Guenther was an updated version of that experiment. If so, it was damned good. Even back in the Sixties most of the kids couldn't tell whether they were talking to a real shrink or a computer program. And as for Little Pointy—yeah, Ed Guenther had me going, all right.

"You've been quiet for a long time, Webster. You still with me?"

"Okay, I'll play a little longer. What's next?"

"A lot of people think that there *is* something on the other side of the wall. You know? Maybe you do go *splat* but maybe that isn't the end of everything. What do you think?"

Oh, Jesus, I thought, this whole thing is a put-up job courtesy of Jehovah's Whozises or the Church of Jesus Cripes of Latter Day Ain'ts or the ghost of the Reverend Gene Scott.

"No, it isn't," Pointy's non-voice said in my head.

"Oh, is isn't, isn't it?" I actually picked up the remote and brandished it at the TV set. Then I put it back down. "Okay, pal, you tell me: What the hell *is* it?"

"Think of it as a free sample," Pointy said. "Or a bouquet of free samples. As if you were at the ice cream parlor and they weren't too busy and the teenaged kid in the funny hat handed you one of those tiny little spoons and invited you to try out every flavor that appealed to you."

"Okay," I moaned. "I give up. Whatever you have to show me, let's give it a shot."

The point of light danced away from me. Its color shifted from the plain brilliant white that had started out and shifted through the spectrum. I saw every color I knew about and a bunch that I had never seen before. I didn't even know the names of some of them.

Little Pointy retreated toward the screen and I followed him, like Peter Pan following Tinker Bell, or maybe like that little kid getting sucked into the TV set in *Poltergeist*. Little Pointy was gone and there were no more messages inside my head, at least for the moment. Instead there was music, nothing but music. Man, was it ever familiar!

I tried to figure out what it was. Something by Gustav Holst or maybe Ralph Vaughn Williams. They were buddies anyhow. Two kings of what is sometimes uncharitably referred to as picture postcard music. At least it wasn't *The Planets*. Not that I despised that piece, it was just too damned popular. How many times did I need to hear it?

But this, I realized, was the third movement of Holst's *Beni Mora*. Yes. The Algerian street music. The quotation from the famous, anonymous street musician who played variations on the same four-note sequence for—which musicologist do you trust?—

two hours, four hours, six hours. Old Gustav ran through a legendary 163 changes on the tune, and listening to it could either put you into a hypnotic trance or send you screaming from the room.

I was lying on a bed and I could hear my own breathing. I looked up and there were faces around me. I think I felt some pain in my body but it was so far distant that I hardly noticed it. Somebody was whispering and somebody was crying and the room, which had been brilliantly lighted at first, was slowly growing dark even as the pain in my body was growing more and more distant.

Breathing was an effort and after a while I decided that it wasn't worth the trouble and I stopped. The room grew still darker. The faces around me grew faint. Something white rose from the direction of my body, of the pain which had now ceased altogether, and then the light disappeared altogether.

I was standing at the mouth of a tunnel. I tried to look back, to see from whence I'd come, but I couldn't do it. I started walking forward into the tunnel. It was cool and pleasant in there, or at least not in the least unpleasant, and I could hear the four notes of the Holst composition, the full orchestration behind the wooden Arab flute, repeating those four notes over and over, yet not repeating. Instead, there was variation in the notes every time the musician played them.

For a moment I thought of Ed Guenther and his gift, of the work I'd done for him at Silicon Labs, of Miranda Nguyen, the woman who worked with Ed Guenther and the astonishing ideas she had offered in the past. She'd been working with electronic analogs of DNA codes. It wasn't my field but I knew enough to remember the four basic molecules that combined and recombined endlessly to create all of evolution.

What if the four factors of DNA and the four notes of Gustav Holst's 1910 composition and the four elements of Greek philosophy were all the same?

I walked through the tunnel for what seemed like a few seconds or maybe several billion years and then I realized that I was approaching the end of the tunnel. The light up ahead was a single glowing point. Maybe it was my old friend Little Pointy.

Little Pointy.

I loved Little Pointy.

I started to run and the brilliant point of light became a bigger speck and then a glowing disk the size of a BB, then a dime, then the moon and then I was there.

People clustered around me. I thought I recognized their faces but whenever I tried to focus in on one I lost track of what I was doing. They were all talking at once and I couldn't understand a word. Everybody seemed to be smiling, pleased to see me, but it was all so confusing.

Then I felt something cold and wet in my hand and I looked down and it was Louisa May Alcott, nuzzling my hand and looking at me, her bushy tale swaying happily from side to side and I started to cry again and I heard those four notes, those damned four notes from Gustav Holst's Algerian street musician and I was getting pulled head first out of there, out of wherever there was. My head was spinning and my ears were ringing and I was sitting in an easy chair in front of Ed Guenther's gift TV set wearing 3D glasses and trying to get damned Gustav Holst and his damned Algerian flautist out of my head.

Something that wasn't a voice asked, "Did you like that, Webster?"

I said, "Fuck you, Pointy, what the hell was that all about?"

"Would this be a good time for a word from our sponsor?" Point asked.

I said, "Get the hell out of my head."

Pointy said, "A lot of people have had that experience or one a lot like it. Some have even come back to tell the story."

"Yeah. Including me."

"Including you, Webster. I'm not saying that's what your future holds, although if it is, you'll live to a ripe old age and died a peaceful death. Does the prospect appeal?"

"Where's my brandy?" I realized that I didn't have to look at the TV set with those 3D glasses. Looking around the room, I could pretty well see everything. I located my snifter—actually, Martha's snifter—and took a sip. It helped me get back into the real world.

Pointy said, "Of course there are a lot of other ideas of what happens. You really ought to try a few." He paused. I think he was waiting for me to say something but I didn't. I could hear a siren in the distance, a fire engine racing to douse the flames in somebody's kitchen or maybe a police cruiser in hot pursuit of a car full of fleeing felons.

Somehow none of that seemed to matter very much.

I could hear a clock ticking. Pretty soon nobody will know what you're talking about when you use that expression. All the clocks in the world will be digital. They won't even whir any more. They'll just flash, *12:01, 12:02, 12:03 . . .*

"Some people think that the next world isn't such a nice place at all. Everybody except the chosen few wind up getting toasted, and I don't mean in a good way."

"Right. Everybody's out of step but Johnny."

"Just for your information, here comes a little taste of what they have planned for everybody else."

I shook my head, started to demur, but before I could tell my new friend, Thanks but no thanks, I was off and riding again. All to the tune of those damnable four notes of Gustav Holst's.

You ever wonder what Hell is like? I don't mean the cartoons of little red guys with horns and tails and pitchforks. Those are more amusing than frightening. And deep thinkers who say there's no physical torment in Hades, it's just separation from the presence of God that makes the damned regret their sins. Maybe we do each make our own Hells. Mine was pretty literal.

One day I was out for a walk near the opera house and suddenly found myself writhing on the sidewalk. I felt as if something had hit me—*wham!*—but it hit me all over, all at once. Fortunately I was wearing clean clothes and looking respectable, so nobody took me for a drunk with the DT's or a hebephrenic having a psychotic episode. Somebody called a cop, who called an ambulance, and pretty soon I was lying in a hospital bed with a morphine drip in one arm.

Turned out my pancreas had blown up on me. In case you're unfamiliar with this unglamorous organ, it's the body's own chemical laboratory. It specializes in manufacturing digestive juices and shipping them off to the stomach where they get to do their job.

Once in a while, though, it can go nuts, start exceeding its production quota by something like 10,000 percent, and spewing nasty gunk all over your innards. I don't mean to be excessively graphic about this, but what happens, in effect, is that your body starts digesting itself from the inside out.

That hurts.

Okay. That's what Hell was like, only instead of just coming from my belly, the pain was coming from all over. Physical pain, moral pain, emotional pain, intellectual pain, you name it. More pain at any moment than anyone could ever tolerate, except that it doesn't last for a moment, it lasts forever.

Got me?

Gustav Holst's picture postcard music, namely that Algerian street minstrel with his four-note repertoire, rescued me from Hell.

I sat there looking for Little Pointy because I wanted to wrap my fingers around his nonexistent neck and throttle the son of a bitch.

Not that I really believe in Hell. If there is a God and he really loves us one and all, as the preachers are always saying, I don't see how God could consign anyone He or She or It or They love to that kind of torment. Especially forever.

Something was coming out of the TV set. Not a point of light. Not now. I don't know what had become of Pointy, if he ever even existed except in my mind, but something was, how to put this, *oozing* from the screen.

It puddled up on the carpet, lapped over the edges of my shoes, and started to take some kind of shape.

Eventually it was a tall, slim, blonde woman. Her hair cascaded down her back in ringlets. Her face held a kind of ethereal beauty that transcends mere movie star good looks. She wore a translucent white robe that hung to the floor.

"You are the Princess Zoralda," I told her, "and you have come from the Planet Uxalot where all beings live in perpetual harmony and joy to invite me aboard your UFO and take me home with you."

"Oh, piss off," said Princess Zoralda, morphing back into my old pal Little Pointy. "Thought you'd bite on that one."

"Did you really? Come on, pal?

"No, really. You'd be surprised how many people believe in Princess Zoralda from the planet Uxalot. Surely you remember the Heaven's Gate bunch, The Two, the wackos who decided there was an alien spacecraft hidden behind that comet? Put on new Nikes and sweatpants and went up to the mommy ship on wings of cyanide. Who knows, maybe they were right."

I said, "I don't think so."

Pointy said, "Me neither. But you can never tell."

We kind of looked at each other for a while, as much as a point of light can look at anyone. Then Pointy said, "You ready for another one?"

I took a sip of my brandy and said, "Sure. So far you haven't showed me anything that appeals very much."

Pointy said, "You ain't seen nothin' yet, baby." He dropped the needle on the LP (yeah, yeah, never mind) and that weird four-note flute piece started up again. I had enough time to put my brandy snifter down before I was snatched out of my easy chair and wafted off into another afterlife adventure. I remember hoping that this one would be pleasanter than Hell had been, and more credible than the Princess Zoralda from the planet Uxalot.

Maybe it was. Or maybe not. I'm not really sure.

See, I don't think I'm a Christian. Born and raised in Northern California in the latter half of the Twentieth Century, I was exposed to plenty of religion, from people peddling magazines door-to-door to wild-eyed zealots preaching in the park to pulpit-pounding pastors of megachurches hyping their glassy-eyed zealot followers to gather up their Uzis and their families and get ready to march off to fight in the final battle between Jehovah and Satan and by the way don't forget to leave something in the collection plate as you go out the door.

The more of that stuff I had pounded into me the less of it I believe. I'm sure that Jewish hippy had some good ideas about living the good life but I don't go for the miracles and the resurrection and all of that.

Well, but water into wine was a good trick. Not sure how the Christian teetotalers deal with that, but never mind, never mind.

Pointy took me by the hand and whisked me into the TV again and I blinked in amazement at my surroundings and at my companion.

"I say, old man, are you all right?"

"Eh?" All I could think of to reply, I'll admit not exactly a clever line, but still, "Eh? What's that?"

"Why, my poor old fellow. You must have dozed off over your port and cakes. I fear you've been working too hard. Do you think you need some time off, Sloat?"

Sloat. Well, he knew who I was. And I knew who he was, but that only made me feel more puzzled. "Sorry, Holmes. But never mind, never mind. What were you saying about . . ." I let my voice trail away, hoping that he would pick up the thread just there, for in truth I had not the foggiest notion what he was talking about.

"I was just comparing the official document so kindly loaned to us by Inspector Gregson with the street version reported to us by our friends the Irregulars."

"Ah, yes," I put in. "And with regard to what do these differing stories relate?"

Holmes turned on his heel and gave me one of his appraising looks. "I refer to the disappearance of Her Majesty's personal pet, the basset hound Rollo, from the royal kennels at Balmoral." His brow wrinkled with concern. "Surely you have not forgotten this morning's conversation with my brother Mycroft and Her Majesty's personal equerry at the Diogenes Club."

"No, no, Holmes, of course not." I went to the window and peered out into fog-shrouded, gas-lit Baker Street. A hansom cab rolled past, the sound of its wheels clattering over the cobblestones and the hooves of the creature pulling it clopping steadily in the London night.

I turned back to face my companion. My mind was racing. Had I fallen asleep? Was this all a dream? Or—no, now I remembered. I was sampling different images of the afterlife. I suppose some people would enjoy reincarnation as fictional characters. It might be fun to share those adventures with the Great Detective, stalking across the moors of Scotland, confronting madmen and enemy agents and the master criminal, the most dangerous man in London, Professor Moriarty.

Of course there was the question of Dr. Watson. Maybe somewhere in Ed Geunther's disk there was a Sherlock Holmes track, a piece of write-your-own-adventure, role playing game software, that let the user take part in a case.

Or maybe this was all coming out of my own subconscious. I'd been a Sherlock Holmes fan as a kid. My Dad had a huge book with the complete Sherlock Holmes stories in it, all the short stories and novels. I must have been eight years old when I came down with scarlet fever. There was a real scare in our town, kids getting sent home from school, doctors coming to their houses. Doctors still came to their patients' houses in those days.

I had to stay home for weeks. I read the whole book from start to finish. I was beside myself when I came to the end of 'The Adventure of Shoscombe Old Place' until my Dad said I could just go back to the beginning of 'A Study in Scarlet' and read the whole book again.

Well, I hadn't read a Sherlock Holmes story in, what, thirty years at least. But come to think of it, 221b Baker Street might not be a bad address for the afterlife.

"You'll have to forgive me, Holmes," I managed. "Of course Her Majesty must be beside herself with anxiety for the welfare of her pet. Have the abductors of the royal canine announced their terms for Rollo's return?"

"Indeed they have, Sloat, indeed they have!" Holmes crossed the room in two lengthy strides and thrust into my hands a piece of cheap foolscap on which a message had been placed in the form of words cut from newspapers and crudely attached with mucilage.

Even as I reached to take the paper from Holmes I felt myself slipping away, lifted out of that world to the accompaniment of four notes sounded on an Arab flute, four notes repeated over and over yet never quite repeating exactly the same pattern of sound.

Little Pointy grinned, or he would have grinned, I'm sure, if he'd had a face. Somehow in my mind he was grinning. "Ain't this fun?"

"Is that Heaven?" I asked him. "Playing Watson to an imaginary Sherlock Holmes?"

"Is there any other kind of Sherlock Holmes? You're not one of those poor souls who write letters to Baker Street asking Holmes to help find their lost brooches or make their husbands love them again, are you?"

"Don't be ridiculous. I can tell the difference between what's real and what's imaginary."

"Can you? Actually, can you? Am I real? Are you? *Cogito, ergo sum?* Poor old Monsieur Descartes. I can arrange for you to meet him, if you'd like, Webster old boy."

I shook my head, or thought I shook my head. Once you start down that street the only end is a room with soft walls and rounded corners. Instead, I said, "I guess anybody can have an idea of Heaven."

Pointy grinned again, or would have if . . . oh, you know the drill. Okay. Pointy grinned again. "You ever hear the story of the fundamentalist missionary and the Eskimo family? The more he ranted about hellfire and toasting forever on the devil's own griddle, the more his host kept saying, 'Yes, yes, that's where I want to spend eternity!'"

I managed to stand up and walk around a little. My hindquarters were getting numb from all the sitting, and I'd been reading about the dangers of too much sitting, embolisms and all that. I said, "You know what I'd like to do in the afterlife—assuming, that is, that there is such a thing?"

Pointy said, "No, Webster, I don't know. Suppose you tell me."

I said, "Nope!" I was going to show that I was smarter than a glittering point of light that probably wouldn't even be there if I took off my special glasses.

And fuck you very much, Ed Guenther.

"I'll just sit back and have another sip of my brandy. Would you like—oh, I'm sorry, I guess that wouldn't be possible would it? Anyway, I tell you what. I'm getting a little bit weary. Suppose you hit me with your best shot and then we'll call it a night."

Pointy said, "Fair enough, Webster old boy. Let's see. We have the Muslim paradise. Days of wine and virgins appeal to you? How about the Christians? We've been over that already, haven't we? Still, though—fluffy clouds, golden harps, people wandering around like hippies in robes and sandals? No sale?"

I swear, if that point of light had been a salesman in an automobile showroom he would have been coming at me with the classic line about, "What would it take to put you into a shiny new Charioteer V-8 with air, MP3, GPS, and . . ." But of course this wasn't an auto showroom and he wasn't a car salesman so he said,

"What would you like to try?"

I said, "Tell you what, I'll roll the dice if you will."

There was a moment of silence. Then Pointy said, "Roll the dice? Me, roll the dice? No hands little me?"

I just sat there.

Pointy sighed. I think he actually sighed. "Tough audience," he grumbled. Then, "Okay, let's give 'er a whirl and see that happens."

I could almost hear the late great Lawrence Welk signaling his band of merry pranksters. Anna Won, Anna Too . . .

Horns, donkeys, Arab street vendors, the distant cry of the muezzin, a wooden flute, and—

I was standing on the flight deck of a little spaceship and from the sights I could see beyond the view-ports we were way, way out in space. I mean, not just far from Earth or even from Sol. Not even outside our galaxy. I mean, we were way, way into deep space—and beyond it.

I used to sit in on some blue-sky sessions at the lab. Ed Guenther liked to get the superbrains together after hours, sometimes in his office, sometimes in the cafeteria, most often at Albert and Paddy's Bar and Grille in Fremont. The establishment was run a fellow named Harry Slotnick. Nobody had ever seen Albert or Paddy, but Slotnick insisted that he was just a hired hand, the place had been founded back in the 1950s by Albert Einstein and Patrick Houlihan.

Harry Slotnick used to hand out tee shirts to his regular clientele with a picture of Albert Einstein and Patrick Houlihan toasting each other in Irish whiskey. You couldn't buy one of those shirts for any price. Just keep showing up the A&P and after a while, if Harry took to you, he'd give you the shirt.

There was even an A&P baseball cap, or at least legend had it so. I've never seen one.

Anyway, one wet Friday after the lab had closed, Ed Guenther and Miranda Nguyen from Silicon Research, Alberto Salazar from NASA-Ames, Bobby Armstrong from NIMH, and I had settled in for a happy session of generously lubricated speculation. Topic *du nuit* was, What happens if you get to the very edge of Einsteinian space-time and keep on going?

Conservative view was, you'd just swoop around and head back in, whatever "in" meant in that context. In other words, once you reached the end of space, you'd discover that there was no more there, there.

Shades of Gertie Stein!

But Miranda Nguyen said she wasn't convinced of that. She thought you could pop right out of our cozy little four-dimensional space-time continuum and travel through a *fifth* dimension where ordinary four-dimensional universes floated around like air bubbles in a fresh stein of beer and pop back into a four-dimensional universe, our own or another, pay your money and take your pick.

Then Bobby Armstrong, our resident headshrinker on loan from the Feds, rapped for attention. "I read this story once," Bobby started.

Everybody moaned.

Bobby is a science fiction nut. Not only that, he's an *old* science fiction nut. Any time anybody claims ownership of a new and startling idea, Bobby comes back with, "I read this story once," and he'll give with a full citation, volume and issue number, of some story that was published in a pulp magazine before any of us were even born, that had exactly that idea in it.

Now Bobby said, "This story, it was called 'The Living Galaxy,' by Laurence Manning, *Wonder Stories,* September 1934. This space ship gets outside our galaxy—nobody knew there was more than one, back in 'thirty-four—and the astronauts look back and they see tentacles and pseudopods and they realize that our whole galaxy is a living creature and we're just a tiny speck, less than a cell, inside this creature. And of course if there's one of these beings wriggling around in hyperspace then there have to be more of them. Then the great Ray Bradbury came along with a story called 'King of the Gray Spaces' in 1943 . . ."

Ed Guenther said, "Enough already, Bobby, for God's sake, we'll take your word for it."

Okay, okay, I don't want to turn this into just another one of those tiresome conversations-in-a-tavern ditties like Clarke's White Hart stories or Robinson's Crosstime Saloon or that one I once read called "At the Esquire." Point is, in my dream or hallucination or whatever you want to call it that Little Pointy had dragged me into, there I was on the flight deck of a little spaceship called *The Comet*. There was a crew of five but only two of us were human. I was the captain and pilot and my co-pilot and faithful friend and companion was a gorgeous raven-haired beauty named Joan Randall who could have passed for 1940s glamour queen Ann Sheridan's twin sister.

Then there was a seven-foot-tall robot named Grag and a rubbery hairless android named Otho and a human brain in a transparent cube filled with nutrient fluid. The brain had once belonged to the brilliant Simon Wright. Simon could see with photo-electric eyes and speak through a circular diaphragm.

We'd been pursuing the mad would-be universal dictator Zohak -Yei. He'd been reported on a thousand worlds in a hundred galaxies but at last we'd tracked him down to an asteroid that he'd taken over in one of the spiral arms of the Andromeda Galaxy. He was reported building a machine that would send out antigravity waves throughout the universe, disrupting the mental and physical processes that had kept galactic peace for ten thousand years.

Once chaos reigned the Legion of Zohak-Yei would descend on the settled worlds, forcing every civilized race to submit to Zohak-Yei's cruel dictatorship—or perish in an orgy of madness and destruction!

Planets and stars flashed by our tiny ship like snowflakes in a winter storm in the Sierras as we drove on toward Zohak-Yei's distant lair. Our cyclotrons whined at an ear-splitting screech as we drove them to the danger point and beyond. The universe outside the windows of our tiny ship flashed and tumbled as if the very gods were protesting our audacity.

The cyclotrons' scream modulated into a weird musical note. Then another and another and—

I was sitting in front of the TV set. The screen was filled with countless whirling colors. A single brilliant point of light hovered in front of me, circling like an insect seeking a place to settle.

"That was a good one," Pointy commented.

I said, "Can you see everything I—what should I call these experiences? Dreams?"

"I don't think so. Visions, maybe. Your language is kind of thin when it comes to describing, ah . . ."

"Right." I think I actually smiled. "The indescribable."

"Anyway, you seem to have gone from versions of the afterlife that your various pulpit-thumpers like to rant about, to a lot more personal idea. But I guess it's true, isn't it?"

"Isn't what?"

"That everybody makes his own heaven or hell."

"I guess."

"You're looking kind of peaked, Webster." Pointy bobbed up and down a couple of times. If he'd been human I think he would have been nodding. "Want to call it a night?"

I lifted my hand to look at my faithful old Timex. The Oyster that Martha gave me for my birthday I keep in its box and take out for special occasions. I couldn't read the darned thing. Either the hands were whirling around faster than I could see, or they were standing still at quarter to yesterday or half-past tomorrow.

"In a strange way," I told Pointy, "I'm actually having fun. Let's keep 'em rolling. One or two more, anyhow."

Pointy said, "Okay, Web. It's your funeral." He stood there, pulsing away. "It's your funeral," he reiterated. "Get it? Afterlife. Funeral? Oh, never mind. Talk about trying to work a dead house." Pause. "Dead house—get it? Work a dead house? Man, are you ever stiff!"

I remember when my little ray of sunshine used to come home from first grade and share knock-knock jokes with me. I never understood them but she did for sure and she'd explode in hysterical laughter that was so joyous I'd find myself close to tears with amusement and joy just to be with her.

So don't tell me about laughter, Pointy. I know what laughter is all about.

We were down 14-13 with five seconds on the clock. The Scorpions had the ball on our two-yard line. If our kicker hadn't missed a conversion the score would have been tied but as it was, barring a miracle, we didn't have a chance.

Somehow it was the era of leather helmets and sixty-minute men and water-boys rushing onto the field during time-outs with buckets of water and ladles to keep the players from passing out. Rovers Stadium was packed for the big game. Must have been three thousand people there. Cheerleaders jumping up and down in their sweaters and pleated skirts and bobby sox and saddle shoes, shaking their pompoms and yelling for all they were worth.

The Scorps could have had the victory for the taking, just snap the ball and run around for five seconds and the game would be over but their quarterback was a nasty character. He wanted to rub it in. He figured they could push in for one more touchdown on the last play of the game, rack up an extra six-pointer just to rub our noses in it.

Their center snapped the ball and both of their ends circled around into our backfield in a crossing pattern. The quarterback sent up a soft spiral into the end zone. Their two halfbacks converged. I was the lone defender right there. I didn't know which of the two receivers to cover so instead I ignored them and leaped as high as I could, just as the ball dropped toward the turf and into my hands.

I ran straight ahead, jumped over the writhing pile of linemen and into the Scorpions' backfield. I think they must have been shocked by the sudden reversal of fortune. Five or six Scorpion players headed for me but even before they could get their bearings I had put the better part of ten yards between them and me. I was running as fast as I could, desperately working to drag air into my lungs as I pounded up the middle of the field toward the distant goal posts.

Somehow I heard the cannon go off marking the end of playing time but I kept on running. If I stepped out of bounds the game was over. If I was tackled the game was over. There was nothing I could do except keep going, keep going, keep going, keep going. I heard four notes sounding over and over, over and over with each step I took.

There was one figure between me and the goal line. Through streaming, stinging sweat I recognized the Scorpions' quarterback. When everyone else on their team had run toward me, the quarterback had run toward their own goal line. He was standing on the goal line now, jumping up and down, shouting something at me. I couldn't hear him but I could read his lips. "Come on, you yellow-belly," he screamed, "come on, I'll smash you to bits!"

I was at the twenty, then the fifteen, then the ten.

He started straight for me. He launched himself into a flying tackle, his two arms outstretched like the mandibles of a giant, murderous spider. There was no way I could dodge around him. If I met him head-on we would go down in a tangle of arms and legs short of the goal line and the final score would still be Scorpions 14, Rovers 13.

I ducked my head, bounded into a front-flip. With my right hand I clutched the football to my belly. With my left hand I straight-armed the Scorpion quarterback in the center of his grass-stained jersey. I bounced into the air, cart-wheeling forward and crashed to the ground—in the end-zone.

Cheering fans rushed onto the field. The referee whistled frantically but there was no controlling the crowd. No way we'd have a chance to kick the conversion, but it didn't matter. Final score: Rovers 19, Scorpions 13.

I felt myself being lifted up, hoisted onto the shoulders of my teammates, carried around the field in triumph. I knew there was going to be a party tonight at the frat house. I had time to shower and put on some clean clothes and head over to the head cheerleader's sorority house to pick her up before things got rolling. I knew I'd had the greatest afternoon of my life, and I was going to have the luckiest night.

I started whistling and without my being conscious of it I realized that my whistling had turned into that four-note sequence and I was staring at Little Pointy with a dumb-but-happy grin on my face.

"Want to quit?" Pointy asked.

"I don't know." I pulled the 3D glasses off, laid them on the arm of my easy chair, and walked out of the room.

"Hey," I seemed to hear Little Pointy calling plaintively although, of course, I wasn't really *hearing* him at all. "Hey, where are you going? Web, Webster, Webster Sloat, what are you doing?"

I walked through the parlor, then the foyer, then out of Martha's beautiful Queen Anne Victorian. I carefully locked the door. I stood on the sidewalk looking up at the house. It's painted a bright, cheerful yellow. The gingerbread is white. Even at night there's enough ambient light on the street to show it off.

I walked to the corner like a good citizen of San Francisco and crossed the street. There's a park across the way. Probably dangerous at night but God watches over madmen and I felt about as crazy as I ever had in my life. I wandered through the park. Through the darkness, for five or ten minutes or three or four hours. I have no idea.

There was mist in the air and the few streetlights spaced along the block crated a row of ghostly nimbuses. Every so often a car would slide past, a pair of headlights approaching and then a pair of taillights departing. I drank lungful after lungful of cool, moist, delicious air.

After a while I crossed back, climbed the steps, unlocked the front door, made my way to the TV room, settled into the easy chair and clamped the 3D glasses to my head.

Little Pointy started to do a little jig in front of me, then started to talk to me. I said, "Shut up." He did.

I slid into that other reality. I looked around and realized that I was sitting at the folding bridge table with a bed-sheet covering it that served for elegant dining in the tiny apartment that I'd shared with Beloved Spouse so long ago. She was standing at the stove, wearing a shirtwaist dress with an apron tied over it.

I felt something cold nuzzle my hand and I looked down into the big liquid eyes of Louisa May Alcott.

Beloved Spouse turned from the stove and placed a dime-store dinner plate in front of me, smiling proudly. I picked up my knife and fork. I looked at my meal. Burned liver and yellow wax beans and green string beans.

I had found heaven.

www.ingramcontent.com/pod-product-compliance
Lightning Source LLC
Chambersburg PA
CBHW030809310726
48980CB00006B/429/J

* 9 7 8 0 9 7 2 8 5 4 5 7 3 *